A CASSANDRA KRESNOV NOVEL

JOEL
SHEPHERD

23 YEARS ON FIRE

an imprint of Prometheus Books
Amherst, NY

Published 2013 by Pyr®, an imprint of Prometheus Books

Cover illustration © Stephan Martiniere
Cover design by Jacqueline Nasso Cooke

Inquiries should be addressed to
Pyr
59 John Glenn Drive
Amherst, New York 14228–2119
VOICE: 716–691–0133
FAX: 716–691–0137
WWW.PYRSF.COM

17 16 15 14 13   5 4 3 2 1

Library of Congress Cataloging-in-Publication Data

Shepherd, Joel, 1974-
    23 years on fire : a Cassandra Kresnov novel / Joel Shepherd.
       pages cm. — (A Cassandra Kresnov Novel)
    ISBN 978-1-61614-809-6 (pbk.)
    ISBN 978-1-61614-810-2 (ebook)
    1. Kresnov, Cassandra (Fictitious character)—Fiction. 2. Androids—Fiction.
I. Title. II Title: Twenty-three years on fire.

PR9619.4.S54A615 2013
823'.92—dc23
                            2013022406

Printed in the United States of America

CHAPTER ONE

Ari tried to avoid Kobayashi Square; there were too many monitors. He walked from the rail station about the square perimeter instead, down Jin-Hai Street and across Pier, grateful the traffic monitors weren't set to bust a person for jaywalking.

It was cold in Anjula, several below freezing, but if he walked fast and kept his woolen hat down over his ears, he found it bearable. There was old snow on the curbs, tucked in the places the sweepers missed, or in sidewalk gardens where grass or shrubs tried to grow. All quite odd for a Tanushan, accustomed to that city's tropical location on planet Callay, and temperatures that rarely chilled even on winter nights. He was missing the warmth now, as the prospect of returning to it drew closer. Six months now he'd been without it, stuck here on the outer rim of Federation space, in this sprawling port city built foolishly too far south of the equator.

But in other ways, Anjula was not too different. The night streets buzzed with artificial colour, advertising hoardings, network displays, bars and theatres advertising their latest sin. People crowded the sidewalks, unbothered by the chill, some of the women even with light stockings and otherwise bare legs that Ari shivered just to look at. Here about Kobayashi Square, where transport networks clustered and VR simulation joints were famous, the crowds were sometimes huge. Tonight, they were just large—a Sunday, in the universal Federation week. In a few hours, the crowds would dwindle further. Monday was a work day and by midnight, Anjula's ten-million-strong buzz would have declined to a low murmur. Fewer people were better, for what was planned, however little sympathy he had for them.

It was the most surreal thing, to walk these streets of a huge city, on a world whose population now approached a neat three hundred million, and to know that he was about to bring it all crashing down. Well, not him alone, he'd have help. Quite a lot of help, in fact. But it had been his idea from the inception, several years planning, and lately six months of field work. And none of these people, out on their Sunday night entertainments, had any idea what was about to happen.

Sandy knew she'd hit atmosphere when the aeroshell ceased shaking. That was odd—typically reentry was a fiery affair at nearly thirty thousand kilometers per hour, but a covert insertion fired thrusters before atmospheric contact, slowing the pod to a near hover, then hit troposphere at just over five thousand, barely fast enough to make a jolt in whisper thin air. Otherwise, a series of coordinated fireballs over Anjula might have made the defences suspicious.

After two minutes of falling, she blew the shell off and took a look at where she was. The altimeter said sixty thousand meters, well high enough to see the curvature of Pyeongwha's horizon, if it hadn't been pitch black. She was descending somewhere in excess of Mach two, the air not thick enough to sustain a candle flame even if the howling gale wouldn't blow it out again. She flipped her helmet visuals to ultra-v and got some lovely colours—hot lights below, cities along a crescent-shaped coast. That was Narata, an island, perhaps a thousand kilometers end to end. Upon the far horizon, more lights— Abanda, the mainland continent. Anjula was on Narata, off the coast; a big port city, ideal for a world surfaced eighty percent by water. Its lights below were brightest, sprawling up the coast into fragmenting smaller dots: fishing towns, villages, seaside resorts. Too cold for bikinis now, though.

Spread-eagled, she looked up and around for her support. Helmet vision found them pretty fast, dark shapes falling against an even darker sky, the nearest just over a kilometer. Sandy did a slow spin and finished her count at fifty-two . . . there were fifty-six in the drop, she imagined the other four were fine, helmet visuals weren't as reliable as her bare eyes, but at this altitude she had no other option. Reentry trajectories were notoriously unreliable, a few random atmospheric interactions and you could end up tens of kilometers from where you should be. But the shadow crew that had inserted them had got it down to something of an art, and in free fall you could always correct your descent once unshelled.

She did so now, leaning forward to create a glidepath. Spread across the night sky about her, armoured figures followed her lead.

At thirty thousand meters Anjula was filling her view, patchy with broken cloud. She called up maps and overlaid them, quickly getting a match. From there, navcomp told her what was what, and she'd been committing most of Anjula to memory for the last few weeks. She could laser com her teammates to talk to them without frequency pollution, but Anjula was said to be paranoid enough these days, and a network of low intensity lasers above the city might just be visible enough to the kind of telescope that paranoids might have down there. It was nearly impossible for them to spot the suits, though, armoured with Tanusha's latest stealth materials plus low-intensity opti-cam, not strong enough to turn a soldier invisible at close range, but black against a black sky? Even if a telescope did get very lucky and spot one of them, they were coming down so fast now they'd be grounded before anyone figured out what to do about it.

Ten thousand meters. The central parks were clear now, a chain of natural lakes left untouched by the encroaching sprawl of city. North, Taizhou hills. South, Xanh Harbour, and big docks for shipping, intricate shapes against the water. Not a planned pattern of hubs and spokes like Tanusha, but an organic, random mass. Ari said it was quite pretty.

She passed an airliner at five thousand meters and climbing, and counted several more below, circling toward one of the two major airports. Below that, even now at an hour after midnight, lots of city air traffic. Anjula was big enough that it never truly slept, just dozed.

At two thousand meters she got her first signal reception, a mass of short-range frequencies, strengthening as she fell. Bandwidth increased rapidly, and she sorted fast until her suit latched onto the agreed upon network—an ultra-band used primarily for uplink advertising, nearly unjammable. Trust the advertisers to pick that one while leaving the hospitals with low-band junk.

"Come on, Ari," she murmured, as the ground rushed up fast. "Be there." Suddenly, she found the encryption. Flash-zoomed on internal vision, saw a mass of codework and interlocking structural components that could only be Ari, with open gates just waiting for the right mate-up . . .

She provided it, and with a flash she was in, and a broad network across the entire city of Anjula blew open before her like an unfurling flag. One thousand meters. She chose a building roof and aimed for it, as her team-mates appeared in quick succession upon the new network—tacnet was propagating now, using the Anjula advertising frequency as its operating base, and so much faster than usual as it found Ari's little markers and built on them like some crazed climbing vine on a trellis.

At five hundred meters the thrusters kicked, which felt a little odd at these speeds, but she quickly found her balance and settled down toward the rooftop. She kicked harder a hundred meters up, decelerating from two hundred to fifty kph at impact, and jogged quickly to the edge for a view. The building was only fifteen stories, there wasn't a heck of a lot of super high-rise in Anjula, just masses and masses of middle-rise fading out to suburbs. She was two blocks from the southern-most central park, perhaps two Ks from downtown, and almost exactly where she wanted. Her eyes told her that she was all alone, and none of the sparse traffic on the road below had seen her descent. If it weren't for tacnet, she could have believed she were just a lonely soul on a lonely rooftop in a cold and unfamiliar city.

About the city, her soldiers were landing. Tacnet showed them down, reporting ready. Surely somewhere, someone would notice the small thruster flare and report something . . . a note to a friend, a video recording, a query to an authority. Ari would be watching that, patched into all the local comnets, sifting traffic for telltale phrases or images. So far, nothing. Sandy looked, but even with her enhanced vision, she could see nothing across the jumble of rooftops.

Tacnet showed the last unit down, fifty-six plus her.

"This is Snowcat," she said. "First wave target and lock."

Ari and his local network of rebels had selected the first wave of targets. Pray he got them all right. Sandy activated the suit's launcher, allowed tacnet to allocate her its share of the targets, then waited for the final locks to come in. They did.

"Fire."

Three missiles leaped over her shoulder, then kicked away as primary thrusters activated. They zigzagged like crazed fireflies, weaving across the rooftops. Now she could see her team's presence in Anjula, tiny bright dots appearing across the skyline like illegal fireworks on Chinese New Year. They wove and dodged, headed for targets at a variety of ranges, never aiming at what their launcher was closest to, confusing the defences. Micro-munitions, a recent addition to Callay's production lines, barely bigger than a fist, but fast, accurate and nothing micro about the charge.

She could see the flashes before she heard the booms, casting shadows in the night. They multiplied, random flares, then the sound waves struck with familiar, hypnotic resonance. Boom, b-boom, b-b-b-BOOM, boom. For a moment, it was like being back on Sao Joaquin, watching the latest

Federation counter attack roll through. But she was the Federation now, and this fight was to liberate a world, not take it.

BOOM! Something struck just up the road, a fireball rising and debris raining down. A com node, possibly, the fibre links were underground but wireless transmitters were on rooftops like this one, as were backup satellite links and first-redundancy laser com relays. They whittled Anjula's communications down, limiting options, reducing response times and creating confusion. Now the defence grids would be activating. Time to move.

She unshackled her rifle and jumped; thrusters kicked her into a low flight over the next buildings until a nice corner building loomed up with a rooftop garden. Toward the parks she could see huge fireballs rising, those would be defensive gun emplacements, secondary explosions as the ammunition cooked off. Further north, behind the tall towers of city centre, more big explosions. Parliament defences and government buildings. There would be collateral from those explosions and others, mostly civilian. It couldn't be helped.

Tacnet was slotting them in to secondary targeting now, armscomp found her one and she fired a missile as she landed, with no real interest in where it went. She ducked amidst garden trees and took a knee with a view.

Tacnet was incorporating the local network now, and she could hear/see/feel the local traffic going crazy. Perhaps a million calls to emergency services, media networks abruptly going live, police, hospitals, fire departments . . . and no doubt security services too, but those weren't on any accessible network. Or, not yet.

"*Okay, I'm getting a CNS response, very active, all units standby.*"

That was Ari, tracking Central Network Security as it tried to lock its own tactical networks into place. There was no way of knowing exactly where they propagated from until they went active.

"*I have police on the streets at A-35 by H-16,*" came another, as tacnet immediately located that grid reference and highlighted it. "*Multiple vehicles, looks like a convoy.*"

"*Don't hit it unless it's para,*" came Vanessa's reply. She was only coming online now, her tacnet functions took longer to propagate, leaving the first "fire" command to Sandy. But now, she was in charge. "*Police just cause confusion.*"

If they're not equipped for this sort of fighting. Most weren't. They'd run the simulations many times, and Sandy concurred—they were actually more use alive. Emergency services, too. Sandy would have vetoed shooting at them, anyhow. Yet, happily, fire trucks blocking the roads served every purpose except the defence of Anjula.

"Airborne at C-9 and V-3. Unspecified security vehicle."

"Kill it."

And so it went. Pyeongwha security would go red now, but they weren't equipped for this kind of assault; it would take them time to get assets in the right positions to be effective. In the meantime, Sandy had a facility building to reach. She couldn't head straight in because Ari thought the network defences were too advanced, and could be degraded through phase one of the assault. Give it a half hour, he insisted, and he'd have her a path inside.

Ari sat in Moon's residence and observed the chaos. Moon sat alongside, working multiple display screens and VR uplinks at once, Hideger beside him. Across Anjula, they had a network of perhaps a hundred—rebels, activists, hackers, local Anjulans and other Pyeongwhanians pissed at the system. They'd planned this for months, some of them years, and a few, decades. Now it was finally on.

Beyond the windows were flashes of light, and shockwaves that shook the glass. Power flickered and restored, and air traffic shrieked overhead as flight control sent vehicles low on emergency lanes to escape the field of fire. A pointless measure; civvie aircars were hardly the target.

Conversations clamoured in Ari's ears, network operators locked into their various infiltrations, attacking security barriers, police communications, primary information channels. Two minutes ago an old fashioned TV network had attempted to go live from a building top, only to lose uplink feed a moment later, from hacking or explosions. VTS, the government network, had crossed to live broadcast a minute later, only to receive a warhead through their studio window, then static. Who had authorised that strike, Ari didn't know. Things were happening too fast, target assignments flashing new onto tacnet by the second.

He let the team do their job. There would be plenty of time for recriminations later. He was after bigger fish.

"Okay, here they come," he declared, watching the network defences spiral out from hardpoints along the com grid. The major institutions knew they were under attack. They'd have a defence plan to seek out the infiltrators, erase their networks and if possible, discern a physical location so their SWAT teams could take them out. That could mean a warhead landing in his lap, or anyone's lap, at any time. "I'm running counter, let's see if this works."

His counter measures were packages inserted covertly into various supposedly high security com nodes. Those com nodes now relayed attacks from Anjula's security institutions, unaware they were feeding data on their composition straight back to Ari. Within seconds he had an array of network points highlighted for tacnet. A simple publish sent them through.

"Hello Jailbait, I'd like these dead, yesterday if possible."

Vanessa wouldn't bother replying, and didn't, but after a pause of a few seconds he saw a new cascade of orange and white flashes across the urban horizon, and a whole series of network lines abruptly died. Then the sound reached him, a thunder like stampeding elephants, shaking the windows and walls.

"Dude, those are some fireworks!" Moon announced, wide eyed, as fingers flew across his interface.

Some of those security networks had used servers that weren't in reinforced locations. Some were in office buildings, where micro-munitions could surgically remove single or multiple offices, and all hardware within. Network barriers that could be snuck past when no one was looking, but were impossible to simply tear down by hacking alone, now disappeared. It was cheating, of course—hackers were supposed to hack barriers, not simply destroy their mainframes. But he'd ceased to be a simple hacker a long time ago, and now played by different rules.

"Good work," he said. "I've got barriers down all over the place . . . team, let's get inside before they transfer functions and reestablish."

Now it was a genuine fight. Sandy's target was beyond the CBD, by the northern edge of the most northerly park. She'd not wanted to land closer—confusion was a part of the assault plan, and that region was heavily guarded. But now, she had a trek ahead of her.

She leaped across several blocks, keeping low, scanning for anything that moved. There were quite a few civilians and ground cars. When she'd first heard "jetpacks," she'd nearly resigned on the spot. Those contraptions just put you on a slow, fixed trajectory that the dumbest armscomp could blow from the sky. But these were jumpjets, it had been insisted, for short, varied bursts of flight like the grasshoppers for which they were named. Still she didn't trust them, and stayed as close to the rooftops as possible.

Tacnet showed airbourne security vehicles trying to make their way from suburban bases to downtown, and getting blown from the sky. That would limit defensive deployment options. Others were trying to move out by ground, and that was more effective, if far slower. She headed for one now, grounding in a small city park between buildings to break up her flight path, then leaping again through the trees.

She landed on a rooftop seven stories up, looking onto a street afire with ruined vehicles and collapsed building fronts. Tacnet showed her a couple of likely culprits ahead, and she leaped after them, zooming vision on their newest targets—a couple of personnel carriers. It wasn't always easy to tell where they'd come from; some of the police and security stations through the inner city had armoured depots that micro-munitions wouldn't touch.

They were under fire when she landed, two FSA suits on neighbouring rooftops pouring fire onto the street below. They hadn't seen the UAV zooming around behind them for a shot, Sandy armscomped it in midflight, pulled the trigger, then landed by a skylight as the UAV screamed tumbling into a building a block away and exploded.

One of the APCs was afire, men scrambling from the back, Sandy locked a grenade on the other and blew its top turret, then ducked back as fire came at her from across the street. Suddenly a viewfeed from one of her friendlies showed AMAPS on the road, running through halted civvie traffic with that ugly, birdlike gait. Sandy's friend blew one of them to hell with a rifle shot, but suddenly there were missiles in the air and everyone jumped.

Sandy's rooftop blew up just after she'd left it, and she took the flying vantage to put multiple rifle rounds into another running AMAPS on the street below, but one of those missiles was still going, streaking about in a circle as it tried to reacquire. It picked her, and Sandy turned, shot it from the sky, and crashed onto a rooftop ventilation system with less grace than she'd have liked. Snipers snapped at her from across the road somewhere, two of them, armscomp calced and showed her where in a split second as she came up on her feet and fired twice, then dropped a free fall grenade over the edge.

"Blinder!" she advised her wingmen as the phosphorus detonated, and any sensitive lenses focused that way abruptly burned out. She went over the edge a second later, blew another AMAPS's CPU apart with a headshot, hit the jumpjets in mid-fall to land sideways and rolling as another AMAPS tore the street apart with its twin cannon, firing blind. Sandy and a wingman hit it with grenades simultaneously and it disappeared in three directions at once.

Sandy left, disconcerted that she'd dented a thruster, but otherwise unscathed. Happily, no one else tried to shoot at her as she sailed with her two companions toward a new landing. Watching snipers' heads explode was not pleasant, and if the only enemies that shot at her from now on were mechanicals like those Armoured Mobile Anti-Personnel Systems, she'd be happy.

UAVs were now proving a pain in the ass. Pyeongwha's military was restricted, like all Federation worlds, so they had few assets that qualified as full-blown military. But that left "para military," which Sandy knew from experience could include pretty much anything if you classified it cunningly. On her leaping trek around Anjula downtown, she counted five types in the air, two of them supersonic, one of them high altitude recon, and two others slow and hovering and hiding behind buildings. She disliked those most of all. She could track and hit high-motion at anything up to Mach one with barely any assistance from armscomp, but while Mach one was very visible, even she couldn't hit what she couldn't see.

She covered her teammates' blind spots as they moved, as they covered hers, and they leapfrogged forward in the most old-fashioned of infantry manoeuvers, covering about half a K with each jump. Police and para-military were getting more snipers into high buildings now, and some with missile launchers, but those were going to have trouble tracking FSA suits in opti-cam. Even so, armscomp started registering regular near misses, mostly in the air. True to Sandy's infantry prejudice, grounded meant cover, and cover meant "safe." In the old days, there'd been something called the "air force." These days, modern weapons and armscomp turned most aircraft into flying bull's-eyes.

They were closing on North Park when Anjula began closing down the advertising frequencies, having realised how the attackers were using it against them. Ari simply transitioned them to one of the emergency services sub-frequencies, and tacnet propagated all over again. They could keep frequency jumping all night until Anjula shut the whole lot down, but then the city would be as blind as the attackers, who could then just switch to their own coms and battle through whatever jamming was thrown at them. Defending took a lot more coordination, and if Anjula's assets couldn't talk to each other, they were screwed.

Sandy paused on a rooftop long enough to track and fire a missile at a high-altitude UAV, then was startled by civvies on a neighbouring balcony peering out to take a look. She refrained from shooting, leaped instead, and scanning nearby air traffic on tacnet found one vehicle loitering suspiciously and warned her second wingman about it. There were no rooftops she liked the look of, ahead, so she grounded on the road instead and pressed herself to a wall. At fifteen thousand meters overhead, the UAV blew up. So did the cruiser she'd warned about, when a door opened to reveal security with a launcher.

There were displays and advertising everywhere at street level. Sandy realised she was in one of the entertainment strips, wall to wall graphics and dancing images. All deserted now save for several cops huddled by their cruiser, staring fearfully. Sandy ignored them and leaped again, and was immediately shot at by someone down below . . . low caliber, she didn't bother shooting back.

Ahead was a big tower, and she crashed through a tenth story window, scattering chairs in an office. Ran out into the corridor in case someone sent a munition through the window after her, fast down a corridor then kicked in a door, activating building security alarms. That brought her to a window with a view. Ahead was North Park. To the right of that, the Domestic Affairs Building. It looked like it was built to withstand a nuke, which wasn't far from the truth. Around it were gardens, all trip-wired and armed to hell, then high walls. Flames rose from several points around it, indicating it had been subject to some early strikes, but she'd studied the preliminary schematics that were all Ari's folks had smuggled out, and wasn't especially encouraged.

"Ari, I want an active schematic on Primary Target, real time if you please. No guesses." At another time it might have felt a little odd; she hadn't spoken to him directly for half a year now. No, dammit, at any time it still felt a little odd. "Alpha formation, make a perimeter and hold," she added to her wingmen. The other three would be joining them shortly, she hoped.

"I've still got a few barriers remaining," came Ari's reply. *"Just hold for a little."* A little what, Sandy nearly said, but didn't. She was military, her brain didn't process "a little."

She smashed the window and jumped out instead. She fell, and the side of the building behind her exploded. Smaller neighbouring buildings gave cover for her landing, and she hit the street hard, then moved quickly along a sidewalk as burning debris and shattering glass tumbled about her.

"*Someone missed an emplacement,*" said Han, one of her wingmen.

"You think?" Sandy muttered. Probably it'd seen her break the window and fired just late. That was a happier thought than it having been about to fire anyway, and it being just dumb luck that she'd jumped when she had. Han lit up the offending emplacement for tacnet, saving his own ammunition, as elsewhere about the city, missiles leapt skyward. Ten seconds later, as Sandy sheltered at a corner, another explosion tore the air by the DA building.

"*Active countermeasures nearly got it,*" Han observed. Sandy watched a replay of what he'd seen, a storm of micro-flares about the gardens, settling now amidst the trees and bushes. Enough to distract most missiles, but not Tanushan tech, evidenced by the new smoking crater beneath one wall where the emplacement had been.

"If countermeasures are still active, they'll have just about everything up, save the big emplacements," Sandy observed. "Anyone running or flying in there is dead. Ari, either you get that defensive grid down or find us another way in."

"*Um, okay, hang on a moment . . .*" Between familiarly gritted teeth.

The front of the DA building exploded. Even though Sandy was not in direct line of sight, the intensity of the flash, and then the boom, made her duck. Then, amid the rain of debris onto neighbouring blocks, she looked up, and saw an especially large missile contrail.

Sandy suppressed a smile. "That you, darling?"

"*I told you,*" said Vanessa, "*never go anywhere without clean underwear and artillery.*"

"Yeah, well my underwear is now less clean than it was," said Han.

It was the Trebuchet system. Vanessa had insisted on bringing it along, descending on UAV mounts and sparing several troops to spend ten minutes of phase one setting it up somewhere hidden. God knew how long they could now keep it hidden, but for the moment it had proven a far-sighted insistence. Vanessa's operational policy had always been that obstacles were not obstacles once you'd blown them up. Facing the collapsed front facade of the DA building, Sandy found the logic hard to argue with.

"Let's go," said Sandy, targeting her three remaining missiles at surrounding department gardens, then leaping. At max power the jets pulled nearly nine Gs, and she did a fast loop over buildings, screamed low across a road and into the debris cloud of multiple explosions. Still something hit her, and she nearly crashed on deceleration and landing, digging a knee-down furrow in the turf, laying rifle and grenade shots down at everything that might be an emplacement. She continued putting down fire as Han and Weller tore in to more dignified landings, and then, just a little late, Rhian and her pair.

"*Sorry we're late,*" said Rhian, as they crashed through debris into the DA building. "*Got into a tangle.*"

"I know," said Sandy, ducking beneath collapsed steel beams, the ground an unstable mess of crushed concrete. "Let's see what we've got."

What they had was smoke and dust filled corridors, nothing working, and only the fuzziest network reception. Sandy recalled her pre-stored schematic, which was hardly precise, but it said the basement ought to be accessible from elevator shafts ahead. If that blast hadn't crippled or collapsed everything.

"*Sandy,*" said Ari in her ear, "*network.*" The connection clicked, and suddenly she was in, a vast expanse of complicated electronic schematics overlaying her vision. This was central grid, the command foundation that Anjula always pretended didn't exist. Pyeongwha was a free world, they said. Democratic, free trading, law abiding, a self-evolving society that no outside force had the right to dictate terms to. So why did it need a central network regulator, and hidden ministry compounds—the public discussion of which would get a government worker disappeared? To defend freedoms, Anjula replied, on the rare occasion they spoke of it at all. But the freedom to do what?

At a central point there were indeed elevator banks, two of them large, for cargo. Nothing worked. Han smashed the doors open and peered down the shaft, while Sandy accessed some interesting functions on her schematic.

"The shaft's booby-trapped," she observed, as they began unsealing from their suits. "Gas won't bother us, but there's a microwave projector that will clear your airways real good."

"Microwaves," said Khan. "That's so evil supervillain."

All six of them were GIs. There had been about fifty arriving on Callay over the past few years, mostly high-designation, escapees from the League who were following Sandy and Rhian's example and claiming asylum. Rights activists had taken up their cause, and each year more turned up at Gordon Spaceport. A few with network capabilities, advanced like hers, appeared almost right on Sandy's doorstep. Most volunteered for military or paramilitary, that being the only work they knew. A few non-combatant designations had found high level civvie jobs, most in data processing or technology of some description. And a few, more concerningly, had become loners, and struggled.

Sandy got her helmet off as the rest of the suit unsealed and disassembled. The big chest plate came off first, then the arm rigs that allowed her to hold up the enormous mag-rifle, then the heavy backpack/power source which she lowered to the ground. The leg-exo shed, like a crustacean losing its shell, and the whole rig, thrusters and all, slid to an untidy pile on the floor. Her light under-armour was her regular rig, plenty tough enough for infantry work. It now had a hole through the left side of the chest plate, where the building defences had hit her on the way in.

Khan saw it. "That go through?"

"Bit." Sandy flexed an arm with a grimace. "Maybe a rib. I'm fine." Disconnecting the assault rifle from the mag-rifle, a tiny thing by comparison, but just what she needed at close range. Without the helmet, she just had a headrig—like a headband with eyepiece, earpiece and insert plugs at the back—rigged in turn to signal boosters in her backpack. More grenades from storage, and twin pistols in her back holster, and she was right to go. "Ari, can you cut power on the shaft?"

"*No, but I have a schematic for that microwave.*" It flashed up. Sandy peered in the shaft and saw the relevant points on the wall, maybe twenty meters down. Scrolling through visual spectrums, she could also see the laser grid defences.

"Lasers," she said. "First person down there will discover the correct use of the word 'decimated.'" She strode to another shaft, and smashed through the doors with a single punch, then pulled them aside.

"There's a correct use?" wondered Han.

"To divide into ten equal portions," said Rhian, also armed up and covering a corridor. "She hates it when the reporters don't know what it means."

"It's Latin," said Weller. Someone up a corridor pointed a gun at them. Weller shot him in the head before he could fire. "Deci as in ten; decade, decimal, decahedron."

Sandy put a grenade through where Ari's schematic showed the microwave's power source was. Her schematic flickered, shielding wobbled then failed, and she hacked the lasers, too. Unable to deactivate them, she fired them instead, and they tore the sides of the shaft, and each other, to sizzling pieces.

"Let's go." She jumped.

CHAPTER TWO

Han was a 43 series, Dark Star. Sandy had met him once, briefly, in operations now nine years back, when they were both on the wrong side. Chinese by cosmetics, he was a specialised point man, a clear thinker, and overwhelmingly right-handed. He'd survived the Dark Star culls that had sent Sandy running for the Federation, tranquilised in an isolation cell until some unknown League techie had woken him up and smuggled him onto a freighter. More good Samaritans, a Christian group, had brought him to Callay and alerted herself and various rights groups, who'd all watched as CSA and others debriefed him and argued over asylum.

"Nice guy," Vanessa had told General Dal in their formal prep, in selecting the final assault squad. "Bit dopey. Does what he's told, vague on details, but absolutely disciplined and very dependable. Just don't let him make decisions on his own."

"Not like we haven't seen that before in GIs," Sandy had added, wryly. Back on old Earth, American soldiers had once been called "GIs" because every piece of kit they'd been issued was stamped "GI," for "General Issue." When League's industrial war machine had begun issuing front line units not just with kit, but with fully sentient synthetic soldiers, they'd been called "GIs" too, for the same reason. The acronym had stuck, its meaning forever changed.

Khan was a 47 series, and had never seen actual combat in the League. Too experimental, apparently, he was only about eight years old, which meant at his long-gestation designation, he'd only been active for about four. Three of those had now been on Callay. Again, a group of League defectors had brought him with them before he was evolved enough to think for himself, hoping to get a better asylum deal for themselves if they brought a high-des GI along. That made some security folks nervous—Khan had never actually defected, like Sandy, or even reached the conscious realisation that the League truly sucked for GIs and a lot of other people, like Han. And Khan had become truly smart, socialised and borderline devious when he chose. If anyone could fake it, then sell you out to his old League friends, Khan could.

"Showbiz Khan," Vanessa called him, after his flashing smile. "He'd be command material if he had more experience. Wait and see how he responds to the real thing, then we'll make a call."

Ogun was a 40, of African cosmetics, bald and dour-looking. By designation that made him kind of dumb, but Sandy wasn't so sure. Certainly he didn't say much, including about how he'd gotten out. But all the psychs agreed that he hated the League with a passion, and wasn't smart enough, or devious enough, to fake it. The Federation opposed the League and that was good enough for him. His loyalty was beyond doubt.

"Great team player," was Vanessa's assessment. "He just knows where to be. Individually, not so much."

"A lot of the lower designations are better team players that their supposed superiors," Sandy had added. "Thus proving that selfishness is a higher intellectual function."

"Ha," spoke Vanessa. "Apply that theory to a five-year-old."

Weller was an odd girl. A 44 by designation, European by cosmetics, she claimed to have been injured in a major battle eight years ago, left for dead in a ruined city, and nursed back to health by Sufi mystics who'd found her there. Both her injuries and her devotion to Sufism backed her story, but Sandy still found something about her strange.

"Her detachment is almost sociopathic," Vanessa had observed. "But that's unfair, because she's quite a nice girl. She just, you know, doesn't seem to make the distinction between people, events and emotions."

"I think 'autistic' would be more fair than 'sociopathic,'" Sandy had said. "Not uncommon amongst GIs either. But she's a good soldier, I'll take her."

Rhian Chu, of course, was Sandy's old buddy, and a quite intriguing individual. Upon first arrival in the Federation, Sandy wouldn't have trusted her with a combat command any more than Ogun or Han, but she'd grown enormously since. A 39 by designation, she wasn't technically supposed to be that smart, but these days Sandy would have backed her over a lot of higher designations. To prove the point, she'd recently completed an advanced postgrad on child psychology and early development, and aced it in a tough class.

"It's sad she's still a soldier," Vanessa had observed. "She's got far more to offer childhood studies and education than she does here. But she's got to make that call for herself, I can't do it."

"I said I was coming," Sandy had sighed, "and she was pretty much unstoppable from then."

Last of these final, elite six, was Cassandra Kresnov. GIs had been coming in from the League for four years now, experimental ones with the self-awareness to realise the injustices done to them. Though two had emerged as challengers, and one of those was certainly her equal in intellect, there were still none who came close in combat. Weller had quoted Hindu scripture after seeing her fight—Vishnu from the Baghavad-Gita: "for I am become death, destroyer of worlds." Sandy was one of a tiny handful of 50 series GIs ever made. Certainly she was the only one serving the Federation. It was hypothetically conceivable that further advances could make a more effective soldier, but Vanessa, for one, doubted it.

"Babe," she'd said, "if it's Pyeongwha versus you, I pick you."

"Well that's sweet," Sandy had replied, "but you know better than anyone it doesn't work like that."

"Bullshit it doesn't," Vanessa had said with a smile. "I've got an entire assault plan that counts on it."

Under the DA building was a cavern. It led to a maze of caves beneath Anjula, well known by the first settlers over two hundred years ago . . . in fact, it was one of the reasons why the city had been placed where it was. Into the caves had gone power plants, waste management systems, and various emergency facilities—a whole underground infrastructure. Then, from eighty years back, access had been increasingly restricted.

It had begun by accident. A local biotech firm had made some genome alterations to counter a strain of nasty Pyeongwha native neural diseases. It worked, and the genome adjustments had created an interesting additional benefit—an enhanced ability to assimilate what had then been a new and innovative neural-cluster uplink technology. Those were synthetic-organic themselves, the kind of thing the League had been playing with at the time, later largely banned in the Federation. But on Pyeongwha, they'd led to a noticeable increase in productivity, ingenuity, and—its proponents claimed—social harmony. So popular they'd proven, that governments had been elected to promote, and later mandate, certain functions. A new phase of human evolution, they'd called it. Theories had abounded on how the natural mechanisms of organic evolution were now adapting themselves to NCT, as Neural Cluster Tech was called, leading to a virtuous circle of technological and biological improvement.

NCT proponents built the technology into a vision of prosperity, and hadn't taken criticism well. Soon NCT on Pyeongwha was cultish, non-NCT subscribers didn't get into good schools, or get good jobs, and were accused of pushing down "national competitiveness." Others were told they promoted "social disharmony." Twenty years ago, they'd begun disappearing. Escaping "subversives" had told horror stories of covert "social reorganisation" programs occurring beneath the ground, and pleaded with the Federation Grand Council to do something. But that Federation Grand Council had been locked away on Earth, and only interested in keeping the trading lanes open. Pyeongwha was wealthy and productive, and action would be expensive.

Then the Grand Council had shifted to Callay, where the fate of Federation colonies meant far more than just economics. Finally, five years after the relocation, a decision had been made. Fleet had wanted to do it the old fashioned way, strangling and pounding from orbit, but Callay's former CDF, now refashioned into the new Federal Security Agency, had had other ideas. Callayan and Tanushan technology, long a driving revolutionary force in Federation civilian tech, now moved into military affairs. With a new cadre of side-switching GIs leading the push, FSA commanders were adamant that now, things would happen differently.

Differently hadn't included getting pinned down straight out of the elevators. There were caverns here all right, heavily engineered with gantry walls, great pipes and electrical assemblies running everywhere. Not some kind of military base, just a big city's underground infrastructure, but Anjula was certainly protecting it.

Sandy covered on one side of a big cargo doorway, arranging her various magazines and grenades where she reckoned she'd need them. Her squad were spread across the industrial space, exchanging fire with intense resistance in the cavern beyond. Sandy saved her ammo; anything she eliminated here would just be replaced. She had an objective, and any firepower she expended that didn't directly help her get there was wasted.

"*Cap,*" said Rhian on uplinks, "*they've got an AMAPS up high somewhere, another low to the left, there's no angle on this doorway.*"

"Doesn't matter, go around it," she replied. "Take the squad, Rhi, you're in charge. Get their damn power plants offline, we can shut down half the city from here."

"*You're going alone?*" She didn't sound that surprised.

"You know the sims in tight spaces, once they realise they can't get me, they'll flank me, everything will come down on my wingman, any way they can. I'm really better at this alone."

"*I know.*"

It was one of the stupid ironies about being the galaxy's most effective 50 series GI—she was a very talented commander, yet even better in a shooting fight. In situations like this, where the objective was imperative, support only slowed her down, and all her command skills were for nothing.

They moved, Sandy down a side corridor, then up some stairs to a gantry overlooking the cavern. It was guarded, she shot two soldiers defending it, crushed the skull of a third with a casual passing elbow, then proceeded, while running, to put bullets through the exposed faces, throats and armour weak spots of another five troops at various points about the cavern. The AMAPS Rhian had spotted was on her level now, turning with twin cannon spinning. Sandy leaped and spun, switching the rifle to her left hand to nail its sensors with a grenade while the right angled upward with a pistol to shoot two men on a gantry above her. She skidded on her back, put another grenade in the AMAPS, leaped for the overhead gantry, silenced two more shooters in mid air, then ducked into a side tunnel before the second AMAPS tore that gantry to pieces with its cannon.

Anyone who got in her way, and was armed, died. If Rhian had come with her, she'd have lost her by now anyhow; coordination at these speeds was nearly impossible. The biggest worry now was booby traps, always the biggest threat to GIs. She sprinted down corridors, literally bouncing off walls to make corners at speed, leaped down stairwells, and crossed open spaces so fast guarding soldiers barely had time to aim before she was gone. If they were lucky, she didn't bother killing them on the way through. In combat mode, even she wasn't entirely certain what her subconscious would process as a threat, and simply didn't have time to think it through at length.

Her mental schematic helped, too, it wasn't always perfect, but it gave her a general idea of what lay ahead. It told her a door blocking the corridor was thin enough to grenade and dive through the hole, while another one would be faster for her to go around. Automatic gun emplacements guarded a junction, so hair-trigger that she didn't dare try and shoot them even with her reflexes. She hacked a ventilation system instead, blasting one with cold air, causing others to shoot the vent, which blew out the region's power and caused a defensive grid flux. That was all she needed to hack one's control system and blow the other emplacements to pieces. She was twenty-two years old now, positively ancient in GI terms, and she knew a lot of tricks.

The corridors opened onto proper caverns, metal giving way to rock, and here there was a full squad with multiple AMAPS, heavy weapons, the works. First thing, from the shelter of an engineering approach, Sandy hacked and shut down half the lights. The other half came down with a couple of well-placed grenades, heavy supports crashing to the cavern floor, sending soldiers running in the engulfing dark. Then, dark as the night that had suddenly descended, she simply jumped in amongst them.

It was a horror, the only light came from misused AMAPS floodlights that glared and blinded as much as they illuminated, and muzzle flashes and explosions, everyone firing and only one target, which was never where or what its opponents thought it was. Sandy barely had to shoot more than a third of them, mostly they shot each other as she skipped, rolled and wove amongst them, a bullet here, a punch there. Most commanders did not realise how numerical superiority could be a curse until they ran into high-designation GIs. They were still dying once she'd gone, racing into the complex they'd been defending—a hive of steel and glass emerging from the rock. She shot a window, leaped three stories and crashed through office glass, confounding anyone who'd expected her to take the door.

Civvies screamed and ran, and Sandy ignored them, save for one woman, dressed like a manager, whom she abruptly headlocked against a steel corridor wall. "Where's the containment facility, I want the people. Where do you keep them?"

And followed the woman's trembling finger, down the corridor in a flash. This place was medical. That immediately creeped her out. NCT was medical, certainly, and required a lot of ongoing research. Anjula insisted that it was all above-board biotech, but refused Federal inspectors who wanted to probe further for illegal tech. This place looked like a giant steel-framed hospital, built into a natural cavern like a beehive might fill up a spider's hole with honeycomb. Everywhere were secure doors requiring keycards or iris scans, though Sandy found that network hacks or hammer blows did the trick as well.

She skipped through rooms to cut between corridors, and found vast labs, high tech analysers, rows of test tubes and refrigerated containers. Partly, she was dimly aware past the combat reflex, it creeped her out because many of her own worst nightmares came from places like this—too many bad memories of combat patches, upgrade surgeries or the ubiquitous "checkups." She'd been conceived in a place like this, no doubt. It wasn't something she liked to think about, and even Tanushan psychs were accustomed to her changing the subject.

A couple of guards surprised her at a doorway, she took both by breaking bones without killing, and used one's keycard to open a secure door as he shrieked. This room had refrigeration units. Big ones, from floor to ceiling, with fancy screens that displayed the vitals of the people within. Because . . . they were *people*, it registered now as she slowed her pace a little. Rows of them, men and women, old and young. The network in this region was proving stubborn, so she accessed at a local data point, downloaded rapid codes, then fed them up to Ari, confident he'd find a delicate way through where she'd just break things and make a mess. This information, they needed intact.

Into a neighbouring room, past more refrigeration units, dimly aware that Ari was swearing in her inner ear. She really wasn't processing on that emotional level yet; she'd cut that out of her world, unable to handle that and the job she was here to do at the same time. He was seeing the same thing she was—armscomp had cameras on her headset, and he was reading and no doubt recording those images. Someone in the room with Ari, in the background, sounded like he was crying.

Through another door, and here were surgical tables, with great automated surgical units hovering like mechanical spiders above the slabs, arms affixed with every cutting and scanning and stabbing tool known to medicine, plus tubes for the blood and grilles on the floor to flush away the mess . . .

At that moment all the doors slammed shut and armed soldiers sprang up beyond the adjoining control room windows, no doubt thinking it a fine trap they'd led her into. Sandy shot them all in slightly less than half a second, and leaped into the control room through shattered glass. She accessed physically with a cord and socket, and accumulated codes got her into memory files and recent activities, and now she could see bodies on the slabs, machine tools whirring, skulls sliced open to probe the mysteries of NCT within, and why it didn't seem to work on some defective people as well as Anjula's leaders thought it ought. Everyone had thought the situation on Pyeongwha was bad, but no one had quite expected this.

"Oh, you got 'em Sandy," Ari was saying, choked with furious emotion. *"I'm getting all this and we're putting it out to broadcast in a few seconds. You fucking got 'em."*

"These memory files are too big," she heard herself saying. "There's got to be years of files in here. Surely this whole facility can't be for this."

"I think it might be," said Ari. *"It would explain a lot, these last fifteen years or so . . ."* And he broke off, to calm the sudden clamor for names from the crying man in the room with him. There would be plenty of time to search the database for names later, he assured that man. They'd find everyone, every last man and woman, no one would be forgotten.

Sandy didn't know how she felt. It was more than just combat reflex, which made it hard to access emotion. She just felt . . . numb. She'd wanted to be on board precisely because of this, and the prospect of a very worthy cause. But now that she was here, she couldn't figure if she was glad to be here, or if she'd regret it forever. Perhaps, like so many things in the lives of soldiers, it was both.

"Sandy," came Rhian's voice, *"you've still got several hundred security personnel in there with you, and maybe a thousand civvies. Do you need some help mopping up?"*

"Help?" Sandy disconnected and moved through a side door. A security man on the far side tried to shoot her, but between his finger tightening on the trigger and the gun going off, Sandy was no longer where she had been. She punched him in the head, not an especially hard punch as such things went, but the wall three meters back was sprayed with skull, blood and brains. "No," she said, continuing down the corridor. "I think I can handle it."

Admiral Alemsegad's shuttle arrived in the cold dawn, upon the landing pad within the bowl-shaped rooftop of Anjula's Parliament, with engines screaming and thermal scales popping from reentry heat. Assault shuttles were always a menace to the eardrums. On polite official visits, VIPs would land at the spaceport and take an atmospheric shuttle to the Parliament, and not bring their direct-from-orbit beasts down on the roof to frighten local residents and damage their windows. But this was no polite visit, and Vanessa was there to meet him, thankful her helmet would save her senses from damage.

The admiral wore a spacer's jumpsuit, jacket and a uniform cloak, swirling out the back in a blast of frigid air amidst his armoured Marine escort. Vanessa popped her visor and saluted. The cold on her face was enough that she wished she hadn't.

"Commander Rice," she identified herself. The admiral saluted, and she gestured him to walk with her.

"Sitrep," he requested.

"We have Anjula for now," she said, leading him through the blast doors into the holding area, signaling whoever was watching the monitor to cycle the doors. Probably it was one of their AIs. "Anjula rebels hold much of the Parliament network function, and now we physically hold most of the building . . ."

"Most?" Alemsegad interrupted.

Vanessa shrugged. "A few quarters holding out. We haven't the manpower to mop up completely, they weren't attacking us so we sealed them off. Now that you're here, feel free to finish up."

The admiral nodded, and gave a signal to the Marine captain at this side. The captain relayed something, and four from the admiral's ten-strong contingent hurried ahead as the inner doors squealed open.

Vanessa led the admiral after. "Parliament wants to speak to you," she continued. "They want to know by what right the Grand Council attacked their world."

"President Tao?"

"Vice President Hakana," Vanessa corrected. "Tao's wounded." The admiral looked at her. "We had to shoot our way in. They were trying to reestablish network control. Shit happened."

The admiral made a face. "Hakana then. Who's in charge now?"

Of the rebels, he meant. It was necessary protocol. The Fleet wasn't allowed to intervene in any Federation world's affairs except in exceptional circumstances. One of those circumstances was the event of civil uprising and loss of governmental control.

"His name's Moon," said Vanessa, as they walked down a wide, gently bending corridor, office doors on the right, windows offering a view across the Anjulan skyline to the left. Smoke rose in columns, across a cityscape unusually clear of air traffic. "University professor and tech wizard. He'll be acting president."

"Well," said Alemsegad, "now I am. As the senior Federal representative, I'll be acting president until a governor arrives, and you'll be my security chief."

"Yes sir. You'd not rather use a Marine?"

"You've been planning this for months, we just got here. I'll need your knowledge."

"Yes sir."

Alemsegad smiled. "Don't worry, Commander, I'll not keep you long. Just until relief arrives, maybe a week."

"Damn," said Vanessa. "I'm gonna miss Tanusha fashion week."

"Seriously?" asked the admiral.

"No," said Vanessa. Alemsegad actually grinned. Word was, he didn't do that often.

The planning/debriefing session in the ex-president's office that evening was of informal attire, but as deadly focused, as one would expect from a bunch of war veterans who cared less about procedure than results.

Sandy sat by the big, bomb-proof windows with her feet up, in a reclining chair with just a jacket over a bra-top, her side swathed in bandages. The DA building defences had indeed taken a rib, which had stopped them from taking a lung. The rib would heal, she was assured, but it needed to breathe, and have as little pressure on it as possible. A straight human, of course, would have lost most of her chest cavity. Also present were Vanessa, Ari, Admiral Alemsegad, Moon, Marine Captain Reddy, and Choi, a colleague of Moon's, formerly an Anjulan police officer of considerable rank.

"Streets are pretty quiet," Choi was saying, with that East-Asian stilt to his English that was the standard Anjulan accent. "I'm not a social psychologist, but there's going to be a big problem assimilating this. Many won't accept it. Right now they're stunned, they don't know how to process it. But that doesn't mean that when they do process it, we'll like how they do it."

All com networks had been taken over, forced to run footage of Sandy's discoveries, and the discoveries that were now continuing to pour out from the Marines that had now taken over the underground facility. Ari had suggested they just run the footage live and unedited, with jerky visuals, foul trooper language and all. Certainly, it was more effective that way, more authentic to a disbelieving public. On another channel were Anjulan rebels, transmitting from a Parliament office, scrolling through lists of names and inviting Pyeongwha citizens to come forward with names of their own, with photographs, medical records and DNA samples, if possible. They were getting a lot of response, but it was not overwhelming. Most of the security forces, the occupiers agreed, had not been eliminated, but had merely gone to ground, sheltered by the populace. Even with these new revelations, it was unclear which way the population would go.

"It's just the most fucking amazing thing," Ari said, a steaming cup of chai in hand, looking worn and dazed. He had a moustache now, which Sandy didn't think she liked. And he looked older. "The whole thing's a giant, collective, mutually-agreed-upon brain fuck. I mean, they knew. They had to have known, there were so many clues, so few other alternatives . . ."

"Oh, they knew!" Moon said loudly, shaking with emotion. "They all knew, half the damn population!"

"It's a feedback loop," said Ari. "In most societies the population splits fifty-fifty on any question, but the genetic modifications made here didn't stop once NCT took off; they accelerated. They were genetically pre-selecting the most well-disposed toward the technology, and those changes were in turn shaping the direction of NCT itself. Like a feedback loop on an unsecured microphone—sound produces vibration, vibration produces sound, round in circles until all you're left with is out of control squealing."

"It's no different from what we've seen in human societies before," said Vanessa. "It's just another variation of authoritarianism. We've just never seen it interact with technology like this before."

The footage from preliminary debriefings in the medical facility was the most chilling of all. Ordinary men and women, highly qualified, family people with no apparent psychological disorders, who saw absolutely nothing wrong in their daily work. Not in the killing, not in the experiments, and not in some of the truly horrific things that were emerging on the lower levels.

"All human psychology has a natural inclination toward consensus,"

Sandy said tiredly from her reclining chair. "NCT is a technology that actively creates consensus. With uplink technology it works like a kind of mass telepathy, a collectivisation. And it's exhilarating, I bet. Made them heaps productive, wealthy, talented. I worried about it all the time in GIs. Tacnet and instantaneous communication is just so immersive, some come to not like the real world half as much. They'd rather stay connected all the time.

"You add that to the genetic tinkering they were doing, actively breeding out the non-NCT compliant as an economic and social measure . . . at some point it just reaches some really scary place that the rest of us unconnected just can't process; a place where people start to practise mass slaughter and not see the problem. Their value structure is completely consumed into the NCT network."

"There is a report," said Alemsegad, his lanky frame lounged on a chair. His manner was sparse, inscrutable, his sentences short. Ethiopian heritage, Sandy guessed. "A classified report. Fleet Intelligence. On NCT and brain structure. The network software was changing brain structure."

"All uplinks do that," said Ari. "Ours too."

Alemsegad shook his head. "Not just increasing existing pathways. Overall structure, composition, processing order. Actively, short term, not long term."

"Shit," Vanessa murmured, almost as fascinated as horrified. "Really?"

"Write new software, new brain structure appears. Two years, maybe less. So, at what point does the brain write the software? Or the software write the brain?"

Silence in the room. Moon and Choi looked particularly uncomfortable. Almost certainly they'd had some form of NCT augmentation. The technology was variable, as were degrees of augmentation. Many non-compliants had rewritten their implant software, dialed it down, and escaped the worst effects. But nearly everyone on Pyeongwha had it done. It'd been mandatory for twenty-four years now, and semi-mandatory for another forty before that.

Neural cluster tech wasn't so different from League synthetic biology, though. Human psychology had been adjusting to neural implants for a long time now—several hundred years, with the more basic tech. League tech copied natural brain function to the degree that the human brain did not recognise it as foreign, and that caused the brain to naturally rewire itself, certainly, in ways that were still surprising many researchers, growing new pathways to cope with network information flows that could never occur in nature. NCT was different in that it allowed a lot more two-way interaction, telling the brain what to do in ways that League tech, being purposely more passive, didn't.

Could synthetic biological implants cause a brain to rewire itself to look more like the implant and less like the original brain? As an entirely synthetic entity herself, Sandy didn't like the idea. If regular organic brains were that rewritable, what did it say of a GI's chances? And yet, she thought, it might explain some things. League researchers designing GI tech for the war hadn't been like peacetime scientists, sharing information in the spirit of open discovery. They'd been shut away in massively funded, isolated institutions, concentrating on the sole purpose of building better fighting machines. Sandy knew from experience they'd been less than honest about exactly what they'd discovered, and how GIs really worked—even with each other.

"I don't buy it," Sandy decided. There was still a moral issue at play, after all. "Blame the technology. Maybe NCT leans them in one direction, but people still get to choose."

"And you didn't hear it from me," Alemsegad finished, giving Sandy a long, skeptical look. That didn't surprise her. A lot of Fleet officers remained cool toward her. They'd thought the Federation's war against the League had been a war to defeat the scourge of artificial humanity—GIs, like her. That it had actually been about liberating, or presenting the choice of liberation, to the most advanced GIs, was not something that a lot of them accepted. She could see it in his eyes as he looked at her: I lost all of those good friends for this?

"So how do we do this?" Vanessa asked Moon and Choi. "You two know the place. How many of the population are as hardcore as the administration?"

"It's not how many are that hardcore," said Choi, shaking his head. "It's how many are prepared to accept an alternative. When something is your whole world, it's hard to believe it's not true, even when someone shows you proof."

"There will be conspiracy stories," Moon agreed, nodding vigorously. "They will make up tales about how the whole thing is a Federation plot. Probably they won't believe the facilities are even real, or say we made the whole thing up."

"And that gives a resistance movement enough of a foundation amongst the populace to mount a guerilla resistance," Captain Reddy summarised. "Could go on a long time." Alemsegad looked at him. Evidently they'd had this discussion before. "Could lose a lot of people on this rock."

"Could stop following orders and stop calling yourself a Marine," the admiral replied. Reddy looked at his boots. "We only control Anjula, anyway. Let's wait for the rest of the planet. I've heard it's not as bad away from Anjula, out in the rural belts."

Choi and Moon looked skeptical, but did not argue.

"Or we could find a way to use NCT against them," Ari suggested, deep in thought. "I need to think about that for a bit."

Soon they departed, everyone with much to do except Sandy, who'd been told to rest. Ari waited too. Vanessa lingered in the door with a look of concern, then departed with an encouraging smile at Sandy.

"Hi," said Ari, hands in pockets.

"Hi," said Sandy, still reclining. It had taken something out of her, that fight, combat reflex hiding from her that she'd nearly lost a lung. Now the masking agents had worn off, she was worn out, and didn't much feel like sitting up straight, much less standing. "You did good. Saved a lot of people."

"You, too. How were the hoppers?"

"Amazing tech. Revolutionary technology for sure, we pinned down an entire city with just fifty troops and good network support."

"There'll be a counter-technology though, there always is."

"Yeah."

A silence. Ari looked at his feet, a familiar, nervous mannerism. Sandy sighed. She really wasn't good at this. She was drastically civilianised over what she'd been when she first arrived in Federation space, but still she had her limitations. Being a good soldier meant knowing what those limitations were.

She heaved herself reluctantly to her feet, muscles aching, walked to him, and put her arms around him. He put his arms around her too, carefully. For a moment, they held each other. Then she kissed him on the cheek.

"It's okay, Ari," she told him. "You know I don't make scenes. I'm not mad. You're free to live your life, don't worry about it."

He gazed at her, with those intensely browed, intelligent eyes. "Sandy, you know, I wish that I could . . . I mean, I wish it didn't have to . . ."

"I said it's okay. I understand."

"I don't think you do."

Sandy's expression hardened just a little, her head cocked to one side. "You're not going to make this difficult, are you? Because you know I don't like difficult."

"But everything's always difficult," said Ari. "That's the point." His comebacks were always so fast. She had the quickest reflexes of any living thing, but sometimes, talking to Ari, she felt overwhelmed and sluggish.

She chose not to reply.

Ari sighed. "Look, Sandy." He took her face in his hands, one of the very few people who'd dare. One of the very few who knew her well enough to know that there was really nothing to dare. "I love you. I'll always love you. Just because we're no longer . . ."

"Yeah." She still didn't really understand that bit. She wasn't accustomed to being left. She'd never really understood what all that meant until now.

"I just needed that part of my life back, at this time, that's all."

"It's okay, Ari," she insisted. "You're allowed to have your reasons. I forgive you."

He didn't leave. She wished he'd just leave, that would be easier. But he stood there, and gazed at her, as though she were the most confusing, confounding problem his hyper-intelligent brain had ever struggled and failed to comprehend. Well, she knew how that felt. Then, finally, he kissed her on the forehead, and left.

Vanessa came back in the door as soon as Ari went through it. She hadn't departed, merely waited outside. That made Sandy more emotional than the exchange with Ari had. She hugged her friend, who hugged her back.

"You okay?" Vanessa asked.

"Yeah. Twenty-two years old, I guess it's about time I learned what it's like to get dumped." She wiped her eye. "Stupid thing to worry about now. It's not like there aren't more important things."

"You've got to live, Sandy. Life doesn't just stop because things in the universe suck. You and Ari were good together. It's worth feeling sad about."

Sandy released her and gazed out the windows. "You never seemed that surprised, though."

"Well it's Ari. And you, I mean, neither of you are that predictable. And look, you're still so young, you've only been a Federation civilian for what is it now, seven years?"

"Seven," Sandy nodded.

"And you were with Ari for five and a bit of those, which is longer than most people gave you. But let's face it, everything for you is still a bit of a learning curve. Chalk it down to experience and move on. This shit's happened to all of us; it certainly happened to me."

"Yeah." Vanessa was divorced, shortly after Sandy first met her. She'd not seen her ex-husband since, not even heard word of him. Given their working circumstances, Sandy knew she and Ari weren't going to get the same clean break.

"Besides which," said Vanessa, arm about her, "you'll always have me."

Sandy smiled. "Only you go and get married again, and leave me all alone in my house . . ."

"Oh, poor Sandy," Vanessa laughed. "As if seeing me all day every day for work isn't more than any sane person could bear."

CHAPTER THREE

T rue to his word, Admiral Alemsegad only kept them a week, until Marine and Army reinforcements arrived. After that, the FSA assault team were free to return to Callay on the first available cruiser.

Sandy recovered fast; she'd need the bandages for a while yet, but the damage hadn't affected a joint or moving part, so her mobility was relatively unaffected. Mentally, from the combined effects of events on Anjula and finally seeing Ari again, she was less unscathed. She had several mandatory tape sessions, where the shipboard psych ran invasive readjustments through her short term memory—standard for all soldiers to prevent the onset of post-traumatic stress, and it worked pretty similarly for GIs and straights alike. It helped her sleep, though truly, like most tape-adjusted vets, she had no idea if she was actually susceptible to PTSD or not. Common theory was that GIs weren't, thanks to the response-deadening effects of combat reflex . . . but then, she'd seen GIs blow themselves to bits rather than face an upcoming fight. Twice. And she'd heard of a number of others.

Whatever the cause, she still felt off, and so resorted to her old League-side medicine: fucking. GIs of any designation were largely immune from jealousy and other inconvenient emotional strangleholds, so Khan and Han were obvious choices, and lucky for her, both volunteered simultaneously. It had been a long time since she'd done anything as wild as two at a time—League-side, she supposed, when life had been simpler, and life expectancies considerably shorter, leading to more enthusiastically wild entertainments of the kind.

The orgasms were incredible. And it bothered her a little, because Ari had been a good lover, and they'd had some great sessions together. But there were things a straight human man simply couldn't do, like experience some of her more wild and powerful manoeuvers and live to talk about it. On her cramped shipboard bunk, she embraced alternately Khan or Han, and really went for it, and felt so liberated that she did not have to worry about harming either of them, let alone killing them, as could easily happen when she truly lost control. No more careful sex, then—Vanessa had told her to make the most of where life took her, and this was one obvious advantage. She kept the two men busy for nearly an hour, until finally collapsing, sweat-drenched and exhausted, on a bunk with torn sheets and a newly-bent frame.

After a shower, she called on Vanessa, a short walk down a narrow, dog-legged corridor to the small gymnasium. It felt weird to be on a combat ship again, where she'd spent so much of her previous life. The faintly stale, recycled air, the low overheads and the emergency acceleration slings lining the corridors set off all sorts of memories, some fond, others utterly unwanted. That she was bandaged, with a healing hole in her side, returning from a fairly nasty fight with the after-effects of trauma tape in her head, and the recent recipient of a truly awesome fucking, all combined to amplify the effect.

Vanessa was belted into a weights machine, lifting about five hundred kilos' worth of resistance with her legs. That was somewhat remarkable to watch of such a small girl, and a good two hundred kilos more than she'd have managed perhaps a year ago. Sandy herself, of course, could do comfortably ten times what the machine could offer without breaking. That wasn't what made GIs dangerous, however—it was the fast-twitch, high velocity release of all that power.

"Good to be back amongst your own kind, then?" Vanessa asked her with a grin, sweaty and not-particularly-strained, as Sandy sat on a bench alongside.

"You heard?"

"I walked past your door half an hour ago. Sounded like you were trashing the place. Are the boys okay?"

Sandy smiled. "They're fine. And quite talented too, if you'd like a turn."

"Oh no," said Vanessa, still pushing. "Happy monogamy for me. If even you could manage it for four years, I'm sure I can."

"Even me," Sandy repeated, taking mock offence. But her heart wasn't in it. Vanessa saw. "What's wrong?"

"Oh, nothing." She thought about it for a moment. "I think I'm reverting."

"To what?"

"To how I was. I'd thought I was progressing. Maturing as a person. I was learning civilian life, I had a steady boyfriend, I actually made a pretty good girlfriend too, at times."

"You did," Vanessa agreed, nodding.

"I mean, I wasn't pushy or demanding. I could be fun, I'd drag him out of his comfort zone often enough to make his life more interesting, and he seemed to appreciate it."

"He did."

"I'd thought that was the direction I had to go. To move away from what I'd been, as a League soldier. A drone."

"Sandy, you were never a drone."

"Oh, we all are at some point. All GIs. Some of us grow out of it, that's all. I'd thought I was growing, but now I'm back to old ways. Fighting, fucking . . ." She shrugged, and ran a hand through her wet hair.

Vanessa stopped with the weights, unstrapped herself and sat up. Sandy tossed her a towel.

"It's not the sex that's bothering you, is it?" It was more a statement than a question. Vanessa always saw through her. Given a choice between her and any shrink, Sandy chose Vanessa every time. "It's the fight."

"I killed a lot of people in that fight," Sandy said somberly.

"Me too. So what?"

"It usually bothers me. Last year, when I took out that idiot at Larion Park . . ."

"Who was holding a room full of innocent people hostage with explosives and firearms, thus saving at least twenty lives, yes?"

"Yeah, but it bothered me. The guy was a mental case, the system failed him, his family were so upset . . ."

"And all those soldiers in Anjula had family, too," Vanessa interjected, "and no doubt they'll be very unhappy, as well. Sandy, they were part of a system that was massacring thousands of innocent people. We stopped them. You saved a lot more than you killed, and . . ."

"I know," said Sandy, with a calm stare. "That's the point. It doesn't bother me at all." Vanessa frowned a little. "I mean, I think about them now, and truly, I couldn't give a rat's ass."

"Well that's good then," said Vanessa, switching the machine over so she could do reps with her arms.

"I don't know. I began life not caring, because all GIs start off as drones, like I said. Then I realised I did care, but couldn't do anything about it. Then I realised the League sucked, and I could do something about it, so I did. I just . . . I just got used to the idea that my guilt, or conscience, or whatever you want to call it, was a sign of my evolution as a person. And now, I go cut a swathe through Anjula's finest, and I just don't care. And it's not just the tape, I'm sure of it."

"So you're scared that you're turning back into a version of what you were when you were younger, in the League?"

Sandy sighed. "I don't know. Maybe."

"Because your boyfriend left you?" It was one of Vanessa's familiar, sharp little underhanded jabs.

Sandy's lips twisted. "Yeah. I guess."

"Look." Vanessa hooked her arms over the machine's handles. "It's tough for you right now, I know. And not just with Ari, that's bullshit—with all these other GIs pouring down on you from the League the past few years. You feel responsible, you worry about them, there's all the legal and political shit. And you're worried about how it's all going to turn out. I don't just mean facts on the ground, I mean more broadly."

"Yeah."

"I mean, I'm a straight, organic human. All the literature's been pretty much written on me and my kind. But you guys . . . Sandy, you ever just think that however you turn out, that's what you're meant to be? Maybe it's time to stop worrying about what you ought to try and become, and just accept what you are."

"Vanessa, you know better than anyone. There's a whole bunch of things about what I am that I don't like."

"So let me tell you this—there's a whole bunch of things about what you are that I absolutely love. And I don't just mean as your friend, I mean in general. As qualities everyone could learn from. As improvements to our species."

"Including Anjula." Drily.

"Including Anjula," Vanessa declared, with a very firm nod. "Yes. Absolutely including Anjula. Someone has to do it, Sandy. Be proud of it. And fuck lots of guys, and continue to like too many different brands of coffee, and be addicted to surfing like a junkie, and just be what you are, and stop fucking worrying about it."

Vanessa tossed the towel back at Sandy, who could have caught it, but let it catch her in the face instead. Vanessa glared at her, then settled back down to do her reps. Sandy watched her. Nearly three hundred kilos, with the arms of a girl who, unaugmented, would probably struggle to do forty.

"So, how does the upgrade feel?" Sandy asked her.

"Awesome," said Vanessa, with real pleasure. "The tech's incredible. It's not so much the extra strength, it's the speed and endurance. I nearly got a mid-des GI's score on the last combat course I did."

"I know," said Sandy. "I'd say you were eighty percent what I'd expect a mid-des like Khan to do."

"And I've gotten faster since then, too," Vanessa said smugly.

"Only your command skills are so much better." Sandy was relieved about that. It kept Vanessa further to the rear. Plus, there was something faintly unnerving about watching Vanessa's transformation, and her pleasure at its results. "Exactly what are you trying to become, Ricey? And are you aware what it's going to cost? "They haven't found an upgrade for command yet."

"Nor wisdom, nor humour, nor good sexual technique. But I'm sure they're working on it."

The trip took two weeks. Vanessa wanted to go home to her husband. Rhian wanted to go home to her husband and her three adopted kids. Han, Weller and Khan wanted to go and see their friends, other GIs newly arrived from the League, and see how things were progressing. Sandy wanted that, too, but there would be plenty of time for that later. First, she wanted to go surfing.

The problems began at Balaji Airport. Balaji was the airport Fleet used to avoid crowding up Gordon, the main civilian port. It was nestled in a shallow valley, two hundred kilometers from Tanusha, far enough that the environmentalists didn't protest at all the trees to be chopped down. For all Fleet's increasing scale on Callay, now that the Grand Council made Callay the administrative center of the entire Federation, Balaji remained some-what rural—some big structures mostly underground to guard against orbital strike, a small accompanying town, and only averaging perhaps twenty shuttle flights a day, as Gordon retained all of the station traffic. Balaji only took independent shuttles from interplanetary vessels that did not go through station customs first. Normally, that caused no one any problem.

"What d'you fucking mean we have to go through customs?" Vanessa snarled at the airport official who'd informed them. They stood in the middle of a vast underground hangar where they'd all expected an aircraft of some description to take them into town. Instead, there was a Fleet officer, accompanied by some government people in suits.

"I'm sorry," said the officer, "but we're informed by the Callayan government that the crew of all foreign vessels must pass through customs first."

"Foreign? We're Federal Security Agency, which is based on Callay . . . how is that foreign?"

"If it's not a Callayan national entity, it's foreign," one of the suits explained.

"Um, excuse me?" said Yeoh, who was the unit's leading Intel officer, pushing to the front. "I actually have a Masters in law from Kannan University, and that's just not correct . . . clause182b was inserted into the Callayan constitution following the relocation, and it states that all Federal security personnel based on Callay shall be regarded as Callayan citizens for arrivals and departures."

Everyone looked hopefully at their antagonists.

"Our information is that you need to go through customs," came the reply. Exclamations of dismay.

Yeoh would have taken it further—the studious young man almost laughing at the stupidity of it all—but Vanessa stopped him.

"Don't worry, kid," she told him, "the president's just fucking with us. Won't matter what you say."

And so, sixty FSA troopers and nearly a hundred and twenty support staff, newly disembarked from a journey of thirty-three light years and a great military success, found themselves sitting in the sun beside the big elevator leading down to the big empty hangar, waiting for a customs inspection. A few played ball games, a few board or video games, or watched movies or caught up on Tanushan news and events that they'd missed in the past few months. Most simply sat, or lay in the sun, and enjoyed the warmth they'd missed while in space or, briefly, on Pyeongwha.

"I hate this fucking government," Vanessa said, sunglasses on, lying at Sandy's side on a patch of green grass off the taxiway, surrounded by their soldiers. "I want Neiland back."

"Fat chance," said Sandy. "She makes more money a year consulting than we make in twenty, and she lives on a beautiful river with her porch literally over the water. She got out at just the right time, you couldn't drag her back."

Callay's president now was Vikram Singh, having disposed of Neiland in a political coup nearly two years ago. Establishing the Grand Council on Callay had chewed through Callay's budget, disrupted long held financial goals, and of course, cost far more than Neiland or anyone had promised. Then loopholes had begun appearing in Callay's laws, special deals for foreign worlds, for Fleet troops, for new embassies, all the things that needed to happen for Callay to become the central Federation world, but smacked of an erosion of sovereignty to Callayans unaccustomed to such things.

Portions of the Fleet had practically declared war on Callay five years ago, and were only defeated in what historians now called either the first, second or third Federation civil war, depending on which writing of history you preferred. Now the Fleet had control of spaceplanes, and Fleet Marines wandered Tanushan bars, occasionally causing trouble as hard-drinking Marines sometimes could. And then the GIs had begun turning up. One GI was an interesting curiosity. Two, when Rhian had joined Sandy, was tolerable. But now it was fifty and climbing. The religious radicals who hated GIs had faded but not disappeared, and now raised their voices once more. The Federation loyalists, who'd fervently hated the League precisely because of GIs, were also unhappy, as were all the biotech conservatives. And a lot of ordinary Callayans, who may or may not have come to accept the presence of Cassandra Kresnov, now worried that while one or two GIs might be an acceptable risk, fifty could be stretching their luck. And where would it end? Even Sandy didn't know the answer to that.

Vikram Singh had been Neiland's Education Minister, until Neiland's numbers had begun to slip badly on accumulated concerns. He'd taken power in a typically craven fit of backstabbing, and now promised a hard line against the overreach of new Federal agencies, promising to defend Callayan independence against all comers, be they Federation or League. To Sandy's astonishment, she now found herself associated by many with both. Well, the first was true, at least.

"Let's launch a coup!" a soldier shouted, flat on his back and chafing to see his family again. "Fuck it, we just knocked off one planetary government, let's make it two!" Loud cheers from the troops.

"Hey!" Vanessa yelled. "None of that! Not even in jest, I'm serious!" They quietened. "If someone heard that, God forbid in the media, we'd be fucked!"

Silence settled. Vanessa checked her internal visual for the time.

"Half an hour," she muttered. "How long do you think they'll keep us?"

"Vikram's just trying to show who's in charge," Sandy said calmly, arm behind her head, using the rucksack for a pillow. "Could be another half an hour, could be five hours. Either way, he made us wait, we only moved when he wanted. He makes his point, he wins."

There was an election coming up, too, due in three months. President Singh had to justify his faction's betrayal and removal of Neiland, who though unpopular at the time, had still won two previous elections and led Callay through some truly tumultuous times.

"I don't like him winning." Vanessa got up. "Let's go."

"Balaji won't let us leave," Sandy reminded her from the ground.

"Balaji won't let us leave by air," Vanessa corrected. "If we take the highway from here, we'll be home in ninety minutes."

Sandy smiled, and also got up. "We'll catch shit for skipping his customs inspection."

"Do you give a shit?" Sandy shook her head. "I don't give a shit. Better that than him winning. Now, transport for two hundred. Any ideas?"

A network scan showed them a number of charter companies in the area, running bus tours for tourists, as the countryside was quite beautiful. Vanessa called a human operator, and managed to wrangle up four busses over the next couple of hours, at a reasonable fee on Federal credit. Various suits scrambled to stop the troops as they walked to a gate, and were cheerfully ignored. Vanessa was right. Balaji airport could only stop them from leaving by air, and Vanessa herself had security access to get through the gate.

The busses arrived shortly, capacity of sixty each, and everyone piled in. Once on the regional highway, speed accelerated to 150 kph, through valleys and across wild, sloping hillsides and thick, green forests. Spirits were high, and there was singing, and joking around. Sandy kept an eye on the network, and sure enough, there was soon an unmarked flyer following them overhead, transmitting on heavily encrypted frequencies. She pointed it out to Vanessa, who grinned, and pointed it out to the rest of the bus, to much hilarity. Every soldier liked to win. Against the president of Callay, who was an asshole, winning was especially sweet.

Sandy got home mid-afternoon, grabbed her board and wetsuit and went straight to the beach. A sea breeze made the surf a bit messy, but it was wonderful to just be out on the water again, bobbing in the swell, with nothing about but sun and breeze and the roar of breaking waves. This was Kuvalam Beach, well north up the coast from the suburban encroachments that had made the main Tanushan beaches unpleasant for serious surfers. Tanusha grew so fast, and she could hardly begrudge its sixty-two million inhabitants their share of her favorite part of Callay—its coastline. The developments weren't even objectionable, no gaudy high-rises or marinas, just pleasant suburban neighbourhoods and protected parks by the beaches.

But there were literally thousands of people in the water even on workdays like this one, which was to a surfer what Tanusha's crowded sidewalks were to a jogger. Even out here at Kuvalam where the landscape was almost completely wild there were lots of people in the water, but most were surfers, and so long as they didn't cut in on her waves, she didn't mind. To live in a big city was to learn to tolerate others, even out on the water.

Returning to her spot beyond the break after her sixth decent ride, she sat up on her board and saw a surfer paddling toward her. Something about his stroke was familiar. Powerful, she saw, as he effortlessly burst over the top of a breaker and kept coming. An African man with strong shoulders. She vision-zoomed, and was not particularly surprised to see who it was.

"Mustafa!" she called, not as displeased to see him as she'd have thought. "I didn't know you surfed?"

"I don't!" he replied. "But you learned rather quickly, so how hard can it be?"

He sat up beside her, with only a slight wobble on the unfamiliar board. It was a short board too, and only an idiot or a GI would come out in surf like this on a short board if he wasn't experienced. Mustafa Ramoja, of course, was the latter.

Mustafa was still League. He was ISO, League Intelligence, a senior attachment to the League's Tanushan embassy. Callayan and Federal Intelligence knew he'd gotten up to things he really wasn't supposed to, but hadn't expelled him, partly on Sandy's assessment that he was actually quite helpful at times, and partly because everyone felt safer when they knew where he was. As GIs went, he was exceptionally rare—technically a higher designation even than Sandy. Not quite the combatant that she was, though not by much, he was the only GI Sandy had ever met that she had to concede was a match for her in intellect. And on her less self-important days, grudgingly, probably somewhat more than that.

Mustafa gazed at the shoreline, the long stretch of sand, and the nearby rocky bluffs that broke up the coastline and gave each beach its separate identity. "It is very pretty," he conceded. "I can see why you come here so often."

Sandy smiled, amused at the small talk. "So, why did you follow me today?"

"Oh, come now," he said. "Can't old friends just catch up and talk? I'd have invited you for a coffee, but I knew I'd be keeping you from your surfing, and you wouldn't thank me."

"You want to know about Anjula?" Sandy tried her second option.

Mustafa was amused. "Well, yes. If you wished to discuss it, that would be nice."

"As League Intel, you probably know more about what was happening on Pyeongwha than I do." Mustafa shrugged. "What would you like to know?"

"Oh, a whole bunch of things you're not allowed to tell me." A big swell rode them up, then down the far side. "I hear the assault went well?"

"Very well, thank you."

"And your president still doesn't like Federal Security Agency treading on his toes."

"He should have thought of that before supporting the relocation." She glanced over her shoulder. "Excuse me, this wave looks excellent, back in a minute."

She lay flat and took off paddling. The wave was a nice six-footer, standard for Kuvalam, and she put on a few moves, nothing fancy. As with most things physical, it wasn't the technical challenge that drew her to the activity. Plus, she'd been told she could sometimes be identified from a distance when she showed off—there were things she could do on a board that even augmented humans couldn't. The price of anonymity was mediocrity.

Paddling back out, she saw Mustafa trying a wave. He judged the drop nicely, stood up fine, then put too much weight on the back leg and the board took off, dumping him behind it.

"Not so easy after all," Sandy suggested as she paddled in beside him.

"How many tries did it take you before you could stand up?" Mustafa wondered.

"First time. Bigger surf than this, too."

"Show-off."

"I'm not a show-off. You asked me a question, I answered it truthfully."

They rolled under another big breaker that swamped them. "Don't be troubled," she added as they emerged and resumed paddling, "you're doing quite well for a non-combat model."

Mustafa was only partly amused.

"So you're happy in the Federal Security Agency?" Mustafa asked as they resumed their seats beyond the break.

"It was only ever a secondment," said Sandy. "I'm still CSA."

The rearranging and disappearance of security agencies was a source of some discussion and exasperation on Callay. The Callayan Security Agency alone weathered the storm, Callay's preeminent central institution for all high level security matters. Its SWAT teams had been temporarily folded into the short-lived Callayan Defence Force, which had been necessary when it looked like parts of the Federation Fleet were about to declare war on Callay. But with Fleet now supporting the new situation, the CDF's position had become untenable, as a Federal-level military organisation effectively in competition with Fleet, and with overlapping jurisdictions.

And so the CDF had joined the fledgling Federal Security Agency, which in turn had replaced the old Federal Intelligence Agency that had caused Sandy so much grief upon her first arrival on Callay. The FIA had collapsed, largely due to events Sandy had been central to, and been replaced by the FSA. There were too many old FIA folks in the FSA for lots of Callayans to feel comfortable with, however, so sticking the CDF onto it had been a good way to boost colonial control of the old-Earth institution.

Sandy, Vanessa and Rhian had gone with the CDF to the FSA at first, then realised just how infrequently the military arm of the FSA was actually going to be used, and that most of their time would be training and paperwork. They could train better in CSA SWAT, by doing actual missions, and so the present arrangement had emerged—several FSA arms, one based on Callay, each of which would stay "current" with their skills by working most of their time in local SWAT teams. The CSA had certainly been glad to have them back; they'd been rebuilding their SWAT teams, but standards had slipped, and undesirable activity on Callay—in Tanusha, in particular—had increased. They'd been even happier that their returning troopers had brought a lot of their new toys with them, acquired in the FSA and earlier in the CDF, when Callay had been arming fast.

"And you've heard of the new lawsuit by the Rainbow Coalition?" Mustafa pressed.

"Which one?"

Mustafa smiled. "The one charging the CSA with becoming a planetary military force, and demanding it disarm."

"That's not my favorite," said Sandy. "I like the more recent one charging the FSA with war crimes on Pyeongwha and Anjula."

"That was fast. I had not heard that." Mustafa wasn't nearly as interested in Callayan pop culture and local affairs as she was. "Well, I suppose that's the danger when you conduct any operation that kills civilians."

"Oh they'd be charging us with war crimes if we'd only killed mass murderers," said Sandy. "A lot of pacifists on Callay aren't actually pacifists, they're just cheering for whoever we're against. We'll answer in court with those tapes we got of the victims."

"You really think they'll care?"

"No," Sandy admitted. "I'm sure most pacifists would prefer that mass slaughter continued, they only object when we try to stop it. It's just another totalitarian ideology, they all cling together. But we can win most of the Callayan population these days. They're far less pacifist than they were."

"They just don't vote for presidents who support you."

"Actually, no one's voted for Singh yet," Sandy reminded him. "That's three months away. The population's leaning to Callayan nationalism, sure, which puts it at odds with the Grand Council and everything Federation. It was inevitable. But that doesn't mean they'll oppose what we did in Anjula."

"This strikes me as a painfully ad-hoc situation," said Mustafa. "The Callayan president takes a populist stance against the FSA, but most of the FSA troops on the Pyeongwha mission are actually his own CSA troops on temporary assignment. Can you keep wearing two hats like this?"

"Sure," said Sandy. "It just proves what a dumb fuck the president is. We're trying to narrow the gap between Federation member worlds at the Federation government level, and he's trying to widen it. Even though his own world is now the central world of the Federation, and all his institutions are becoming integrated into it whether he likes it or not. He's cutting off his nose to spite his face. Fingers crossed for the election."

"Not that the alternative looks much better."

Sandy smiled. It was too much to expect Mustafa to have anything positive to say about Callay's present situation. "Maybe. But the way you dispose of idiot politicians is like how you eat an elephant—one bite at a time." Another wave was coming, nicer than the last. "Excuse me, back in a minute."

This one gave her a huge eight-foot drop, from which she launched immediately into a cut back, a top turn, then a high floater off the lip as the whole thing collapsed beneath her. The roar of exploding foam humbled her with its power. She liked that. Perhaps she needed it. Humility, for someone like her, was sometimes infrequently encountered.

She thought back to recent sex, her first time with someone other than Ari in a long time. She didn't like being in charge all the time. It got tiresome. Ari was her intellectual equal, and in some things superior, but in other things . . . what had Vanessa said? Nice to be back amongst your own kind? What was "her kind" anyway?

Mustafa had tried another wave. This time he lost it right at the top, and fell eight feet off the lip with a crash that would have made Sandy wince if she hadn't known what he was.

"Most intelligent beings of any kind need to fail several times before they succeed," Mustafa observed as they paddled back out together.

"Well you've certainly got the failing part together," Sandy observed mercilessly. Advantages against Mustafa were rare and precious things, to be enjoyed to their fullest.

"Actually," he said as they resumed their seats beyond the break, "I've come to ask a favour."

"Ah," said Sandy. "Now we get to it."

"It has come to ISO attention that an individual has come to Tanusha, whom it would be in all of our interests to see apprehended."

"A GI," Sandy told the gathered CSA chiefs, the display screen filled with all the information that Mustafa had shared with her. "Goes by Eduardo."

"Designation?" asked Naidu.

"GI-4337-HK. That's pretty high; 37s were about the fifth successful variant on the 43 series, known to be a little unstable on three of seven main psych-axes. There were a few non-combatant 4339s made for Intel and service functions."

"Poole is a 4337," Chandrasekar observed.

"Yes," Sandy confirmed.

"Unstable, you say."

"Poole's eccentric," said Sandy. "No signs of instability."

Chandrasekar shrugged. "Just saying."

Sandy gave him a longer, displeased look. Chandrasekar was unbothered. They all were these days, all these CSA old hands; she didn't intimidate any of them. Which was nice, because it showed how intimately she was trusted, and how many friends she had. But sometimes, it came with disadvantages.

"How did he get in?" Lodra asked.

"Stealth approach to farside, then hiked in."

"Not many ships stealthy enough to get through our grid," said Alam with a frown.

"Which implies whoever put him in is well equipped," said Naidu. "One of the Torah Systems."

The Torah Systems were everyone's problem these days. Seven years ago, the old League regime had collapsed, replaced with a new government that grudgingly accepted its defeat at the Federation's hands. Several League systems, only made viable by the centralised economics of the war effort, had been abandoned as the League's economy shrivelled. Reports from those systems had not made pleasant reading. Whole cities had imploded, civilisation collapsed, rampant violence, along with disease and even starvation.

Federation humanitarians had wanted to intervene and help, but the Torah Systems were still nominally League territory, and a Federation push there could potentially restart the war. The League said it had everything under control, and everyone played along with that pretense in the name of peace. Meanwhile, the Torahns died.

Until recently, when a semblance of new authority had emerged. New Torah, they called themselves. The more astute media commentators thought "New Terror" more appropriate. Media of any kind were not welcome in New Torah, and several intrepid outsiders who had penetrated inside, to attempt to find out what was going on, had never returned.

What was known was that New Torah had military tech, and lots of it. Those systems had been the engine room of the old League war machine, and were now stuck with lots of weapons industries, and no one to sell to. Sandy had always wanted to know if those weapons industries had included the capability to make GIs. Mustafa and other League officials had always insisted otherwise. Sandy remained unconvinced.

"Seems likely," Sandy agreed. "Ramoja says Eduardo is not here on League authority, yet it seems that unlike some others, neither is he here to defect. Exactly what options that leaves open, Ramoja won't say, save that it's better we find and grab him before we find out the nasty way."

"Any idea why Ramoja's talking now?"

Sandy shook her head. "You know what it's like whenever the ISO tell us anything. It's pointless speculating why they're telling us until we know more. Usually their intel's good; they know we can make their life real difficult if they screw us with bad info. Let's just grab Eduardo and then start speculating." There were nods around the table, no one disputing. "He's given us some uplink codes, apparently recent, and a very short psych profile. The summary of which is 'unstable.'"

Another glance at Chandrasekar. Chandrasekar raised his eyebrows, innocently.

"Well," said Director Ibrahim from the head of the table, "I think that concludes whatever useful discussion we can have. Let's take this information and get to work. Cassandra, I'm presuming you'd like to be included in the ongoing investigation, should your other activities not preclude it?"

"Yes," said Sandy, not at all surprised that Ibrahim anticipated her wishes. "The FSA's on wind-down for the moment, and SWAT are doing quite well without me."

"Well, insert yourself into the investigations construct at the earliest, I'm sure they'll be happy to have you. And Cassandra, good job on Pyeongwha." His gaze was very intense, and sincere. "An excellent conclusion to a truly serious problem, and well worth the cost."

Nods and loud approval from around the table. Sandy knew what Ibrahim said was true for herself, without needing to be told. Yet it still surprised her how much better she felt to hear it from his mouth, and to hear the approval of these men and women whose opinions she respected.

"Thank you," she said, with genuine gratitude. "All of you."

"Cassandra," Ibrahim added, "if I could speak with you before you leave."

She waited until the others had gone, and the door shut behind them. Ibrahim, Sandy was always pleased to see, looked little changed and little older than when she'd first met him. He had one of those faces, angular and big nosed, Afghan and statuesque. He'd have looked old when he was young, but now hardly seemed to age.

"Well," he said, with a faint smile. It was affection, as much as a man like Ibrahim ever showed in this professional world. Sandy treasured it. "Good to see you back safely. Not that I had any doubt of it."

"Good to be back safely." Sandy never commented on her chances. Others thought her more indestructible than she knew she was. Even she needed luck, and she'd been lucky on Anjula, and lucky in every fight she'd been in. One did not toy with luck by pronouncing oneself safe from harm.

"There is a conference next month," said Ibrahim. "Closed to the public and media, experts only. The topic is GIs in the Federation. I'd like you to be the keynote speaker."

"Hmm," said Sandy. She'd never done public speaking, unless one counted the occasional TV interview, Senate questioning or, of course, command addresses to her troops. She thought keynote speaking ought to be easier, since no one would be shooting at her. Hopefully. "Who qualifies as an expert?"

"Oh, very many people who probably do not qualify as such," said Ibrahim, with a faint smile. "But you'll get that at every such gathering."

"Rainbow Coalition?"

"No. No politicians, no activists. Academics and experts in the security field. Field expertise only, no one without it gets in."

"You can enforce that?" Sandy asked with a raised eyebrow.

"You've become very cynical in your time here," Ibrahim observed with amusement.

"I believe the word is 'experienced.' But sure, if you ask, I'll do it."

"I don't hear much enthusiasm. It should be a positive exercise, I believe there is significant progress to be made, simply by education. The recent arrivals on Callay are mostly doing very well; a study of that progress, presented by yourself, ought to help that process of education along."

Sandy sighed. "I've become wary of injecting myself into these debates. It becomes about me, and we lose focus on the issue."

"Cassandra," Ibrahim replied, with that impressively mild-yet-firm tone he had when delivering a lecture, "I'm afraid you cannot avoid becoming a spokesperson on this issue, at least among the experts. Not if you wish to remain as heavily involved in the matter as you presently are. And as your immediate superior, in your primary capacity as a CSA operative, I then become accountable for your actions, for they involve the CSA as well by virtue of your employment here.

"Now, I am happy to support you on this, not because of our friendship but because I genuinely believe that your approach is most constructive, and the best course for Callayan security. But my responsibility for your actions directs me to make you available, from time to time, for a more direct interrogation from those who consider themselves to be the CSA's peers and colleagues, and in some cases, its oversight."

"You give a good lecture," Sandy told him.

"I do, don't I," said Ibrahim.

Sandy glanced at the tabletop. "You're right, of course. As always. But it's not the protocol I have a problem with. It's that I'm being asked to argue for a position I'm not sure I entirely support." She looked up, and met his gaze. "I'm arguing for Callay and the Federation to accept further asylum applications, perhaps even encourage more high-des GIs to come, if they wish. But I really don't know how safe it is. Maybe we're just lucky so far, that fifty-plus have come and they're all relatively sane. But then there was Jane . . ."

"Yet Jane was precisely what she was intended to be," Ibrahim countered. "From a security standpoint, it's the unstable ones we're concerned of. If we know what they're going to do, we can counter it, even if those intentions are bad. It's the ones that pledge one thing, then change their minds, that do the most damage, and we haven't had one of those yet."

"But you trust me so much," Sandy said, leaning forward on the table. "And you should, because I'm yours, I'm Callay to the bone. But I'm being taken as a representative of my kind. Of GIs. And they're not all like me. Some of them are assholes. Others are unstable. Some have poor or non-existent moral judgment. I've seen it, and sometimes it's even made me doubt myself and what I am. You got lucky with me, and maybe with these others—the very fact that they wanted to come to the Federation in search of freedom shows they're a self-selecting group. I don't think you'll get that lucky with the rest."

"So you'd like to argue for greater restrictions," Ibrahim suggested, with a considered frown.

"I'd like to argue for the very, very careful processing of asylum claims.

This isn't like accepting refugee claims from some poor sods from New Torah who only want a place to raise their kids in peace. GIs can't have kids, we don't think in terms of society so easily. Morality and ethics are all very sketchy, and even when strongly held, they're shallow, easily manipulated."

She thought of Pyeongwha, of League uplink technology that rewrote human brain function. Was it the right time to raise that fear as well?

"Then that's what you should argue," said Ibrahim. "These people will welcome a considered and even-handed argument. If you argued to trust every GI ever made, they'd respect you less."

"And in doing so I undermine my own advocacy for current policies," Sandy finished. "Because you don't win a policy argument by making the other side's case for them."

"Politics does have that way of dividing the issue, then polarising each side," Ibrahim admitted. "All that I can advise you is to always stand for the truth. The truth can be difficult, but if you have faith in the decency of people, and in the rightness of your cause, then it is the only option possible."

Sandy smiled. It was what Ibrahim did—resolve difficult issues with an appeal to moral certainties. You're not in control, he reminded her. You can't play the system. Just do your best, and the rest is up to fate. Or in Ibrahim's case, to Allah.

"That's good advice," she said. "I'll remember it."

She rose to get up. "Cassandra," he said. "One more thing. I may not be Director of the CSA for very much longer."

"Oh, no. The circulation fanatics aren't finally winning, are they?"

"Circulation" was what they called the natural cycle of top officials in big organisations, as the head stepped down and was replaced by the next in line. Before Callay's troubles had begun, it had been the way things were done— the Director of the CSA would serve for three or four years, then stand aside for his deputy. "Circulation" filtered downward, allowing the queue of eager ladder-climbers to move upward, making everyone happy. Until something happened that ensured the CSA was genuinely, seriously needed for something, and everyone realised that the man currently at the head of the queue was significantly better at his job than any of his would-be replacements.

Next-in-line had been Ulu N'Darie, five years ago, but she'd pointedly resigned in order to end that argument, and had taken up a senior post at a think tank instead. She wasn't Ibrahim's equal in this job, she'd stated quite plainly, and nor were the next four rungs down, and probably never would be, and the CSA was simply too important an institution to be changing horses now or into the foreseeable future. It hadn't stopped some of the most eager ladder-climbers, however, from claiming that Ibrahim had been there too long, and it was time for a change.

"No," Ibrahim said. "No, I do love this job for all its challenges, and would not normally have any intention to leave. Unfortunately, as with most things, these choices in life are never entirely up to any of us."

Sandy frowned, awaiting an explanation. Ibrahim's lips pursed. It was emotion. Upset. Ibrahim almost never showed that.

"My wife Radha is ill," he said finally. "A rare form of cancer."

"Oh no," said Sandy. Shocked.

"If it were one of my children or grandchildren," Ibrahim continued, a faint quaver in his voice, "well, I love them as dearly of course, but they have families of their own now, and do not require my individual attention in the same way. But Radha has been my partner in life for nearly forty years now. Children leave home, yet we have always been partners, and always shall. And if I must step down to care for her, then I must." He smiled, weakly. "I have always lived by the creed that all individual concerns must be measured against the greater good. Now, I find that philosophy tested."

"Callay be damned," Sandy agreed. "Take care of your wife."

CHAPTER FOUR

"**H**ello Siddhartha," Sandy said ten minutes later, piloting her cruiser through busy Tanushan skylanes. "I'm researching Type QL neural cancers and treatments. What can you tell me?"

A narrow face peered in her display. Siddhartha was another of Ari's friends, a senior figure in a research laboratory connected to some huge biotech firms and Callayan teaching hospitals. Like many such people, he frequently played around the edges of the Federation's crazily complicated biotech laws. Also like many of them, he was very pleased to be friends with Sandy.

"*Almost always terminal, I'm afraid. Is it someone close to you?*"

"Close to a dear friend." Sandy had met Radha Ibrahim a few times, and thought her wonderful. A gentle lady with a fearsome intellect, her law practise took lots of pro-bono cases, from local unfortunates to League immigrants, to recently, several GIs hoping for asylum. "Are treatment chances any better in the League?"

"*Well no, not that I'm aware. It is always the question, isn't it?*"

"Always," Sandy agreed. Advanced biotech was restricted in the Federation, least it be abused. That meant that the Federation forewent many treatments that could cure terminal cases, and the black market buzzed with illegal and semi-legal treatments. "Why haven't the League found a cure? There's not that many incurable cancers left, are there?"

"*No,*" Siddhartha agreed, "*but the body keeps inventing new ones. We keep doing things to our biology and biology always fights back. Something like ninety percent of the disease fatalities in the Federation today are from things that didn't exist two centuries ago, disorders that we basically invented as a corollary to all our new treatments and enhancements. Or responses to alien environments and diseases, of course. Type QL cancers are one of these, and for whatever reason, the League doesn't have any more answers than we do right now.*"

"It's a dysfunction of the occipital cortex, isn't it?" Sandy pressed determinedly.

"*Uh, I think you mean the occipital lobes.*"

"Whatever. That's near the parietal lobes, I recall."

"*Well, yes.*" Siddhartha was always nervous trying to explain the latest neuro-biology to laymen. Even most neurobiologists didn't understand it themselves without the assistance of enormous VR constructs and AI revision to sort out all the pieces. "*What are you thinking, Cassandra?*"

"Well I'm obviously no neuroscientist, but I've read enough about my own origins to know that my brain function is pretty advanced around there. And that there's more overlap between my synthetic brain function and human biology than in nearly any other organ."

A pause. "*Are you suggesting what I think you're suggesting?*"

"I'm not suggesting anything. That would probably be illegal."

"*Probably.*"

"But you know, I've been having these awful headaches lately. I think I need an expert of your caliber to take a look and see if there's something wrong."

"*Well actually, headaches and brain function are completely unrelated . . .*"

"When can we meet?" Sandy said sourly. Trust the neuro-nerd to miss the point.

"*Ah, well, tomorrow at six, if you come in then I could . . .*"

"I'll send you the address, and you make your way there inconspicuously. Okay?"

"*Yes. Certainly.*" With a mixture of trepidation and excitement.

Sandy disconnected. God knew what she was doing. But it was her damn brain, she could do with it what she wanted.

She found Poole at Anita's third residence (of the ones she knew of). It served as a kind of halfway house for GIs, to assist them in making their transition into Tanushan society. Civilian manners were often confusing, and it was better for them to enjoy each other's company for a few years, most agreed, until it was decided where they'd go next.

The house was a mansion in a secluded neighbourhood, nine bedrooms, surrounded with thick gardens and tall walls for privacy. Sandy wondered just how much money Anita and Pushpa were making these days, as she uplinked to the complex interface and completed fifteen ID locks just to open the front door.

The layout was wide and modern, big rooms with sunken floors and lots of glass; a minimalist, Japanese inspiration. Sandy wandered, finding no one obviously home, and uplinked to the house network. There were two people upstairs, noisily fucking. Weller and Khan, by the sound of it. And one person in the rear room, playing piano.

Sandy went that way. Poole's piano was above the step-down to an indoor garden, a big square hole in the floor. On the other side of window glass, a long pond along the outer wall, in which big, native fish swam. Beyond that, a field of high, green bamboo. Poole played quite intricately, hands flying over the keys. Sandy thought it sounded beautiful. She stopped by the garden in the floor, and listened.

Poole played on, knowing she was there but not really caring. Or whatever Poole thought at such moments; no one really knew. He was shirtless, his torso as sculpted and muscular as any combat GI, like a regular human gymnast . . . only Poole would retain that shape regardless of how much he exercised or ate. Male and female GIs were different in basic structure, just like regular humans. Males packed more synthetic myomer muscle onto the same length of bone, and weighed more accordingly. Males thus tended to have better long-term power, better endurance, and could take more punishment. But large muscle mass tended to preclude the most sensitive fast-twitch reactions, so females tended to have marginally faster reflexes and better short-term accuracy, to say nothing of more explosive, short-term power generated by sheer speed. There were so many other variables gender was often drowned out, but broadly speaking, if you wanted something particularly heavy lifted, you asked a man. If you wanted something particularly strong broken, you asked a woman.

"Who is that you're playing?" Sandy asked finally, deciding she didn't have all day to wait. Poole sometimes played for hours without pause.

"Jiang Shuangchao," said Poole, still playing.

"I like the sound. When was Jiang Shuangchao composing?"

"Late twenty-first century." He could talk and play incredibly technical things at the same time. Regular humans couldn't. "She was a leader of the revivalist movement. She didn't like all the modernist stuff of the time, so she wrote stuff she liked instead."

"Ah," said Sandy. "I knew I liked it. I like the revivalists."

"No one at the time appreciated her," Poole added, hands flying on the keys. "They said she sounded too much like older guys, Beethoven and Mozart and stuff. Only after she'd died did people realise how good she was."

"Yeah," said Sandy, leaning on the wall alongside. "Cause when she was dead, she became just another dead composer. People are dumb like that, they always think their era is unique, and everyone should act unique because of it. Only once it's passed does everyone realise it wasn't."

"It's sad no one liked her when she was alive," said Poole. "She became very famous after she died. Everyone played her, everyone agreed they'd been dumb not to like her before. Some say she was better than Beethoven."

"Sometimes people don't see what's in front of them. They have this idea in their head, this framework, and all information they take into their heads has to fit into that framework. Those people had an idea that no new composers were allowed to compose like Beethoven. If someone did compose like Beethoven, then surely it couldn't be any good. Even if it was good, even if it was better, they'd still deny it. They wouldn't allow it to be true. Lots of things are like that, even today."

Poole kept playing with no sign that he'd heard, or that what she'd said had registered. She had an obligation to get her fellow GIs thinking, in the hope that they'd absorb something and become a little better equipped to handle their new world. And she had an obligation to Callay, to find out what her fellow GIs were thinking, in case one of them was seriously not coping. The problem with Poole was that no one knew if he was coping or not. He rarely stopped playing long enough for anyone to find out.

"Poole? There's a rogue GI in town. We think he's from New Torah. He's the same designation as you, his name's Eduardo." Poole kept playing. "Poole?"

Poole stopped. He stared at the keys, as though the sudden silence affronted him. "I can never get it good enough," he murmured. "Always it's flat."

"It sounds wonderful to me," Sandy offered, in all honesty.

"It doesn't have the expression. You listen to Jiang Shuangchao, there's so much expression. I can copy it, but I can't create it."

"Hey," said Sandy. She put a hand on his bare shoulder. "Are you okay?"

"You love music," said Poole, and looked at her for the first time. He had blue eyes, within a strong, young, handsome face. Dark hair, shaved short. He looked for all the world like all the other combat GIs she'd known. But he wasn't. "You're the smartest GI ever commissioned, you love music and arts, yet you never learned to play. Why not?"

Sandy gazed at him. "I suppose I'm scared I'll mess it up," she confessed.

"How can you mess it up? You're almost technically perfect at any physical thing you do. You find most sports boring because you almost never miss. I bet you'd play better than me, even, and you'd barely have to practise."

Sandy felt uncomfortable. Why hadn't she learned? She'd had it suggested to her often enough, most recently by Vanessa's new husband, who knew more than a thing or two about music. Because Poole was right, she didn't even need to learn. She could probably just do it, just like Poole played now without sheet music, just reading off the uplink visual in his head. Probably he'd never even played this piece before.

"You're scared the emotion won't be there, aren't you?" said Poole, his blue eyes searching her face. "That you'll sit down and pour yourself out onto the instrument, and nothing will resonate back. That the only sound will be this dull, empty thud."

Sandy stared at him, feeling cold. A little frightened, in fact. She didn't know what to say.

Poole put his hand on hers. "Don't worry," he told her. "I know what that feels like. That's why I sit here and play. I'm listening to the resonance, trying to find that emotion. Maybe it'll tell me who I am."

And Ari had left her. Had she done that? Even Vanessa had once accused her of not feeling love like a regular human. GIs didn't get jealous, and she'd thought that was just socialisation too, but even now she thought that if she were still with Ari, she could probably handle Ari screwing other girls and have no problem, so long as he let her screw other guys as well. Which was most unlike straights, who were neurologically programmed to pair-bond, however inconsistently that programming actually translated into real life. She'd thought she'd grow into love with Ari, and get devastatingly jealous when he flirted with other girls, but she hadn't.

Were there limits to how socialised a GI could become, in a civilian world? Did it mean she'd only ever have successful relationships with other GIs? Or what did "successful" mean, if it could only define promiscuity? Promiscuity was a very low setting on the bar for success, surely? Even now she was upset that Ari had dumped her, certainly, but not devastated. Just confused, and hoping, she admitted, that he'd come back from Pyeongwha soon, and they'd be able to resume their old friendship, just minus the fucking. Was that wrong of her? Shouldn't she be torn apart, if she was wired correctly? And was it wrong of her to be mildly relieved that she wasn't? She loved him, certainly, but there were plenty of people she loved, yet didn't sleep with. Yet every regular human girlfriend who'd spoken to her on the breakup insisted that a good, clean break was essential, and that she should see him as little as possible from now on, if at all. But that was stupid. Ari was still Ari, and she was still herself, and everything could still be somewhat like it was before, just without the sex. Couldn't it?

"Hey," she said to Poole, feeling a little lost. "I'm single now. You want to go upstairs?" It always worked for her, at least in the short term, when she felt like this. Perhaps it would work for Poole also.

"Thanks," he said. "But I really want to finish this piece."

Vanessa had about as much interest in chasing after a rogue GI as she did in watching the latest immigration debate. She was having time off, as were most of the FSA squad upon their return.

"Sandy," she said determinedly, attending to the barbeque in her bikini top and sarong, "have some food and come for a swim. Let Chandrasekar catch the damn GI. That's what he's good for."

They were in the backyard of Vanessa and Phillippe's house. Kids splashed in the pool while adults ate and talked on the grass, or on the verandah. Mostly Vanessa and Phillippe's extended family; they hadn't gotten around to kids of their own yet. Soon, Vanessa said airily, whenever the question came up.

Rhian was here too—in the pool of course, with the kids, playing games. One of those was her stepson Salman, who was six. The twins were with Rakesh, a big, handsome guy who worked at a construction firm, was a talented minor league footballer, and loved kids as much as Rhian did. Salman was Rakesh's from a previous marriage. The twins had been adopted from some struggling League system with too many orphans. They were girls, just recently walking and quite adorable, now fetching their father various playthings on the grass, and looking pleased with his delight at their generosity.

Perhaps this was why she was feeling a bit morose, Sandy thought wryly. Her two best friends, both women, were recently married, and displaying alarming signs of impending domesticity. While she herself seemed to move in the opposite direction. She wasn't even sure that she wanted domesticity, it was just that watching Vanessa and Rhian slowly slide into it made her feel . . . well, left out.

There was another reason for feeling morose, of course. "You heard about Radha?"

"Yeah. Horrible. And," Vanessa added, with emphasis, "absolutely nothing we can do about it by feeling miserable."

"I'm not miserable."

"Crap, you've been miserable since Anjula. The happiest I've seen you in months was just before the fight."

Sandy frowned. "That's not true."

"Well okay, that's unfair. You weren't happy, just . . . alive. Buzzing. You had that spark in your eyes, the one that scares journalists and gives real men erections." Sandy restrained a grin. "Yeah, that one." Vanessa pointed tongs at her, knowingly. "You've got down time. Take it."

"Down time is when I feel worst," Sandy admitted. "I like being busy."

"Me too, just not always with work." One of the kids said something very rude to her playmates in the pool. "Isabelle! Auntie Rhian may not mind you using that word, but I do! Use it again and there'll be trouble!"

"But I learned it from you!" came the retort. Sandy smothered another smile.

"You fucking didn't!" said Vanessa.

Phillippe emerged from the house with a bowl of potato salad in one hand, a bottle of wine in the other. "How's that looking?" he asked Vanessa, his cheek on her head to peer at the barbeque.

"Pretty good, I reckon."

"Don't burn the chicken. Those ones are for the kids, they don't like it too crispy . . ."

Vanessa swatted away his attempt to take her tongs. "My barbeque," she told him. "Go and give advice on something you're actually good at."

Phillippe grinned, and kissed her, and departed with the salad. It was Vanessa's bossiness that he liked so much, Sandy reckoned. Phillippe was one of Callay's three leading classical violinists, and moved in a world of elegant, feminine ladies who felt no urge to take command of the barbeque and arrange lunch dishes like a military operation. Small and pretty, with short, dark curls and an elegant jaw line, Vanessa could have passed for one of those women if she'd wished. But Vanessa was deadly strong, foul mouthed, bitingly funny, and went through life with the energy of a bouncing rubber ball.

Phillippe had met her at a concert function, and been instantly smitten. Sandy had been there too—they'd had tickets courtesy of some very wealthy friends—and she'd seen it happen. In their first two minutes of conversation, Vanessa had managed to insult him, challenge him, make scathing fun of several fellow attendees, all in the happiest of good humours, all flashing teeth and sparkling eyes. Sandy had never seen a man melt so quickly, and had excused herself with a wink. And Phillippe was dashing, handsome, talented, and more than a handful for most merely mortal women . . . save for Vanessa, with whom he could suddenly barely keep up. Obviously he loved it, and her, and Sandy couldn't have been happier for them.

She watched him leave. "I haven't the heart to tell him you're a lesbian."

Vanessa laughed, and shoved her tongs under Sandy's nose, threateningly. "You'll find that in a fit of rage I become so powerful I can take even you down."

"Sure. If I were a pork chop."

"I haven't thought that way about women in years," said Vanessa, returning to her meat.

"Hmm," Sandy agreed, sipping her wine. "When I was with Ari, I'd think about other men at least six times a day. But sure, if that's what you need to tell yourself . . ."

"Well okay, I think about it. But it's just not that interesting any longer." She seemed perfectly serious.

"Well observe," said Sandy, smiling. "The magical vanishing homosexual."

Vanessa grinned, then shot Sandy a hard look. "When did you become such a dry wit?" Sandy snorted. "I just found the right person, that's all. If Phillippe was a girl, I'd probably be telling you I had no need for men anymore. It's quite nice to know that the emotions can drive the sex drive, and not the other way around. Makes me feel in control."

"Hmm," said Sandy, amusement fading.

Vanessa looked at her, suddenly concerned. "Oh, hey, I didn't mean that."

"No, right," Sandy brushed her off. "I wonder that myself. About myself."

"You'll find the right guy someday," Vanessa said firmly. And added mischievously, "You're too damn hot not to."

"I don't know if I want the right guy. I think for the next few years I'll just settle for a wide assortment of penises, and give preference to none."

"The thing with penises," said Vanessa, "they have a habit of moving in and spending your money."

"So long as they cook me breakfast, I don't care." Sandy frowned. "What's the collective noun of penises anyway? Or is it peni? A gaggle of peni?"

"A flock?" Vanessa suggested. "Maybe a swarm."

"A parliament," said Phillippe in passing back up the stairs, and the girls doubled up laughing in his wake.

"He's wonderful," Vanessa said as she recovered, wiping her eyes. "Isn't he wonderful?" Sandy just sighed. It was only funny because it struck too close to home. In the pool, kids were shouting. Then came that word again. "Right, Isabelle!" Vanessa shouted. "I warned you!"

She handed Sandy the tongs, then turned and sprinted to the pool, leaped a final five meters through the air and hit the water in a flying dive. There followed much splashing and squealing and protesting kids. Sandy wondered if Phillippe had entirely thought through the consequences of marrying an infantry grunt. Their own kids, when they arrived, would learn a lot of interesting vocabulary.

Sandy turned, and found Phillippe watching from the balcony, stars in his eyes. "She's wonderful," he beamed. "Isn't she wonderful?"

Sandy smiled. "You're a few years late to the fact," she sighed. "But yes, she is." And sculled the rest of her wine, wishing that some of its legendary effects on regular humans carried over to GIs.

CHAPTER FIVE

Sandy was woken at three in the morning by an uplink alarm. It was the CSA, requesting her presence immediately. Sandy got up, dressed quickly, stuffed her usual two pistols into belt and jacket holster respectively, grabbed a makani juice drink from the fridge and went outside, allowing the house minder to lock up behind her.

A CSA cruiser was landing in the narrow, stone-paved street between high brick walls—when SWAT said immediately, that meant now. The howl would wake the neighbours and no doubt provoke some angry calls, but the CSA did have flight clearance even in no-fly security zones like Canas special protective district, in the event of emergencies.

Sandy got in and they took off immediately. She didn't recognise the pilot, and sculled makani juice fast—caffeine only worked on GI physiology half as well as makani juice. They flew five minutes through the sprawling high-rise sky, then landed upon a high tower pad where a CSA flyer was waiting. Sandy switched vehicles and found herself in the back with SWAT Two, ten troopers in full armour, led by Captain Arvid Singh.

"Hey Arvid," said Sandy, hanging on the overhead as they lifted off immediately. "What's the deal?"

"Eduardo," said Singh from his command chair. He hadn't been on the FSA raid and was pissed about it, but he was senior SWAT team leader these days, Vanessa's old job, and Tanusha couldn't afford to have all of its senior SWAT officers offworld at once. Sandy hooked into the flyer's network and found tacnet already up, coordinating with several other units about a park in Montoya. One of them had a visual.

Imagery blurred before her eyes as she changed resolutions and zoomed. Then resolved upon a man, in plain shirt and cargo pants, sitting on a park bench. At three-fifteen in the morning, in the dim glow of a park light, with no one else around. Sandy checked the visual match, but there was no mistaking it—the man's face was the same as Mustafa had shown her in the data package. He wasn't active on the net, so they couldn't check his uplink patterns . . . likely they'd be impenetrable anyway, League GIs normally were. But it could only be him.

"Not exactly inconspicuous, is he?" Sandy observed. "How was he acquired?"

Singh shrugged. "Montoya's a high security zone. You sit alone on a park bench at three a.m. long enough, someone will scan you and see if you match a database. He did."

"Hmm," said Sandy. SWAT Two were still looking bleary-eyed, a few yawning, so they'd all been woken and assembled—SWAT worked on a roster, so squads knew if it was their turn to be on call, but still it took some time. Maybe a half hour to get everyone here. She'd taken ten minutes, so they'd waited twenty before calling her. Once Eduardo had been IDed, SWAT would have been called immediately. "So he can't have been there more than . . . forty-five minutes?"

"I was thinking a trap," said Singh. In monotone, because it was that obvious, but procedures said you had to be absolutely clear in prep.

"Hmm," said Sandy. Navcomp said they'd be there in three minutes. "Have we got a sniper scan?"

Vision flashed up, a full graphic of the park and neighbouring buildings. The only possible sniper vantages were covered and cleared—there were enough cameras around to do that thoroughly. It was possible Eduardo had support hidden in the buildings, but if they made a sudden move there'd be warning. Warning for someone who moved as fast as she did, at least.

"Not much of a trap," Singh admitted. "I suppose you want to take this?" With resignation.

"Sorry, Arvid. I really think I should."

They landed on a tower a kilometer away, and a police car was waiting to speed her to the park. She got out at a secluded corner and walked. Tanushan parks were lush and green, fragrant with tropical vegetation. Trees dripped with recent rain as she walked a main path. Puddles reflected dim city light. Insects fluttered around park lights. Bunbuns and native possums crawled in the trees. On combat reflex, it was a lot of distraction, sharp motions that made her eyes jump from one potential target to the next. GIs weren't really designed for natural environments. On combat exercise in Callay's wild forests she was forever within milliseconds of assassinating cute and furry animals left and right. The little buggers kept surprising her.

Eduardo saw her coming. He couldn't miss her, since they were the only two people in the park. His hands were visible, elbows hooked over the seatback. Sandy's belt holster was closer. He'd know what she was, watching her approach. GIs could usually recognise each other just by walk or stance, sometimes right down to the designation.

Sandy walked to the bench by Eduardo's side. The bench was wet, so she touched the evaporator on the seatback, and watched the moisture steam and vanish. Then she sat.

"I've been told your name's Eduardo," she said. "I'm Commander Kresnov." Eduardo wasn't really looking at her. What he was looking at, she couldn't tell. He was good looking, like most GIs. Tanned skin, dark hair with a short cut, military style. God knew how these cosmetics were decided, the ethnicity of appearance and names. GIs had to fit in to the regular population, and the regular population of nearly all colonial worlds, League and Federation alike, was racially diverse.

But it was always amusing when Federation media assumed she could speak Russian, or could name more European classical composers than Indian ones.

"How did you find me?" Eduardo asked finally.

"You're about a kilometer from the Grand Council Congress," she told him. "This whole neighbourhood is new—this park, the buildings, streets, everything, less than a year since it was all opened. And of course, it's all wired with surveillance." She paused, peering at him more closely. "But I think you knew that."

He moved, and with a twitch a pistol was in her hand, down in her lap, angled up at his neck. Eduardo kept moving, slowly, and stretched an awkward kink.

"I like the moonlight," Eduardo explained. Sandy frowned. There was no silver light from the moon tonight. She didn't want to look up to see, and take her eyes off Eduardo, but a quick uplink calendar check confirmed her observation. The moon had set two hours ago.

"I'm told you came from the League," Sandy tried. "Why did you come here?"

"Rinni and Pasha."

Sandy frowned. "Who?"

"I came for Rinni and Pasha. Came to see them."

Sandy opened her mouth to ask further, but was interrupted by Singh. *"Sandy, Rinni and Pasha are a kids' TV show. My kids watch them all the time."*

"Eduardo," Sandy said carefully, "are you telling me you came all the way to Callay for a kids' TV show?"

Eduardo wasn't really responding to her. Just sitting, and gazing at the park, and lights of tall buildings that rose beyond the trees. She didn't think it was an act. This GI wasn't entirely there. There were as many possible reasons why as with a regular human.

"Who are Rinni and Pasha?" Sandy silently formulated to Singh.

"They're friends. A boy and a girl, they go to school together. It's funny, like all kids shows, but the idea is that they're just friends, but of course they're really more than that. You know, teenage romantic tension."

"Yeah." Well, she'd heard of it. And to Eduardo, "Why do you like Rinni and Pasha, Eduardo?"

An uplink activated. A gentle touch on the local net, a contact on her barriers. Attached was a tiny little picture file, far too small to hold some kind of code bomb. Sandy accepted it, and a picture opened upon her vision. It was Eduardo, and a girl. A GI, Sandy guessed, by the look of her. They had an arm around each other and looked cheerful, posing for the picture.

"She's very pretty," said Sandy. It was redundant, since nearly all GIs were pretty, but it seemed the right thing to say. "Who is she?"

"She's Pasha," said Eduardo. "I'm Rinni."

"Oh." Sandy's heart began to thump. It wasn't excitement. Cold dread, more like it. Something here just felt very wrong. "Eduardo, where is Pasha now?"

"They were going to take her." He took a deep breath. The breath shuddered, with obvious emotion. "It's not good when they take you away. I'm here now."

"You came from New Torah, didn't you?" Sandy pressed. "Did they send you to Callay? Did they take your friend, your Pasha, and make you come to Callay? Did they threaten to do something to her if you didn't?"

"He wants to kiss her," said Eduardo, very sadly. "He wants to kiss her, but he can't. You know?"

"Eduardo," Sandy pressed urgently. "I'm a GI like you. I came from the

League. I belong here now, and I have many friends. They can be your friends, too. Would you like that?" She took a risk, and placed her non-gun hand on his arm. "This can be your home too, if you want."

He turned and looked at her for the first time. His stare was unfocused, but not stupid. Dazed. "You're not as pretty as Pasha."

"No," Sandy said quietly. "I don't suppose I am."

"Will you go and get her? If I help you?"

Sandy felt helpless. This, she'd been dreading. For years and years. "I'd like to," she said earnestly. "I'd like to very much."

Eduardo smiled. And began convulsing.

"Eduardo?" The convulsions grew worse. Sandy grabbed him. If she hadn't been a GI herself, the convulsions would have smashed her bones. A flailing arm crushed the chair back of the bench, and Sandy threw herself on top of him to pin him. "I want an ambulance!" she yelled, not bothering with internal formulation. "Whatever leading biotech surgeon you can get, he's in trouble!"

Immediately she could hear a cruiser coming in; they'd had one on standby for rapid transport in case something happened. Eduardo's eyes were rolled back in his head, his mouth foaming. And then he stopped. GIs had no jugular pulse, so Sandy put her ear to his chest. The pulse was still there, but galloping.

She tried a violent network access, but the barriers were hard, unresponsive. She reached instead for a pocket, withdrew an ever-present access line, clicked it into the back of her own head, then rolled Eduardo to get at his own inserts . . . and her fingertips felt hot, melted metal. It was smoking, the inserts entirely melted through the skin.

Oh, God. She slumped back and sat on the path as the CSA cruiser howled in to a landing on nearby grass, landing lights flashing. Gull doors opened and medicos rushed to her, and the lifeless body of her newest friend.

Sandy sat in the observation chamber, elbows on knees, and watched the coroners work. They had tools set up especially for this—laser cutters that could saw through even a GI's synthetic tissue and bone. Scanners showed a clear picture, and visual diagnostics programs tried to make sense of what they saw. The CSA knew a lot more about GI physiology now than it had a few years back, and one of the coroners was actually a leading biotech surgeon, a civvie but security cleared. They cut efficiently, removing a piece of skull.

Some years ago, no one would have dared sit near her and offer comfort when she was in this mood. Now, Singh came by, recently showered post-armour, and sat beside her and asked how she was. Not great. He put an arm around her shoulders and just sat with her for a while, watching the monitors. Naidu likewise came and asked, and Chandrasekar. Ibrahim was elsewhere, probably briefing politicians. These days he had to do more of that than he liked.

Then Vanessa arrived, and took Singh's place as he left. "It's the kill-switch," said Sandy.

"I know."

"I don't know who triggered it, there was no transmission. It just melted his brain."

"Yeah." Vanessa clasped her hand.

"I think he was sent here to kill someone. I think he was being black-mailed, and now he refused, and they killed him." Vanessa's gaze was very worried. "I swear I'm going to find who did this." Her tone, like her mood, was utterly black. "I'm going to kill them. I don't care if there are hundreds, I'll kill them all."

The biotech surgeon's name was Sasa. She sat at the end of the briefing table, with the intense, slightly exhausted look of someone trying to process a lot of information in a short space of time. About the table, CSA command sat and listened.

"Well," said Sasa, "it's hard to tell exactly what they did to him. But it looks like one of his memory implants was converted into some kind of a control matrix. There are two kinds of memory implants—real memory and cybernetic. What the real memory implants do is compile a copy, like a fac-simile, of memory triggers—for a smell, a sensation, there's a pattern firing of neurons that the brain instantly recognises and uses like a key to unlock particular memories. Real memory implants don't actually store the memory itself, they store the key that helps the brain to unlock that memory from within its natural, organic memory. Unlike cybernetic implants, which store electronic, virtual memory like any computer.

"Eduardo's real memory implants seem to have been compiling this fac-simile copy of memories into a pattern. My guess is that something in that pattern triggered the killswitch."

"You're saying that if he ever had the wrong kind of thought, it could trigger the killswitch automatically?" Sandy asked.

Sasa looked a little unnerved by her stare. "Um, yes. Well no, not exactly. It's . . . it's a pattern. It's very complicated, but brainwaves create memory triggers in patterns, which can be compiled into three dimensional displays in a memory implant. It's not a single thought that will trigger the killswitch, it's a certain frame of mind."

"Traitorous thoughts," said Sandy.

"Yes." Sasa fidgeted. "More likely. Your own implants have been inspected?"

"I'm clean," said Sandy.

"And your own killswitch?"

"I said I'm clean."

In a tone that left silence around the table.

"We've managed to make some nano-scale inroads into Cassandra's own killswitch," Ibrahim said for Sasa's benefit. "It hasn't been disconnected, it's too well integrated into her brainstem, but the trigger is now less sensitive, and one of our experts feels the micro-battery charge may be susceptible to degradation over the years. Her implants have been so heavily shielded now that it seems highly unlikely anyone could trigger the killswitch by remote."

Sasa nodded. "There's something else odd," she said. "The brain struc-ture's a little different. The neural groupings just aren't where we'd expect in some places. It's almost as though the brain was developed using one of the alternative generation methods."

There were puzzled faces about the table.

"Getting synthetic synaptic tissue to behave like a real brain was always the hardest thing," Sandy explained for the table. This part of GI physiology she did know. "They tried many different methods. We still don't know how the process of narrowing it down worked, but there's evidence they started with lots of different methods, then boiled it down to a couple that worked. One method is mainstream, and was used to create just about every GI ever made. And the other created me, and Mustafa, and Jane—the extra-high-des GIs. What Dr Sasa is saying, aren't you doctor, is that this is neither of those two."

The doctor nodded, brushing African braids back from her face. "This looks like a third generation mode," she agreed. "Which we didn't actually know the League were still working on."

"Because they're not," said Sandy. "But New Torah is."

More silence at the table. "The League government insists otherwise," Chandrasekar ventured.

"They say a lot of things."

"Cassandra," Ibrahim ventured. "Do you have proof, besides Eduardo?"

"No," said Sandy. "But I'll get some."

Sandy walked into the safe house's wide dining room unannounced, and various important people turned to stare at her.

"Excuse me," the head of a very large communications firm asked, "but who is this?" Mustafa Ramoja rolled his eyes. Some of the guests did recognise her, with murmurs and gasps.

"I'm sorry," said Mustafa, "I wasn't expecting company, but it seems the CSA has sent some anyway. Perhaps we can do this another time."

"Anyone thinking of reporting my presence here today," Sandy told the gathering as they hurried for the doors, "might want to reflect on how I know who all of you are, and where all of you live, and how none of you are really supposed to be talking to the League without a Federation government representative present."

Doors opened and they filed out. Mustafa just watched Sandy, with resigned respect. Sunlight spilled through big windows onto a spartanly modernist floor, wide and spotless. Polished slate here, then two steps up to polished timber, and a bar. The look was so League, Sandy thought. So "future." If one were stupid enough to presume that one could decide what the future looked like.

"Have you any idea," Mustafa asked her, ascending the two steps, "how long it took me to get that group together?"

"Far longer than it took us to find out you were doing it," said Sandy. Security came into the room from the outside, wondering what the problem was. They took one look at Sandy, recognised her, and paled. Wisely, they made not even a twitch toward their weapons.

"It's all right, Trudi," Mustafa sighed, walking behind the bar. "She gets past even the best of us. You can go." The security guards left, and closed the doors. "Though I had thought our security here a little tighter. You didn't trigger anything?"

Sandy shook her head. "Tanushan IT is superior even to the League, I've learned new tricks while I'm here."

"It does make sense, I suppose. Drink?"

"Whisky. Straight." Being unaffected by alcohol didn't mean she didn't enjoy the biting taste. Mustafa poured. "New Torah's making GIs, I see."

"Do you?" He poured a glass for himself, and walked to her. "You'd be the first person to see that."

He tossed the glass to her, whisky and all. Sandy caught it neatly in her fingertips, and not a drop spilled.

"You knew what he was," said Sandy, watching him closely. "I'm sure you were under orders to bring him in yourself. Yet you sent us after him. Why?"

"I've no idea what you're talking about."

"Unless you wanted us to know what your government won't admit," Sandy continued. "Unless you went against their express orders. But you'd never do anything like that, would you, Mustafa? Disobey an order? From the most moral, enlightened government in the human universe?"

Mustafa walked to the windows and gazed out. Linked into the room network by means of devious infiltration even a League safe house was not equipped to stop, Sandy sensed the network suddenly change. Autistic mode. Sandy walked to his side.

"Disobeying one's government," Mustafa said quietly, "is not the same as abandoning one's people."

"Ah," said Sandy. "So you're following ISO orders. Which somewhere along the line have deviated from the League government's."

"Politicians can be stupid."

"Tell me about it."

"I wanted you to help Eduardo," said Mustafa. "I did not wish him dead, though it's not exactly surprising. Either way, New Torah needs to be stopped."

"And you think that the Federation might do it?" Sandy asked incredulously. "With the risk of war, with your mob still claiming New Torah as their own?"

"No one really controls New Torah today," said Mustafa. He was very grim, with none of his usual elegant amusement. "Our government abandoned them on the pretext that those systems were not economically viable. Well, now it turns out that New Torah has found a way to make itself economically viable. Only now, League administration doesn't want to hear about it. New Torah is too difficult and too embarrassing. We abandoned a lot of people to an awful fate when we left. Millions of people."

"And now they wouldn't have you back even if you tried," Sandy surmised. The safe house was obviously ISO run from top to bottom for Mustafa to be talking so openly, even with the network systems jammed. She did not mind League officials hearing her, but Mustafa would. "How bad is it?"

"Well, first," said Mustafa with a hard edge of sarcasm, "most systems descended into bloody turmoil and economic collapse. The wealthy, the elite, the most well educated all found passage elsewhere. Those left behind were hardnosed working class, often without families, attracted by high wages and the prospect of fortunes. The Torah Systems were not a place to go for those interested in a grand vision of civilised virtue. There were many good people, just not enough."

"Frontier worlds," Sandy agreed, nodding. "We have them here, too."

"So you can imagine who takes over." He sipped his drink. "And who they kill as soon as they take power. Those are military industrial worlds; the only resource they have is weapons. It became incredibly brutal for several years, then a new stability emerged. There are several factions prominent now. They call themselves corporations but in reality they're crime gangs. Incredibly well-armed crime gangs. They do business like regular corporations, but they solve contractual disputes with assassinations and minor wars. There are no laws or morals, only winners and losers."

"And League administration feels they're not worth the trouble," said Sandy.

"Yes, because League administration's judgment is so infrequently flawed." The sarcasm was like nothing Mustafa had directed toward his government within her hearing before. "Like judging the Torah Systems unsustainable in the first place."

"Maybe they were right," Sandy suggested. "Maybe they were unsustainable for a civilised government. The problem with uncivilised governments is that they often do quite a good job where civilisation has failed."

"Yes," Mustafa agreed, darkly. "New Torah has been quite successful. They now threaten to become a major problem for the League. The ISO pleads for action, yet the government is too wrapped up in domestic issues, and insists otherwise."

"What kind of major problem?" Sandy asked.

"New Torah is redeveloping ship-building capability," said Mustafa. "Warships, to compliment the small merchant fleet that they have currently."

Oh, thought Sandy. It wasn't often that she scooped the highest levels of Federal intelligence with something major. She'd enjoy seeing their faces when she told them. But that was the only happy thought in the information. She was no fan of the League or its new government, but the instability of what Mustafa was describing promised no good for anyone.

"Wealthy inter-system crime families posing as planetary governments and building military class starships," she said. "What could possibly go wrong?"

"And building GIs," Mustafa added. "That, too." Another scoop, though a long suspected one. She felt no joy at all at this one.

"How many?"

He shook his head. "Uncertain. Quite a few. They're not all that good at it, though. Lots of experimentation." His voice grew tight. "Failed attempts that do not immediately die."

They stood together for a while in silence.

"You can feel that, can't you?" Sandy said quietly after a moment. "That's rage. Or outrage, perhaps. You haven't experienced what I have, from the wrong end of when GI policy goes wrong, so you might not recognise the feeling. There are laws here protecting newborn human life from experimentation, incredibly strict laws. For GIs in the League, nothing."

"It's not League government that's doing it," Mustafa countered.

"That's debatable, and you know it. There was plenty of it going on during the war, too. And you know that also."

"And what if," Mustafa asked, "by preventing such experimentation, advances were slowed to such an extent that advanced GIs like you or I did not exist?"

"We're both like the children of rape victims, Mustafa. The child bears no blame at all for the act of his creation, but that does not excuse the horror of what befell his mother."

Mustafa sighed. "I cannot accept such a narrow and pessimistic view of our existence. The League's experiments were with strict controls. They did not churn out misshapen monsters before arriving at us . . ."

"That you know of."

"And I know an awful lot more than you. The experimentation was at laboratory and simulation level only, and failures never achieved consciousness."

"Bullshit," Sandy snorted. "You know I don't believe that."

"Your experiences in the military have clouded your reason," Mustafa said calmly. "You suffered great mistreatment, it's true. But those were the people who used GIs, not those who made them." Sandy said nothing. "With New Torah, however, your anger is justified, and shared by me."

"That's wonderful," said Sandy. "The question is, what are you going to do about it?"

CHAPTER SIX

Sandy took a train to Montoya. She liked to do it sometimes, to remind herself of the people it was her job to protect. They filled the maglev, a predominance of South Asian brown, the rest an equal mix of white and black, as was Tanusha's immigration pattern. They wore interlink visors, chatting silently or out loud on calls, or read books or worked. One elderly Sikh gentleman, clearly an eccentric, read a real, worn paper book. Some sat or stood with friends and talked, but this was largely a working crowd, 10 a.m. on a Tuesday morning, travelling alone in working attire.

None recognised her, in her baseball cap and sunglasses. The city sped below the windows, very green, now passing low-rise roofs of suburban neighbourhoods as the track curved toward a high-rise urban cluster. There the train slowed, almost soundlessly, from over 200kph to very little. Tall buildings slid past, then the base of a mega-rise, towering the best part of a kilometer into the sky. On the streets here were crowds on well-designed pavements, busy streetfronts alive with shops and cafes, roads jammed with centrally regulated traffic. The details still amazed her, even after so long. As they approached the elevated station, a huge screen advertised Ramprakash Road's latest musical hit, an extravaganza of dancing girls and dazzling colours. Then the station, doors of the tube sliding open, people coming and going. People on the platform. A mother with kids in an automated stroller. Tourists consulting a display map. A young guy with dreadlocks and a guitar case. At least six hundred people on this platform alone. Maybe five thousand in the open-tube body of the maglev.

Sometimes, if she allowed herself to think upon it, the scale of the responsibility was more frightening than the dangers of the job itself.

At Montoya, the station stopped five hundred meters from the Grand Council Assembly building. Sandy took the stairs down to street level instead of the escalator, and marvelled at how the whole neighbourhood looked so permanent, when just five years ago it had been forest. On the sidewalk, she walked, as the buildings gave way to grassy parks—a three hundred meter security buffer about the Assembly perimeter, and the reason the maglev station was as far away as it was.

The Assembly was a monster, far larger than the Callayan Parliament. Architects stated it was inspired in part by the old coliseum in Rome—a huge circle, with straight walls a hundred meters high, inset with huge pillars and grand atrium entrances. Somewhat larger than the coliseum, then, but Sandy reckoned the Romans would have loved it just the same. That old building had been a place where contestants fought and died for the entertainment of crowds. The Grand Council Assembly was less bloody, and (its critics complained) less entertaining, but most of those familiar with it agreed the comparison was apt.

About it, all roads terminated. Ahead, Sandy could hear the shouting of crowds. Then she saw them, protestors at a gate, a great mass spilling onto the neighbouring grass. Some police riot vans blocked them, and more cops in armour, plus a few in huge, intimidating walkers—metal gorillas with human drivers, ten feet tall with dispersant foam cannons in powerful fists.

She detoured to walk past them. There were banners and placards, and lots of shouting. About five thousand people, she reckoned, switching to a network link from a nearby camera, which gave her a good overhead view. A CSA passcode gave her a police feed, which estimated about the same. News networks, anything up to twenty thousand . . . predictable overestimation, that was. But five thousand was plenty. The rule of thumb was that anything over two thousand, in party town Tanusha, indicated a serious hot-button issue.

"What do we want?"

"Justice for Pyeongwha!"

"When do we want it?"

"Now!"

Some might have found the chant amusing. "Pyeongwha" was Korean for "peace," an optimistic name for a new world. So the protestors demanded "justice for peace." Which to Sandy's mind was precisely the trade they were proposing.

Sandy picked her way through the crowd. Many were young, a lot looked like students. They didn't look like Pyeongwha ex-pats, though—Pyeongwha immigration patterns had given them a sixty-percent East Asian demographic, while East Asians here looked about the usual Tanushan ten percent. Plus they just looked like Tanushans. Even the crazy, fringe types were just a little too well dressed to be convincing—jewellery clashed with dyed T-shirts, and brand name shoes completely ruined the effect of ascetic robes or lungi.

The crowd silenced to hear a speaker with a megaphone. "These Federal warmongers have attacked and raped the peaceful world of Pyeongwha!" A roar of displeasure from the crowd. "Pyeongwha never attacked anyone!" Another roar. "Pyeongwha is a major exporter of Neodymium, currently one of the most valuable rare metals in the Federation! This is nothing short of a Federal coup to control the Neodymium trade, for which the innocent people of Pyeongwha are being murdered in their thousands!"

Sandy recalled the "medical" facility beneath Anjula. The bodies, the storage facilities. The skulls being sliced open. Some of those people had been conscious at the time. The peaceful world of Pyeongwha? Peaceful to whom?

She reached the front of the crowd, pushed through the thickest concentration, and flashed her badge at a policeman. He let her through, and she passed through police lines and barricades to the perimeter gate. There an armed officer gave her a more thorough network scan.

"Good morning, Commander," he said cheerfully as the scan results showed him her identity. "Lovely day for a protest."

"Isn't it always," Sandy said sourly. The officer grinned.

She started up the path from the gate, through the lovely gardens that, as always, were a front for massively overlapping security layers. One false move within this perimeter, and even a GI could be dead at the touch of a button.

Suddenly a girl was chasing her, a cameraman in tow. Dammit, Sandy thought to herself. Smaller protests were so common the media usually didn't bother to send reporters directly, and in the throng she was good at blending in. But now, on the grounds, she was conspicuous.

"Excuse me! Commander Kresnov!" Sandy thought of walking faster, but that always looked bad on camera. Media training kicked in and she slowed, took off her glasses, and fixed her most pleasant, agreeable expression. The girl came alongside, very excited. "Commander Kresnov, Sushma Sen, KIN Network." That was a big one, with Federation-wide distribution. The cameraman arrived to zoom on Sandy's face, holding the automated mount steady with a light touch.

"Hi," said Sandy.

"What brings you to the scene of this enormous protest?"

Enormous? "I'm not at the protest, I'm at the Grand Council Assembly."

"But you came in at the side exit, right by the protest, when most VIPs go through the main entrances. Are you impressed by its size?"

VIPs? "I'm very pleased to live in a society where this kind of free expression is encouraged," Sandy gave the rote answer.

"The protesters are angry at the apparently unprovoked military invasion of Pyeongwha. Were you yourself involved in the invasion?"

Invasion? Military? Unprovoked? "I'm not allowed to comment on that kind of stuff."

"Some commentators on the invasion have noted that you haven't been seen around Tanusha for the past month and more."

"Neither has Santa Claus," said Sandy with a smile. Defuse with humour, her media trainers encouraged. "I'm fairly sure he wasn't on Pyeongwha either."

"So what have you been doing this past month?"

"I've been not commenting on things I'm not supposed to talk about." Halfway to the Assembly steps now, just keep walking and don't fuck it up. Who gave this idiot a grounds pass anyway?

"Can you comment on the progress of your GI friends as they wait for their asylum claims to be processed?"

Friends? Not all of them were. "Well, it varies on a case by case basis. I'm not a lawyer, so I really can't say anything worth listening to about their prospects. But I'm confident that the system will give each of them a fair hearing."

"A number of prominent commentators have accused the presence of GIs in Tanusha as being responsible for a rise in violence. After the shooting in Denpasar last week in which seven people were killed, there's a lot of fingers pointing at GIs and those who sponsor their asylum claims as promoting a general culture of violence which might inspire some unstable people to violent acts."

Oh dear God. "Well firstly," she said with entirely commendable calm, "not all GIs have a combat designation. We weren't initially even created with combat in mind. That came later with the advent of the League-Federation War. A number of those GIs currently seeking asylum in Tanusha are non-combat designations. Secondly, I think that murder is a very serious charge, and we should level charges of murder against actual murderers."

"But if GIs are all peaceful, why are the vast majority of them, including yourself, taking up military or paramilitary jobs after gaining citizenship here?"

Un. Fucking. Believable. "Surely being a soldier doesn't necessarily make one violent?" She was almost able to keep the scorn from her voice, as she mounted the steps to the security entrance. Almost.

"Thank you, Commander," the girl called after her. Her repressed smile showed what she thought of such unsophisticated logic.

"Hello, Commander," said the sympathetic security guard as she handed over her guns for him to register and hand back. "Sorry about that. She got the press pass from someone in the public affairs office. Nothing we can do."

"Dear fucking God," Sandy replied. "I think my IQ just dropped ten points."

Chandrasekar was already in the Intelligence Committee room, waiting for things to start. He gave her a sardonic look as she picked her way through System Ambassadors and clusters of attendant staff, greeting those she knew with a smile and a handshake.

"You came prepared, I trust?" he said as she reached her seat at his side. The raised eyebrow was for her jeans and jacket as much as her lack of briefing papers, but she was always active duty, and formal attire for women sucked, so it was her habit to flaunt the dress code and come in "native," as some called it.

"Can I borrow a comb?" she asked, taking her seat. Chandrasekar immediately produced one, only to see from her grin that she was teasing. The CSA's Investigations chief was always exceptionally well groomed, with big, vid-star hair and neat moustache. He scowled, and put the comb away.

The Grand Council Intelligence Committee was where the Federation's senior government officials were briefed on the Federation's most secret and sensitive matters. People took their seats, Ambassadors at the oval tables, staff against the walls behind. The decor was nice, polished wood and big leather chairs, but there were no windows, and absolutely no media or public access of any kind. This was the most secure room in Tanusha. There weren't even security cameras in here. Sandy's uplinks were completely blank; nothing registered on any frequency. Cybernetics ensured that records were kept, of course, but even those implants were fully registered with building security, and all recordings shared and documented after each session. Any of those recordings that showed up in any place they shouldn't would launch an immediate high level investigation, which could easily land an offender in prison or worse.

Chairman Ballan got the session underway with the usual procedurals, during one of which Sandy spoke up to announce to all present that she was armed at the table, as was Deputy Chandrasekar. A pointless announcement, but procedure demanded it.

"Good," said Ambassador Honiker from Argos System. "I always feel safer when you are."

Sandy enjoyed the Grand Council Committees far more than Callayan Parliament Committees of late. Grand Council politics were more benign, for one thing. There were no parties, only loosely defined factions that varied from issue to issue. Each of these ambassadors' native constituencies were many light years away, and while media from each of their worlds were present to apply pressure, the ambassadors themselves were mostly not elected. As bureaucrats rather than populists, they were not prone to the kind of political showboating that had caused Sandy so much grief on Callay.

The resulting atmosphere was not so charged with factionalism and grandstanding, debates were more sensible and leisurely, and people in general more friendly and collegial. And yet, for all the lowered temperature, the stakes here were far higher than most matters discussed in the Callayan Parliament. That building represented just one world of a hundred and forty-three million. This building and its ambassadors represented the entire Federation, now twenty-seven-billion-plus strong.

This session was on New Torah. Sandy told them what she knew, with no mention of Mustafa, then Chandrasekar joined in with accumulated background on New Torah's seven systems and four inhabited worlds, and which of its so-called governments were doing what to whom. Then, there were questions.

"Commander Kresnov," said Chairman Ballan. "You yourself aren't just a policy analyst, you're a policy executor, in the security field at least. If I can put it that way."

"That is one way to put it," Sandy conceded wryly. Some others smiled.

"So I think it might be useful, in this location where we can discuss actions and consequences so freely, to discuss options. If I were to ask you for your policy recommendation on New Torah, what would it be?"

"Aggressive intervention," said Sandy. "Immediately."

"You're aware of the many consequences of that policy, of course?"

"Of course. And I don't want to make light of them, the consequences would be very serious. I don't need to explain them to anyone here. All of you have had careers in government far more diverse than my own specialty. But my specialty requires me to focus on the consequences of *not* intervening.

"Firstly, there's the ship-building capability. Now, a Fleet Captain would give a more expert opinion than mine, but I'm pretty sure most of them would say the same thing—New Torah's so-called governments are little more than crime gangs, and the prospect of crime gangs with military starships is simply unacceptable. The League should be told that either they deal with it, or we will."

"Wouldn't the League be a more likely target than us?" another ambassador asked.

"Maybe," said Sandy. "But that's like hoping the predator eats someone else instead of you—maybe it will, maybe it won't. The definition of security is not leaving things to chance, hope is not a viable security policy. Secondly, crime gangs are attracted to money. You've all seen the briefings detailing New Torah's increasing involvement into Federation trade, businesses and technology. We're far wealthier than the League, especially now, and we're probably more naive of the risks. If I'm a Torah crime gang looking for easy profits, I come here. With a starship that can achieve approach velocities so high it can kill continents."

"They'd never use that," said someone else. "Crime gangs are safer than religious or ideological radicals. They're rational actors because we can always kill them back, and they do care if they die. They won't commit suicide."

"Yes," Chandrasekar added, "but hell of a way to start a protection racket." Grim nods around the table.

"Thirdly," Sandy continued, "there's synthetic biology, GIs in particular." She took a breath. "Now I can't claim objectivity here, not even close. But I think the arguments are compelling whether objectively made or not. New Torah makes GIs. There's an argument for humanitarian intervention right there, but I'm not naive enough to suppose that the suffering of an unknown number of artificial people will warrant direct intervention where the suffering of millions of natural, organic humans has not.

"But New Torah has starships now. Eduardo got to Callay. He was supposed to perform some covert function, we don't know what, but evidently he was a strong character who bravely resisted his masters' crude attempts at programming, and died for it. We might not get so lucky with the next GIs. We've already had one new generation GI, whom you'll know from previous reports went by the name of Jane, who was utterly programmable. New Torah doesn't have that technology yet, but they might acquire it. GIs in the wrong hands can do a lot of damage. We've all seen it happen in this city."

"We do have quite a few friendly GIs now as defence," someone else answered.

"Sure, but I can't defend you against everything. I can only fight GIs once I know they're here, and sometimes I'll only know that after the damage has been done. And even I'm not invulnerable. A bad intelligence breach could put me in real danger, particularly from GIs in Tanusha that I'm not prepared for."

Or a simple sniper, she could have said. She wasn't bullet proof, only bullet resistant, and if the caliber was big enough, and she didn't know it was coming, she was as dead as anyone else. But even in this secure room, she wasn't about to start announcing her weaknesses in public.

"And further," she added, "and this is by far the most dangerous point of all, GI technology is not static. I'm the most advanced combat GI so far, but I'm twenty-two years old now. League didn't work on the technology beyond me for political reasons mostly, and for the fear that I wouldn't turn out to be loyal, which was proven a correct fear. So maybe I am the final say in GI psychology, because at least I'm stable—Jane was the other way of doing it, but the book isn't written with her any longer. She had to evolve further before we'd know one way or the other."

Which was, of course, why Sandy had let her live, when she had assuredly deserved to die. Or that's what she told herself.

"But if New Torah starts pressing that technology forward once more, taking it beyond where the League basically stopped, then the whole ball starts rolling again, and we're back where we were when the Federation declared war on the League. Artificial humanity is potentially reconcilable with organic humanity, I think, although that solution is yet to be written. Perhaps that's the chapter we're writing here on Callay, with myself and the other refugees.

"But artificial humanity is not reconcilable into civilised human society when its direction is controlled by a bunch of brutal crime gangs who are only interested in using their fighting abilities to advance their own monstrous criminality. That's my greatest fear. Artificial humanity is capable of the same wonders and joys of life as regular humans. But New Torah will turn us into monsters, to the point that one day the only thing we'll be good for is extinction."

"How many do you have?" Sandy asked Allessandro Ballan after the briefing. A staffer brought her lunch: a bowl of very decent pasta and a glass of red. They were in Ballan's office, just the two of them, his staffers occupying the rooms outside. From here they had a view through polarized glass onto the inner courtyard of the Grand Council Assembly building. Circular walls and offices rose high around the garden below, thick with native trees. In the garden's center, a large skylight made a glass ceiling for the Assembly chamber below. Sandy had personally protested that architectural choice—any assault team had outside access directly to the core of the building, rendering the entire complex vulnerable, to say nothing of the damage that could be caused by an attack with heavy weapons. She'd been assured the high tech defences would guard against either eventuality, which was bullshit, and she'd nearly written an editorial to a news service saying so, when no one else would listen. But the Tanushan media, she'd learned from long experience, were not her friends.

Ambassador Ballan followed her gaze, and smiled. "Still concerned for the Assembly's safety?"

"My FSA team could be in here in ten minutes," she said flatly, eating pasta at the office table. Ballan received his own bowl, and joined her. "I've got it all documented for the aftermath: how I protested, how the CSA backed me, how we were overruled, everything. The investigation will find it useful."

Ballan chuckled. "You've become very cynical in your old age."

"I keep getting accused of that. I think the word is 'experienced.'"

Ballan was the ambassador of Nova Esperanca, a world of eight hundred million situated close to League space. That proximity had put Nova Esperanca front and center in the war, giving Ballan a strong security background. He was well respected, and a natural choice for Chairman of the Intelligence Committee.

"Currently," he answered her question, "we have thirty-six. We need sixty percent of member worlds, there's fifty-seven of those at present, so we need thirty-four."

"Slim margin," Sandy murmured.

Ballan nodded. "Of course, it will be a priority vote, so it might take a while." Meaning that Ambassadors would have to consult with their home governments before voting. That could take up to two months. Voting to authorise assertive military policy against New Torah was not a non-priority matter.

"So it should pass?" Sandy asked.

Ballan shrugged. "Never certain. But most likely, yes."

"Then what?"

"Then we convene a policy cabinet on the issue, and all the member worlds will select whomever they feel most qualified to represent their interests. Much like the war against the League. Only we hope it shall not be so serious this time."

"Won't the member worlds all have some kind of domestic vote first?"

"Oh, no," said Ballan dismissively, around another mouthful. "We're not voting to authorise a war. Only to move to a potential war footing, in the hope of dissuading both the League and New Torah from current actions. I personally doubt it will go any further than that; the League cannot afford our displeasure now. We'll twist their arm, and force them to deal with New Torah themselves."

"What if they don't?"

"Bridge, crossing, the old cliché."

"So if we had to take more aggressive action," Sandy pressed, "it could take more months to be authorised. And then we probably would need all the member worlds to have their own separate vote . . ."

"Some of them would demand it, yes. Others not."

"And in the meantime we'd just have to hope New Torah doesn't see all this going on, and decide to hit us first."

Ballan gave her a look of heavy-lidded concern. "It would rather solve the debate."

"Wouldn't it," said Sandy, with displeasure. "At what cost?"

Ballan sighed, forking more pasta. "There is another issue that could derail us. The action on Pyeongwha has occurred very close to this new vote, and some of those worlds who voted against it are still smarting from their defeat . . ."

"Even despite what we found?" Sandy was too wise by now to be incredulous. This felt more like contempt than incredulity.

"Some worlds do not like a strong Grand Council taking military action against member worlds," Ballan said reasonably. "Callay itself is one such world, having voted against the action only to lose the vote, to the displeasure of President Singh."

"Trust me," said Sandy, "I noticed."

"It's simply not the Grand Council that many people envisioned and wanted. The institution was supposed to be benign, but then came the war. Now that the war is over, people wanted it to return to their original vision, an institution of peaceful compromise. Instead, we find ourselves taking one aggressive policy decision after another."

"And because of everyone's reluctance," Sandy added, "something like six hundred thousand people on Pyeongwha have died when it could have been stopped."

"Is it up to six hundred thousand now?" Ballan murmured, aghast.

Sandy nodded. "It was industrial scale. We've found another six facilities so far. Their records indicate they were going at a solid forty thousand a year this year. It had been escalating upward for the last few decades. It started off as just a handful of murders a year, then grew exponentially. Kind of like NCT itself."

"It doesn't seem possible, does it?" Ballan gulped his wine.

"Oh, I think it does," said Sandy.

"Perhaps you're less naive than I."

"Or perhaps when you're the product of an industrial war machine like I am, and you've then seen the people who created you treat this wonderful creation like something they scraped off their shoe, you realise that with human civilisation, pretty much anything is possible."

Ballan smiled faintly. "Having seen the abuses you've seen, it's a wonder you're not a pacifist."

"Having seen the abuses I've seen," Sandy replied with an edge, "it would be a wonder if anyone could *remain* a pacifist."

Ballan nodded thoughtfully. "So tell me this," he said. "The Federal Security Agency. You're a member of both it, and the Callayan Security Agency. Can this continue?"

"Right now we don't have a choice. The FSA is new, and while there's plenty of intel analysts and desk jockeys, they're short of serious muscle. We're still recruiting, but there's always been a shortage of good paramilitary people on Federation worlds, and from there the next step up is Fleet. And a lot of Fleet Marines don't really like the FSA because of all the old CDF hands like myself and Vanessa who shot up a bunch of Fifth Fleet people five years ago."

"To say nothing of all the former-League GIs now in the FSA as well," Ballan added.

"Exactly. So if the FSA is to have an arm with muscle, that can carry out strikes independently of Fleet, we're really stuck with ex-CDF and CSA people, because there's not enough of the others yet to fill the numbers. And if we strip all those people out of the CSA at the same time, the CSA's left with nothing, and with all the threats on Callay at the moment, that's not feasible. Thus, we're all working two jobs."

"It's just that when we moved the center of the Federation from Earth to Callay," Ballan explained, "we swore this kind of blurring between the Federal government and the local would end."

Sandy shrugged, shovelling pasta. "That's life."

"You can't just step up recruitment?"

"Oh, we are. But the technology we're using these days for augmentation is getting very advanced. Previously, maybe three percent of the population had the right genes and physiology to handle the upgrades, but with the most recent stuff it's down to less than one percent. We'll expand that as genetic mods improve, but that'll take time. Plus, if we're recruiting from all member worlds directly into the FSA, that's a huge leap for a rookie. We'd rather recruit from experienced pools like the CSA. We're working with a number of them to fast track interested personnel, but again, it takes time."

"And you're adamant we can't let Fleet carry out operations like Pyeongwha on their own?"

Sandy made a face, shaking her head. "It's not just me that says so. Look, Fleet Marines are good, but they don't do what we do. Marines are an arm of the Fleet, and Fleet's strategic—they go after big installations, stations, ports, command centers. They hit and hold, and their units are kind of inflexible because they have to be, to concentrate firepower on specific objectives.

"FSA are more tactical. On Pyeongwha we worked in small units, we coordinated with civilian groups on the ground, we had a whole range of targets and objectives, and we really took tacnet coordination to a whole new level . . . like I said, our augmentation's getting very high tech. Fleet haven't caught up yet, and I don't know if they're interested. Marines see tacnet as a coordination tool; FSA uses it like an offensive weapon."

"Interesting," said Ballan. A staffer hurried into the room, bringing a tablet, which Ballan read, signed and sent. "I'm also a little concerned at how for all the FSA's supposed intelligence expertise, they keep being trumped by the CSA. Take this latest news on New Torah."

"Well, the sources are on Callay," Sandy said. "And the CSA knows Callay better than anyone, obviously. But also, Ibrahim is just the best."

"I know."

"And Director Diez . . ."

"I know." Ballan put down his fork and picked up his glass. He sipped, and looked at her for a long, considering moment. "What would you say to replacing one with the other?"

Sandy sighed. "If it weren't for the fact that his wife is dying and he wants to retire to look after her, I'd say hurray."

Ambassador Ballan wanted her to meet some Fleet Intelligence officers whom he respected, to talk about New Torah from Fleet's perspective. Sandy went, despite having ten other things that needed attending, more because one did not say no to Ambassador Ballan than for any great enthusiasm for Fleet Intelligence. The Grand Council Assembly Director was Li Shufu, who was the closest thing that the Federation had to an overall president. Second to him was Ouchi. Ballan was number three, and as chairman of the Intelligence Committee, and highly respected in Fleet, arguably more important in security matters than the other two combined.

Walking the hall with him certainly reinforced that impression, as several staff accompanied him, including one young, pretty female staffer who was newly promoted, and staring about in wide eyed glee at all the big architecture and important people. Security walked with them, and Ballan excused himself from Sandy's company to talk with a senior staffer about something unrelated.

Then ahead, Sandy saw the journalist, Sushma Sen, waiting for them. She refrained from groaning, and was pleased at least that the cameraman was not also present. One did not interrupt Ambassador Ballan in mid-conversation with senior staff, so Ms Sen intercepted one of the other staffers, with whom she seemed friendly, and walked with them, talking.

She wasn't sure what happened next, but at one moment her ears caught one of those odd sounds her subconscious was specifically programmed to isolate, and the next she was tackling Ambassador Ballan to the ground. Just a millisecond before the explosion detonated, she recognised the sound as a cybernetic charge.

It blew its wearer to pieces, chaos and smoke in the hallway, then she was up with both pistols drawn as several people came out of hallway doors front and rear, armed. Sandy dropped them, guns blazing both ways at once. Then the secondary charge went off and sent her flying into the far wall.

She rebounded immediately, shaking her head clear, hair smoking and clothes in tatters. One gun was gone, the other no longer working, and several more armed people were rushing her and firing.

Sandy ducked, half-spun as bullets whipped where she'd been, then kicked off the wall to shoot herself at the opposing wall like a projectile. She bounced off to take one runner down with an elbow through the chest. The next swung at her and she grabbed the arm and threw—too hard, the arm came off in her hand, so she went low for the third's legs, upended him and put a fist through his skull before it hit the ground.

That gave her his weapon, which she took, and put bullets through the heads of two more down the hall's other end. The armless man was still alive, and would remain so for a little while despite jets of arterial blood, so she put six rounds through his chest to be sure.

Then Assembly security came running, too late for what had obviously been a suicide mission, even if there had only been one human bomb. She yelled at them, in case they didn't notice the network telling them who she was. That was when she registered she wasn't wearing much any longer. The second charge had removed her jacket completely, and most of her shirt beneath. Her jeans were now shorts, legs shredded. She still had hair—GI hair being, like most things, somewhat tougher than the organic equivalent—but still she was smouldering.

Only now was she noticing how dark it was, smoke everywhere, walls blasted, the fire retardant still not activated because nothing was on fire after the initial explosion. She ran back to check on her group. All of them were down. Ballan was alive but unconscious; she'd saved him from the first blast, and he'd then been lying flat for the second one, which she'd caught full in the face. Two others looked like they might make it—a security guard and the young staffer. Probably he'd tackled her and saved them both, but still it looked nasty, flesh shredded and amputations necessary. The others were all gone, two of them literally, just bits and pieces blasted about the hall.

More security were rushing in, a few of them checking on the bodies of the attackers.

"Leave them!" Sandy snapped, and strode over. Security backed off in awe at this apparition that strode from the smoke, half naked, scorched and blackened. Sandy knelt by a body, and remembered her interlink cord had been in her jacket. "Someone get me a cord!"

A cord was produced, and she snapped it into an insert socket—her head, then the corpse. That was always creepy, accessing a dead network construct, but she was hardly in a mood to be squeamish. It didn't take long to find what she was looking for.

"Everyone from Pyeongwha in the building gets arrested!" she yelled. "Right now! Everyone who's been there on holiday gets arrested! Everyone who has family there gets arrested! Everyone who has NCT installed in any form, gets arrested!"

"But we'd already done that," one security man protested.

"Yeah," she muttered, "that's what I thought, too."

CHAPTER SEVEN

She sat in FSA medical. The scanners circled the table where she sat in her underwear, while several FSA meds checked her over. Sandy watched news reports on uplink. She saw lots of emergency vehicles parked around the Assembly Building, and flyers in the air. Reporters talking to camera; God knew why they did that.

Then the footage again. No one knew how the media had received it, only that the now-late Sushma Sen had had some kind of fancy cybernetic upgrade done that allowed her to record vision, like a GI might. It had activated during the attack, and the footage now had found its way to the media, who found little squeamish in displaying the last sights of a dead woman. The footage had been cleaned up a lot, yet it showed enough—walking in the corridor, then a blast and everything going sideways. An attempt to rise, then a second blast, and down again, this time for good. She'd been lying there, probably dead, with the implant still recording. Through the smoke, the final image was clear—Sandy, an indistinct yet clearly female figure, unloading six rounds into a wounded attacker on the ground.

They were now asking if the execution of a wounded prisoner was justified. God knew how they came to the word "prisoner"—she hadn't arrested anyone, and with cybernetic explosives even corpses were threats until disposed of. She'd just killed him so he couldn't self-terminate, if he'd been loaded, which it turned out he hadn't. Just that first one, a passing female staffer with several false ribs, loaded as a human bomb: one blast for effect, then a second to scythe down anyone resisting the firearm attack.

A few commentators made the sensible point, but a few more condemned that killing as excessive. Over and over, they played that footage—a female GI, standing over a wounded man, impassive and fearsome, putting six rounds through him without blinking. Could a GI have caused this attack, other commentators wondered? Possibly one of those seeking asylum?

Great, thought Sandy. Barely an hour later, and the media were already spinning to try to make this her fault.

"Well the scans don't show anything," said Hueng, one of the meds. "I'm sure you must have some kind of blast concussion, but our equipment can't find it. I suppose we have to let you go."

"Good," said Sandy, and moved to get off the table.

"Uh!" Rhian said loudly, from where she'd been waiting by one wall. She shook her head at Sandy, sternly, and indicated she lie down. Sandy snorted, and did so. "Here's an old trick, doc. Sometimes, you have to use your hands."

Rhian dug her fingers and thumbs into various pressure points and gauged Sandy's response by voluntary and involuntary means. It wasn't hard to do. A hiss of pain usually meant something tight.

"They're pretty much the same pressure points a chiropractor or physiotherapist knows," Rhian explained to the curious meds. "Synth-alloy myomer will contract hard after a blast, just like any impact, but strains won't show on scans. You have to feel for it."

Hueng took over. And probably enjoyed it somewhat more than Rhian, as Hueng had a pretty obvious crush on her, and she wasn't wearing much. Another time, she would have teased him, or flirted. Now, she just watched the uplink images repeating before her eyes.

Someone found her some spare clothes, and she dressed, then left to find Rhian in the adjoining analysis room. Salman was there, sitting on a stool as a med lady showed him how the microscopes worked. Rhian had been with him, Rakesh working, the twins with Rakesh's parents, when news of the attack came through. Another mother might have panicked at the thought of letting a six-year-old wander into this world, but Rhian knew better than most what was safe, and was adamant that experiences were important for kids, even unsettling ones. With all the security around the FSA compound, which was brand new and alongside the Grand Council Assembly, Salman was certainly having an experience. And sure as hell there were no Pyeongwha-born or connected people here.

"Aunty Sandy!" Salman said upon seeing her. He looked anxious. "Did you get hurt?"

"No," said Sandy, dismissively. "I'm fine. I have a few bruises, that's all."

"Rhian said someone tried to hurt a Grand Council Ambassador."

"Yeah," she sighed. "It happens sometimes."

"If you got hurt," Salman said sagely, "you should go to a hospital. But this isn't a real hospital." With a look around at the lab equipment.

"He was at the hospital when the twins had some checks," Rhian explained. "He knows what a real hospital looks like."

Sandy squatted opposite the young boy. He looked a lot like his dad, which was to say that one day he'd be a big guy, and handsome.

"Well," she said, "you know what I am, right?"

"You're in the CSA!" With considerable awe. It was nice to know that someone still thought the CSA was cool. Still much cooler than the FSA, which might upset a few people in this building.

"Yes I am. But what else am I?"

Salman thought about it. Then realised what she was getting at. "You're a GI. Like Mum."

At that word, Rhian beamed. He didn't use it all the time, but lately more and more.

"Yeah. I'm a GI. And do you know what that means?"

"That means you're strong and you protect people from the bad guys."

Sandy nearly burst into tears. It astonished her, but suddenly her eyes hurt badly, and she had to wipe them to keep her vision clear.

"That's right," she agreed, her voice tight. "Your mum and I keep people safe. We're synthetic. That means we're made of different stuff from you and your dad, but we're real people just like you. If we get hurt, we have to go to a place that has equipment that can make us better. Ordinary hospitals don't usually have it, so I come here."

Salman nodded enthusiastically. "I know," he said. "Dad told me about it before."

Just like that. Sandy recalled all the hand-wringing angst when some Callayan media outfit had discovered that one of Callay's new GIs was adopting children. That one had gone on for weeks. Luckily no one had spilled Rhian's name, a fact helped by all of Rhian's underground friends helping to sweep the networks of details the media shouldn't know, and the promise of a lengthy jail term to anyone publically naming a CSA operative without authorisation. But the debate had been typically stupid, and Rhian had obviously been hurt, however she denied it.

How could a child accept a synthetic person as a parent, they'd asked? What damage would it cause to do so? Hell, Sandy had once asked those questions of Rhian, herself. But Salman just called her Mum, and that was that.

Rhian always said she preferred the logic of children to adults, not because it was escapist, but because it often stated truths that adults were blind to. Now, Sandy was seeing what she meant.

"Come on," she said, and scooped Salman up. "I'll walk you and Mum to your cruiser, then I have some things I have to do. Are you going to have a party this Holi?"

"Yes," Salman said happily. "We're going to have water pistols, and we're going to make everyone wet!"

"Oh that sounds like fun. Can I come?"

"Yes!" said Salman, even more happily. "And Auntie Vanessa too, can she come, too?"

"You know," said Rhian as they left the med room, "I sometimes think he's getting an unrealistic view of women. His three main examples are all grunts."

"At least he thinks we're fun," Sandy said firmly.

"What does unrealistic mean?" asked Salman.

The interviewee was a young woman, no more than twenty-five. She was an Anjulan facility employee, European, moderately pretty. She had a small nose stud, standard fashion accessory on many worlds, and wore a light, peach-gloss eye shadow. She had the blood of thousands on her hands.

"*Can you describe your job in the facility?*" asked an interviewer, off screen. Her voice was measured. Sandy had heard that tone many times, in professional psychs, constructing an angle of attack.

"*I was in prep,*" said the girl.

"*And what were your responsibilities, in prep?*"

"*I would prepare the subjects.*"

"*Prepare them how?*"

"*I'd put them in a sedated state. Then I'd prepare them for the procedure.*"

"*The surgical procedure?*"

"*Yes,*" said the girl.

Sandy sat in a comfortable reclining chair, with a grand view of night-time Tanusha. This was one of Anita and Pushpa's apartments. They had numerous, which formed a valuable support network for all the curious causes the two very-wealthy businesswomen found it necessary to support. Sandy herself was one of those causes, as were most of the GI asylum seekers.

"Where did you get this from?" Vanessa asked Pushpa. She'd excused herself from Phillippe's company, citing an evening with the girls—any excuse to get away from one of Phillippe's functions with the various music-supporting VIPs that she found so awful. Sandy doubted Phillippe had any problem with Vanessa's absence—when Vanessa was unhappy, she had a way of spreading it around.

"Ask me no questions," said Pushpa around a mouthful of ice cream, "and I'll tell you no scurrilous half-truths."

"Ah," said Vanessa. Ari was still on Pyeongwha, leading the FSA's investigations. These interviews were strictly not for public release, but mysteriously, a bunch of them were now making the rounds on a string of pirate network sites, the kind that propagated themselves in a dozen new locations every time the authorities shut one down. This was a new interview that wasn't even on the networks. Yet.

"*Did it concern you at all that these were ordinary people?*" asked the interviewer. "*Pyeongwha citizens, like you?*"

The girl shook her head. "*They weren't like me.*"

"Disassociation," said Anita, watching the screen with wide, transfixed eyes. She had a mohawk now, dyed various colours, and unorthodox jewellery. Among her many unofficial qualifications was psychology, which she'd acquired by being one of Callay's best uplink software constructors.

"*How were they not like you?*"

"*They were rejectors.*"

"*What is a rejector?*"

"*A rejector is a traitor,*" the girl insisted, with a flash of anger. "*NCT is Pyeongwha's greatest achievement. It makes us strong against our enemies. Rejectors are traitors who try to destroy everything good in Pyeongwha. They serve our enemies, and they must be fought.*"

"Notice the language," said Anita. "The overuse of the first person plural, we, our, us. Collectivists always do that."

"Nothing you don't hear from radicals here," Pushpa said skeptically.

"*Some of our research suggests that many of these rejectors, as you call them, were not actually opposed to Neural Cluster Technology at all, nor to Pyeongwha society,*" the interviewer continued. "*Instead, it's more that their brains were not structured to best adapt to NCT. So they weren't making a conscious choice to reject NCT, it was just an accident of biology.*"

The girl just looked at her blankly. There was a chilling pause. No one in the room spoke.

"*Does this distinction mean nothing to you?*" the interviewer persisted.

"*What distinction?*"

"*The distinction between someone who is consciously betraying everything you claim to be defending, and someone who merely, through no fault of their own, does not have the biology to assimilate Pyeongwha's NCT regime.*"

Another long pause. "Good God," Anita murmured.

The girl finally shook her head. "*I don't understand your point.*"

"*So there's no distinction in your mind between the different kinds of people you dealt with in prep?*"

"*A traitor is a traitor. Pyeongwha society works a certain way. They knew that. They chose another path, and all societies have the right to defend themselves from those who attack them.*"

"And so all resistance or non-compliance becomes attack," said Anita. "Thus justifying anything Anjula does in response."

"Hell, politicians do that here," said Pushpa. "You brand a political attack with something morally unacceptable—racism, sexism, qualificationism—to try and make your opponents shut up."

"Attacking free speech isn't the same as mass murder," Vanessa replied.

"I'm not saying it's the same thing," said Pushpa, spooning another mouthful of ice cream, "I'm just saying that you can observe the same rhetorical mechanisms at play in all societies. The consequences of those rhetorical mechanisms may vary wildly, but the mechanisms themselves all come from the same places and the same logic."

"Sure," said Vanessa, "but that just leads to some soft civvies in places like Tanusha, who've never seen a real blood and guts disaster up close, thinking that all this shit is basically equivalent—freedom of speech here, mass murder there. It's not."

Pushpa held up a pacifying hand. "No, you're right, I agree. I'm just saying."

Sandy smiled. Pushpa and Anita were from what was, in Sandy's opinion, easily Tanusha's most intelligent segment of society—the freewheeling, free commercial, free everything underground. It made everything they had to say worth listening to. But Vanessa knew things they didn't, first hand, and argued like a grunt—straight for the throat every time. What Vanessa liked about Anita and Pushpa was that they'd actually listen to a mere grunt, unlike many far more "capital Q" Qualified individuals who found security personnel irredeemably blue collar and beneath respectability.

"Okay," said Siddhartha, finishing the final screw that connected the brace to Sandy's neck. "That's all ready."

Rhian came across and peered at it. It was a simple enough device: a brace mount for an extremely strong, slim needle. The whole thing was rigged with microsensors, to measure every fraction of a millimeter.

"I'd rather Rhian did it," said Sandy.

"Oh, no," said Siddhartha, "the needle is so exceptionally small you'll barely feel a thing. It shouldn't cause you any reaction."

"I don't care," said Sandy. "If you're poking around in the spinal column of a GI, anyone within arm's reach is theoretically at risk. Rhian will do it."

"I'll do it," Rhian agreed. "What do I do?"

"Oh, it's all preprogrammed," said Siddhartha. "You just need to activate it here," pointing, "and keep an eye on the screen here to make sure the program works as written . . . and if it doesn't, tell me immediately, because we only use these to sample normal humans, and while I'm sure the needle is strong enough, with a GI you never know."

"It should be fine," Rhian said confidently. She knew quite a lot of medical-type stuff these days beyond even her early learning expertise.

"I agree," said Anita, knowing as much but for different reasons. She dashed for a bottle, poured Sandy a vodka, and handed it to her.

"Won't do any good," Sandy reminded her.

"I know. It just seemed appropriate."

Sandy sculled it and gave the glass back. Then she called up her full internal network diagnostic, so she could look at everything on overlaid vision and be certain nothing would be affected.

"Ready?" Rhian asked.

"Yeah, fine," said Sandy.

She felt the sting of first penetration. Then a strange, numb pain.

"Okay?" Rhian asked.

"Like I imagine an insect bite would feel, if I could feel insect bites. Is it going in?"

"Slowly," said Rhian. A pause. "Very slowly."

"What's the resistance meter?" Siddhartha asked anxiously.

"Seven four two," said Rhian. "Is that high?"

"Ridiculously high. But it should withstand up to nine hundred."

"Seven nine one," Rhian corrected.

"The needle's not going in?" Sandy sighed. It was predictable. All GIs were made tough. Herself, even more so. Her internal schematic was unchanged.

"No, wait, here we go," said Rhian. "It's going in." Sandy frowned. The pain was unchanged. That she felt it at all told her how unserious it was. Serious pain kicked in combat reflexes, which dimmed everything with natural painkiller—direct relief in the neural centers themselves, a redirecting of neural activity, not crude drugs in the bloodstream. "And now it's out."

Siddhartha stepped back in to undo the fastenings and check the sample.

"Oh yes," he said, with some excitement. "That's a very nice sample. Absolutely tiny, just a single molecular cluster. But more than enough to work with."

"Now," Vanessa said sternly, "no sharing with anyone."

"Oh, absolutely," said Siddhartha, nodding his head as the fasteners came away. "The sample won't leave my lab, and will be locked in the most secure facility. Diamonds are not as well protected." And Siddhartha was boss of his company, unlisted, with no superior to answer to.

"Diamonds are nowhere near as valuable," said Anita.

Sandy rubbed her neck as Siddhartha packed up and left, very anxious to get back to his lab.

"I get the feeling he's going to have a very late night," Pushpa observed once the door was shut. She'd put the ice cream back in the freezer, and was now started on cream whisky. Sandy was certain that if it weren't for intestinal micros, Pushpa would be considerably plumper than she already was.

"No sleep for forty-eight hours, I bet," Anita agreed.

"He's a good guy, though," said Sandy, taking some chocolate and a glass of red, and settling onto the couch next to Vanessa. "Ari's known him a long time, says he's always been above board. Absolutely obsessive, but then all the best experts are."

"Well," Anita said brightly, pouring herself a drink, "I propose a toast! We all just broke the law!" Small cheers. "Including some very senior Tanushan law enforcement officials. I propose we toast a fine day for the restoration of sanity to the Federation's biotech laws."

"I accept your toast only on the hypocritical grounds that everybody does it," said Vanessa, raising her glass.

"My point exactly!" said Anita.

"I and Rhian accept your toast on the basis that we're both walking violations of countless laws anyway," said Sandy.

"Precisely!" said Anita, very pleased, and drank. Sandy reflected on how much the Federation had changed in the seven years she'd been here. Back then, this would have been a very serious breach of law indeed. Now, not so much. Technology swept ahead, irresistible as all progress, and in that respect, the League's vision of human society was certainly winning.

"Still interesting to speculate," said Pushpa. "How much do you think that sample could fetch, 'Nita? Three bil?"

"Oh, at least," said Anita. "Taken from Sandy, easily." A Callayan dollar was fairly strong, but Tanusha was expensive. Most people made about forty thousand before tax, but an average apartment cost two hundred thousand. A house, five hundred. A nice cruiser, six hundred and up. Anita and Pushpa's little software company, Sandy heard, turned over perhaps thirty mil a year . . . with just ten employees. They'd had plenty of chances to grow it larger, but preferred it exactly this size.

"Three billion dollars?" Rhian asked, blinking.

"Easy," Anita repeated. "I mean, that's the most advanced neural synthology ever made, that we know of. The stuff we know works, anyway. The proteins alone would be three billion. I reckon if we organised a little auction we could probably get it up to five or six. All the big companies would bid through proxies and stitch up finances somehow. They can afford it."

"And they might get very little for it," Pushpa added. "Or more likely, they'd unlock completely new markets spanning the entire Federation, and six billion would be an amazing bargain."

"If I'm so fucking valuable," said Sandy, "why am I poor?"

"Because you're honest," Anita laughed.

Pushpa nodded, pointing a finger. "There's your mistake," she agreed. "If you'd been selling bits of yourself to the right people, you'd make us look like paupers."

"You're not poor," Vanessa teased her. "You earn twice the average wage and your accommodation is rent free, plus tax benefits for CSA personnel."

"I feel poor," Sandy complained.

"That's not hard in Tanusha."

"And seriously, Sandy," said Anita, "if you'd like some extra money, make me some software!" She'd been pestering Sandy on this for years. "You're a software magician. You have capabilities even I can only dream of, you could make a fortune if you wanted. I've even checked the CSA rules, and there's nothing stopping you from making some extra money on the side, so long as it's not security related. Look, I've got a couple of little barrier booster replication functions I've been working on, but I can't get the bandwidth frequencies and field depth to match in their current matrix . . . you rock at that kind of thing. Do that for me and I'll get you an equivalent percentage cut of the final product when we put it to market."

"Who's it for?" Sandy asked.

"Logistics company," said Anita. "Nothing security related."

"Logistics interfaces with central traffic control," said Sandy. "Central traffic has AIs parsing their code line by line. They'll find it. You know how AIs are with unusual patterns . . ."

"And it's not security related, so they won't care!"

"But it is security related," Sandy persisted, "because like all centralised routines, central traffic has security routines running all through it, many of which activate in the event of emergency, which I know because I actually helped write a few of them, with no additional boost to my salary."

"Well that's just dumb, Sandy," said Pushpa from her seat, a comfortable round lump in lime green salwar kameez. "No one works for free."

"It was a part of my job, included in my current salary. And here's the kicker: if there were an emergency, the first person they'll ask to parse the code is me. I'm even better on League-specific patterns than AIs are, so I'd be writing on the appearance of my own code, written privately for your logistics company, in my report."

"I can't see how that would mean you've done anything wrong," Anita said stubbornly.

"No," said Sandy, "it just looks really, really bad. 'Nita, there's very little in this network that doesn't interface with security protocols at some point.

All the stuff I write looks very specific, it's very different from anything else. I use different processing routines to write it. And a lot of that process is kind of automatic. I process cyberspace like I process anything in three dimensions, without really thinking about it."

Automatic. She thought of Poole playing the piano. Complaining that he couldn't get the expression right, that it sounded flat, emotionless. Poole could play the piano the same way that Sandy could target ten ways at once in a firefight and hit all of them—it was instinctive, the processing of situational information at a very rapid speed, translated into mechanically precise action. GIs had very little conscious control over any of it. That was what made it so effective. She didn't need to think about it—if she did, she might miss. And she never missed.

That was what Poole had been trying to do at his piano—to wrest back conscious control from the subconscious routines that dominated so much of a GI's brainspace. To assert conscious domination of the automatic subconscious. To insert emotion, on purpose, into the mechanical precision of fingers flying over piano keys. That was why he played for hours on end. To try and inject variation, on command. GIs did not do variation well. She was designed to shoot things. Variation, in shooting things, meant missing.

Was that the real reason why she didn't want to write software for Anita? Like the real reason she didn't want to learn to play music? Hidden under all her excuses, was she really frightened that, laid out in her creations, exposed for all to see, would be patterns so automatic and predictable that everyone would immediately know it was her? Because GIs were truly that predictable—not genuine, free personalities at all, but controlled and automated collections of subconscious routines? And not all that different, in fact, from the brainwashed suicidals who had attacked her today, and slaughtered thousands on Pyeongwha?

"Hey," said Vanessa, gently. Whatever Anita had said in reply hadn't registered. She'd just been sitting, and gazing at nothing. "You okay?"

"Yeah." Sandy ran a hand over her face, tiredly. "I just had a really bad day."

Vanessa put her head on Sandy's shoulder and snuggled close. It was a big advantage for female soldiers, Vanessa had once observed. Both sexes knew that some things could never be made better by talking. But girls, at least, were not embarrassed to cuddle.

Sandy thought of the bodies in the hallway, of Ambassador Ballan's staffers, even of the annoying journalist. She'd had post-stress tape, of course, so the memories did not knock her sideways. But still she had to wipe her eyes.

"Fucking Anjulans," she said, with a glance back to the girl frozen in mid-interview on the display. "They got what they voted for and most of them aren't technically brainwashed. Sometimes I think they all fucking deserve it."

"That's not why we hit them," said Vanessa against her shoulder.

"No." Sandy put her cheek in Vanessa's hair. "No, we had to stop it spreading. But even so."

Her own mood disturbed her. She felt so much more compassion these days for people on her side. Far more than she had back in the League. Living in Tanusha had shown her previously foreign things like family, children and friends. She knew the depth and breadth of what had been lost, even for people she hadn't especially liked. But for her enemies, she felt less and less. Did that mean she was becoming less human, or more?

"I just hope Siddhartha finds something that can cure Radha," she added. "Something good should come from today, at least."

"If that means we can promote Ibrahim to FSA Director," said Vanessa, "it'll be a net win for Federal security."

"And a net loss for Callayan security," Rhian remarked.

Vanessa shrugged. "Maybe. There are some good options. But maybe it's time we started putting the Federation first, not just Callay."

"I'm not sure I feel comfortable amongst all this patriotism," Pushpa remarked.

"Well, you refrained from muttering rude remarks about Ibrahim," said Vanessa, "so there's hope for you yet."

On some matters, the underground and law enforcement would remain forever far apart. Like on the necessity of a lot of law enforcement in the first place.

"Well, I was going to say," said Pushpa, "I'm surprised you're not more involved in the investigations, Sandy. I mean, they're not even sure if Ballan was the target. It might have been you."

Sandy shrugged. "Perhaps. But there's nothing I can do. I'm not investigations, I'm not static security, I'm kept deliberately ignorant of most of the security procedures in the Grand Council, like most people. I'm a shooter, a combat specialist. I just sit here and wait for them to tell us how badly people fucked up."

"Pretty badly," said Vanessa, leaning forward to pour herself another drink.

"Well, it's an inside job, pretty obviously," said Anita, looking at Sandy. They were the two main software experts in the room—Pushpa was talented, but business was more her field. She handled the money and lined up the jobs.

Sandy smiled faintly. "Like I'm just going to discuss Federal level security with you," she teased.

Anita made a face. "It's just not fair that there's no known way to get a GI drunk."

"Thank God for it, too," said Vanessa. "I mean, can you imagine?"

Sandy was mildly offended. "I think I'd be a very good drunk."

"A good drunk who can bend steel barehanded."

"I think I'd be a friendly drunk," Sandy corrected, thinking about it. "A very friendly drunk." She grabbed Vanessa.

"Hey!"

"I think I'd cuddle too much and do inappropriate things."

She tried to bite her neck. Vanessa yelped and fought back, with new augmentation that their sofa could not handle, and overturned.

"You idiot," said Vanessa with affection, as they lay in a laughing heap on the floor.

"Hey, wow," said Sandy, looking at Vanessa's drink. Even after their scuffle and the fall, she hadn't spilt a drop. "That's crazy. Your hands are nearly as good as mine now."

CHAPTER EIGHT

A month later, Sandy hung from her knees in the CSA gym, and pulled on the steel U-beams in the floor. Muscles rippled and tensed, as she began to heave upward, slowly at first, waiting for the unpleasant catch of pain in her rib. Today it was almost gone, just a dull tingle that was more a memory than anything real.

She tensed up further, locked her knees hard, and really gave it a pull. Anti-projectile-armour strength alloy squealed and groaned. They'd had it installed in the SWAT gym several years ago as a Christmas present, walked her in with her eyes closed and revealed it to her—custom designed steel beams driven into alloy-reinforced walls to a depth of four meters and surrounded by buffers of hard, synthetic rubber so the walls didn't crack—the kind of engineering usually used to hold up freeway overpasses. Now she could hang and pull, and stretch nearly every muscle out fully without breaking any equipment. Muscles ripped tighter and tighter, swelling and flexing down shoulders, abdomen, thighs and buttocks, with a release of synthetic endorphin into her system that felt quite exhilarating.

She held it for a full minute, intensifying one muscle group after another. After thirty seconds, she could feel the heat of high-intensity combat myomer nearly burning her skin. After the full minute, she was dripping with sweat, her body temperature reaching levels that would be dangerous if sustained. She stopped when the forty-centimeter-wide beam she hung upon started to squeal from two meters deep in its wall socket, and she dropped to the floor. Of course, she was now completely surrounded by gym rats, watching with the same expressions motorsport enthusiasts wore at rocket racer weekends.

"What?" she laughed at them, and sat to stretch out. Most of them were men, all SWAT colleagues and friends, but some of the newer ones were still unaccustomed to seeing her do this. Among straights she usually pulled her punches, literally and figuratively. But exercise was a universal human requirement, organic or synthetic.

"How's the rib?" Kohla asked her.

"Excellent," she said. "Wow, I haven't been able to do that for a while." A side effect of the endorphins, of course, was that surrounded by this many fit men, all staring at her in her gym clothes, she was struck by the predictable urge to grab one of them and take him somewhere private. But she was very senior here, and took her job as commander and mentor very seriously. These guys were not GIs, fraternisation could harm them, and the thought was never more than entertaining whimsy.

"Can I help you with that, Commander?" asked Banipal. His colleagues laughed and egged him on. Banipal was new and young, a good soldier and not shy with any woman.

"Absolutely," said Sandy, seated with legs splayed, grabbing her toes. She had to grit her teeth, and Banipal's hands on her back helped. Flexibility was never the strongpoint of any GI. "Just keep your hands above the waist or I'll have you up on charges."

She repeated her stretches several times, then strolled with a towel about her shoulders to check on Vanessa, who was sparring with young Yusuf, who was huge, powerful and heavily augmented. Like Vanessa, his augments were the latest ALK series, and for all the enormous size difference, the big guy had his hands full. Whenever he kicked, Vanessa went low for a pivot leg. When he tried to grapple, she'd sumo-push and shove his 120-kilo frame straight back like he'd been kicked by a horse. Even Sandy found it unnerving, to see how strong Vanessa's slight frame had become. She'd always been fit, but now she was ripped, and under the natural muscle, Sandy's trained eye could find the swelling at reinforced joints, where muscle sheaths had been severely bulked up, and muscles themselves interlaced by growth myomer not too dissimilar to Sandy's own, taking the strain off the organic tissue and adding serious power.

It wasn't even "cyborging," as the underground called it, because ALK series augments were League-derived and completely organic . . . just "synthetic organic," meaning nothing that occurred naturally, but still technically alive in ways that fused with new host organisms. If the host's biology was compatible, it would colonise the new implants and fuse with them in much the same way a coral reef would absorb a sunken ship, artificial fusing with organic to become part of the same, living system. This was true synthetic biology, the foundational technology that had eventually given rise to GIs, and true to all the earliest fears of its opponents, it was loose and increasingly legal in the Federation.

Even so, given the restraints of the sparring ring, Vanessa was always going to lose eventually, and Yusuf got her down for good and pinned her. In a real fight, of course, Vanessa would have more weapons and more options, and less qualms about maiming her opponent. As always in combat between straights, women's chances improved as rules were removed.

"Pretty cool, huh?" Sandy asked her, as Vanessa climbed back to her feet and repeated a few fast combinations.

"Amazing," said Vanessa with a grin. She bounced a few times, went for a sip of water, then resumed moves with Yusuf. This time she circled, dangerously fast. When Yusuf lunged a little too far, she went sideways at a speed even Sandy found hard to follow, grabbed a wrist to pull him a little further forward, then caught him with an open handed right to his sparring helmet. It rocked the young man to the ground, to exclamations from those watching. Yusuf took a few seconds to get up, then grinned at her, shook out the cobwebs, and gestured to go again.

"I don't like it," said Sandy to Captain Hiraki, finding him at her side. He was shirtless, scarred and tattooed, hands down the meanest-looking guy in SWAT. The kids called him Shogun, without really knowing what it meant. "I know they can both take more punishment now without danger, but offensive power always increases faster than defensive. Someone's going to get hurt."

"Soldiers must train," said Hiraki. "Accidents happen in all training. This is not more dangerous than a live fire exercise."

"No, but it's *another* dangerous form of training. I don't like them multiplying."

"You worry too much," said Hiraki, with utter disregard. "We are not GIs. When we train, there are risks. This is our profession, and we accept them. If it bothers you, close your eyes."

"Thank you," Sandy said sourly. "You're a great help."

"You're welcome," said Hiraki, and applauded Yusuf and Vanessa's next exchange.

Hiraki's subtext, of course, was specifically that he thought she worried too much about *Vanessa*. Which was probably true, and unavoidable. The stronger and more invulnerable our bodies, he'd told her once, the weaker and more fragile our minds. It was the very fact of human weakness, in other words, that created human strength. If people could never feel pain, and never know defeat, they would have no need for courage or character. Upon which philosophy Hiraki beat himself into shape every day, with the toughest training regimen Sandy had ever seen—not because he wanted to be invulnerable, but rather because he sought, in bashing himself against his limitations, to breed the strength, hardness and resolve to overcome them.

"He's calling you soft," said Sergeant Raf Tufau from her other side.

Sandy smiled. "I guess it's progress to know there's one person on Callay who thinks I am."

"You think that's progress?" Raf asked.

"Yeah. The most exciting time of my life was when I realised I could actually be more than just a killing machine. Some of you guys might get your kicks trying to turn yourselves into one, but I came to the Federation to become more human, not less."

"Strength is the most human thing there is," said Hiraki, still watching the fight. "And it's softness that places all the rest in danger."

"If strength was all we had," Sandy said firmly, "there'd be nothing for the strong to defend. What brings you here, Raf?"

Raf was SWAT Five, and they were detailed for equipment maintenance right about now. "Maintenance is boring," said Raf.

"And?"

"So we found you a sport. Why don't you come and see?"

She and a number of others followed Raf down to the equipment bays, where flyers and cruisers filled hangar bays, and the occasional robot roller scurried by from one storeroom to another. Heavy equipment whined and echoed.

"I won't like it," said Sandy.

"I promise you, you will." The few girls in SWAT called Raf "dream boat," partly to tease him, and partly because they meant it. Tall, handsome and mild mannered, he'd chosen the CSA over stocks and trading, though rumour was he had a lot of money invested. Vanessa thought he'd probably end up running the whole show some day, if he didn't get bored first.

"Like that time you introduced me to darts," said Sandy.

"Well, that was just an experiment," Raf explained. "I wasn't sure you could hit a bull's-eye from across a crowded bar with your eyes closed and talking to someone else, but it turns out you can. Now we know."

"And then there was volleyball."

"Well, the game is better served when you don't leap five meters in the air before smashing the ball into a corner at two hundred kilometers an hour."

"I took off behind the line. It was legal."

"Surely even a GI can understand a concept like 'the spirit of the game'?"

"The game only works because it has rules," Sandy said testily. "If the rules can't sustain an interesting contest, there is no spirit because there is no game."

"Well, come on, you did enjoy playing football."

"Only because you lot look so funny crashing into each other." And it was entertaining watching them trying to tackle her. She hadn't the heart to tell them she'd been barely out of first gear all game, and at one point, actually doing homework on her uplinks while dodging and passing. If she'd actually wanted to score, at any given moment, they couldn't have stopped her.

"Well then," said Raf, stopping before a storeroom door where some other members of SWAT Five had gathered. Some of them had industrial paint spray, in jumpsuits stained with colour, and great rolls of scotch tape. They all looked very pleased with themselves. Sandy looked at them with great suspicion. "Allow me to introduce you to something new."

He pressed the door button, and it opened. Within, smelling strongly of recent, fast-dry paint, was an empty concrete storeroom, with perfectly symmetrical walls. There was a precisely horizontal line, bright red, upon the far wall. On the side walls, it angled downward a little, and was not present at all on the rear wall. On the floor were more lines, dividing the room into two boxes against the rear wall, within which were too smaller boxes against the side walls.

"May we present, racquet ball!" A cheer from those who'd painted the lines. "It's like squash, only we figured you'd probably break a squash racquet." Someone produced two racquets, like tennis racquets only with no neck, and shorter.

Sandy sighed, and took one. A fast demonstration of why her automatic motor skills made this sport utterly boring for her also, and she'd be out of here. "Fine," she said. "What do I do?"

"First," said Raf, "you find another GI." Han stepped forward, unzipping his jumpsuit. He was assigned to SWAT Five at the moment. Sandy was pleased to see he'd been helping with this utter waste of time, and seemed in good humour. "Then, you stand in one of those small squares, and hit the ball against the front wall." He tossed her a ball, orange, rubber and squishy. "It has to land in this other big square here, that's the serve, to start the point. Then you rally. If you let the ball bounce twice, you lose. It only has to hit the front wall once, and stay below this high line up here, otherwise you can bounce it off whatever walls you like. And you have to stay out of the other person's way, and not obstruct them as they try to reach the ball."

Sandy stepped to the small square, thinking about it. She looked about the court. She couldn't hit it too hard, to land in that square, but after that, anything went. And no matter how hard she hit it, the ball would just keep rebounding, back into the middle of the court.

She blinked, gazing in amazement. The very dimensions of the court neutralised the GI power advantage. However she smashed it, the ball would come back. So she had to keep it below the high line . . . but that was a dumb rule, given that GIs could easily reach the ceiling.

"Okay," she said, with dawning enthusiasm. "First GI rule change. The high line is out, we're allowed to bounce it off the ceiling."

"Done!" Raf beamed.

"Now, all of you out. Someone could get hurt."

They hustled out the door, leaving a couple of tiny vid units on the wall by the doorframe. Those broadcasted on open frequency, so any passerby could access and watch.

Sandy and Han began playing. Quickly it became obvious that the game needed more changes—power was counterproductive. The object was to get the ball further away from your opponent, so finesse was needed to drop the ball into a far corner. But GIs were fast, and the court far too small. It was simply impossible to drop the ball anywhere a GI couldn't reach it before bouncing twice.

"We need to put power back in the game," Sandy announced after a rally that went on for four minutes straight and began to get dull. "If you can hit the front wall twice, with a single shot, you win."

That livened it up immediately. Both Sandy and Han could smash the ball at the front wall so hard, it would fly to the rear wall, then hit the front wall a second time before bouncing twice. That now became the object, with shots ripping the air like bullets. Intercepting a wildly bouncing ball travelling at up to four hundred kph was actually difficult, even for Sandy. To do it, she had to concentrate so hard she slipped into combat mode, vision tracking on multiple spectrums, reflexes hairtriggered. Often, to hit the ball she'd have to throw herself and roll. Soon evolved a new strategy, to end each dive near a wall, then shove off at just the right moment and fly across the court in mid-air to intercept the next one. Soon it was not just the ball that was shooting and bouncing off the walls, but the players, literally.

But they kept getting hit by the ball, travelling by now so fast it was impossible even for GIs to avoid.

"If you get hit by the ball after a fair shot," Han decided, "you lose."

That was a stroke of genius. Now they could aim at each other, so long as the ball hit the front wall first. Strokes became target practise, each of them dodging frantically aside from a ball that was travelling considerably faster than the rubber bullets sometimes used to take down rioters, then recovering to try and hit it off the rear wall on the slower rebound. Aiming straight at the front wall was often impossible; they'd have to shoot at the rear wall first, or side walls, or ceiling, and hope to impart enough trajectory and power to hit the front wall as well. Playing was like sharing an armoured room with a high velocity ricochet, ripping and fizzing in all directions at once. Sometimes the players collided, in spectacular default. If they'd been regular humans, even augmented ones, bones would have been fractured.

They broke racquets instead, then an unbreakable rubber ball exploded. Each time, the door opened and a new one was thrown in. They kept score, and Sandy won two out of every three points with a recurring mathematical precision that was almost spooky. At times, Sandy found herself making genuine mistakes, so hard was this game to master. It was one of the few things she'd ever done that stretched her to the genuine, exhilarating edge of her abilities. There were times that even she forgot where those edges were, and here, she found them once more. It was like a self-knowledge session with a psychologist, only fun, and useful. And finally, after Sandy had won three sets straight and actually cracked a concrete wall by kicking off it too hard, they stopped.

"Good game," said Han, grinning and dripping sweat. Being male, he wasn't as tired as she was. But also, he was that tiny bit slower, and had lost. Though that was far more her designation than any structural implications of her gender.

Sandy laughed, exhausted and buzzing. She hadn't had this much fun doing something physical since she and Han had done something else physical, on the way back from Pyeongwha. And several times since, though they didn't talk about that. She opened the door and led him out.

A big crowd was gathered, maybe a hundred people filling the hangar beyond the hallway. Someone had put up a display screen, better resolution for straights than an uplink visual, and they'd all been watching. Now they cheered and yelled with an enthusiasm that astonished her.

"Holy fuck!" Raf greeted them, the well-comported young man not usually a big swearer. "That was fucking insane! We just invented a new sport! GI racquetball! We're rich!"

Sandy wondered how long it would be until someone put the footage on the net. Oh well—she'd come to Tanusha to learn, and finally, after seven years of bemusement and disdain, she'd finally learned to like sport. Or one sport, at least.

She was on her way home when uplinks registered an incoming call. The signature was unfamiliar, so she circled it, analysed, and traced its routing. Its user was pretty clever. The route went all over the place, but she had routines that could break barriers in the actual carrier networks, another of those things that would freak the media if anyone knew she possessed them. The carrier networks told her exactly where the call was coming from, and she traced the source to a person, walking on the street. No, not walking, it was moving too fast. But the network wouldn't tell her how. An unregistered vehicle?

It intrigued her enough to open the link. "Hello."

"*Commander Kresnov?*"

"Who are you and what do you want?"

"*My name's Justice. Justice Rosa, you might have heard of me.*"

"Can't say I have." The vehicle, whatever it was, was averaging thirty kph in Petersham District, five minutes' flight time away.

"*I wrote a few books. Best sellers. Plus I write columns.*"

Great, a journalist. "I'm sorry Mr Rosa, I'm sure you'll appreciate that if I gave interviews to all the journalists who wanted to speak with me, I'd spend my days doing nothing else."

"*I'd like to speak with you about Operation Patchup.*" Fuck. That wasn't a name she wanted to hear upon the lips of journalists. "*Can we do that?*"

"Where?" Sandy asked impatiently. A link came through; map coordinates.

This should be adequate. And yes, I'm aware you don't want to be seen, and if I value my safety I should come alone.

Justice Rosa's coordinates led to a garden amphitheatre in a park. It was one of those beautiful little Tanushan public spaces, a pagoda stage surrounded by intimate terraces, the whole lot over shadowed by the huge, gnarled trunks of centuries-old trees. The lower terraces held a scattering of children and parents, and on the stage were school dance rehearsals, a common sight about town.

Sandy looked about the terraces. Higher up were various other people, some reading, some working on portables, others watching the performance. One man stood out immediately. Leaning against the winding roots of the tree alongside him, was a bicycle. She climbed toward him, and he indicated to her. No one else paid her any notice, and with her cap on, she wasn't easy to recognise.

"Don't see many of them here," said Sandy, nodding at the bicycle.

"Oh there's quite a few of us," said Justice, sipping a water bottle. "You cruiser passengers just fly too high to notice." He was a tall rake of a man, ethnicity indistinct, somewhere between Indian and African; brown skin, a lean face, curly black hair. He smelled of sweat and deodorant, and his bare legs were strong.

Sandy sat on a step. Justice's look was . . . different. Not frightened, not excited. Like he knew what she was, had seen it before. And more than that. He had a depth to him.

"You were in the war," she said.

He raised his eyebrows. "Impressive." On a chain about his neck was a swastika. Another common thing in Tanusha.

"You're a Jain?" Sandy asked. A nod. "So, not a soldier, then. War correspondent."

"Even more impressive."

"How long for?"

"Five years. The last five. I was an author before that, not really a journalist. I volunteered to be a correspondent, and some media folks liked the idea of my name on the byline. I won an award for coverage on Goan."

He seemed very keen to mention his awards and writing success, Sandy thought. "I was on Goan," she said. "On the other side. Only two months, though. Feb to March, 2539."

"Six months, October 2538 onward. You ever go near Rachongi? Daria Road?"

"Many times. Fed Fourth Army put its Intel assets there."

"And Dark Star chased Intel assets in particular," said Justice, nodding. "They didn't know you knew they were there. My best contacts were Forth Intel."

"We probably passed within blocks of each other."

"I'm surprised I'm still alive," said Justice.

Sandy shook her head. "It was all a fuckup on our side, even worse than yours. The whole city was crawling with traps. They tried to use us as regular recon in the worst areas. I kept losing highly trained strikers to fucking pointless objectives. I wasn't going onto Daria Road. We called it Hell Strip. We just hovered, and waited for targets of opportunity."

"And so now," added Justice, "I want to talk to you about Operation Patchup, and I'm wondering again if it's safe for me to ask."

"I don't know what you think you know about me," Sandy said edgily, "but I didn't do that kind of thing even when I was on that side."

"I'm pleased to hear it," Justice said easily. "Not everyone in the Federation seems convinced of it, though."

"Mostly journalists," said Sandy. "My approval rating on Callay actually runs between sixty-five and sixty-nine percent."

"It's not that high for GI immigration, though."

"Hell, even I'm not certain if I'm in favour of large scale GI immigration. But sixty-five to sixty-nine percent of Callayans generally approve of me, that's been consistent for five years now. And after the Assembly attack, I actually went up to seventy-two."

It turned out most Callayans actually liked having security personnel who shot walking bombs first and wondered if their rights were being violated later.

"You seem very confident of those numbers," said Justice. He seemed to Sandy a very serious man. He didn't pay her as much attention as most journalists would, staring rapt at her face, in search of some penetrating insight. His eyes wandered from her to the children performing on the stage, and back again. It was a Kathak dance, North Indian. The kids looked very cute in their costumes. Some other kids played instruments, mostly drums, and a teacher counted out the rhythm.

"I have to be. When the numbers are high, I get left alone to do my job. If they fall, I'm in trouble."

"They're not what the polls I'm aware of indicate."

"I have better polling."

"Ah," said Justice. "Interface polling." Among Sandy's underground friends numbered those who had pioneered polling techniques that polled not people, but network activity. There were complicated algorithms that could calculate people's interests, biases and opinions by monitoring general network activity. Sandy didn't pretend to know how it worked, but she'd seen some very scientific research that proved the results significantly more accurate. They could even predict future trends, given certain circumstances. "That's illegal."

"Illegal to publish, not illegal for private use."

"You're a publically employed official. You're not using it for private use, solely." But everyone did it, and these distinctions were hair-splitting to say the least.

"Yeah, well, fuck you," said Sandy. "What are you going to do about it?"

Justice smiled. As though he'd learned something important about her, and where her limits were. Well, perhaps he had.

"Operation Patchup," he said. "Is there really a secret plan to intervene in New Torah?"

"Sounds interesting," said Sandy. "Even if something like that were true, why should I tell you?"

"Because the public have a right to know."

"Everything?"

"Nearly everything."

"Tomorrow's lottery numbers? My credit details? Your most private secrets?"

"Obviously not," said Justice, now with a slight frown. As though whatever he'd been expecting of her, it hadn't been this. "But the Federation has been engaging in some very aggressive policy-making lately. Take Pyeongwha. When the government that you live under decides to start attacking and killing other members of the Federation to achieve its policy ends, surely that's relevant to ordinary people in the Federation in a way that your credit details and my private life are not?"

"Don't play dumb," said Sandy. "Security policy doesn't work if every bit of information we have is made public. You covered a war, you know that as well as anyone."

"This is another war we're potentially talking about, and the public have a right to be informed."

"There is no plan to make war on New Torah," Sandy said firmly. "I can state that categorically. Nor on the League if they don't act on New Torah. There's nothing happening that would require a major public debate, and as for strategy, we'd be stupid to tell anyone how we're playing that. Besides, out of curiosity, how did the public vote go when the choice of whether to go to war against the League was put to them?"

Justice sighed. "There wasn't a vote."

"Exactly. Democracies elect leaders to make these decisions for them. The people in power make decisions as best they can, and wear the consequences. There's just no workable time or procedure to let everyone have a vote, especially not over these light years in the Grand Council. If the public don't like it, they can vote them out at the next election."

"After it's too late."

"So what?" Sandy asked incredulously. "You know how difficult it is to make decisions in committees or cabinets of fifteen people? You want a decision-making cabinet of twenty-seven billion people?"

"After what I saw on Goan," said Justice, "I swore that if I could ever do something to prevent another conflict like it, I would. Given that conflict is the only reason you exist, perhaps you feel differently about it."

"Yeah, because we GIs got such a bargain from the war," Sandy retorted. "In about nine years of fighting, I lost ninety-three people under my command— that's in units rarely larger than twenty soldiers, our turnover was that high. Not all of them were friends, but a lot of them were. When you extend the number to include friends not under my command, including non-GIs, it goes into hundreds. GI lifespans during the war were measured in months, even for high designations. My team was a bit longer because I was better at it, and because after a while I just took fewer risks, to the point of disobeying direct orders on occasions. And if that weren't enough, I found out toward the end that my own side were knocking off the rest of us, because we'd be a political inconvenience to them once the war ended.

"Regular soldiers at least had a chance to lead a real life for a little while before they died. My guys never got to do even that. My first real memories are combat. I only discovered what real humanity was about later. The first real children I saw were huddled in ruins, screaming over their dead parents. I work security on Callay because I want to prevent that kind of thing. And people like you make that job more difficult. Don't you go around claiming some kind of moral superiority over me because you once saw a few dead people on Goan. That's pathetic."

Justice studied her for a long moment, with serious eyes. "I'm sorry," he said then. "That last comment about you was unfair. I see I haven't done enough research on you, and that was a mistake."

"A common enough mistake among a certain segment of Tanushan society," Sandy conceded.

"But I stand by everything else I said. And unless you can give me a very good reason not to, I'll go ahead and publish what I already know."

"Which is?"

"An organised campaign to pressure the League to deal with New Torah itself. Beginning with treaty revision, then moving to shipping lane access, then moving to Fleet overwatch of New Torah space, if League still don't agree. Cancelling all trade restoration talks, political exchanges, the works."

Sandy kept her face blank. She couldn't let him know how good his information was. She pulled a small portable from her pocket and uploaded a file with a fast mental link. Then she handed it to him.

Justice took it, and accessed—third party units were useful where one party didn't necessarily trust the other enough to make a direct link. But Sandy could see the file as he watched it, at the same time he could.

"This is just one of our bits of intel from New Torah," she said. "No one without a security clearance has seen it, that I know of."

The file was from a visual augment, a recording of someone's vision. This person was sprinting down a dusty street. Buildings were ramshackle, industrial, with rough signage and dirty windows. In the street, many other people were running. Some entered a doorway, and the file-viewpoint followed.

Within was a workshop, equipment crates and shelves, the viewpoint running past other people crouched, terrified and armed. Then it slid behind some shelves and hid. There was a lot of shouting back and forth, and some fast, frightened close-ups of people sweating, checking weapons, asking for more ammunition. Arguments in several languages, some wanting to run, another retorting angrily in Mandarin.

"He's asking them where the hell they're going to run to," Sandy said. They'd had the audio cleaned and translated.

In the street outside came shooting. Concentrated bursts, not random sprays. Rhythmic crashes, like footsteps, coming closer. More shooting. Sandy's mind automatically translated a picture for her, return fire, cover fire, heavy reply, dead. Cover fire from a different angle, return fire, dead. The viewpoint owner's breathing was harsh and frantic, sheer terror. A fast glance across the workshop showed more people . . . and Sandy paused the tape.

"See the guy there, by the cooler?" she said. "That's a GI."

Justice frowned, shading his eyes. He reached for some sunglasses—not everyone's visual cortex switched as effortlessly between simulated vision and real sight as she did. Justice put on the shades and blocked out the light.

"You can tell?" he asked.

Sandy nodded. "So tell me this. Why's he defending a bunch of regular humans? If he was manufactured by the other side?"

She resumed play. Explosions blew the front of the workshop apart. Then lots of shooting and too much chaos to see clearly. She paused again on the brief glimpse of what attacked them—AMAPS, huge, scary things with rotary cannon arms, hailing fire onto cowering civilians. Then the feed vanished.

"Just another day in New Torah," Sandy said quietly. Justice took a deep breath, and took off his shades.

"Who were they?" he asked.

"Some neighbourhood that pissed off one of the companies. They got taught a lesson. That's how the system works now."

"But the Federation isn't interested in helping these people," Justice said cautiously. "They're about protecting the Federation's interests. These people won't be helped directly at all."

"Maybe not," said Sandy. "But there is stuff we can do, and will do. Trust me on that."

"After the League abandoned them, they won't want the League back."

"If they had to live under threat of this," said Sandy, pointing to the portable, "after a while the League's return might look pretty darn good. Look, I can't guarantee that anything we do might make a positive difference. But while I can't tell you exactly what we're working on, I can tell you that we're trying. And if you go talking about this right now, in public, you blow up a big political shit storm that could scuttle everything before we can get it right, and you condemn everyone on New Torah to a future like this, indefinitely, with no hope of outside help or change."

"The last foreign ministers are due in tomorrow," said Justice. "They're here to vote on it, aren't they? The new trade bill's just a cover."

Sandy said nothing.

"Tell me this, then," he said instead. "Do you want to help mostly because of these poor people we see suffering here? Or because of that GI hiding behind the water cooler? It seems to me you have a lot of unfinished business with the League. First they made you, then they betrayed you, and now they're doing the same to others. Or, New Torah is while the League does nothing and denies it. And here you sit, helpless, wondering if other GIs are out there going through far worse than even you did, and wondering further if there isn't some kind of closure to be had. Confronting the system that made you? Perhaps destroying it? Bringing justice to those that deserve it? Saving those like yourself who need to be saved?"

Sandy smiled faintly. "Make a good book, wouldn't it?"

"It might."

"If you hold off on publishing what you've got, I'll give you the fully authorised story. My story. Or this part of it, at least. That's the best I can offer you."

CHAPTER NINE

Private astronomers noticed the new arrival first of all, out past Vamana, the sixth and smallest planet of the Callayan system, an unexpected jump point for any Federation vessel. It broadcast no ID, closing very fast, and generated enough trans-radiation that they thought it might be quite large. The media picked it up, and soon all the channels were issuing live coverage, filling the airwaves with unfounded speculation. The system defense grids were activated, and Fleet placed on high alert. Anything that big, travelling that fast from jump, could kill a planet.

In reality there was nothing to worry about—it would still take several days to arrive, and Callay's defensive stations were well positioned to turn the arrival to radioactive dust well before that, along with any ordinance it fired. Fleet itself was an extra safety net. But determined not to miss a dramatic opportunity, Callayans responded with "end of days" parties, spontaneous prayer services, and groups of robed crazies roaming the streets, yelling at everyone to harmonise their chakras before it was too late. Zoroastrians slaughtered goats in public parks, and were promptly arrested for animal cruelty. Hari Krishnas danced in shopping malls. Buddhist monks drew huge mandalas with coloured sand in public squares. Sufis gathered at shrines to sing praise of Allah. And Hindu holymen did whatever the hell they felt like, as had been their way for thousands of years.

Sandy thought it all wonderful. With a day off, she took several of her GIs to a street dance party, to show them how much fun their adopted home could be. A full kilometer of road in Kotam District had been shut down, filled with live dance and music acts, some traditional, some techno or fusion, and all incredibly rhythmic as one would expect from a society obsessed with parties and celebrations, nearly two-thirds of whose population traced ancestry to South Asia or Africa. Word had gone out on the net, and soon all of Tanusha's amateur drummers were gathering on the dance road—there were thousands. Nearly every school kid learned tabla or bongo at some point. Soon professional acts and amateur but talented enthusiasts were mingling, and the noise was incredible.

Different sections of road gathered about different acts, which grew and swelled as new drummers joined or left. The rhythms were not only loud, they were intricate and would shift organically, as appointed leaders led to a new change, and the rest followed by osmosis. Thousands of people danced as the sound shook their bones, half naked and sweaty. The sheer adrenaline of the sound and movement was intoxicating, and Sandy danced with the rest of them in her surfer-chick short top and board shorts—her most comfortable civilian identity, the one that let her be sexy without having to indulge impractical feminine fashions that would never be her style. To her delight, her GIs all joined in—they were that kind of group anyway, that being why she'd brought them. Several looked utterly astonished, like virgins having great sex for the first time, or children having their first taste of chocolate. Incredulous delight.

They stayed, as some people left, but even more arrived, and the drumming continued well past midnight and only got louder. They split up, and went from group to group up the road, each with a different character. Some Tanushans were now arriving dressed up, some even in Mardi Gras costumes, others in various festival extravaganzas that Sandy did not recognise: sequins and feathers and crazy, sexy things that left breasts bare and backsides shaking. Amongst the cool crowd there were even mostly-naked, ash-smeared Sadhus, stoned off their heads and dancing crazily toward alignment with nirvana, dreadlocks flying. Sandy flirted with total strangers, her big sunglasses on and confident she wouldn't be recognised in the night's confusion. There were now sparklers and miniature pyrotechnics going off, plus the flashing lights of professional rigs, and besides, most Tanushans knew her serious in uniform, not sweaty with her hair flying. In addition to which, there was quite a lot of mind-altering substance being consumed, some eaten, drunk or smoked, others uploaded in uplink connections, much of it illegal and as at least nominal law enforcement she should probably have said something, but what the fuck, the world was ending.

At dawn came word that the unidentified vessel had revealed itself to be the *Eternity*, a League ship bearing government envoys, their communications damaged in jump, with sincere apologies for any nervous moments their unannounced arrival may have caused.

"Who are they kidding?" said Rami Rahim on his crazy live show, still

Sandy's favorite Tanushan entertainment personality. Dancers had been linking to him on and off all night as he jumped coverage from one Tanushan party to another. "Callay hasn't had this much fun since the last ice age." And had then sent roving reporters to go and find various crackpot religious figures to see if he couldn't arrange some kind of calendar of impending global catastrophies, so all Callayans would know when the next cool party was on.

Some among the tired, departing crowd were unhappy because *Eternity's* identification meant the dancing stopped. Sandy was unhappy for different reasons.

"Fucking League envoys," she told her group of departing GIs, as they headed for the maglev in pale, morning light. "Pity they fixed their coms, better if we nuked them."

"Hear, hear," said Khan, shirtless, with lipstick smears on his cheek and a happy smile on his face.

Eternity arrived in orbit three days later. The day after that, Sandy was attending the conference Ibrahim had put her up to. It was held at the Colonial Institute, a Callayan policy think tank which occupied levels eighty-five to ninety of the Surat Tower in Surat District. The gathering numbered about three hundred, Callay having become a center for think tanks in the last five years, it being the one place besides Earth where Federal-level policy makers could be reliably found in numbers.

They had plenty of people there to tell the attendees how the current bunch of GIs were little threat, and plenty more to make the case that by granting GIs asylum, the Federation was potentially inoculating itself against the further, aggressive employment of GIs by the League, by making the League worry about the loyalty of every high-designation GI they produced. Already there were propaganda efforts going underground through League society, with slogans like "the League makes them, the Federation sets them free." Sandy knew that she herself, had she heard something like that, would have been skeptical about her own side's intentions a lot earlier than she had been.

What they didn't have was someone to tell them about the League's GI production facilities, something she'd been accumulating intelligence on over the last five years. Ibrahim thought it nice she had a hobby, and encouraged everyone in Intelligence to indulge her. Director Diez of the FSA was less enthusiastic, but as all the necessary intelligence sources were heading for Callay, the CSA had probably better information than the FSA anyhow.

After her talk, she took questions from a very crowded room, before a massive view of the skyline.

"The League's official pronouncements on their GI production levels have denied retaining any research capability," asked one person. "You're saying they're lying?"

"Yes," said Sandy. "I'm not even sure they know where all of their production and research capacity is. It was all centralised under Recruitment in the final ten years of the war, but Recruitment then dismantled everything before the new government took over. They never found all the pieces again. And to this day I haven't heard any reliable intelligence on the whereabouts of Renaldo Takawashi, to name just one prominent researcher."

"What are your thoughts on the speculation he might be in New Torah?" asked another.

"It's one of several sobering possibilities." Should have killed the old bastard when I had the chance, she thought. "The problem is, like I said, they're working on mind control. I proved to them that GIs are unreliable because we make up our own minds. But just now on Pyeongwha we've seen an entire civilisation of human beings go into a state of mass homicidal paranoia because of League-related uplink technology. If New Torah is working on this stuff again, it's not just GIs who might get more dangerous, it's everyone."

The door at the room's far end opened, and some people in suits walked in. Sandy knew immediately something was wrong. They looked official, and they strode up the aisle through the audience without looking for a seat.

"Commander Kresnov," said one, "I'm Special Agent Gilberta Sullivan of the Special Investigation Bureau. I'm here to inform you that you are under arrest under the war crimes act of Five Junctions Treaty, for the suspicion of war crimes against League personnel in the year 2542."

In the audience, people began getting to their feet in astonishment. Gilberta Sullivan— more than half the SIB's agents were female—stopped by the speaker's podium, holding a piece of paper.

"Will you please accompany us, Commander."

Sandy sighed.

"Excuse me," said a CSA agent in the audience front row, "what the hell is this about? War crimes?"

"Commander," the special agent insisted. "Now, if you please."

"It's *Eternity*," said Sandy, holding up her hands to placate those in the audience becoming increasingly angry. "They've concocted something to accuse me of through the war crimes act . . . Henry, could you contact the Director for me? I'm technically not supposed to once I'm under arrest."

She stepped down from the podium. Sullivan was holding handcuffs. Sandy turned around to let her put them on, as the room erupted in conversation and protest. Some more CSA agents looked furious enough to jump on the SIBs, but Sandy shook her head at them as she walked up the aisle and out of the room. The SIBs were no doubt hoping she'd do something rash, and she'd then be charged with the real retaliation, rather than the insubstantial crime.

Once in the SIB cruiser, however, she snapped the handcuffs to scratch her nose. "Commander, you're resisting arrest," said Sullivan, seated opposite as the cruiser took to the air from the mid-level hangar.

"I've got an itchy nose," Sandy retorted. "Want to scratch it for me?"

Sullivan didn't bother trying to put more cuffs on her. The whole thing was for show—the timing in front of the audience, all of it. And pointing guns at her was, of course, not wise.

"You know," said Sandy, "I'm surprised it took them so long."

"To find a bunch of innocent people you killed and charge you with it?" Sullivan asked coldly.

"No. For a bunch of cold-blooded murderers to realise that in a contest between the devil and me, the SIB would side with the devil every time."

At SIB HQ they put the cuffs back on. They led her through the main offices, SIB agents standing and watching her, like zoo employees watching some dangerous animal recently recaptured. Some looked very happy, as though her being here represented some great triumph. How the SIB had got to this point, even the CSA's best behaviouralists weren't entirely sure. It was like Pyeongwha, but without the murders, or the NCT.

They put her in an interrogation room, at a desk before one-way glass. Sandy snapped the cuffs once more, tore the manacles off her wrists, and rejected the chair to lie down on the table instead—interrogation room chairs were always uncomfortable, and she had a typical myomer-twinge in her lower back and hip.

The building network was surprisingly open to her, so she accessed the news nets. And there she was, without vision, but some talking heads were already deep in conversation about the SIB's charging the CSA's Commander Kresnov, an artificial person, with war crimes from year 2542 of the League-Federation War. It was one of the peace articles, controversially included in the League surrender—controversial in part because it had not been an unconditional surrender, because the Federation had no intention of occupying League space. That would be far too expensive. Conditional surrender entailed conditions, of course, and the League had demanded theirs in full. One of them was that if League officers were to be held accountable for war crimes, Federation officers must be also. Thus, an exchange process had been worked out, where evidence by either side would be considered in full view of both.

Eternity must have brought evidence of some sort. Sandy was pretty sure she knew what. There were only a few institutions that could enforce such matters; war crimes were on a high Federal level that went over the Callayan police force's heads, and given that the accused was CSA herself, the CSA couldn't do it. That left the SIB, everyone's favorite law enforcement bureaucracy, who never saw a moralising, semantic piece of nonsense they wouldn't try their damnedest to enforce. Especially if it involved putting Kresnov and the CSA in a bad spot. One of the SIB's favorite judges must have signed the warrant, and rather than doing it quietly and in consultation, the SIB had chosen to barge into her convention talk and do it in public.

Clearly it was a diversion. The League wanted her out of the way. There was only one big thing she was involved in that might provoke a League starship to come all this way with trumped up charges of something that, if Sandy was right about its nature, the League would usually prefer to keep quiet. Sandy wondered what else *Eternity*'s envoys were up to in Tanusha, at this very moment, when everyone's attention was elsewhere. Frustration set in. Ibrahim had better send someone fast.

Her seekers brought back further net hits, and she scrolled through them—no details about the charges yet. That didn't surprise her; she hadn't been told, either. Some commentators were calling for her resignation anyway.

Some were vigorously defending her. Most of those were independent media. The establishment, Sandy had long known, was a lost cause where she was concerned. Thankfully, the establishment had been proven wrong so many times on security issues, most Callayans didn't take them seriously.

Another hit caught her eye—a video link, and she opened it.

Super cool vision!, it said. *Sandy Kresnov, Callay's hottest soldier babe, spotted dancing at Kotam Road party!*

The vision was clear enough, and it was indeed her—hard to recognise directly in the crowds and flashing lights with her shades on, but if you paid attention . . . Sandy smiled. As with most things physical she was a very good dancer, and looked good doing it. Here on the vision, someone was spraying the dancing crowds with water, everyone dripping and having a blast. The vision lasted thirty seconds, then cut. There could have been more, close-ups of her face, or tits, but there weren't. Someone had taken the trouble to make her look good without being too intrusive, and released it just when her public image could most use the support.

Her smile grew to a grin. She could almost get emotional at how her strongest supporters here, most of them anonymous civvies she'd never met, consistently came to her defence. No, dammit, now she *was* getting emotional. She wiped her eyes.

Ibrahim did better than send someone. Barely thirty minutes later, he came himself. She was led from the interrogation room back into the main offices, where Ibrahim very pointedly returned to her her ID and her guns, in full view of all the SIBs who'd watched her come in.

"I invoked emergency privilege," he answered her unasked question, in the backseat of his cruiser as they flew into a cloudy midday sky. "You're essential personnel and they've no business arresting you. The charges won't be so easy to dismiss, however. It's going to cause a stink for quite a while I'm afraid."

He looked at her, questioningly. "I'll tell you later," she promised.

"A lot of very awful things happened on all sides of that war," said Ibrahim. "Many of them are far too readily politicised by those seeking to make a political point against the other side."

"Don't," said Sandy, shaking her head. "Don't abandon your objectivity just for my sake. I value it too much. I'll tell you, and you can judge. You all can. Just not right now, because it was intended as a distraction, and it will be."

Ibrahim pursed his lips, and nodded. "Very well. When the current noise has faded, you can speak when you wish."

"They're after Operation Patchup, aren't they?" said Sandy. "*Eternity*'s envoys?"

Ibrahim nodded. "Somehow they found out, or suspected. They're from League Interplanetary Affairs, so they're government."

"What else are they doing, aside from discrediting me?"

"Making threats. Resumption of war seems the main thing."

"They can't afford it," Sandy scoffed. "They had riots on five worlds in the past three months, law and order problems everywhere. The only business sector booming over there right now is domestic security."

"Of course. But the foreign ministers are all here, and foreign ministers, like chickens, are best frightened in groups. Safe to say that the resumption of a war everyone in the Federation thought we'd won is not a popular proposition, not even to risk it."

"But it's not a risk," Sandy retorted, "the League physically can't do it. They'd lose in weeks. The economy's collapsed and they've nothing left!"

"Well yes," said Ibrahim, smiling at her naivety. "We rational security types know that. Foreign ministers consider their reelections and begin to cluck and lay eggs."

"Fuck!" Sandy exclaimed. "God damn our fucking useless security. How did they find out just the moment to send their special envoys to Callay and make threats?"

"Probably the same way that your journalist friend found out here, only weeks ago. There are many worlds in the Federation. Keeping secrets on all of them simultaneously is hard, and beyond our control."

"You don't seem that surprised," Sandy accused him.

Ibrahim shrugged. "It's politics."

Sandy frowned. "You don't seem all too upset about it, either."

Ibrahim smiled. "When have you seen me upset?" Then he waved a hand. "No, don't answer that." He seemed almost . . . cheerful. He saw her looking, and sighed. "Radha had her tests this morning. I just came from the hospital. The cancer is in remission."

Sandy stared. "It worked?"

"It seems to have."

Sandy didn't know how Siddhartha had done it. The technology was far beyond what laymen could even begin to comprehend, save to say that Radha's cancer had been caused by one of those new cellular mutations humanity had picked up in response to generations of uplink augmentation. As synthetic organisms, GIs were packed with various synthetic microdefenses that copied human biology while breaking all kinds of normal biological rules—natural/synthetic fusion, like so much League tech. Some of that stuff could be synthesised and recreated in new, custom-designed cells and proteins to do all kinds of other stuff in regular humans. Siddhartha's massive VR computer systems had calculated which bits would work on what (as there was no chance of a human holding all that data in his head) and come up with some drugs. A week ago, he'd applied them himself. Today was Radha's first checkup.

"How much reduction?" Sandy asked, holding her breath.

"Eighty percent." Ibrahim was beaming. Sandy laughed, and did something she'd never done to her boss before, hugging him, and kissing him on the cheek. Normally she valued the solemnity of their relationship far too much, and did not wish to belittle him, nor the rock-like reassurance of his guidance. But today, it was obvious, he didn't care a bit.

"Oh that's wonderful," she said. "Perhaps we should both break the law more often."

"Allah does not like me to break the law, I am certain," said Ibrahim. "But his first command to every husband is to care for his wife."

"It's a stupid law, anyway," Sandy added. "I bet Allah thinks so, too."

Ibrahim laughed, a very rare sound indeed. "I bet he does."

Sandy was very pleased Ibrahim had chosen this day to find out Radha's good news. It saved her from being quite so depressed when it became clear that the Operation Patchup vote was collapsing.

She sat in Grand Council offices with some leading aides, FSA and CSA agents, and several academics who had all been leading the way on Patchup the last month, and waited for the final meetings to conclude. Every ten minutes someone on their side would message one of the group with bad news—the debate was swaying the wrong way, foreign ministers were uncommitted, making excuses, going back on carefully worded arrangements that their permanent ambassadors had been writing the past month. There was a conversation going, here in the room, about how they might yet find some way to intervene, or do something with New Torah, once it became finally clear that Patchup was a non-starter.

Sandy didn't contribute much, sitting and watching the usual summer mid-afternoon rain pouring down. She thought of Eduardo, and the picture of his female GI friend. She still had it in memory storage, and recalled it now to look at once more. The girl could have been Sandy herself, League-built and young, like Eduardo. Perhaps four or five years old. What had she known, at that age? Almost nothing, and her memories were very vague, almost non-existent. Like dreams.

She knew she should have been more concerned for the broader security issues. New Torah was a threat, in so many ways. And the Torahns themselves were suffering and dying. But if she was honest with herself, she knew that wasn't the reason for her growing obsession. GIs were the key to this, she knew they were. The technology could go in directions that would give her no peace for the rest of her life, nor her GI friends. Eduardo had ended up here, and others would follow. She'd hoped to escape all this, but increasingly she knew she couldn't.

But she'd broken out. She hadn't obeyed her masters. Neither had Eduardo. What was going on out there? Who exactly in New Torah was making GIs, and for what reasons? She wanted to save them, but knew it wasn't so simple. Some of them simply didn't deserve to be saved—not their fault, they couldn't help being what they were, but that didn't make an emotionless killbot any more sympathetic. But the others, the high designations like her . . .

What if they could be turned against their masters, like she'd done for herself? What contribution would that make, towards solving the overall security problem that New Torah presented? She didn't dare raise it here. People would look at her crazy. GIs were a problem, not a solution. They'd think she'd gone all Moses on them, "let my people free," leading them to some promised land.

Well. Hadn't she? Just a little bit?

Mustafa walked in. The security agents in the room grasped that significance, and stared at him. The others didn't notice, and continued their glum discussion. Mustafa headed for Sandy, and beckoned her to a corner. Sandy knew it wasn't even worth asking how he'd gotten into the Assembly Building. Mustafa had ways.

"Director Diez," he said quietly.

Sandy frowned. "Director Diez what?"

"Told one of my agents. Who told League government. Who sent *Eternity*. Which scuttled Operation Patchup."

Sandy stared. A thousand thoughts went through her mind. She found the most relevant. "Why tell me now?"

"I only just found out. I had suspicions, which I acted upon. And I was right, though the exact source was a surprise, I'll admit."

"And you'll give me evidence? We can't move on Diez without evidence."

"I know. You can have it immediately."

"Damn," said Sandy, looking out the window to gather her thoughts. The room's agents were still watching, wondering what was going on. Their hearing enhancements weren't as good as hers, then. "We'll have to do this quietly, can't let the media know it came from you."

"Surely the Director needs to spend some more time with his family," Mustafa suggested.

"Yeah," said Sandy, darkly. "Damn, I'd love to throw him in jail." She considered him more closely. "You wanted Operation Patchup that badly?"

"ISO did, certainly," said Mustafa. "Now there will be trouble."

"League governments excel at trouble," said Sandy, and walked to the agents, to set up a group call to Ibrahim.

It went down quickly. Sandy wasn't even there; the FSA handled their Director internally, and sent him home on leave. Now they were stewing on Mustafa's evidence, she knew. It was uncontestable—encrypted files only the FSA Director had access to, traced to the possession of one of League Embassy's staff, who was, Mustafa shared with them, ISO and well connected with various League politicians. That last was a big breach by Mustafa. ISO never revealed information on the whos and whys of Embassy postings. Until now.

She landed her cruiser now near her own home—Canas high security district, not only where she lived, but where various high ranking Grand Council figures now lived as well. She found Ambassador Ballan in a reclining chair in his rear room by an indoor fish pond. A sunroom, with glass windows and rooftop, streaked with drumming rain.

"Cassandra!" said the Ambassador from Nova Esperanca, putting aside his reader. "Please have a seat, Ana come and say hello, Cassandra's here!"

Ana was Ballan's teenage daughter. She gave Sandy a tight hug, as she did every time she saw her, then rushed to get them some drinks and snacks. Ana knew her father was only alive because of Sandy. She'd been thinking of a career in environmental management, before. Now, she was seriously considering security.

"You're looking well," said Sandy, as they sipped fruit lassi Ana had brought them.

"Not so bad," Ballan admitted. "I'm looking forward to leaving the house in a few weeks. Margarite has promised me a football match."

He still wore a robe, with lots of bandages beneath it. The last time Sandy had seen him, he'd joked he had enough synthetic micros in his body to start their own evolutionary patterns.

"I hear we have an FSA problem," said Ballan.

"We do," Sandy affirmed. "It does present an opportunity."

"It does indeed." Ballan thought about it, sipping his drink. "Will the CSA agree?"

"They won't like it," said Sandy. "Hell, I won't like it. Or not all of it. But in the time I've been working with the FSA, I've come to appreciate how important it actually is."

"There's nothing like a dysfunctional organisation to make you appreciate its importance," Ballan agreed. "It's only the ones that work well that get taken for granted."

"And treated with contempt," Sandy added, thinking of the protestors. And the SIB.

"Will Ibrahim agree to go?"

"I think so. We've spoken of it."

Ballan raised his eyebrows. "You have?" Sandy nodded. "And?"

Sandy smiled. "My confidences with Ibrahim are unbreakable. Let's just say I'm confident he'll take the position if offered. It is just down the road, really. Its jurisdiction overlaps with his current responsibilities. And now that the Grand Council is on Callay, I'm sure most Callayans will feel safer with an FSA that actually works."

"Except for President Singh."

"He doesn't count."

She went home for dinner—Thai curry she'd cooked the night before. Home felt empty. It had been her, Vanessa, Rhian and Ari living here together. Then, within the space of a year and a half, it was just her. Various of her GI buddies came over often enough, sometimes to visit, sometimes for a night or two. Particularly the men, of late. But they all liked to live together in big groups, as they were familiar from the League, while she was too senior ranked to be allowed to live with so many potential security risks even if she'd wanted to.

She'd never minded solitude before—had sought it out in fact, in the League, where quarters were crowded and time alone something to be treasured. Then she'd come to Tanusha, and wound up in a communal living environment, which felt something like she was used to, only much more fun. And now she came home to no one. Not even Jean Pierre, Vanessa's little pet bunbun, who now clambered at night through the trees surrounding Vanessa and Phillippe's house.

She ate dinner in front of the display, flicking through various news items her seekers had identified as interesting to her. She put music on—something African. It reminded her of the Kotam Road party, and the end of the world. There were a couple of bongo drums in the corner, previously Vanessa's, but left for Sandy in light of Phillippe's overflowing supply of instruments. Sandy thought of Poole and his piano. She could play drums, surely. Rhythm was instinctive; all fighters knew rhythm in one form or another. Timing, punctuation. Surely she could play drums as easily as she picked up racquetball.

"But what if you're hoping for emotion, and all you get is a dull, empty thud?" she heard Poole say. The food tasted sour in her mouth. She turned off the music, and the TV, and gazed at nothing.

Vanessa called, her interlink codes as familiar as her voice. *"Hey babe. How's things?"*

"Okay. How was your day?"

Vanessa proceeded to tell her. It was typical of days when they didn't see much of each other, though there weren't many of those. And sometimes even of days when they had, and one would call the other in the evening to continue a conversation from earlier at work.

As Vanessa talked, Sandy checked her uplink messages, left by people whose concerns were either not urgent, or who didn't know her well enough to access her direct link. Most were work, a few social, and one . . . one's ID codings she didn't like at all. Not in her in-box.

She opened it as Vanessa talked—Vanessa wouldn't hear, and Sandy could listen to two conversations at once. Sometimes three, but only if two were boring.

"Hello Ms GI," said a male voice. Unfamiliar. Trying to sound sinister, with amused self-importance. *"I see that the Director's wife got better real fast. That's good to hear. But now I'm concerned, because you broke the law, didn't you? That's very naughty of you. I wonder how many people in this city would like to know that both you and your precious Director broke the law?"*

Sandy sipped her drink. *" . . . so Hashmi comes back to me with the wrong fucking manifest,"* Vanessa was saying, *"and can't understand why that pisses me off so much . . . do you know Hashmi?"*

"Worked with her," Sandy confirmed. "Bit of a ditz."

"Yeah no kidding. So I send her to get the A2 manifest, and you won't fucking believe what she said . . ."

"Now I'm a reasonable man," the faux sinister voice continued. *"Nobody needs to know what you did. But I'm a part of a very respectable organisation in Tanusha, and we control access to the kinds of things you and your Director are pushing. I'm a businessman; I might even let you in on a cut. All very quiet, you understand? You don't really want to be in my business, because it's bad for your reputation. Better you hand your business over to me. Otherwise some friends of yours might end up getting hurt. You're a very popular girl. You can't protect all your friends, can you?"*

"So then Rajendra comes in," Vanessa was continuing, *"and of course Hashmi's his favorite, and he's upset at me that I yelled at Hashmi, so now I'm dealing with two five-year-olds, as though one weren't enough . . ."*

Sandy got up, still listening on both sides of her brain, and put her meal back in the refrigerator. Then she went upstairs to her bedroom and opened the closet.

"If you want to talk," the man's voice continued, *"just return this call. Peace, Commander."*

Sandy searched for an outfit. She actually had a few that went all the way into feminine and impractical, not that she ever wore them, but shopping with female friends had a way of sometimes degenerating into a spree of wasted money. Tonight . . . well, she couldn't go completely slutty, she didn't want too much attention. She just wanted to blend in with a very different crowd.

"*So I heard the SIB arrested you!*" Vanessa said cheerfully as Sandy dressed, her own story ending. "*In the middle of your conference talk!*"

"Yeah, I'm actually not allowed to talk about it," Sandy half-lied. The rule was that she shouldn't, but it was well understood that those rules rarely applied to Vanessa. "So it'll make for a very interesting tale in a few days, but not right now. Sorry."

"*Are you okay?*"

Sandy smiled. Vanessa of course had led off with her own story first to cheer her up; it was the war crimes charge she was most concerned about. Not that she'd believe a word of it, of course, but she knew how, with Sandy, to approach these things sideways. "I'm fine. I'm just going to go out for a few hours."

"*Romantic rendezvous?*"

"Not that I'm aware of. There's just a show I'd like to see."

"*You want me to come?*"

"No," Sandy scolded. "You stay at home with your poor husband. I already feel guilty for how often I drag you away from him."

"*Well, okay then. What are you wearing?*"

"And here I thought you were no longer a lesbian."

Vanessa laughed. "*I was never a lesbian, I was bi. But it wasn't that kind of question. What are you wearing?*"

"Nirvana" was probably the least original name for a club Sandy could think of. This was Tanusha, where hedonism, faith and consumerism were interchangeable, and there was a Nirvana fashion label, Nirvana hair stylists, a Nirvana jewellery outlet, Nirvana chocolates and, of course, a Nirvana series of VR sex sims that she'd heard were good, but wouldn't work on her because VR sims never did. Besides, none of it was as good as a very old rock band by the same name she'd found archived many years ago.

Much better than the crap she could hear booming from behind the doors of the Nirvana club. She faked a serious ID to her portable, which she flashed at the bouncers after skipping the long queue. They scanned it—big, heavily augmented dudes who these days were getting more dangerous by the week. In case the ID didn't do it alone, Sandy put a hand on her hip as she waited, pulling aside the leather jacket to reveal the bra top underneath, and a lot of very shapely, hard midriff. Rhian and Vanessa had insisted she buy the top. It was an obvious fit for her, and they were both perhaps a little jealous. Not that she was actually big, she sometimes teased them, it was just that she had a pair. There was no way the bouncers would recognise her, her hair fuzzed up from the fifteen-minute salon treatment, half her face hidden behind large, fashionable shades. Bouncers didn't care about faces, just net IDs, clothes and bodies.

The bouncers let her through, to disgust and exclamations from the queue. Keeping the daughter of a senior Tourism Department bureaucrat waiting could have consequences. She strode in, hips swinging, feeling just a little stupid but knowing that her usual stride set off alarm bells with some well trained bouncers, the ones who knew combat augmentations when they saw them. She pushed through the doors and network-scanned, finding several ways into the Nirvana club's construct, all of which turned out to be lure traps. No matter, she backed out and kept searching.

Inside, the club was like clubs everywhere—dark with flashing lights, booming music and dancing crowds amidst holographic effects on dry ice. Dancing girls writhed on platforms about the walls in fluoro body paint. All the lights jumped and flashed abruptly in time with a music change, and all the dancers changed with it. Sandy guessed it was all very hallucinatory and dream-tripping for regular humans. But flashing lights and crashing sounds reminded her brain too much of battle, and she half-slid into combat reflex, separating bodies and motions into clear, distinct locations and patterns. This was why high-end VR never worked on her either; her brain kept breaking down the routines into component parts. Sometimes even with paintings, she couldn't appreciate the picture because she was too busy noticing the brush strokes.

She moved through the crowds, eyes flicking from face to face, then up at the higher balcony, and the people there. She knew this was the place. The signature on the message she'd received was too clear. The biotech laws were changing fast, but all kinds of advanced biotech was still illegal on Callay and in most of the Federation. Illegal meant underground, and in Tanusha, the underground controlled most of the trade. Usually they just did business. Many of them, like Anita and Pushpa, were entirely above board, and only dabbled in the illegal stuff in their after-hours, like most of the population. But then there were the gangs, who insisted they were businessmen too, but as they traded in illegal stuff, they tended to deal with disputes in illegal ways as well. Ways that involved sticks and knives, and sometimes even guns. Clubs made an excellent cover for activities—a hangout for all the usual characters, and part of a perfect laundering system that began in entertainment and gambling, and extended eventually to biotech services and even property. From her time with Ari, Sandy had come to learn a lot about it. From her time in SWAT, she'd busted up a few of them, too.

That time had given her some interesting codes as well. She tried a few of them, working at the pulsating barriers before her internal vision until one faded and admitted her. Her personal tacnet compiled a building schematic for her, but she didn't access too far too early. She wasn't a sneak like Ari. If she went all in, she could gain control of pretty much any network function she wanted, but she'd set off every alarm as well, and smash them all into submission.

She climbed the stairs from the dance floor to the upper balcony. Big men in suits let her through, not in the habit of turning back girls who looked like her. The upper balcony was full of them, sexy, pretty things drawn by the shine of jewellery and the smell of cash. Most were wearing a lot less than Sandy, but Sandy's athletic curves made tight, sparkle-pattern jeans look hot enough. And black leather against her mostly bare torso beneath . . . hell, even she found that sexy. She slipped easily between them, feeling the gaze of the men on this VIP level slipping over her, and knowing that so long as she kept the hips swinging, it was like a force field that would prevent them from seeing. Men like these weren't accustomed to women like her in places like this, and would assume she was like these others. It was a mental block, stopping them from recognising her. She'd had a similar experience as a soldier in the League. Here, they expected her to simper. There, they'd expected her to obey.

She moved through the doorway from the balcony, and kept strolling. In side rooms, men and women gambled, or drank, or did fancy VR, or fucked. All just expected that she was where she should be. A man fondled her ass in passing. She whacked his in reply, playfully, and kept going.

Next floor up? Her schematic suggested so. Lots of net traffic, and the heaviest encryption. She'd break it, but she didn't need to know what was in it, just where it was. She took the next stairs, and came up on the higher corridor.

There, walking toward her amidst a group of serious dudes, was Adash Radni. Handsomely dressed in the Tanushan style, smart suits with open collars, expensive and informal at the same time. Jewellery, but not garish, not vulgar. Here even gangsters had style. Designer facial hair, laser trimmed in lines so sharp they nearly bled. They did not walk, they strolled—gaits that cried out with heavy augmentation. Most people, confronting this lot coming down a club corridor, would stand aside. All men, of course. Tanushan underworld gangs didn't do gender equality; the men were disinterested and the women even more so. Sandy was always astonished at the number of women who liked it that way.

A few of the group looked up from their walking conversation and saw her. Most ignored her, too frequently surrounded by pretty girls to bother checking out one more. But one noticed, and frowned. Then froze. Radni seemed to smell something wrong, and looked up also. He saw her. Sandy calmly took off her glasses.

"Oh fuck!" said someone, with real fear. Like they'd strolled into the wrong patch of Callayan jungle, and found themselves staring down a hungry sabre cat. Only worse, because people had actually been known to survive sabre cats. The look in Radni's eyes was all guilt.

"What'sa matter, Radni?" she asked him. "Live in Nirvana but scared of dying?"

Too much augmentation had a way of giving men false confidence—they pulled guns on her. Sandy went through them in a blur, scattering bodies and smashing bones. One went through a side window, another crashed off a wall, she cracked a knee ninety degrees the wrong way, made a new elbow for an arm where there hadn't been one before, and shattered a shoulder with a careless twist.

Several more had stun batons, and twirled them with adrenaline charged expertise as Radni and a few others ran away. The network exploded with alarms, meaning everyone would come running. Sandy hardly minded. The baton wielders were seriously fast, even by her standards of measurement. She couldn't take augments like this lightly, not in these numbers. It would test her. Kind of like GI racquetball. Tests were fun.

She jabbed repeatedly for the non-stunning grips, broke a finger, blocked the baton's spin then broke its wielder's ribs, used his body for leverage to come up and over on his partner to smash his arm with a kick before he could even swing. They collapsed to join the others on the ground, some of those still conscious screaming in pain, but nothing life threatening. She wasn't here to kill, just to scare. Badly. She walked, hips still swinging even now, and entirely too amused with herself.

Another man was backing off before her, hands held up, palms empty, eyes wide. "Hey, it wasn't my idea. It was Radni's. I told him it was stupid to threaten you. I'm sorry. I'm really sorry."

"Fair enough," she told him. "Run away." He did, past her and back down the way she'd come.

The schematic showed the room beyond was big and filling with activity, her hearing catching lots of panicked yells. Radni hadn't expected she'd be here, hadn't expected she'd do this. No one ever predicted her, only Vanessa and Ibrahim. Truthfully, she kind of liked that. Now, with resistance awaiting her beyond the door, she hacked the building's lights, flicked them off, and uploaded her own happy music to the big backroom speakers. Nirvana, the real deal, first a twirl of bass intro. Then, as someone overrode her hack to put the lights back on, the drums and heavy guitar kicked in.

Sandy went through the door before anyone's eyes could adjust to the on-and-off lighting, their hearing suddenly blasted by rock and roll. A few with guns tried foolishly to shoot her, and were felled immediately by the pistol she'd taken from one of the men she'd dropped in the corridor. She took legs, arms and shoulders, then put bullets through where her schematic showed the power mains would be. Half the lights went out again, sparks exploded and small fires started.

A couple actually came at her, either drugged insensible or so hyper on adrenaline augments they couldn't stay away from a fight once started. Cage fighters, she reckoned as she spun past one and into his buddy, whose middle she crushed with a flying knee, then caught his arm and twisted, popping the shoulder. Underground fights, big augmentation, big money, frequent fatalities. Another leaped at her and she took him from the air with a spin kick that sent him cartwheeling over tables.

"Radni!" she yelled, as someone behind to her left risked raising a pistol in what he thought was her blind spot. Sandy put a bullet through his shoulder without looking, then saw Radni trying to ascend a loft staircase up one wall. She grabbed a big table, spun and hurled it, two hundred kilos flying through the air like a Frisbee to destroy the stairs just before Radni, sending him tumbling back down.

Several of his men tried to block her path to him, bravely, with knives and clubs rather than guns. Nirvana hit her favorite, thrashing chorus, and she took them gleefully apart, nothing spectacular, just short, brutal and close, blocks turning into grabs and twists, blending into spins and jabs, then a drop-and-scythe that took another's legs. She took limbs only—limbs would mend—and avoided the head shots that might not. Bones broke in time with the rhythm, and then she was at Radni, who was picking himself up from the base of the stairs. She grabbed him by the collar, lifted him, then carried him to the bar and slammed him down.

"Radni," she said to him, quite calmly. An uplink command turned the music down. "You don't seem to understand. I am, without challenge, the baddest, meanest thing in this city. Sometimes I don't think you comprehend that, because I'm such a nice girl and I usually play by the rules. Sometimes you think I'm so constrained by those rules, you can do anything, and I won't touch you.

"Now, you can threaten me all you like. And I'll laugh at you, because actually trying to hurt me is fatal, and you know that. So you think you can go around me, and go after the people close to me instead."

She tightened her grip on his throat, to give him a taste of her power. His eyes bulged.

"So let me make this clear. You. Don't. Threaten. My. Friends." Double pause. "Ever. I will bury you. I will smear you and your comrades all over these walls. I will destroy everything you have, then burn the ashes. And if you tell the media I was here, or if you come after me in some other way, I have lots of CSA friends who hate you, who'd love to investigate a whole bunch of activities in your organisation we haven't bothered to investigate so far."

She hacked his uplink with a powerful override. It was painful when she did it, unlike the more subtle artists, and he winced, gasped and writhed. She downloaded files, pictures, linkages. Stuff the CSA had compiled. The

Tanushan black market was so extensive that going after the likes of Radni on everything was a legal maze. Usually the CSA just drew lines in the sand, and went after them only when those were crossed.

"Do you understand me?" she asked him. He nodded weakly. "I'm sorry, I can't hear you."

"I understand you," he whispered hoarsely, files opening before his eyes that he had no control of. Images of things he'd done, or that his organisation had. Faces, names he'd rather not see discussed in public. No doubt it was frightening enough just to have one's uplinks hacked so comprehensively. Like someone else taking over your brain. In a combat GI, it was just as much a military function as straight shooting. "I apologise. It was a mistake."

"I'm glad you think so. I'm going to let you live this time. Don't try me again. There is no defence against me, in this city. Be very, very certain of that."

She left him splayed on the bar, and walked away. "I apologise to everyone else I hurt," she called to the room of groaning, broken bodies, tossing the borrowed pistol aside. "Your boss made a bad call, you were just collateral. Please be certain he makes better calls in the future."

She tensed leg muscles, then sprang for a high window. She flew across the room, smashed the glass whilst grabbing the ledge, then leaping upward as the schematic showed her she could for the roof. That gave her a platform to leap to the neighbouring roof, and from there down to a rear lane.

Then she walked, zipping up her jacket, back out onto the street. Night-time pedestrian crowds, talking, laughing, searching for entertainment along the glaring light and displays of Tianjin strip. No one paid her any mind.

An hour ago, she'd been feeling . . . not unhappy, no, but melancholy. Now, she felt good. She buzzed, limbs loose and mind alive, like in the aftermath of really good exercise, or really good entertainment. Or really good sex, perhaps . . . but no, that was a more laid back, lazy feeling. This was jumping, vital. She felt like dancing. Maybe she would. There were at least forty or fifty really good concerts in Tanusha on any given night, and she was out now, and dressed for it.

This wasn't normal, she knew. Plenty of regular humans enjoyed a fight, but not like this. Cage fighters after a winning bout found ecstasy in relief and triumph. Her brain didn't do triumph. Triumph implied the possibility of losing, and the exultation of not losing. It was certainly possible that the fight wouldn't have gone as well for her; there were plenty of opponents, and under-world augmentations were becoming truly military-class. But it never really occurred to her either way. She just didn't do all that subconscious Freudian stuff—not the fear, not the yearning, not the desperate desire to prove herself. She'd never had a childhood, had never developed all of those complexes. She just was.

And what she was, was this. In the moment. One pace, one mood, all the time, no wild swings. Her desires were basic, fundamental. Food, love, sensa-tion. Violence. There were times when it haunted her. There'd been a time she'd cried to the heavens in denial, and sought a life built on anything, any-thing at all, but that.

And then there were times when she knew it to be the most fundamental core of who she was. Like now. Know thyself, the holymen advised. She'd been on that journey all her life. Well, this, she knew. And tonight, at least, so much of the confusion was gone.

Vanessa pushed into the debrief office, and found it already full. Most of the CSA's seniors sat on chairs, while Sandy sat on a bench by the holo display. The chairs were all full, but Chandrasekar stood for her. Vanessa waved him off, and leaned against the wall instead. Chandrasekar rolled his eyes, took her by the shoulders, and put her physically in the chair. Vanessa could have resisted, but just grinned, as did the room. She'd been on alert standby half the afternoon on a bit of random suburban crime with uncivilised weapons. The cops had settled it peacefully, and now she was just back from her shower, and rather tired.

"Okay," said Sandy. "Now that your shower has finally finished . . ."

"Oh, shut up," said Vanessa, stretching her legs in her comfortable tracksuit.

Sandy smiled. She wore her usual civvie off-duty wear, jeans and jacket. There had been a time, attending lots of Grand Council committees, when she'd gone for girl-suits, but she'd never liked them. Light cloth felt as fragile as silk, to a GI. She liked tough clothes that wouldn't easily tear, and felt uncomfortable in anything less.

"I've never told the whole story about how I left the League," she said. "I'm not sorry about it, and I'm not apologising. Every veteran has something they don't want to talk about, not with anyone. But since the League have decided to call it a war crime so that our enemies here will prosecute me on their behalf, that's a luxury I no longer have.

"Combat GIs had rehabilitation facilities. We're pretty tough; a lot of battle damage is just patched on the spot and we're ready to go again, even if it sometimes takes a few weeks. But some damage can't be fixed within weeks. It takes months, a full rehabilitation job. So there was a station, back in Tropez System, well back from the contested front. It circled one of the outer worlds. It's mostly mining colonies there, not much traffic; a good place because it meant Federation raiders weren't likely to hit it.

"Everyone in Dark Star knew, if you got hurt bad, they sent you to Tropez. I had a few troops who went, then came back. They said it was great . . . a bit of a production line with GIs coming in and going out, but it was a war; everything had to be cost effective. The tech was good, everyone got fixed, and on the rare occasion someone couldn't be completely fixed, they were assigned a desk somewhere."

She sipped on her makani juice. Someone brought Vanessa tea—white, sugar, a touch of cardamom, as she liked it. Ibrahim preferred coffee, black, and was seated at the rear wall with his ankles crossed. "I had this one guy in particular, Jonti," Sandy continued. "He took a fragmentation mine on a boarding mission. I wasn't sure he'd make it, but they sent him off to Tropez and soon I got a vid message from him, lying in his bed and quite cheerful, saying he'd take a few months to mend but the doctors assured him he'd be back soon enough. So I sent a message back, and we kept in touch . . . nearly a year, it was. He seemed to be doing better with each message.

"By this time, of course, we were losing the war; everyone knew it. Recruitment had taken over GI divisions in League Command, Command didn't like it, there were some good military people there who didn't want some bunch of tight-ass bureaucrats telling them what to do with their personnel. But GI production was expensive, Recruitment had been told to cut back, so they were streamlining everything, making sure Command were doing their bit to save resources. EEMs, they were called. Efficient Employment Methodologies."

She snorted, and sipped her drink again. Vanessa felt for her. She knew Sandy didn't like replaying this part of her life. She did it occasionally, when it suited her, when she needed something off her chest. Otherwise Vanessa left it alone. She didn't have anything like the scale of nasty experiences Sandy had had, but she'd had a few. She was too much the cheerful person to dwell on them, and was always grateful when people declined to prod her too much. Being able to talk about it when you wanted to was good, but being allowed to not talk about it when you didn't was better.

"I was having my terminal falling out with Dark Star at this point. I never actually turned on them until they had my team terminated, but we were engaged in low intensity conflict for maybe a couple of years before Recruitment arrived. I was questioning orders, talking to people I shouldn't, asking inconvenient questions. Then Recruitment took over and we got hard-ass commanders who didn't like GIs much. That was when I began reinterpreting orders and missions as I saw fit, and lying about it afterwards. They were a bunch of stupid fucks. I was having problems with everything by then, not just the conduct of the war but the entire rationale behind it. And everything about GIs; my own reasons for existing.

"We hit a station once, in Eludi System. This Colonel Melak, he was a Recruitment appointee, he ordered us to shake down the station civvies." She looked at Vanessa. Vanessa had heard this story, though no one else had. Vanessa nodded understanding. "We had to divide all the civvies into groups, they were searching for people they thought were intelligence assets, certain professions, engineers, doctors. Rough up any in those categories, make them talk. I said fuck it, you can all go, and put them onto shuttles. Colonel Melak came and threatened me with court martial . . . that was about the fifth time, I think . . . said he'd take my team away from me. I blew him out an airlock, made it look like an accident . . . happens a lot on damaged stations, post combat. My team swore blind he'd pushed the wrong button. They were awesome."

Silence in the room. They were now, perhaps, beginning to understand why League called her a traitor, and now a war criminal.

"You blew him out an airlock for threatening you with court martial?" asked Obango.

"No," said Sandy. "For threatening to take my team away. I kept them alive. If I hadn't done it, one of them would have, only messier, and gotten caught."

Obango nodded warily, not really understanding. Civvies never quite understood how cheap life got in war.

"Anyway," Sandy continued, "even if they suspected, I was too damn useful when they used me properly for them to ditch me. That and some of the research guys like Takawashi had too much invested in me. So the war kept getting worse, and finally Recruitment got so scared of the investigations that would happen in the peace, and the fact that the general public didn't know that GIs as advanced as me even existed, their heads were going to be on the blocks. So they had my team eliminated, made it look like a Federation victory. But you know all that.

"What I never told you was that in the process of going AWOL . . . well, I killed a few people. To get into the League systems, check out a bunch of data. Clear a way out for myself. In doing so, I found some reports on Tropez Station. Recruitment had shut it down a year earlier. It was too expensive, you see. They were winding back GI production and employment anyway, in preparation for the peace; there were too many of us. And now they had to save money, rehabilitating GIs is expensive, so they just shut it down. And all the patients there. It had become a recycling facility. Live, wounded GIs would come in one end, and spare parts would come out the other. So my buddy Jonti, a few others I knew who'd gone there since . . ."

She took a breath. Wiped her eye, and sipped her drink. Oh God, thought Vanessa, barely daring to breathe. She knew what came next. In some things, to her at least, her friend had become quite predictable.

"Those recordings of Jonti were just sims, visual constructs. They'd studied his mannerisms, figures of speech, and the programs had put it together. Could have fooled his mother, if GIs had mothers. And I'd been sending messages to a guy who'd been dead a year.

"I didn't go straight to the Federation. I got out at a crazy station with twice the ship traffic it was designed to handle, whole waves of refugees coming through . . . I stole a limpet, hitched a jump on several big ships, then waited until I found one heading for one of the Tropez mining systems. I went to Tropez rehab station, of course. They let me in, thought I was something else—you know how good I do fake IDs. I got on board, and I cleaned the place out. Then I rigged their reactors to blow, and left. Fleet records here have a few mentions of a League facility lost at Tropez, cause unknown. That was me. I suppose we can update that intel now."

More silence. Vanessa could hear frogs croaking in the CSA compound gardens outside.

"How many?" Ibrahim asked.

"Oh they'd automated most of it by then," Sandy said dismissively. "Just enough to keep up appearances in the lobby. Twenty-two, all Recruitment employees." Another sip. "Plus about a hundred GI regs and a whole bunch of automated defences who were protecting the place. Put there in case a Federation raider tried to take them. Bad publicity that would be. But they weren't expecting one little limpet ship with a four-crew capacity to be a threat."

"They used GIs to defend a GI slaughter house?" Chandrasekar asked incredulously.

"Yeah, regs," Sandy said drily. "They're regs, they do what they're told. They'll shoot their own wounded if ordered, I've seen it. Sometimes they'll shoot themselves."

"A hundred is a lot, even for you," Vanessa said quietly.

"Yeah," Sandy sighed. "Probably the worst fight I was ever in. I gave myself one chance in fifty." She paused. "Guess I underestimated myself. But I had some holes in me when it was over. Bit of a mess. I made a few of the surviving techs help patch me up. Then locked them up, and left."

"Blowing the station behind you?" Chandrasekar asked. Sandy nodded. "After those people helped you? Civilians?"

"Yes," said Sandy. "Recruitment. Manning a slaughterhouse. Several thousand GIs, easy, lots of higher designations among them. Mass murderers, every one."

Chandrasekar leaned forward, very serious. "But, Sandy. Defenseless civilians? Who'd surrendered, then helped you when you were wounded?"

"Not by choice," Sandy said coldly. Dammit Chandi, don't go there, thought Vanessa. But he was too far away for her to warn with a glance. And being Chandi, would probably ignore her.

"Cassandra," he pressed, "you're accused of being a monster. Now, we know you're no monster. I've seen your compassion so many times. But you're asking us to defend you from these terrible charges on the grounds that what you did was actually justified, and I'm just trying to understand . . ."

"I'm not asking you to do anything," said Sandy. "I'm telling you what happened. Whether you feel that makes me worthy of your defence is entirely up to you."

"Fine, just help me to understand how . . ."

Vanessa saw the snap coming just before it happened. "Because they're my people!" Sandy snarled at Chandrasekar, with more venom than Vanessa had ever seen her use. Her eyes blazed, and Chandrasekar shrank back into his chair in shock. "And if you murder my people, you're gonna fucking die!"

Deathly silence. Sandy sipped her juice, not missing a beat. That was almost as scary as the temper. It wasn't an outburst. There was no fast recovery, no recognition of something gone wrong, no apology. As though the fury had always been there, just below the surface.

"Anyhow," she said, in a much the same, though calmer, tone. "That's my story. You're going to want to discuss it, and say things you'd probably prefer I wasn't here for. That's okay. Take your time."

She slipped off the bench, and walked. Her path detoured past Vanessa first, extending a hand. Vanessa took it. It wasn't an apology so much, just a reassurance. "I know you understand," it meant. Vanessa nodded slowly to herself as Sandy walked to the door, and closed it behind her. She did understand quite well.

Chandrasekar let out a short breath. "Damn it," he said softly. "I've never been scared of her before today."

"Rest it, Chandi," said Vanessa. "I'd have done the same thing."

He looked at her, frowning. "Would you really?"

"Absolutely. Without even having to understand what those years were like for her, I know I would. CDF may have folded, but I'm still technically a soldier. If anyone did that to my guys, I wouldn't care who they were. I'd have killed them."

"No chance of a trial out there," Obango added.

"Sure, but that's not it," said Vanessa. "It's just soldiers in war. I don't like doing this to you, Chandi, but I will say it—unless you've been there, you don't know. There's not much I wouldn't do for my guys. If anyone hurts them . . ."

"Most of those the station at Tropez killed weren't her guys, going by what she said," Chandrasekar countered. "Just this one friend of hers, Jonti."

"Which brings in the rest of her life at that point," said Vanessa. "She wanted so badly to believe in the League cause. Every soldier wants to believe in what they're fighting for. But her real investment was in the guys she fought with, not her commanders, not the big picture. And those commanders treated her guys like shit, and threw them away like toilet paper. The resentment built for years, she was trying to justify it back and forth in her own head for a long time, and then when it finally dawned on her that everything up to that point had been a lie . . ." she sighed. She didn't like getting into this with Sandy too much for a reason.

"Well can you imagine the guilt?" she finished. "She's not just mad at the League for what they did to her and her people, she's mad at herself for not figuring it out sooner. Look, she's my best friend in the whole world, and I know her as the kindest and most generous person . . . but that's all wrapped up in some very dark stuff. She deals with it wonderfully, almost all of the time, but it's still there, and even I don't go prodding around in there without invitation. If she's got issues, you can hardly blame her. And unlike all of us, she really is death on legs, and getting mad enough to kill is not just a hypothetical for her."

"Well, I'll be real careful, then," Chandrasekar murmured.

"No that's not it at all," Vanessa snapped in frustration. "She wouldn't hurt a hair on your head, and you know it. It's just that there are a lot of people in her immediate environment who attack and try to hurt her in one way or another, and she has to be very restrained most of the time. When she finally does get a real enemy she can hurt, it's almost a relief. She's not scared of getting hurt herself, she's scared that like the last time, she'll miss something that will cause her friends to get hurt. She tries to protect everyone but she doesn't always know how, and that scares her, because the last time in the League, a whole bunch of her friends died because she didn't figure out what was going on quickly enough. Which is why she hasn't spoken of Tropez Station until now, not even with me, because she can't bear recalling how this horrible thing was going on under her nose all that time, and she didn't pick it. People who threaten her friends just make her furious. That's as angry as she gets. And that's what you just saw."

CHAPTER TEN

Three days of listening to Callay newsfeeds on the way to station convinced Ari that he should avoid Balaji Airport on the way down, and go via Gordon instead. He abandoned the FSA Agents at Nehru Station as they took a runner out to their spaceplane and a direct way down. His own flight would give him a twelve-hour layover; it was the earliest available on short notice.

He checked into a hotel with rucksack and luggage, not accustomed to travelling heavy and despising space travel in general. That last gravity shift had left him more than queasy. A robo porter wheeled his bags up three levels, then along the narrow hall to a little room with noisy ventilation and no windows. Ari had never been an especially outdoorsy person, but now he was desperate for some sunlight. Space was so incredibly big, but every room you stayed in while travelling through it was claustrophobically small.

Locked in his newest cell, he opened a line down to the surface. Check messages? Shit no, he didn't trust orbital uplinks for a second. Everything was filtered. Still, he could call people. He called Ibrahim. Ibrahim was busy, wouldn't be available for a while, could the secretary take a message? He tried Chandrasekar instead, no more luck. Ibrahim, the newslinks had told him on the way in, was being promoted to FSA Director. Working with the FSA of late, Ari knew he should be delighted—the FSA might actually start working properly now. But Ari was Callayan through and through, and the thought of the CSA without Ibrahim filled him with dread. Chandrasekar was being moved up to Director. That wasn't so bad . . . but hell of a big pair of shoes to fill. Hell of a big pair.

He contacted Naidu instead.

"*Ari, dear boy,*" said Naidu, looking rumpled and deadpan as usual on the vidphone. "*You're back, are you?*"

"In orbit."

"*Wonderful, good for you. How's space travel suiting you?*"

"Fucking hate it. Where is everyone?"

"*Chaos down here Ari, everything's in a state.*"

"So what's new?"

"*Quite a lot actually. The old man's in Parliament for confirmation hearings, Chandi's doing all the paperwork, there's war crimes trials upcoming, we've appeals pending, I'm up to my neck in lawyers and we've journalists literally hunting us around the grounds.*"

"Sounds great," said Ari. "I'd like to speak to Sandy. Is she around?"

"*Haven't seen her. Not taking calls lately, can't say I blame her.*"

"Is she okay, do you know?"

"*About the war crimes nonsense?*" Naidu's expression was all disdain. "*Absolutely. Complete beat-up, nothing to it. But as you might imagine, she's not making herself available, and we're facilitating that. How was Pyeongwha?*"

"Frightening," said Ari. "Tell Ibrahim I need to speak with him at the earliest, in his capacity as either FSA or CSA Director, either one's important."

"*Will do,*" said Naidu.

"Oh, another thing," said Ari before he could sign off, "why aren't you being considered for CSA Director? I mean, you're senior to Chandi."

Naidu smiled. "*I'm old, Ari. Being old, I'm quite happy to stay in my little garden and prune the roses, so to speak.*"

"You'd have made a good Director."

"*So will Chandi,*" Naidu said firmly.

"We'll see. See you tomorrow."

"*Yes, and Ari? Don't let the journalists grab you on the way in, yes?*"

Ari slept for a while, then woke to take the shuttle. A trip up to the core, more weightless time as the crowd of civvie passengers was loaded, then a very bumpy reentry ride down. At Gordon he went through customs like everyone else—though his fancy passport did let him skip the queue—collected priority luggage and wheeled it straight for the taxi stand. There were media waiting in arrivals, for whom he didn't know. But him they ignored—they'd tried to do stories from time to time on Commander Kresnov's mysterious lover, but Ari valued his anonymity on par with his testicles. It had been one of several points of friction between them, when she'd wanted to go out, and he'd refused for fear of attention. She wanted to be a normal girl and have fun. He appreciated that. But normality had never been high on his own list of priorities.

The taxi cruiser charged his card some obscene fee and lifted him off the ramp, forest green sprawling away from the spaceport perimeter below. Ahead, across all the horizon, hundreds and hundreds of towers, and air traffic so thick it looked from this distance like mist. Home.

He checked messages on the way in, and got overwhelming thousands. Just too damn popular, he thought, sifting through the masses. Mostly friends and business, which with him was often the same thing . . . a few ex-girlfriends, a few potentially new ex-girlfriends, a handful of death threats, the usual. A bunch of very interesting leads, people who needed to be researched, others begging to be arrested . . . it frustrated him that he'd been away for so long and hadn't been able to deal with it. Like a gardener returned from a long absence to find the hedges untrimmed, the grass knee-high, weeds and dead leaves everywhere. Travelling was so overrated, he'd be quite happy if he never left Tanusha again.

He searched all the network for Sandy, and found not a trace. He tried all the tricks, all the encryption codes, all the hidden markers and trail seekers . . . nothing. Very few people as network-active as Sandy could just disappear like that, not from him, not in his city. She really didn't want to be found.

That left one obvious route. He locked into the CSA's network, past the usual multitudes of querying barriers, then into SWAT and more barriers, and found SWAT One was on deployment in Ludhiana. As active CSA he had codes that could break into even active tacnet . . . which was up, he found, and he dialed into their coms. And called. And called.

It disconnected.

"Oh, come on, Ricey," he exclaimed. "Don't beat me up, this is important."

He tried again. Vanessa would see the indicator light, would know who was calling. Again it went dead.

"Fuck." Girlfriends would stick together. He'd have to take more direct action.

SWAT One was deployed around a large demonstration in Ludhiana District's main park. Or rather a series of demonstrations, Ari thought, flashing ID at ground level security and taking the elevator of a parkside building to the top. The building had rooftop gardens, like many flat-top towers in Tanusha, their coupolas emptied of their usual tea garden patrons, and Ari walked a path to the edge of the rooftop. There on the edge sat several figures in deadly powered armour, rifles strapped to their backs, observing the crowds in the park below with graphically enhanced vision.

Ari identified the smallest, walked up behind and tapped a shoulder. "Go away," said the armour suit.

"No," said Ari, and tapped the shoulder again. Vanessa turned on him, flipped up her visor and regarded him sullenly. "Hi," he said. Vanessa still looked sullen. Ari held up the flower he'd picked from the garden, hopefully.

Vanessa sighed, took it and hugged him. In bone-crushing armour, that wasn't exactly comfortable. "Hey," she said. "Just get back?"

"Yeah." She resumed her seat—a chair from the tea garden—and resumed her vigil. "Fun demonstration."

"Oh, hysterical. See this group over here?" She pointed to a far corner of the park, on the roads about which were a lot of police vehicles and flashing lights. "Callayan nationalists, demanding the FSA be abolished. This group over here," she pointed again, "in the middle, they're protesting biotech and GI immigration, it's like one of those two for the price of one deals. And here nearest us, they're demanding war crimes perpetrators be punished, because violence is bad, apparently. Naturally, they began throwing things at the poor bloody cops an hour ago."

"It's good to be home," said Ari. "So who called SWAT?"

"Whole bunch of death threats, Feddie nationalists threatening Callayan nationalists, pro-biotech anarchists threatening the antis . . . that's your crowd isn't it?"

"Oh, hell yes, where's my black bandana?"

"A few threats looked viable . . . hang on." She clicked on her mike. "Rani, can you just check that fourth floor window, on my grid fix now? I can see movement. Yeah, just keep an eye on it, get a cop to climb some stairs and check on it." She pointed to a chair alongside, and Ari sat. Vanessa commanded this rooftop and all those surrounding; one didn't do anything without permission. "You looking for Sandy?"

"Uh-huh."

"Personal or professional?" Her visor was back down, sunlight glinting off a mean visage, voice a little tinny on the speakers. She wasn't doing it deliberately to distance him, more that she had advanced visuals in that visor, and needed to see. Mostly.

"Never done a good job of separating those two in my life."

"Me neither. You can't have her back, you know."

"I . . ." Ari frowned, not really knowing what to say to that. "I know."

"I mean, I think I know why you left."

"You do?"

"Ari, you were obsessing about Pyeongwha for the best part of a year. You think it's your business. You think all this stuff is your business. You get pissed when people mess it up because you're not there, and they don't do as good a job as you do. So you took it on yourself to save a planet, and relation-ships get in the way. You've never been a relationship kind of guy, anyway. I was amazed you lasted that long."

Ari ran a hand through his hair. "Hmm." She was half right. "Where is she?"

"Plus, you worried about what you'd find, and that that relationship in particular meant you'd lose your objectivity." Okay, Ari conceded, more than half right. Sandy was right, Vanessa had missed her true calling as a psych. "So I'm pissed at you, sure, but I forgive you too, because I was there on Pyeongwha, and that was hard, what you did. So I sympathise, but I'm telling you all the same, you can't have her back now Pyeongwha is over."

"Well, firstly," said Ari, "Pyeongwha isn't over, not by half. And secondly, who says I want her back?"

The visored, armoured face turned to look at him. "I do, because I know you, and every other girl will seem boring to you after her." Well now you're just projecting, Ari nearly said, but refrained. Vanessa returned her gaze to the crowds below. "And I won't let you. She doesn't, you know, emotionalise this stuff like we do. Non-GIs. But that doesn't mean it doesn't hurt. And just because it doesn't affect her in the same way it affects a non-GI, she knows you're not a GI, so she's wondering what you were feeling, and why she wasn't important enough to you, and it's confusing and complicated. She doesn't need this right now, so don't even try."

"Look, you're a good friend to her," Ari tried. "And I hope you'll want to remain a good friend to me, whatever else happens. But there's also business. I need to talk to her about Pyeongwha; she has insights into that stuff. Where is she?"

Ari had always thought surfing would be hard. He hadn't expected that the hardest bit would just be paddling out through the waves. They hadn't looked enormous from the shore, but lying flat on his hired longboard, they towered over him. A wall of foaming water rushed into him, tipping the board up, then upending him. He struggled back on top and resumed paddling, only to be knocked off by a second one while he was still getting his breath back. He swallowed some water and coughed madly, losing breath, while more broken waves sent him back toward the beach. Great, now he was back where he'd started.

He tried again. He was fit—partly from the combat exercises that he'd become very good at since living with Sandy, Vanessa and Rhian had made them seem like a good idea—and partly from the standard micro augments that accentuated every bit of exercise and made it count for triple. The two women he'd been with since leaving Sandy had been suitably impressed . . . which he had to admit he'd enjoyed, because living in a house with three of the Federation's most dangerous women had been enough to knock any man's ego down a few pegs. It had been nice to rediscover that by regular male standards he was pretty buff. Just not buff enough to impress those three. Or maybe they'd just enjoyed teasing him, whatever.

But fit or not, several minutes later, he was still struggling. He rolled under another wave, resurfaced amidst the churning wash, and found he'd gone another twenty meters backward. How the fuck did surfers do it? A man could drown out here.

Suddenly someone was beside him, wet blonde hair and lean, bare arms.

"Hang on," Sandy told him, with undisguised amusement. "Just get on board and kick, watch out for my feet." She grabbed his board's nose one-handed, and kicked and paddled hard. There shouldn't have been enough leverage, but her feet were truly thrashing now, with power that Ari was pretty sure would break his arm if he stuck it in. Watch out for the feet indeed. Soon they were really moving. He only got dumped three more times, and was rewarded each time by her laughing at him.

Finally they were out past the break, him gasping for air as he sat up. "Well I guess I deserve that," he wheezed, and coughed.

"And far more." But she was smiling. Makeup and fancy clothes looked great on some girls, but Sandy looked best like this—natural, hair wet, eyes alive. It was summer, the ocean currents too warm for wetsuits, so she wore boardshorts and surfer's top—a rashie, he remembered some called them,

Australian slang like a lot of sporting terms. Ari thought she looked pretty damn good in more traditional swimwear too, but in this kind of surf, they'd get torn off.

"You're a dill," she told him. That was Australian for idiot. "It's a fairly big day today, and you've never even sat on a board."

"Yeah, well, I wanted to talk to you."

"Looks good on you though," she added, as he wobbled a little on his board. He rode far higher in the water than her, his longboard buoyant, her short board submerged.

"Why aren't you working?" he asked.

"Who says I'm not?" She nodded toward the shore. Ari looked, and saw a strong black man powering toward them on a short board. Every under-grounder who was anyone knew Mustafa Ramoja on sight. For a lot of them, he was an even bigger hero than Sandy, whom some considered a sellout for having abandoned the League.

"Ah," said Ari. "Hello Mustafa!"

"Hello Ari," said Mustafa, smiling. "How was Pyeongwha?"

"Wonderful. Real garden spot." He caught Mustafa's glance at Sandy. "Oh, did I intrude on something? Excellent." He waited, all ears.

"Your news first," said Mustafa.

"You wouldn't find my news interesting."

"I am an intelligence agent. I assure you I would."

"Ari," said Sandy, "Mustafa's currently at odds with the League govern-ment. The whole ISO is." Ari raised his eyebrows at her. Then at Mustafa. Mustafa sighed, as though not particularly happy she'd said that. "If you wanted to talk to me about NCT, Mustafa might actually be able to help."

She gave the other GI a long, hard look. Ari frowned, looking from one to the other. What was going on?

He decided to take a chance. "Well, look, this is not the place to go into detail, with my head full of salt water. It's just that . . . well, I think Pyeongwha NCT is based upon one of the previously unused GI development methods. Brain development. Which means that if New Torah is reactivating some of that tech like we think, it could be real trouble."

Neither GI replied. They bobbed in the swell, and the cool breeze felt a nice contrast to the warm sun. Houses perched on a nearby rocky bluff.

Flickwings circled, reptilian birds, searching for fish. It was really nice out here, Ari decided. This part of surfing he liked. It was just the paddling, the waves and the . . . well, the surfing, that he loathed.

"He's useful," Sandy insisted to Mustafa. Mustafa looked dubious.

"Useful for what?" Ari ventured. Between these two, the insecurity was back—they were both so beautiful, effortless and smart. Why would Sandy want to be saddled with a regular human like him anyway, when she could have men like this?

"Mustafa has a plan," said Sandy. Mustafa did not silence her. "Or rather, the ISO has a plan. For intervening in New Torah."

Ari blinked at her. "Against the wishes of the League government?"

Sandy nodded. "Yes."

"And involving Federation Intelligence assets? The FSA?"

"And CSA, yes."

"Why? Why not do it themselves?"

Sandy smiled at Mustafa. Mustafa scowled. "Because the Federation currently has more high-designation GIs trained for this sort of irregular operation than the League does," she said cheerfully. It was pretty funny, Ari had to concede. "And if this is going to work, they're going to need us."

"A blind drop?" Ari said dubiously.

They sat on temple steps as the waves crashed upon the shoreline, and ate fish and chips from a nearby vendor. Flickwings swooped and squealed across the sand as the sun set behind them, and the sky faded to a dark turquoise. A few people strolled or jogged, or came up the stairs to attend evening prayers within the temple. Within, between rowed pillars, priests led a sonorous drone of song and chiming bells, and flame torches flickered.

"We need reconnaissance," said Mustafa. Several women coming up the steps gave him long looks. Ari was comfortable enough without a shirt, but reckoned that if he were built like Mustafa, he'd find excuses to take it off more often. "We can't do anything without it."

"You're telling me that after . . . what is it, a hundred and twenty years of settlement, the ISO has no intelligence assets left in the Torah systems?"

"On the outer systems, yes," said Mustafa, about a mouthful of fish. "On Pantala, not really. Nothing useful."

"And how is that?"

Pantala was the Torah Systems' only heavily inhabited world, though even that population was sparse. It was the central base of Torahn economics and government, where all the major corporations were based. Its capital city was Droze.

"The corporations control the Pantalan infrastructure," said Mustafa. "That's what we need intel on. Corporate loyalties are strong. If you're not in a corporation, you're just a settler. Their lives are cheap, and they've no access to anything. Those assets we did have amongst them were few, and mostly eliminated."

"But you can't just infiltrate a corporation with outsiders," said Ari.

"No."

"So you'll have to infiltrate the settlers, and infiltrate them with someone capable of bridging that gap between settler and corporation. Someone with expertise in infiltrating hard targets."

They both looked at Sandy. Sandy half-shrugged, enjoying the fish. It was charcoal-grilled and delicious. Sandy loved a good meal. Or a good concert, or a nice sunset. Anything sensory and stimulating. Her brain processed enormous volumes of sensory information. It had been a combat design function, surely none of her designers had imagined it would be the making of a hedonist.

"How many others?" Ari asked, feeling worried.

"Undecided," said Mustafa. "Quite a few. Myself, obviously."

"Obviously. What objective?"

"To see if there's some way of bringing it down from the inside," said Mustafa. "To see exactly what they're up to, and what the threat is. Autocratic institutions are inherently unstable, as you found on Pyeongwha. Often it is just a question of leverage."

"I'll go," said Ari.

"No," Sandy said firmly.

"I'm a good sneak," Ari insisted, "you saw what I did on Pyeongwha, and network capabilities don't get much better than mine . . ."

"I know, but no," said Sandy. "This isn't a free information environment Ari, there aren't these masses of civilian traffic you can hide in. This is a spartan, authoritarian system, most of the sneaking will be physical, and anyone doing the sneaking must absolutely be combat specialist enough to survive any encounters."

"This is a very harsh environment," Mustafa agreed. "The corporations use everything from UAVs, AMAPS and GIs to suppress dissent. At present we think it'll be a GI-only operation, ISO and FSA."

"Well then, I want to help in the setup," said Ari. "I have background in this stuff."

"Excellent," said Mustafa. "Welcome aboard."

"And Ibrahim's on board?"

"Cautiously, yes," Sandy affirmed.

Ari looked at her more closely. "Wait, you mean it'll be deniable?"

"No other choice."

"Oh, damn." Ari felt really unsettled now.

"I'd have thought that an obvious reality," said Mustafa, "things being as they are, politically speaking."

"Ari doesn't like governments sneaking around," Sandy explained. "It makes him paranoid."

"It's a little known fact," Ari offered, "but a guard with a spear was manning a wall in ancient Greece, and someone asked him, 'how do you feel,' and he said 'paranoid,' just before a black-clad commando sent by a nearby island's government snuck up behind and stuck a knife in his throat, and that's where the word paranoid comes from."

"You're right," said Sandy. "That is a little known fact, especially from a man who doesn't know ancient Greece from modern New Zealand."

"That's what we pedants call missing the point."

"I'm unsocialised," said Sandy, selecting a chip. "You know I never get the point."

"And once you heroic types have done the reconnaissance," Ari pressed. "What then?"

"There are internal forces within New Torah that can be manipulated," said Mustafa. "It's not a monolithic regime, it's fragmented."

"You say that like it's a weakness," Ari warned. "Fragmentation has been the core organising philosophy of all human civilisation since the beginning of infotech. There are mathematicians and biologists who'll tell you it's at the heart of evolutionary progression itself."

"I've read all the sociological convergence theories, yes," said Mustafa. "But the fact remains that a fragmentary system gives us a way in, in the way that a monolithic system does not. You had to break down Pyeongwha from the outside. In New Torah we're looking for ways to break it down from the inside."

"And if you can't?"

"We'll find evidence of the threat they possess, assuming they do, and convince my government of the need for action." He gazed at the ocean horizon, and the gathering dark. "We still possess that much capability, at least, to deal with a few rogue systems."

His words were sour. No doubt it hurt, to see the grand ideals of League science, reason and progress fall so low. The League had always possessed a technological edge, but it had not been sufficient to win the war. Technology hadn't made as much impact on space warfare as League scientists had theorised; those physics were hard to bend, and when the Federation put its mind to it, it caught up fast. From there, sheer industrial scale had told a predictable tale in the end.

"I still don't understand why the League can't do it themselves," said Ari.

"It's shame," Mustafa replied. "Our leaders said they'd win the war, and failed. They said synthetic humanity was a wonderful evolution of the human species and no ill would come of it, only to be embarrassed by Cassandra here, and others like her, defecting to the Federation. She's very big news in the League, you know. There's quite a backlash in the general public against those who led the war."

"The loyalists don't like me," Sandy murmured.

"But the loyalists lost their credibility when they lost the war," said Mustafa. "The last thing the League public wants now is another war. And the new leaders don't want to reveal just how horrible things got on New Torah after they pulled out. They'd rather not talk about it."

"Sounds like they've got enough violence under their noses without worrying about Torah," said Sandy. "What's happening on Calico right now? That sounds like major civil disturbance, not just a few poor social indicators."

Mustafa sighed, and scratched his head.

"To be expected in the aftermath of any major social dislocation," said Ari. "The war qualifies. Same through all human history."

"Can't talk about it?" Sandy pressed Mustafa further.

Mustafa shrugged. "Don't want to. Too depressing."

"What did happen on Pantala?" Ari asked, with a very level stare. "Most of what we hear is bullshit. I've heard twenty different versions of the same things. But the ISO knows, don't they? They just don't want to talk about it, either."

"Aren't allowed to talk about it," Mustafa corrected grimly. Several priests came up the sand from the water, carrying surfboards. They wore boardshorts, only identifiable as priests due to their dreadlocks or shaved heads, and a few tattoos. There wasn't supposed to be development right on the beach, but no one had protested a few temples, and this order of Shiva had claimed surfing as a necessary part of worship, a sacred union with the elements. Now that it was built, no one complained. It was low-key and beautiful, made of old stone that looked like it had been growing out of the dunes for centuries, and the priests led all the local efforts to keep the beaches clean.

"The main part of the narrative the commentators get wrong is that the corporations probably aren't to blame," Mustafa continued. He tossed a nearby flickwing a last chip. It snarled and leaped, and attracted thirty others, a flurry of leathery wings. "They controlled all the infrastructure on Pantala. The whole world is a company town, there was nothing else there until big industry moved in. Pantala has the most perfect combination of about thirty main elements used in high tech weaponry. They were pulling it out of the ground cheaply and moving all the weapons industries there—the profits were bigger. The rest of the population came later, and set up cities around the main industrial sites. But there's almost no water on Pantala, and the corporations were the only ones with the capability to ship it down from the poles, so they did that, and it was expensive, but profits were large and no one minded. Then every citizen who lives there needs constant micro-upgrades to deal with the atmosphere, radiation, some nasty local viruses, so the corporations paid for those, too. Living on Pantala was expensive, but no one noticed until the war ended and everything collapsed.

"And all the Torah Systems are just so far away from main League space. Space haulage is expensive, and those industries just didn't make any other products that were still competitive when the freight costs were added. The whole place was only made profitable by war. In the free market they had nothing to sell, and the main industries lost all income all at once."

"That was a nasty decision," said Ari, nodding. "Lots of weapons tech is transferable. Those industries could have made a transition to something else if the League hadn't just cut off all funding."

Mustafa shrugged. "We were broke, and we'd just lost a war. Everything was smashed, we had to rebuild priority systems first, and Torah was never priority anything. We cut our losses. But you're right, there should have been more warning. We'd become so good at ignoring reality, and New Torah was so far away, they just kept thinking wishfully until it hit them.

"All the wealthy folk got out first. All the corporate connections. That created a lot of resentment. There weren't anywhere near enough ships. People don't really think about what it means to be isolated on some of these outer systems. They think they can just get a berth on the next ship back; it doesn't occur to them that if everyone wants to leave at once, there's capacity to move maybe one percent of them, if that. Those berths go to the best connected, that's just how it works.

"Suddenly the weapons contracts are cancelled and the industries have no money, everyone's laid off. Economic collapse. No one panics immediately, they're not uncivilised. Right they say, let's do this rationally. What do we need? We need water. Water comes from polar ice, shipped to lower latitudes at great expense. Who pays for it now that there's no money? Well, the corporations are the only ones with the capacity to make shipments. Who pays them, now that they're broke?"

"Credit from the parent company," said Ari.

"Who's just also gone broke," Mustafa countered. "Torah employees counted for just a few percent of their total workers, they've desperate people everywhere. Torah settlers knew the risks when they settled there, didn't get out despite the warnings. Very expensive to keep them on permanent credit when there's so little prospect they'll ever get that money back. Only in a true crisis do all the folks who complain about corporate profits realise that corporate profits are actually life and death."

"Damn," said Ari. "Can't use the debt markets. Markets need buyers and sellers, who would buy Torah debt?"

"It's worthless," Mustafa agreed. "League government aid was the only possibility. But again, we had desperate people everywhere, starvation on quite a few worlds, and each person in New Torah costs four times more money to keep alive than the average. How do you justify that to those dying under your nose?"

"Could have taken Federation government aid," Sandy said grimly. "They'd have done it."

Mustafa gave a humourless laugh. "If the war demonstrated anything, it was that League pride was worth at least a few million League lives." It was possibly the least patriotic thing Ari could ever recall hearing Mustafa say. "Anyhow, on Pantala, the local administration tells the companies that capitalism doesn't work any longer, we'll have to centralise everything under government control."

"Bet that went down well," said Ari.

"But that's the thing," said Mustafa. "The corporations agreed. They couldn't do anything else, they were all stuck in that mess together, and they wanted to survive, and for their families to survive, just like everyone else. Certainly, centralise the system, it's an emergency situation, everyone has to pull together. But they'd still need to maintain all their own people in senior positions, because reasonably enough, their people were the ones who knew how everything worked—medical augments, water, power, everything. And a lot of scared and resentful non-corporates found that disagreeable.

"So they rioted, to take control for the people. Some used big weapons— plenty of those around, the world's an armament factory. Lots of corporates were murdered, families slaughtered, facilities not just taken over, but some of them even destroyed . . . which on a world like Pantala is like stationers destroying their own life support. So frightened corporates fought back, with even bigger weapons. That just turned into a full-on slaughter, we still don't know the exact figures, but our best guess is that it lasted a month and that ten percent of the population died. Pantala was at nearly five million even after the evacuations, so that's half a million people."

A silence, save for the expectant squabbling of flickwings, the crash of surf, and the continuing chants of evening service.

"That's as many soldiers who died in the fucking war," Sandy murmured.

"But always the way, in all civilisation," said Mustafa. "Wars get all the attention, but in truth nothing kills like bad government, or administrative collapse. The cameras capture the exciting battles, but the true carnage is off stage when no one is looking.

"And from there it just broke down further. The administration was gone, and brutality reigned. With no other way of getting what they needed to live, people either signed their lives to one corporation or another, or tried to take it by force. Corporates themselves took casualties—remember, a lot of the best people had fled, and some of the more humane leaders were killed in the fighting whilst trying to make peace. Humane behaviour was thus discredited, and corporations being competitive environments, there were plenty of slippery-pole-climbers with newly-hardened attitudes determined to show what could be achieved with murderous aggression.

"And it worked, of course, because what we call civilisation is really only controlled barbarism. You take away the control and the barbarism is all that's left. Only now, quite a lot more of the infrastructure had been damaged, and some corporates didn't limit their aggression to the common people, they began using it on each other. And so it all divided again, militant factionalism, companies acting like heavily armed gangs, all fighting over access to the basic sustenance that keeps them alive."

"Only now it's even worse," said Sandy, "because instead of continuing their downward spiral, they've stabilised, and are now going to dump all their bullshit on everyone else instead."

"That was the threat that Pyeongwha posed to the Federation," Mustafa said somberly. "You dealt with that threat admirably, and the greater good was served. Now we must do the same for the Torah Systems, whether our respective governments like it or not."

CHAPTER ELEVEN

The Federal Court was another of those institutions that Callay had not had to bother with before the relocation. Sandy's authorisation gave her a pass to land within the grounds, not far from the FSA Compound, itself alongside the Grand Council. A short drive to underground parking, followed by security checks all the way into main chambers—these were Callayan S-2 security, with whom she was mostly on good terms, and a few of them even bantered.

The halls were modernist, white marble with open walls, indoor gardens and expansive water features beneath giant skylights. And the halls were mostly empty, here in the secure sector, where the general public could not go. In truth, the Federal Court didn't do very much. The Federation remained a federal system—most member worlds jealously guarded their individual legal processes, and very rarely did a case venture this far up the ladder. War crimes, or at least those committed in Federal wars, were one of those few categories that were exclusively within the Federal Court purview, and Sandy was quite sure they were going to make the most of their rare chance to justify all this expensive architecture.

She had to pass into the public space to enter the courtroom, however, and the hall before the entrance was predictably crowded with journalists. No cameras, though. The courts had them built in, with selected footage to be released to the media pool if appropriate. Her lawyers were waiting for her, a grey-haired gentleman named Mohammed Iqbal at their head, one of the CSA's favorites, with four more in his team.

"Hi, everyone," said Sandy with dismay. "So many of you."

"A serious and defamatory charge," said Iqbal, with grim disapproval. "It deserves the most serious retort." He gave her a prim once-over: jacket, jeans . . . and leather boots, her one concession to style. These were worn-in and comfortable, with no heels to speak of. "Formal dress would present the most flattering appearance."

"Good," said Sandy.

Iqbal frowned. "Are you armed?"

"CSA agents on operational duty are always armed."

"Not while this courtroom is in session, they aren't."

"This is not a formal session, it is a hearing," Sandy replied.

"Hearing or not, the Federal Court is Federal property pertaining to Federation law only. The Callayan Security Agency's jurisdiction ends in this hallway."

"Not on security matters," Sandy said calmly. "Section 72, subsection c of the Callayan Federal Territories Act: 'all Federal claims to security may be overridden by Callayan security interests in the event of active emergencies.' The CSA is currently on high alert, which means I'm declaring a state of active emergency."

Iqbal's frown grew deeper, and there was a pause as he checked his uplink, no doubt for a copy of that clause. Then his eyebrows raised. "You've done your homework."

Sandy shook her head. "No, I helped write that clause." Several of the junior lawyers smothered smiles. "Let's just say the CSA foresaw this eventuality."

"And what is the emergency this time?" Iqbal asked.

"This is Callay, Mr Iqbal," said Sandy. "There's always an emergency."

"Her Honour may take a dim view of such argument," said Iqbal, gesturing her to walk with him.

"Yeah, well Her Honour can suck on it."

A few of the journalists called questions to her as she walked through. By the doors, finishing a cup of coffee, she saw the lanky frame of Justice Rosa. She waved her lawyers to go in without her.

"Hey," she said. "How's the book coming?"

Justice looked surprised that she'd stopped to greet him. And perhaps a little pleased. "Which one?" he asked.

Sandy smiled. "It was a glib question. I didn't expect to see you here, I'm told nothing substantial happens in hearings you can't get from the transcript."

"Well that was my thought, too, only I hear the CSA is on security alert." His gaze flicked down to the shoulder holster inside her jacket. "And I see that you're about to venture armed into a Federal courtroom."

"Just last month, someone blew up Ambassador Ballan's entourage in the Grand Council building," Sandy reminded him. "One of the things I keep trying to drum into everyone's thick heads is that real security means that you stop assuming there are places your enemies won't attack you."

"In this city in particular," said Justice with irony. It was one of those tired phrases the experts always used, recently to the point of cliché. Callay, with all its infotech complexity and shifting security frameworks, was just damn hard to secure.

Sandy answered with the other groan-inducing cliché. "Price of freedom," she said.

Justice smiled. "My publisher wanted some tentative titles for the book. I gave her a few, but I have a favorite. I was wondering what you thought."

"Oh yes?" With trepidation.

"*23 Years on Fire*," said Justice.

Sandy blinked. "But I'm 22," she offered.

"When I've finished the book, you'll be 23. Do you like it?"

"I'm not sure yet. Ask me on my birthday."

"When's your birthday?" asked Justice.

Sandy smiled. "No idea."

She entered the courtroom, leaving Justice to fend off journalists wondering what all that was about. Most of them knew that Justice was researching a book on her. It was a decision on her part she'd lately become more comfortable with, since Ari had volunteered himself a fan of Justice's work, and called him "one of the few guys in Tanusha who really understands how this whole mess works." Coming from Mr Mess himself, that was quite a compliment. She had no fears Justice would leak information without her approval—his ego was large and he'd never rob himself of exclusivity. And she'd discovered that journalists wrote and said less bullshit about her when they knew a respected, envied writer was getting the real inside story, and might contradict them in the near future.

Inside the courtroom, Sandy notified the bailiff that she was armed, and showed him both pistols. That drew a lot of looks. Thankfully the bailiff appeared to know Section 72, subsection c, and made no complaint.

Her Honour, when she entered the court, was another matter.

"Name the nature of the security emergency," she insisted, once Sandy explained the clause to her. Sandy was not at all surprised that Her Honour didn't know the clause; most powerful Tanushans were only aware line-and-verse of those clauses that promoted their own power, not those that diminished them.

"That's classified," said Sandy.

"Nonsense," said Her Honour. "This courtroom exists within an independent Federal jurisdiction, Ms Kresnov, and I take that independence very seriously."

"It's Commander Kresnov, if you please, Your Honour."

Her Honour frowned. "The CSA should not think that they can just make up some security emergency whenever they please in an attempt to cow this court into submission." How in the world the mere presence of firearms in her possession could do that, Sandy had no idea. Did they think she'd kill everyone in the room if the court ruled against her? She didn't need guns to do that.

"I can assure you Your Honour, this is not a made-up security emergency. I am currently patched into secure CSA channels and receiving updates on an evolving situation even as we speak."

"That sounds like just another day at the office for the CSA," Her Honour snorted. Sandy refrained from smiling. No stupid woman, this. "I repeat my request that you name the nature of the security emergency."

"It's classified," Sandy repeated.

"I'm tempted to compel you with contempt of court."

"In which case I would be obliged to walk out."

"In which case I could have you arrested."

"No, Your Honour, I think you'll find that under the jurisdiction granted by Section 72, subsection c of the Callayan Federal Territories Act, anyone obstructing or attempting to obstruct a Callayan Security Agency operative in the performance of her duty will be in violation of Callayan security law. In which case it shall be me arresting you."

Her Honour said nothing. That was common in courtrooms, Sandy had discovered—instantaneous recall via uplink could place any number of relevant legal articles before a judge or lawyer's internal vision, leading to many reading pauses. The subsection was all product of Sandy's personal insistence, when the Federal Territories had been carved out of Tanusha's Montoya District, that there be no seams, no gaps in the security infrastructure. No separate rules, separate personnel, the kind of thing that had led to disasters in the past. Federal Territories would be independent in everything meaningful, but to allow them any exclusions from the overarching security architecture was suicide, and not worth the salving of Her Honour's pride.

Her Honour looked at Sandy's defence team. "Anything to add, Mr Iqbal?" she asked drily.

Mr Iqbal stood. "Only that in my informed legal opinion, Your Honour, Commander Kresnov is right. We would be off to a most inauspicious start to this hearing should the defendant lead the Chief Justice off in handcuffs."

He sat, and gave Sandy a look of new respect. "Argued like a good lawyer," he commended her.

"I'm insulted," said Sandy with a smile.

Ari landed his cruiser by the police barriers and jogged into the mall. There was a crowd of pedestrians ahead, behind more police tape. The mall was spacious, apparently open air if not for the glass ceiling ten stories overhead, with lots of indoor greenery growing between. The store in question, next to a sushi joint, was a florist, flowers lined in bright rows before the windows. Lots of garlands. There would be a temple nearby—Hinduism was for florists what Christianity was for wrapping paper . . . only Hindus had things to spend money on all the time, not just once a year.

He skipped under the police tape and flashed his badge at a cop. Through the doorway, police had sweeper wands erected, scanning the crime scene to compile a 3-D image. Cops ran sniffers over surfaces. There was a pool of blood by the counter, and droplets elsewhere, each tagged. Brass casings on the floor, bright amidst fallen flowers. Talking to the police lieutenant was a small Japanese-looking woman. Ari was not surprised.

"Ayako!" he said, and went to her.

Ayako Kazuma looked across. "Hi Ari. Thought you'd be here."

"How's the girl?"

The girl was Yvette White. She was a GI, one of the first to gain asylum in the wave that had followed Sandy. And she was one of the rare non-combat designations, with regular myomer musculature instead of combat myomer, and few physical superpowers to speak of.

"She's bad," said Ayako, "shot ten times, but should survive. Even the non-combatants are tough. How about the law office?"

She'd guessed Ari had just come from there. "Two dead," he said. "Another one might be soon, two more wounded. Regular humans, not so tough. We're locking down everyone in firms that have represented GIs."

"You're sure that's the connection?"

"Never sure, just cautious." He looked about the florist shop. "No surveillance?"

Ayako shook her head. "And not at the law office, I'd guess?"

"It was a grenade," said Ari, chewing a lip. "Thrown from outside." He looked at the blood on the floor. "Damn, trust them to pick on the one that can't fight back."

"Her workmates here said she was aware there might be some kind of threat. But she didn't care. They seem pretty upset, her workmates, I mean. A few of them are at the hospital now, since Yvette doesn't have any family, obviously. They're looking out for her. Seems she was quite popular."

"Yeah." Ari looked about the walls for bullet holes, but saw none marked. Accurate shooter, then—novices firing ten rounds would miss a few, even at close range. Steady hands. But not a GI, or Yvette would be dead. "Sandy tried to get her security a few times, tried to bring her into the fold so to speak. But Yvette wouldn't have anything to do with her. She just wanted to be a normal civvie. She was in logistics in League Fleet, but she wouldn't even take up a civilian equivalent job when she arrived here. Just found herself a job at a florist. Said she liked flowers."

"Well," said Ayako, flipping scan glasses over her eyes to view the latest crime-scene input, "you and your GI friends can be intimidating. Coming here, where everyone assumes GIs are soldiers, I can imagine an office worker might just want nothing to do with that."

"I came in here once," Ari said sadly. "Introduced myself, just wanted to say hi. She knew who I was. Told me to get lost."

Ayako smiled. "Finally a GI you couldn't befriend."

"Oh, there are plenty of those out there. Just not here, yet."

The police lieutenant came across. "What do you think?" he asked them. "Nutter-wallah, or something more organised?"

"The two aren't mutually exclusive," said Ari. "Any ID at all on the shooter?"

The lieutenant shook his head. "Not yet. A few witnesses said male, 180 centimeters, pale skin, no good look at his face. Doesn't help much. Scene-scan shows definitely 180 centimeters, definitely right handed, and definitely a 7 mil. We'll have more in five minutes once it processes some more. So I suppose the CSA will be taking over the case?" He looked glum at the prospect of losing something interesting.

"No," said Ayako. "You can lead, we'll just set up a common file space and pool our data."

"Absolutely!" the lieutenant said brightly. "Ashni, get us a common net space up and running with our CSA friends, hey?"

When good old fashioned crime scenes started accumulating, it made far more sense for the CSA to delegate to the Tanushan police on the ground—they were usually better at the grunt work anyway. The CSA would use the information the cops collected and put it together with the stuff they collected themselves. Sometimes it worked well, but sometimes the cops grew upset that the CSA didn't share as much back at them, and the relationship broke down . . . but it couldn't be helped. There were plenty of great investigators in the police, but crime and security were two completely different fields, and the CSA simply wasn't allowed to share a lot of the classified stuff with anyone outside the security field, which included the police.

Ayako flipped her glasses up, and walked to the doorway. "Walked right in," she said, retracing what she'd just seen on the scene-scan. "Stopped here, looked, saw several employees. Sees Yvette here." She pointed, fingers drawn for a pistol. "Walks, Yvette sees him coming, runs to here . . ." other fingers indicating the spot toward the pool of blood, ". . . and here, with the angle past this display, fires three rounds. Walks to here, firing four more." She stopped, next to the blood pool. "Three more here, then leaves."

"Only a ten round clip?" Ari suggested. "That's unprofessional."

Ayako shook her head. "No, it's very professional if it's a thirty round clip. We've got the city seeded with ultra-mikes. We're not allowed full video surveillance, but with all the interactives by the advertising screens and on the transport platforms, there's microphones everywhere. Ultra-sensitive, we've got them programmed to grab specific sounds. One of the most reliable is magazines clicking together in someone's pocket, or even rubbing against something—a jacket side, a wallet. So professionals tape mags together and pad them with a handkerchief or something so they don't rub . . ."

"So it's harder to grab a new mag," Ari finished, "meaning the hitter would rather keep half his magazine loaded in case he gets pursued."

"And changing magazines is a very distinctive sound."

"That's clever. You're working on devious things in Investigations."

It had been Ayako's big move some while back, when someone had suggested her skillset might lead to more action and faster promotion in Investigations as opposed to Ari's preferred Intelligence. She'd been Ari's partner before that, back when Ari had still been on probation in the agency and untrusted by many. Not that that had really changed. But his old partner's move had paid off. Some were now discussing the possibility of her moving up to what was effectively Investigations' number three in the reshuffle after Chandrasekar had moved up to CSA Director. And of course, CSA Directors almost always came out of Investigations, Intel was considered just too narrow a skillsbase for overall command. It wasn't a bad career progression plan for a former underworld private security contractor who as a teenager had been on the CSA's watch list.

"But it also means that if that's what's going on," Ayako finished, "this hit man knew about the ultra-mikes." And she frowned at Ari. "Speaking of which, why don't you know about the ultra-mikes? You always know everything."

"I've been busy elsewhere," Ari said drily. "You know those microphone setups won't last once the civil liberties people catch on."

Ayako shrugged. "But fun while it lasts."

Ari was scanning as they talked. He could do that on a level that even most highly augmented humans could not. Data rushed before his eyes, familiar network paths, old and new codes tried and discarded, keys and barriers interlocking, opening, rejecting.

Ayako regarded his silence. "What's bothering you?"

"I'm not finding any communications trace linking the legal office attack with this one, but that doesn't mean it's not there."

"Well, sometimes the bad guys are pretty good at this stuff, too."

"But that's not the main thing. Sandy's in court."

Ayako frowned. "The war crimes hearing?"

Ari nodded. "And what better time to go after a bunch of people that she's been helping to protect, than when she's indisposed? And if this is a political statement of some kind, what better time than when she's headline news?"

"You think this isn't over?"

"Not by a long shot."

Mr Iqbal was arguing over the admissibility of evidence. The prosecutor was one Padma Chaury, a known enemy of the CSA, and one of the SIB's favorites. She had quite an amazing array of evidence, including the names and family backgrounds of all the people on Tropez Station who'd died. Mr Iqbal was challenging to discover where that information had come from, since personnel data from League secret facilities was usually, well, secret. Ms Chaury wouldn't say.

Sandy wasn't really paying attention. She was uplinked and watching the data pool grow larger as feeds from multiple crime scenes compiled into an increasingly complex picture. A grenade attack at a legal office that had represented several GIs, the shooting attack on Yvette White, and just now a sniper shot had killed a friend of John Tompkin's at a rented apartment he was sharing with three other GIs with asylum claims pending. The friend was not a GI, had just been visiting, dropping off a suit for Tompkin to borrow for his next court appearance. Investigations had the shooter tracked to a rooftop six hundred meters away, so obviously they had inside information on GIs' residences in Tanusha. That had everyone on high alert, and their families.

Rhian had taken the family to Rakesh's sister's house, and was standing guard herself—that was probably enough, but they'd sent some cops as well. Every GI residence was under guard or observation, UAVs and SWAT units airbourne, sim-scans highlighting possible sniper points, surveillance assets watching those locations in hope of grabbing another hitter. Tompkin was demanding to be included in the operation, firearms and all—the poor guy was distraught. He'd arrived four months ago, was trying to make friends and a good impression on his new home, and one new friend, a guy he'd met at a pub, had just been killed when the sniper mistook him for a GI.

"I think that's it," Vanessa said in her ear, from her command seat in the back of SWAT One's flyer. *"We've got pretty much every connected person secured: lawyers, friends, residences . . . there's not much else they can hit for now. Their best option would be to wait until we've settled down, then try again."*

"It's League," Sandy formulated. *"I'll bet anything."*

"Not the ISO?"

"No. League government operatives, not Internal Security. They're not getting along real well at the moment. My bet is Eternity either came with some new operatives we missed, or its arrival activated some sleepers. Probably they're using some local patsies, one of these wanna-be terror groups who don't like GIs. Train them up, give them money, buy weapons on the black market, and we've got a local terror insurgency running in Tanusha that could last for months."

"I think you're probably right," Vanessa said cautiously, "but that's an awful lot of guesswork from just a few attacks. Let's wait until we catch a few people."

"Sure," Sandy said grimly. "Whatever."

Chaury was now arguing that she didn't need to say where she'd gotten the prosecution's information, because the information itself was obviously true, and the rules of a hearing stipulated that the only requirement for the prosecution was to establish a general "weight of evidence." Fucking lawyers.

Mustafa returned her several recent messages. "It's not us," he told her.

Sandy already knew that, but wasn't about to say so. "Well give me something, or we'll start responding as though it is."

"If anything, it's our government trying to frame us, they know we're working with you on New Torah."

"And how do they know that?" Sandy wondered drily.

"Common knowledge, I'm afraid. Look, we just don't know at the moment. I'm asking around and twisting a lot of arms. The ISO has a lot riding on this too, don't forget." They didn't want to get kicked off Callay, he meant. "But these attackers will likely be Callayans with League handlers, so most available evidence will lead to people you'll have far better data on than we do."

Just like she'd thought, then. But surely Mustafa could get better information if pushed. "Not good enough," she told him. "Do better." And disconnected.

Sitting here was going to drive her insane. Ms Chaury was now presenting evidence that a team of GIs had hit the Tropez Station, presenting radar recordings, station logs and audio files from the fight itself. Extraordinary. League had given her all that? After going to the trouble of doctoring it so meticulously? Until now, League hadn't admitted these black facilities even existed. She leaned over to Iqbal.

"The last three people who tried to reveal information this detailed on League black facilities in the war, all turned up dead within weeks," she whispered. "How is it that she knows this stuff, and has so little fear presenting it so openly?"

Iqbal nodded, thought for a few seconds, then stood up to interrupt Ms Chaury, as was his right in a comparatively informal hearing. He repeated what Sandy had said, almost word for word.

Chaury's response was evasive and uninformative, and Iqbal read some notes on a slate that one of his assistants handed to him while she answered. He showed it to Sandy, eyebrows raised in question. It was a selection of news reports, posted within the last hour, of the attacks throughout the city. Sandy nodded in affirmation and pointed to her ear, the universal sign for an uplink.

"Your Honour," Iqbal cut in again, "I should inform the court at this point that the security emergency that Commander Kresnov alluded to at the beginning of proceedings is just now hitting the news networks. There have been a series of attacks on GIs and those associated with them. Two people are dead at a law office and one recent asylum recipient is severely wounded, among others. And now we have Ms Chaury here, sporting information clearly granted to her by secret operatives within the League government, launching what is effectively the second arm in a pincer attack against League defectors in this city . . ."

"Your Honour, I object to this appalling slander!" Ms Chaury retorted. "To suggest that a courtroom opponent is in any way implicated in something as terrible as murder is below the belt even for Mr Iqbal, and I demand that those remarks be stricken from the record."

Sandy gave Chaury a look of faint, uncharitable amusement. *You're playing with fire, dear. I wouldn't be at all surprised if, once they're done with you, you'll end up like those three others.* Chaury saw her looking, and frowned. Then paled a little, and her eyes darted away, as though guessing Sandy's thoughts.

It was late afternoon when Ari entered the walker shop. The workshop was wide, a plain ferrocrete floor echoing with the clanks and whines of machinery under repair. Tanushan planners loathed industrial estates. These working spaces were stacked in high-rise around a central, empty core, up which large loading elevators brought customers and equipment from the ground. Workshops and factory operators bought or leased either a separate space like this one, or an entire floor with no dividing walls.

Ari watched the walkers as he went, wishing he wasn't so busy—he loved these things. They'd been his first technology passion when he was little, watching the emergency service units parade on a local holiday. The huge, humanoid machines lined the walls, strapped into repair bays, worked over by people or awaiting their turn. On the open floor, a worker was testing one's systems by trying some dance moves, making several tonnes of whining, clashing metal and servos look almost graceful to the beat of music on the speakers.

Ari walked to one unit, worked on by several guys, recognising the tattoos on one's arms. He stopped.

"Hey, Pino!" he shouted over the racket. Pino turned and looked down. An average sized guy but muscular. The arm tattoos were the usual stuff, save for the one on the upper arm, which was Marines. "Come down, wanna talk!"

"What's in it for me?" Pino retorted.

"How about a jelly bean. You like jelly beans?" Pino went back to work. "Or how about a kick in the ass?"

Pino climbed down from the scaffold and landed before him with a heavy booted thud. "What?" He was a white guy; stubble jawed, tough dude, wiping his hands on a rag where hydraulic fluid had leaked on them.

"Where were you this morning?"

"Right here." His accent was offworld. He'd grown up on Trevellian, only settled on Callay after his Fleet service. He'd served with an officer who had family in the walker repair business, and had promised him work.

"Bullshit," said Ari. "You got into work at eight, left at 8:33, got back again at 11:02."

"Bullshit yourself," said Pino, smugly. "Check the worksheet. I've been right here, ask anyone."

"You think I trust a fucking worksheet?" Ari said scornfully.

Pino scowled. "You fucking network freaks, you think you can come around just snooping behind a private business's barriers? You know, I don't care what you think you fucking know, the worksheets say I was here, and whatever you've got ain't admissible evidence."

"Girl got shot over in Patterson at 9:50," said Ari. "Know anything about that?"

"Heard it on the net. Wasn't that some skinjob bitch like the ones I used to kill in the war?" His buddies up on the scaffold were laughing. Places like this employed quite a few ex-military people. Despite appearances, most of them made more than suits, Tanusha having a surplus of suits and not enough grease monkeys. But not all of these guys were ex-Fleet, some were just assholes.

"No, not like those ones. They were military, this one was a civ, non-combat."

"A GI that can't fight? About as useful as a badge on a net monkey like you." Ari smiled. "Did you do it?"

"Sure," laughed Pino, "like I'd just tell you. Wish I had."

"Wish you had what? The balls?"

Pino applauded, sarcastically. "Oh, that really hurts. I bet you'd have done her, wouldn't you? Like that Kresnov bitch, bet you wish you could do her, too."

"Sure do," said Ari, smiling more broadly. "She's hot."

"Friend of yours, isn't she?" Like that was a bad thing.

"Sure is. I'll tell her what you think of her, and the girl who got shot. She's real nice about that stuff. If it turns out you did do it, you might be real lucky and she won't pull your ribs out and pick her teeth with the splinters. But you don't look that lucky to me."

Pino wasn't smiling now. He'd fought GIs close up. Regs, Marines had learned to handle. But in Fleet, tales of Dark Star were like tales of ghost ships, scary stories that could keep a Marine awake at night.

"I bet you would, too, wouldn't you?" Pino said coldly. "Turn on your own kind, for them. Fucking traitor."

"There is no them," said Ari. "They're us. I can't betray what doesn't exist."

"Spoken like a traitor."

Ari knew a lot of good ex-Fleet, and some currently serving ones. The CSA and FSA had quite a few of them. Some were even Sandy's friends, and friends of other, recently arrived GIs. But then there were guys like Pino, tribal in their hatred. On one level it was understandable, GIs were scary to fight again, and Pino had lost buddies. Ari would forgive a guy like Pino far more readily than some others, and he knew Sandy would, too. But Sandy wasn't equipped with the expertise or job description to track guys like Pino, seek them on network forums, listen to their rants in VR seminars, chat anonymously with their buddies, learn where they hung out, who their underground contacts were, who kept their military-tech upgrades in good order, who might be willing to sell them weapons.

Ari kept profile networks, and cultivated them on private processors he wouldn't even let Ibrahim see. He had formulas: capabilities plus contacts plus ideology mixed together with a good dose of psychology and some good old fashioned hunches. He wasn't always right, but he could usually narrow down a huge range of possible suspects to a small sample with an accuracy that baffled most investigators, to the point that there were a few police departments to this day who were convinced that he had something to do with the crimes he'd helped solve, so spookily fast had been his work in finding the culprits. Infotech societies had everyone on record somewhere. Finding them was just the old proverbial needle in a haystack thing. Everyone was data. Ari was good at data. But most of all, he knew how the data corresponded with the real world, and how to recognise the recurring patterns when he saw them.

"Hmm," said Ari, scratching his jaw. "Speaking of traitors, what would you call someone who collaborated with League operatives to do their dirty work?" Pino frowned. "Who's your controller, Pino? You know they have this way of lying about who they are? They turn up in chat rooms, usually they have some avatar tailored to what they know you'll like, like, I don't know, hot girls who race motorcycles? They might select some guy who's a big fan of . . . maybe Sarita Muhkerjee, you're in her fan club yes? With half a million other guys, sure, but narrow that down to ex-Fleet, weapons training, martial arts clubs . . . and she ends up with, well, a guy like you. So she makes an avatar in motorcycle leathers, helmet on one arm . . . sound familiar?"

Pino said nothing. Ari's senses weren't as good as a GI's, but he could detect elevated breathing, increased heart rate. Increased pupil dilation.

"And so you talk motorcycles for a while, and she really knows her stuff, because hey, League operatives really train up. They have these last-gen memory enhancements, so they just soak up information like a sponge, great for spies. She could become a motorcycle expert in just a few hours reading, pass herself off to the real deal like you. And then she asks you about your Fleet time, and you get to impress her with your war stories, and she says how much she hates GIs for what they did to your buddies, and you agree, and she says she can introduce you to others who feel the same way, and who hate it how there's suddenly GIs pouring into Tanusha, and some who might even want to do something about it . . ."

Pino took off running. "And you decide to gather on what you think is a secure VR facility on an underground server that just happens to have been designed by a friend of mine," Ari continued as Pino ran away, then stopped in frustration. "Hey! I haven't finished my story yet, dammit!"

Ari jogged after him.

Pino didn't get far. Down a row of walkers, Ayako stepped in front of him with a pistol levelled. Pino stopped.

"CSA," she told him. "Get on the ground."

"Fuck you, bitch."

"No, fuck you," Ayako disagreed, and pointed her pistol at his groin. Pino got on the ground.

Following, Ari saw the previously dancing walker now advancing on them. "Hey!" he yelled, pointing his own pistol at the walker driver. This was a civvie model, recreational and open fronted as the laws stipulated, so they couldn't be used as weapons. Or, not without exposing the driver to casual marksmanship. The driver stopped. "Back off!" Signals flashed on the workshop net, encrypted and directional. Ari didn't like it. Elsewhere about the workshop, some workers were standing and staring, but they seemed abruptly less visible than Ari remembered. "Ayako, quickly!"

Ayako knelt alongside Pino, pistol at his head, handcuffs in the other hand. With a howl, a big walker engine fired up. Pino lashed at Ayako, and she refrained from simply shooting him as she should have, and took the blow on a forearm, skidding backward. Ari swore, pistol still trained on the first walker as his eyes searched for the second. It broke clear of the wall behind him, and he spun. It was over three meters tall, its driver fully enclosed—a police model, small arms fire at the operator was useless. Ari shot at its knees instead, where exposed mechanisms were more vulnerable.

It charged him. He dove sideways, always the best option with walkers, they were fast in a line but didn't change direction quickly. This one skidded on the flat concrete, then Ayako was darting past on its other side, abandoning her fight with Pino to get behind it.

Ari unloaded his clip into the walker's hip, then ran out of ammo and reloaded, retreating between the legs of other, idle walkers as Ayako propagated a tacnet on their common frequency. He barely ducked in time as a worker swung something big and metal at him from the side, lost his pistol as he spun from the second swing, then sidestepped through the third to take the man's arm and rip it back over his head whilst taking his knee out. A second came at him with a big wrench before he could finish the move, Ari stepped inside the swing, caught an arm, broke the grip, kicked to the groin, then drove the head down onto his raised knee. The first man was getting up, Ari spun kicked him flying into a walker's leg.

Before he could reclaim his pistol, the police walker, now with Ayako somehow perched atop its shoulders and pulling exposed hydraulics with her bare hands, came rushing head first into the parked walkers where Ari covered. Ari ran like hell as tonnes of metal crashed and walkers fell in a tangle, and Ayako came diving and rolling clear across the floor.

Then the first walker was rushing him, fast, and he leaped straight at it instead of sideways. He grabbed the driver's cage, grabbing the man's arm and pulling hard. The machine's arm flailed in unison, as the driver flailed with his other arm, trying to fight Ari off, only making the machine flail instead. Ari punched the man in the head for good measure, and the machine toppled backward, Ari riding it down.

Tacnet propagated fully, and Ayako's registered targets were suddenly visible to him as well. The police walker was extricating itself from the tangle of fallen walkers, and a glance across to find Pino showed him getting into yet another walker, and at least two more activating about the walls.

"Well, great!" Ayako said cheerfully. "You know how to drive one of these things?" She ran and leaped with ridiculous agility onto the back of the rising police walker, to resume pulling out cables—it was only police, not military, and hardly invulnerable.

Ari was already in the workshop's network, accessing fast by reflex. There were override codes for places like this, ways to get into the emergency remote control systems, mandatory in Tanusha to stop people doing dumb things in walkers . . . but here the construct was all modified, without the proper access points. No matter, he hit it with a few basic attacks, caused one barrier collapse, forced it to reassert system dominance to several backups, which in turn opened a new vulnerability which he hit, causing a full-on subsystem meltdown.

And then he was in, full override control, and one of his multitudes of stored programs fit neatly into the void and ran. Control panels emerged and he shut all the walkers down, full immobility. Ayako's ride collapsed beneath her, and she jumped off, a little puzzled.

"Is that you?" she asked, as the other walkers powering up, now began powering down.

"Damn right, it's me," said Ari, walking to Pino's walker. Fully immobilised, he was now trapped in the driver's cage as it stood against the wall. He struggled against the straps and the locked cage, helplessly. "You know," said Ari, "you're an idiot." Pino stopped struggling, and fumed. "Net monkeys always win. You don't play with technology around me. I own you."

Already there were police cruisers landing on the roof, summonsed automatically by the emergency tacnet propagation. Ari finally answered the urgent query blinking on his inner vision. "Seems to be the group that attacked Yvette White, maybe others," he told incoming law enforcement. "Lock down the whole complex, don't let anyone leave."

"I thought you said there'd only be one guy here," Ayako accused him, coming over. A few shop workers were running out the exits, but two CSA Agents couldn't chase everyone. Law enforcement were locked in now and the runners wouldn't get far.

Ari shrugged. "Well, you find one guy, you find many guys."

"Sloppy."

Ari considered her. "That's a hell of a leap you've acquired. ALKs?"

Ayako nodded smugly. She'd always loved her toys, especially the augments. "Wonderful things. I can jump six meters vertical now. Before, I struggled to do four."

"Sprint?"

"A hundred meters in seven point two."

Ari whistled. "Gotta love that new gen biotech."

"Not so bad, yourself."

Ari smiled. He'd kind of forgotten how good she looked, with her Japanese eyes and kick-ass smile. Now he remembered. "Well, you know how I like to keep on top of the latest tech. You still top of your class at the agency?"

"Not quite," she admitted. "Commander Rice soaks up the tech like no one else. We all joke she must have borrowed some good genes from Commander Kresnov."

Ari's little gang of anti-GI nasties revealed little in interrogation, but plenty more unwittingly. There were comnet functions and databases, old history trails through private VR forums that led to other people, and yet more contacts. Within hours there were new police and CSA raids across Tanusha, and a few on orbiting stations as well. Many of those would end up being released—they hadn't done anything they could be prosecuted for, just fraternised with assholes. But it revealed more contacts, and led to some ghosts, the kinds of people even Ari struggled to find, the kind who couldn't be sorted from the networked millions because they weren't registered on any network, or not by anything real.

There were, of course, hundreds of thousands of those, most of them underground, some because they were genuinely involved in illegal stuff, but most because they simply didn't like being registered on any network. Many in the underground provided the service to others, promised to clean up their constructs, limit how traceable they were, encode all their random traffic, enough to send any investigator or advertising AI running in twenty false directions at once. That was mostly legal, with limitations. The generation of completely false IDs, however, was not, and was also rampant in Tanusha. But with so many former-League operatives now living locally, the CSA had become quite adept in knowing what to look for, with them in particular.

Two they found by early evening. Genuine ghosts, faceless men with no believable IDs at all. Both were taken alive, and everyone knew they would reveal precisely nothing. The CSA didn't torture, and besides, everyone knew the Federation had its own operatives out in League space, and didn't want the favor returned to them. These would be held for a while, then swapped when the League caught a few Feddie spies. It happened all the time with no publicity at all.

But two more were untouchable. One worked for a big joint science program, funded by League and Federation alike, the kind of thing that was supposed to signal a thawing of relations and a common purpose in all this new technology flooding the Federation from the League since the war ended. Politically it would be incredibly awkward if this very high profile humanitarian program, featuring some very good visiting League scientists, were discovered to have been infiltrated by nefarious League agents who fed money and weapons to local extremist groups and encouraged them to murder Callayan nationals that the League would prefer dead. But neither could the present League government be allowed to think this kind of thing would just be overlooked.

The visiting scientist in question (more of a bureaucrat, in truth) was instead viciously attacked in the hallway of his apartment building, his wallet and personals taken, then his apartment ransacked. Many valuables were stolen, and some potentially useful security clearances. It had all the hallmarks of an underground gang hit—they did it sometimes to wealthy or well connected individuals with links to biotech, if there was something to gain. Possibly the cops would even catch who did it, and those people would certainly turn out to be gangsters, just doing an anonymous call-in job for very good money. Who the real client was, no one would ever know.

The scientist/bureaucrat had about fifteen broken bones and severe internal injuries. He'd take three months to heal in hospital at least, followed by a long trip home to the League. It wasn't payback, it was just security. Anything less would simply encourage more attacks. That fact had been demonstrated over and over on Callay, and most Callayans were sick of it. And putting these kinds of operatives in what were fundamentally humanitarian programs, and then daring the CSA to disrupt that humanitarian goodness with a public arrest, was really beyond the pale. This was the CSA's protest against foul play, and a warning that there were other ways to deal with such operatives besides a public arrest.

The second untouchable worked in the League embassy. Vanessa was not happy about that. Mustafa insisted he had not known. No one believed him.

"You want me to do it?" Sandy asked her friend as they sat in their cruiser atop a rooftop pad, twenty stories up in Ranarid District with a good view of a bend in the river.

"No," said Vanessa. "You've done this enough. It's my turn."

They waited for the woman to emerge upon the roof of her apartment building across the river, windows wound down, the sounds of city traffic wafting up on a cool night breeze.

"Phillippe complained about me coming out tonight," Vanessa volunteered. Sandy glanced at her. "That's the first time that's happened."

"It was bound to sometime," Sandy supposed. "He's been very tolerant really. Especially for a guy with no background in security."

"Yeah, but that's the point. That's why he likes it, it's exciting to him because it's unfamiliar. It's one of the things I love about him, he's interested in so many things beyond his own little world."

"It's what you've got in common," said Sandy. "You're the most unlikely SWAT grunt, you weren't even much of a tomboy growing up, then you got into business, so you've had a foot in several worlds. And Phillippe's a musician but he's also a big philanthropist, an amateur botanist, amateur marine biologist . . ."

"Amateur everything," Vanessa said with a smile. "Yeah. He's got my enthusiasm for stuff, any stuff. Tonight he just wanted to sit around and read and talk with me. He's reading a history of Carthage, you know Carthage?"

"Sure, North Africa, wiped out by the Romans."

"And he likes my military insights. That's what we do to relax, we sit around and discuss the annihilation of ancient civilisations." Her smile faded. "He was kind of pissed. Me being in SWAT is cool, but this middle of the night stuff I can't even talk about. He doesn't get to enjoy my profession, he just gets to sit alone and wonder where I am. Said it doesn't have to be me all the time."

Sandy shrugged. "Well, it kind of doesn't."

"Crap. On the big stuff, I'm in charge of SWAT, it does have to be me."

Sandy sighed. "Yeah. I guess." Cicadas chirped in a flower box beside the rooftop landing pad. "Call him."

"Against regs."

"I know. Call him. Or text. And tell him I say hi."

Vanessa smiled and did that. Sandy was fond of saying that a dumb regulation wasn't a regulation at all, just a temporary obstacle. Vanessa thought out a sentence, translated to text, and sent. Phillippe, sitting at home, would receive an uplink call, open it and find the message across his inner vision: *Hey babe, I'm with Sandy talking about you. Sandy says hi. Love you heaps. Don't wait up.*

The last bit didn't feel right, but she had to say it or he would.

"You know," she added, "I used to always think I'd end up marrying someone from SWAT. Or from the CSA at least. Same line of work, similar background, you know?" Sandy nodded. "But these days, I'm so damn glad he doesn't do what we do. So glad I can't begin to tell you."

"Yeah," said Sandy, somberly watching the apartment rooftop across the river bend. "I know what you mean."

The woman appeared. "Here she is," said Vanessa, and pulled her glasses down over her eyes. That filtered the natural light, and her inner-vision showed up more starkly against the contrast. She had multiple visual feeds on tacnet, showing the rooftop from several angles. Net monitors showed her all traffic. The woman was hooked into Tanushan traffic net, and making last minute adjustments to her outbound flight from Gordon Spaceport. She hauled several suitcases with her, and a large shoulder bag. A man was walking out behind her, with more bags.

"Yeah, that's definitely Lu," said Sandy. Lu Dongfu was an embassy worker on the trade desk. No one had suspected him of anything. They'd watched him arrive twenty minutes ago at this safe house, and known immediately who he must be coming to see. "Guilty by implication. The only people helping her at this point are those involved, given the League will deny everything. Still want to do it?"

"I'll do it," said Vanessa. "It's my job."

The two figures loaded suitcases into a cruiser. The woman was Paola Ortiz. She'd been at the League's Tanusha embassy for nearly a year, worked in communications, and hadn't been any more suspicious than any other League embassy employee. The general rule was that one in five of them were ISO, everyone knew it, but the ISO were as much a help of late as they were a problem. Ortiz was evidently something else, connected directly to League government but bypassing the ISO. Or so Mustafa insisted. But that didn't mean he hadn't known. Mustafa knew everything that went on in the embassy, whether he admitted it or not.

Suitcases loaded, Lu was about to join Ortiz getting into the cruiser when a call came through.

"External contact," Sandy affirmed. "Coming from somewhere in . . . hang on a second . . . Mananakorn District. No . . . wait, that was a trick, it's heavily encrypted." Vanessa didn't even bother trying to access the analytical functions Sandy was racing through right now, Sandy processed software constructs so fast it made a normal person's brain feel like it was about to explode. "Well, this smells like Mustafa to me. Similar encryption, similar tricks."

"*Who's getting it?*" someone asked from outside. It sounded like Chandrasekar.

"Lu," Sandy said immediately. "I'm not sure if Ortiz has access."

On the rooftop, Lu changed his mind about getting in the cruiser. There followed a fast discussion between him and Ortiz, then the gull doors closed. Lu stood back as the cruiser lifted, running lights flashing.

"Got it?" Sandy asked Vanessa.

"Got it." Vanessa was looking at a simple interruption sequence, chopping into the main datastream of Tanushan traffic control. Traffic control was inviolable. The CSA weren't allowed to play with it under nearly any circumstance, and certainly not for this one. They weren't even supposed to have the codes. There weren't supposed to be any codes for this sort of thing.

The cruiser's flightpath off the apartment rooftop took it out over the river, slowly building up speed as it climbed in an arc.

"Now," said Sandy.

The interruption sequence ran, and quite smoothly and without any alarm, traffic control implemented a temporary override of the cruiser's navcomp. Without even a wobble or a protest, the cruiser nosed down and dove directly into the river, disappearing with a huge splash.

"Well I never," Sandy murmured. "Diplomatic immunity and all."

"Guess traffic control has a few bugs," Vanessa suggested, firing up the cruiser's engines as the windows wound automatically up to a seal. On the far apartment rooftop, a small figure stood and stared at the frothing river where he'd very nearly died, and no doubt pondered that he owed Mustafa Ramoja his life. But Mustafa had saved only one.

Curious, thought Vanessa, powering the cruiser up into the air.

"Hell of a way to unwind from a war crimes hearing," Sandy remarked. Vanessa didn't find that particularly funny.

CHAPTER TWELVE

F SA Headquarters were a touch more stylish than CSA HQ. Things were whiter and glassier, with more natural light. Sandy wasn't sure she liked it—the security was serious stuff, it demanded a stronger architectural touch. Or maybe the League had bred some aesthetic bias into her after all.

Ibrahim was in a meeting, but she wandered in and watched as several of the FSA's seniors sat and talked with him about organisation and personnel. Ibrahim had an open office policy where possible, and if it wasn't classified, anyone who felt they needed to know could wander in to meetings. Most people were so busy they'd only do it sparingly, but security organisations, Ibrahim insisted, were no place for specialists who knew only their own job and no one else's.

Finally they left, a few with friendly greetings to Sandy, a few more guarded. "Seems to be going well?" Sandy observed, taking a seat. The seats were more comfortable here, too—deep, modern leather. From the windows was a great view across FSA grounds to the Grand Council Building.

"There's a lot to do," Ibrahim replied, rubbing at one pronounced cheekbone. He didn't seem too tired, though. Sandy knew he loved this stuff. Radha Ibrahim had told her once that her husband would love his job until it killed him. To Sandy, he'd never looked more alive. "It's actually part of what I wanted to talk to you about. I'd like a report from you on parallel integration."

It was what he wanted to do between the CSA and the FSA. It was controversial, of course. "How long?"

Ibrahim smiled, shaking his head. "Just start writing and stop when you're finished. Two pages or two hundred, I want your thoughts. You have unique insight."

It touched her. "Sure. Though it seems to me the main problem is political, and I can't help that."

The FSA, obviously, was physically located on Callay. That meant the Callayan Security Agency's jurisdiction overlapped with its own. Ibrahim's idea was to integrate the two agencies, keeping command structures separate yet sharing jurisdictions—the CSA's role would expand out beyond purely

Callayan issues, and the FSA's would also expand . . . or perhaps the better word was contract . . . to include local Callayan matters. But as the lawyers and politicians kept reminding everyone, Federal and local planetary jurisdictions were clearly separated by law, and combining them could be unconstitutional. President Singh, for one, was kicking up a stink.

"No one can help that," Ibrahim replied. "Callay is what it is, and the moment we start regretting that is the moment we fail in our responsibilities."

Sandy nodded. "This means Chandi will still actually be working for you, after you so cruelly granted him his freedom?"

"No," Ibrahim said mildly. "Parallel means parallel, who is in charge will depend on whose jurisdiction it naturally falls into. Federal matters, I'm in command. Local, Chandi will be."

"And of course every case you have will be easy to divide like that," said Sandy.

"Yes." With dry amusement. "I'm sure of it. The next matter—the war crimes prosecution are planning an appeal."

Her Honour had rejected the possibility of trial at the hearing, citing the dubious source of the evidence.

Sandy nodded again. "Yes, I heard."

Ibrahim looked at her cautiously. "It could go on a long time. The appeal will be to a full bench this time, which has fewer time restrictions. It could take months."

"I know," said Sandy. Ibrahim was worried for her emotional state. He needn't have been; she was dealing with it quite well. Accusations of being a killer didn't bother her as much as they once had. She was a killer. As were all soldiers, at least in potential. It was just a question of who, how and why. Here, on all three counts, she was comfortable she was in the right.

"The political implications of this are quite severe," Ibrahim continued. "We are under pressure on many fronts, and we've lost what little cooperation we once had with the League government."

"Killing their operatives will do that," Sandy remarked. It had been Ibrahim's order. The press knew nothing. They'd never known Paola Ortiz even existed. FSA and CSA had collaborated to make a cover story about a foreign temporary visa holder who had crashed into the river in a freak user-error accident—it happened occasionally, when smart people tried to override traffic net, usually for fun or a dare. In the FTL era, such personal details from other worlds would take months to check, and most news organisations hadn't bothered. Those few that had would meet screw-ups at the other end from friendly security agencies doing the CSA some favours, and that would be the end of it. As far as Callay knew, neither Ortiz nor her assassination had ever existed.

"Yes it will," Ibrahim agreed. "But the Federation does actually have many ongoing arrangements with the League, including many ceasefire monitoring deals, humanitarian assistance arrangements, a small amount of trade, various joint research programs, exchange programs and the like."

"I know," said Sandy, now a little frustrated Ibrahim was treating her like a kid. Everyone knew this stuff, why was he . . . ?

"And those arrangements are now in jeopardy." He folded his hands, and leaned on the table. "As such, I'm afraid we shall be forced to end all cooperative arrangements with the ISO on New Torah. The mission's off, Cassandra. I'm sorry, but we have no choice."

"The fuck we don't." Her own language surprised her. So did her volume. "We're just going to let them win? This is why they did it, why they gave Padma fucking Chaury and the SIB all that information on Tropez Station. They knew Mustafa was up to something with me and they wanted to stop it. And it's why they sent *Eternity* before that, to put an end to Operation Patchup. So now you're telling me that it worked? And we're going to reward them for their cleverness?"

"Yes," said Ibrahim, gaze level and unblinking. "I realise the sensation must be quite foreign to you, Cassandra, but sometimes the other side wins. And sometimes, our side loses."

"We didn't lose!" Sandy shouted. "You fucking quit!"

Her vision was tracking now, all the way into infra-red. She hated it when this happened, when she got so angry she slid all the way into combat-reflex with no immediate threat of combat. This reflex confirmed every fear of every prejudiced anti-GI campaigner who insisted that she and her kind were not to be trusted. And the worst of it was that when she was like this, she didn't completely trust herself.

Ibrahim never blinked. Sometimes Sandy thought he had a combat reflex too, of sorts. "Cassandra, I realise that this is of some considerable personal importance to you. But understand that however much I sympathise, and share your concerns about New Torah . . ."

"Stop giving speeches," Sandy told him. "Just stop. I know you make impartial decisions. I know you as well as anyone."

"Not quite," Ibrahim said quietly.

"I know you're the guy who'll order ten people killed so you can save a hundred. I know you'll let friends suffer to save other people you don't like. I get it. You're the impartial one, everyone's equal before the eyes of Allah. But this time, you're wrong."

"Right and wrong in this matter are not for us to decide," said Ibrahim. "There are constraints. I recognise them. Apparently you do not."

"GIs are the center of this!" Sandy insisted. "Out there in the Torah Systems, some bunch of murderous lunatics are taking GI technology in directions that could restart a major war, or . . . or lead to Gods know what!"

"At which point we must suppose that the League will be finally forced to deal with it themselves. We cannot police every crime, Cassandra. Not if it means the significant risk of destabilising the very peace with the League."

"What peace? The Federation fought to win! The League surrendered! Now they get to set the terms of peace?" Ibrahim said nothing. "Your problem is that you don't know what my people are capable of . . ."

"Your people?" Ibrahim interrupted, frowning.

"Yes, my people! Artificial people, like me. There are directions in which that technology can be taken that could spell very bad news for all humanity, and I fear that that's exactly what's going on out in New Torah right now."

"You don't know that."

"No, but I work for a fucking intelligence agency, so you'd think I wouldn't be the only person with an interest in finding out!"

"We have assets we can access without having to get directly involved." Ibrahim leaned forward further, very firmly. "Cassandra, I won't allow it. That is the end of the matter."

"It's not the end of the matter," said Sandy. She took out her badge and guns, and put them on Ibrahim's desk. "I quit. Now try and stop me."

Sandy went home. She knew she was furious, and that it was affecting her judgment. But that was not necessarily a bad thing. Emotions were not intrinsically bad or illogical. Someone who ran into a burning building to save people from the flames was acting under the influence of strong emotion, when it would be far more logical to stand outside and watch them burn.

At home she did not bother gathering her things; she could not take so much as a backpack where she was going. She merely grabbed a few electronic essentials, raided her secret stash of storage chips, sunglasses and some hair dye, and left. She walked out of Canas District, feet being the form of transport the CSA would find hardest to trace without eyes-on surveillance. She'd already changed all her personal constructs to her third alternates, and would change them again soon. Her CSA personal contact links were still working. Ibrahim had made no immediate move to shut her out. She was not concerned either way.

She got a taxi to a tube station, paid cash, then caught the maglev to Kochin District, for no other reason than there was a big shopping mall there, and she could lose herself in the crowd, uplinks working overtime on CSA surveillance frequencies in case she was being traced. Those also remained open, but if they were trailing her they'd use something completely unfamiliar to throw her off. She went into a cosmetics store, bought a makeup box, used the bathroom and snuck out the back way into a service corridor. Down back way stairs into the subway system, which ran shorter distances than the maglev, caught it for several stations to a park where she'd signalled a cruiser taxi to pick her up at a transition zone.

That took her airbourne, as she finally managed to propagate one of her best reserve IDs, paid for the taxi ride with it on a separate and equally fake credit line, then did the same at the high-rise hotel the taxi dropped her off at. That checked her into a room with a cool view, which was nice. She liked to have a place to sleep, and safe houses were overrated. She wasn't wealthy enough to afford one, anyway. But this false ID should hold for tonight; she'd polish up another for tomorrow night somewhere else. She didn't need some secret stash of stuff hidden somewhere—being what she was, and having the network skills she had, there was nothing she couldn't acquire on short notice. Including weapons.

First she showered, and dyed her hair black in the bathroom basin. Then she accessed another storage chip and entered a mental VR space with a huge, complex construct that glowed and pulsed now as she activated functions on the test grid. After half an hour of final checks, she contacted Anita on one of those very covert frequencies that private citizens weren't even supposed to possess, given that it parasited off secure government networks.

"Hi, 'Nita. You heard?"

"'Course I heard. Vanessa has us all on alert in case you contact us. She's worried about you, Sandy!"

"I know. Tell her I'm fine and I'll contact her soon, I promise." That was another helpful fact—having so many friends within the CSA, including a few who could probably bring the entire Callayan security network down from the inside if they were angry enough, would limit anything Ibrahim or Chandi might do against her. But it also put her friends under considerable pressure, and their careers in some jeopardy, at least in the short term. Well, she'd deal with that, too. "Firstly I'd like you to look at this. It's a VR linkup so it'll take a few seconds to propagate."

"Of course, send away." Sandy sent. "So you really quit the CSA and FSA? And Ibrahim accepted?"

"He didn't accept, but my passcodes are inactive and it looks like I'm temporarily suspended, at least. I walked out before we could discuss it further."

"Why wouldn't he cut you off immediately? Doesn't he know how dangerous you can be to CSA systems from the inside?"

"No, he's very clever," Sandy replied, "and he knows me too well. He knows I'm more dangerous on the outside because then I'll have nothing to lose. He knows I'll never sabotage the CSA or FSA from the inside while I'm still technically a member."

"Wow, what happened?"

"And he'll know I won't talk about that."

Anita's VR function would be activating now. There was a pause as Anita accessed. Then . . . "Oh my God. Sandy? Did you make this? It's beautiful!"

"It's a secure communications function for a TS-series net seeker. You know how you send them out but their com systems are vulnerable to infiltration and traceback, and then those new 21-8000s turn them into zombies and feed you bogus data . . ."

"You solved the seeker suckers?" With amazement.

"Well, not solved, but pretty much improved I think, for a TS-series anyway." Anita had designed the TS-series seekers, in Sandy's opinion easily the best available. She'd tinkered with them often. "Make a few tweaks if you like, but I think it should be profitable."

"*Oh, hell yes!*" Anita enthused. "*Sandy, this could make you quite a bit of money.*"

"That is the idea, yes. I'm going to need it."

"*And about time, too. Look, I'll work up a licensing agreement to a false ID. That's usually what we do with designers who want to stay outside the system. And I'm prepared to give you ninety percent revenue after Raj-Bhaj Systems takes care of testing and publicity . . .*"

"Oh, come on, Anita, the usual seventy percent will be fine, you're not a charity . . ."

"*Ninety percent and that's my final offer.*"

"And you did design the TS-series, I just built onto it."

"*Ninety percent it is, then. We can pull an all-nighter for tests, make some calls . . . oh, man, the market's just dying for something like this. People have come up with bits and pieces, but an integrated solution's just eluded everyone so far, assuming it works like you say . . .*"

"It does. I've used it myself for a few months, done my own trouble-shooting. They used to crash whenever they ran into any sort of multi-barrier matrix, but I solved that."

"*Planning ahead?*" Anita wondered slyly.

"It occurred to me something like this might happen," Sandy admitted.

"*Well, if it works like you say, we can release it in three days. You should have money within a week. Blank account, you can do with it what you want. Oh, and Ari's looking for you, too.*"

Sandy smiled. "Tell him I'll give him a thousand bucks if he can find me."

"*Ari never really did it for the money.*"

"Tell him a blowjob, then. For old time's sake."

Anita laughed. "*Now, that he might be more interested in.*"

Weapons were easy. The irony was that though firearm ownership was strictly controlled, alloy-microprinter ownership was not, so there were plenty of workshops scattered through Tanusha that could knock up a good custom automatic in half an hour. Ditto, bullets. A basement chem lab could make good powder in no time, and micro-manufacturing had brought the construction of anything up to and including guided missiles and beyond into the realm of a teenager's after school hobby. No one had yet managed to make a functioning H-bomb, but not for want of trying. Sandy had personally sat in on a briefing given to some civil liberties folks who'd complained about all the radiation sensors built into the Tanushan streetscape, saying that there were plenty of legitimate medical uses of low intensity radiation devices that the CSA had no business snooping into. They'd been shown several very close shaves the CSA had intercepted yet told no one about, and the civil liberties folks had left the room ashen-faced and silent. No more complaints about carpeting radiation scanners had been received.

Sandy simply called a friend of Ari's, a techie guy with a serious crush on her, and lots of potential convictions she'd known about for ages yet never charged him for because he was too useful. Two hours later he delivered her a pair of nine millimeter automatic pistols direct to her doorstep, as though she were ordering pizza. All it cost her was a few hundred bucks, and a kiss. Being single, and the guy kind of cute, she made it a good one.

These even had basic interface, she noted as she sat on the bed and checked them out properly, and the six mags he'd brought her. She tried it out, then received an encrypted transmission from elsewhere. She opened, and found a VR link. Wrong format, too—this full-immersion stuff never worked on her. Whoever this was (and she thought she knew) wanted to meet her in a neutral net venue rather than talking directly, which was more traceable. But if it was who she thought it was, surely he'd know her limitations with VR, and share them?

Curious, she pulled her booster from a jacket pocket, plugged in and inserted that socket into the back of her head. Fully reinforced, she lay back on the bed, closed her eyes and accessed.

Full immersion; she could do that in code-space, but here it was attempting to resolve into shapes and colours. Her brain resisted, as it always did, breaking down the constructs into their component parts and codes.

"*Just relax,*" came Mustafa's voice. "*Don't fight it. I found it hard at first, too. But if you take a deep breath, and just focus on the far horizon . . .*"

She did that. Colours resolved more sharply, then textures. It was a big room. An amazing room, with huge columns. Very familiar architecture . . . except that beyond the columns was open air, and a city. She looked around as things resolved further. Almost lifelike. Almost like she was standing there for real. This looked like some kind of palace. Everything was ornamental, a polished, patterned floor, huge vases, gold trimmed furniture . . . and everything was old. Or old-styled; it actually looked quite new, like it had been made yesterday.

From the city outside arose a constant hubbub, unfamiliar, odd. Voices, and clanking noises. Hammers. Wheels on cobbles. Animals. Old noises. No modern machinery. In the palace there was nothing that looked like it ran on electricity. No panels, displays, controls, automated units. This was utterly pre-technological. And yet, wow! she thought, looking up at the huge columns. Look at this building. Amazing to think people had been able to build these extraordinary things in an age when electricity was still two thousand years away.

She walked to a column and looked out at the city. She'd read enough history, and done enough basic sims, that she knew roughly where she was.

"Ancient Rome," she pronounced. "We're somewhere downtown. Oh, wow, look at the detail. This is amazing." The cityscape was cluttered, spectacular, unpredictable. Columns, pillars, temples. Distant neighbourhoods, fine houses, crowded hovels. "Oh, look, the coliseum is under construction. Maybe 75AD?"

"Vespasian's time," said Mustafa behind her. "He gives bread and circuses to the masses."

Sandy looked at him. He appeared to her vision the same as always, leather jacket, jeans, comfortable shoes. Most GIs dressed similarly. "What," she asked, "no toga?"

"Have you ever seen a black man in a toga?"

"I'm sure there must have been. Half the empire was African."

"North African," Mustafa corrected, standing alongside, taking in the view. "But yes, I suppose there must have been senior black Romans. That colour-based racism actually got worse before it got better. Just like sexism probably got worse after Rome before it got better. I remember being astonished when I first learned that. I'd always assumed that history moved in straight lines . . . you know, things were bad, then they improved. But it doesn't actually work that way."

"History moves in waves," Sandy agreed. The sun was low, yellow behind clouds. It looked like summer, though she had no sensation of warmth. She could hear animals below, yet a deep sniff brought no smell. This VR, too, had its limits, though it was far better than anything she'd previously tried. "Callay's actually got more strict gender rules than much of Earth a few hundred years ago. A lot of women just like these more traditional roles. They're orderly, they give comfort."

"Men too," Mustafa agreed. "And who can reproach them, if that's how they wish to live?"

Sandy nodded. "Vanessa gets upset about it, she's more activist. The old word was feminist. But I don't really care. I suppose that comes from being an outsider; I just never really minded if other people's ideas didn't agree with me. But Vanessa was born here. She doesn't always have that luxury."

"I feel we could be at one of those turning points in history now," said Mustafa. "Regarding GIs. The anti-GI forces in the Federation were always right about one thing—artificial humanity does have the potential to change the entire course of humanity. Whether that course is changed for the better or the worse, whether we ride on the upside of the wave you described, or the downside, depends largely now on events in New Torah."

"Yes," Sandy agreed, with relief. It felt good to finally be in the company of someone who really understood. "GIs are like any group of humans. We have strong points and weak points. So long as our development is contained within a balanced environment, we'll have that balance of good and bad in us. But there's no balance in New Torah. I've had nightmares about what I think GIs could become. Those nightmares got worse after Jane. And now they've got worse again after Pyeongwha. That was in straight humans, but it's GI tech. I think Ari knows, though he hasn't talked about much yet. He never likes to share his work until he's finished and certain."

"I should tell you about Ari," Mustafa said somberly. "I feel responsible in a way, for the two of you breaking up." Sandy stared at him. "I gave him some information. Technical data, very advanced quality. It's not my area of specialty so I only understood parts of it. But I thought Ari would appreciate it, and . . . well, as you saw, he became quite obsessive about it from that point on."

"Neural Cluster Technology?"

Mustafa nodded. "Our scientists know the tech. They never followed that particular line of research as far as they might. They saw the dangers and stopped the experiments. Pyeongwha was the first large-population-scale experiment, if you will."

"With technology that rewrites people's brains faster than they can rewrite the technology," Sandy said sourly.

"It works on GIs too, as you suspected. As Ari suspected. It was about that time that he felt he needed distance from you. That an entire planet's fate may hang upon his objectivity."

Sandy sighed. "You didn't break us up. It was always going to be something, with Ari. His actions are his own responsibility, as my actions are mine. But it's good to know where that came from."

"Oh, he was already very interested. He talked with me about it a few times, and he already knew a lot. I steered him a bit further. The ISO has no interest in seeing NCT spread. There are those in the League too eager to revisit it themselves. The ISO disagreed."

"The faceless men behind the fate of worlds," Sandy remarked.

Mustafa shrugged. "Faceless and useful. What do you know about Compulsive Narrative Syndrome?"

Sandy frowned. "It's basic human psychology. About four hundred years old, I think, it grew into a whole family of cognitive laws. One of the founding laws of modern artificial intelligence. What does that have to do with NCT?"

"Neural Cluster Technology interacts with it in worrisome ways. Tell me what you know of the syndrome, so I know you'll understand what I tell you next."

Sandy leaned her back against the column, yet there was no sensation of pressure. If she moved too much, too quickly, the VR would start to break down. The lowering sun half-lit Mustafa's face in profile.

"Compulsive Narrative Syndrome describes the brain's use of pattern recognition to organise information inputs," she said. A person who wondered what she was, studied psychology. That person, studying psychology, very quickly ran into Compulsive Narrative Syndrome. She'd read quite a lot about it. "A narrative is just another form of pattern. There's too much information in the world for us to process all at once; we need to prioritise. So we learn to focus our attention on specific activities, and take in only information related to that activity, discarding all unrelated information."

"Why?"

"So we don't waste brain space processing irrelevant information. The first AIs used to process everything. They didn't know what was important and what wasn't. It was only when they learned to discard irrelevant information, by prioritising the important stuff, that they began to really speed up."

Mustafa nodded. "So it's task oriented."

"Yes. Information not related to specific tasks is discarded, improving efficiency and focus. So to do that we have pattern recognition, identifying patterns that relate certain information as relevant to certain tasks. We do it all the time in everyday activities. If I'm making tea, the teapot, the cups, the water temperature are important. The colour of a chair across the room is not, so likely I won't notice it. I'd be incredibly slow making a cup of tea if I was always getting distracted by things that had nothing to do with the task.

"But the problem comes when people move into abstract concepts, politics, ideologies and religions. The human brain is trained to look for and identify patterns, but in abstract concepts, fixed and unarguable facts are hard to find. So the brain looks for narratives instead, stories that can tie together various ideas and facts in a way that seems to make sense, to make a pattern. And the human brain, always seeking a pattern as a basic cognitive function, will latch onto a narrative pattern compulsively, and use that pattern as a framework within which to store new information, like a tradesman honing his skill, or someone learning a new language. That's why religions tell such great stories, the story makes a pattern within which everything makes sense. A synchronicity of apparent facts. Political ideologies, too. Humans are suckers for a great story because we can't resist the logical pattern it contains.

"When you're learning a new skill, discarding irrelevant information and organising the relevant stuff within that framework is good. But in ideologies, it means any information that doesn't fit the ideological narrative is literally discarded, and won't be remembered . . . which is why you can argue facts with ideologues and they'll just ignore you. They're not just being stubborn, their brains are literally structurally incapable of processing what they perceive as pattern-anomalous data. That's why some ideologues get so upset when you offer facts that don't match their pattern, it's like you're assaulting them. So what Compulsive Narrative Syndrome really says is that being a one-eyed partisan isn't just a matter of taste or values, it's actually a cognitive, neurological condition that we all suffer from to some degree. And it explains why some people's ideologies can change, because sometimes a new pattern is identified that overrides the old one. And it explains why the most intelligent people are often the most partisan and least objective, because pattern recognition is a function of higher intelligence. If you want an objective opinion, ask a stupid person."

"And a lot of people still don't like Compulsive Narrative Syndrome for exactly that reason," Mustafa agreed. "They don't like the idea that all human intelligence is only possible because of bias, and that there's no such thing as an objective opinion. They like to think that intelligence and accuracy are synonymous, when it's more correct to say that intelligence and complexity are synonymous. But complexity is no guarantee of accuracy, and is sometimes the death of it."

"But some biases are good," Sandy countered. "I'm quite happy to be biased toward individual freedom and dignity. If CNS didn't exist, people wouldn't have the good biases or the bad ones, and that would be even worse than the problems CNS creates. Ideological narratives are the only reason morality exists in society."

"That's what Dr Lo Shao-ho argued in his counter theories," Mustafa conceded. "I love his work."

"But CNS is far more than a theory now. Questioning it is a bit like questioning evolution—it's been pretty comprehensively proven."

"And some religious types on Callay still don't like evolution, either. But here's the thing. New Torah is reactivating study on Neural Cluster Technology, for GIs in particular. NCT is good for military uplink tech. It carries a far higher data baseload than current uplinks can."

"I know," Sandy said somberly. "On both counts."

"Ever wonder what it does to the Compulsive Narrative Syndrome process?"

"Yes," said Sandy. "Some friends had some ideas." Ari and Anita in particular. "NCT is almost like telepathy. Technological telepathy. Even emotions are shared, though at a lower level. Ari said there were multiple mechanisms at play on Pyeongwha, partly that the brain's natural rewiring processes were accelerated over several generations by NCT, and partly that there's just a natural synchronicity that develops between closely linked brains. It begins to erode individuality after a while, and thus the society's value of individuality, leading eventually to the creation of hostility toward anyone displaying overt individuality.

"But he also said there was a pattern recognition thing going on. Did you know that Pyeongwha's internal security services were actually stretched before we hit them? It probably made our job easier; they were distracted."

"Why?" asked Mustafa.

"The last decade saw the eruption of a number of extremist movements. Radical right wingers, radical left wingers, religious radicals, you name it. They had bombings, shootings, they had a mass suicide out in Abanda where nearly a thousand people poisoned themselves because of some religious prophecy that one of Pyeongwha's moons would crash into the planet. Three hundred children among them."

"Children aren't linked to NCT until at least ten," Mustafa said somberly, no doubt guessing the answer to his unasked question.

"Their parents killed them," said Sandy. "And this is the most conformist society you've ever seen, everyone loves the administration and pledges undying loyalty to their world and its values. So why the radical breakaways, in many cases attacking that world and its institutions and people?"

"You think it's narrative pattern recognition?"

"Ari does. NCT alters the brain's information environment. Data processing is radically increased, most of it in socialisation. Humans are group animals, evolution programmed us for group behaviour, so that accentuates the conformity instinct even more. There's so much more data to find patterns in, Ari's studied some of the data secretly compiled by psychologists who weren't affected and were watching what was going on. He says Compulsive Narrative Syndrome was just taking off in some social segments. People's brains were becoming hyper-analytical and hyper-focused, memory retention was both increasing and decreasing, on pattern-matching and pattern-anomalous data respectively."

"Yes," Mustafa said somberly. "That matches our hypothetical research exactly. They were being turned into drones."

"Except where a few individuals would suddenly identify a pattern that the mainstream society never tried to force upon them," Sandy continued. "A conspiracy theory, a new permutation of a pre-existing value structure, usually a persecution complex of some sort. Zodiac signs were big on Pyeongwha— it's a cultural thing. No one really took it seriously in a scientific sense, and of course all the star constellations look completely different on Pyeongwha, like they do on every planet. But in one instance, there was a pocket of people based around several cultural centers—sports clubs, a university, a youth center—who somehow identified a pattern from random data that convinced them that Gemini were conspiring against Pisces, first in some sport results, then in placement for some volunteer jobs, then in criminal activity and accidental injuries. It escalated into fist fights, then into a gun battle. One psychologist's report for the police described prison cells filled with about fifteen to twenty individuals who were absolutely adamant that members of this other zodiac sign were trying to kill them for no other reason than their date of birth, because they had selectively latched onto that information that 'proved' it, while ignoring all non-compatible data. And that whole incident started several copycats, narrative pattern recognition spreads like ripples with NCT, it's absolutely frightening."

"Astonishing," Mustafa murmured. He seemed astonished. And grim. Mustafa rarely let his emotions show so clearly.

"Not that astonishing," said Sandy. "There are people here who still insist I'm a League government plant after all these years. And that the League actually won the war and that all this talk of Federation victory is just an elaborate conspiracy to fool people and hide what really happened."

Mustafa nodded. "Conspiracy theories are an obvious manifestation of CNS. The individual buys into the narrative structure of deceptive governments because it allows the individual an illusion of control over uncontrollable events, allowing him to 'take back' and control the narrative from an evil government which in reality has no more control over the events in question than he does. It's an empowerment narrative, feeding off the subconscious fear of disempowerment, which is very common amongst regular humans. It's an exact fit with textbook CNS because any evidence contrary to the conspiracy theory will be interpreted by the subject as just another part of the conspiracy, which thus becomes an unfalsifiable law, impossible to disprove no matter how stupid. It's perfect."

Sandy thought of some of Ari's more wild conspiracy theories, and restrained a smile. He wasn't as self-assured as she was, certainly, but she'd forgiven him for it. It was all that Freudian stuff again, that regular humans did that she didn't.

"Our psychs have been looking at Eduardo," said Sandy. "The killswitch that killed him looks like it was triggered by the structural realignment of his thought processes away from what his creators intended. He didn't have NCT, though. I think that's the next step. New Torah corporations are only interested in GIs as weapons. NCT will improve their soldiering effectiveness, no doubt, but it could also create new forms of mind control. I'm not going to sit and wait for it to happen."

"Me neither," said Mustafa. "And my superiors continue to feel the same as they did before. New Torah needs to be stopped. But we need more high-designation GIs for the job. Are you still in?"

Sandy nodded immediately. "Yes."

"Even if it means defying Ibrahim?"

"Yes."

CHAPTER THIRTEEN

Ibrahim sipped coffee and watched the sun rise from the Director's office atop the primary building of the FSA compound. The skyline looked different from here, visible across only half of the sky, as Montoya District was on the present day perimeter of Tanusha, along with most of the new, Federal institutions. The CSA compound had been south-central, with towers on all sides.

Uplinks and his desk screen showed him the switchover nearly complete. It was a huge task, recalibrating the entire Federal Security Agency network to an emergency, alternate mode. For the few minutes while it was happening, nothing worked, communications were down, passcodes deactivated. And when it came back up again, everything would be new, and all the old codes and passes would need to be reissued. Right now, that was the least of his worries.

Tselide came in from the neighbouring room. "Done," said the FSA's network chief. "All done, it looks good."

Ibrahim nodded, sipping coffee. "Do you think she can break back in?"

Tselide shrugged. "Technically I don't think there's much she can't break into, not even this network. But there's no way to do it quietly. She'll give away her location, her status, everything. Normally that would be no advantage to us because we'd already know where she is—shooting her way into the complex, as she's designed."

Tselide's expression was anxious. Ibrahim shook his head in reply to the unasked question. "No, we're a long way from that, here."

"Director, Commander Kresnov isn't the only one with network access we have to worry about. And I don't just mean the other GIs. I'm a lot more worried about Agent Ruben and Commander Rice, to name just two."

"I know," said Ibrahim. "We're dealing with that."

"They're being arrested?"

"Only if they leave me no choice."

"The phrase isn't arrest, it's 'watch and contain.'"

"Arrest is too public," said Vanessa, fully armoured, in the command seat of her flyer. "Sandy's a public figure, Callay's security is undermined by the scandal if she's arrested. She's the hair-trigger on a whole bunch of political landmines Ibrahim can't afford to trip."

Not the least of which was that she was the single most useful asset either the CSA or the FSA possessed. Behind her, SWAT One were watchful. The atmosphere was tense in a way Vanessa had only rarely seen before.

"*Ricey, tell me we're not going after Sandy?*" Captain Arvid Singh sounded very worried.

"Only Ibrahim can tell you that," Vanessa replied. "Right now, it's a standoff. Ibrahim and Chandi have reconfigured the entire FSA and CSA networks, even I'm locked out right now. We've got independent tacnet, but all the encryptions are different. I can't access anything off the main construct."

"*Yeah, well he doesn't trust you, does he?*"

Vanessa exhaled shortly, thankful the main network changes would also render this tacnet communication entirely silent. "I think there's a lot of people he can't trust right now. Han, Weller, Khan and Ogun didn't show up to work today, for one thing."

"*Well you could expect that with the GIs. What about Rhian?*"

"Rhian's here. She's on standby with SWAT Six." She was a section leader in SWAT Six, technically second-in-command. "So I guess SWAT Six is out of the question, too."

"*Ricey, this is ridiculous.*" Arvid had always had that knack of stating the obvious. "*I'm not shooting at Sandy, Sandy's not shooting at me, she's sure as hell not shooting at you or Rhian, and you and Rhian both would rather resign and become pole dancers than shoot at Sandy. Is that about it?*"

"Yeah," Vanessa sighed. "That's about it. 'Cept for your prejudiced assumption that I'd hate to pole dance."

"*You wouldn't? 'Cause I could arrange that. Are we on the verge of mutiny here or what?*"

Vanessa thought hard. Sandy had accused her in the past of getting too emotional, but now when the stakes were highest, she felt very calm. She'd always been like this—under pressure was when she thought clearest.

"No mutiny," she said. "Ibrahim knows all of this. He won't force the situation, he knows he can't rely on us against Sandy." *Because I fucking will resign and spill it all to the media*, she left unsaid. "He'll use other assets. And he'll keep us busy and occupied on alert so we can't help Sandy, either."

"Would you help Sandy?"

Damn, wasn't that the question? As much as she loved Sandy and would sacrifice her career in an instant if that love demanded it, they were still somewhere short of that. And she was also a loyal servant of Callay, and believed wholeheartedly in duty and service, and putting aside personal concerns for the greater good. If Sandy had gone nuts and was trying to kill Ibrahim, or the president, or trying to harm Callay's security in any serious way, that would be different. But this, currently, was just dumb. Sandy was still as loyal to Callay and dedicated to its security as she'd ever been, with an intensity that rivalled even Ibrahim's. It was just that she and Ibrahim were having a very lively disagreement over how that security should best be maintained with respect to New Torah.

"Someone should grab them both by the ear and tell them to sort it out like grownups," she muttered. "Just sit tight, Arvid, I've got some calls to make."

She checked their location—circling somewhere over west-central Tanusha, at two thousand meters and well above the regular traffic.

She made a connection. "Ari," she said without preamble, "I think Ibrahim's going to have to use SIB to go after Sandy. Any movement there?"

"He'd be stupid to," came Ari's voice. *"She'd never fire on CSA or FSA. I wouldn't be so sure about that with SIB."*

"Any idea why he's suddenly going after her, when he didn't stop her leaving the building after she quit yesterday? I mean, he hasn't even accepted her resignation yet."

"I think she's been in contact with Mustafa. That was her whole point—she's still working with him on New Torah, and after Ibrahim's forbidden it, that gives him his excuse."

"And where are you on this?"

"You know, that's a fucking stupid question." Click, and he was gone. Well, that gave her a clear enough answer. It couldn't be easy on Ari. He'd worked with Ibrahim longer than he'd known Sandy; Ibrahim was the only authority figure Ari truly trusted and respected. But evidently, that didn't mean much when it was Sandy in question. And on the matter of New Torah, Ari probably thought that Sandy was right and Ibrahim wrong.

"Christ," she muttered to herself. "This is like civil war without the shooting."

Sandy sat cross-legged and barefoot in the Durga Temple, with a view past many rows of square columns to a city park. On the other side was downtown

Patna—busy sidewalks, traffic and crowds, with a continual smattering of people coming up and down the stairs and into the forest of columns. Here on the park side it was quieter, just a few people sitting, talking, reading or working on mobile devices.

Weller sat nearby, in deep discussion with a local priest about the intersection between Hinduism and Sufi Islam. A dedicated Sufi, Weller was the only GI Sandy had known who was deeply religious. And like any good Sufi, she was very good at finding points of commonality between Islam and every other faith, particularly Hinduism. Both she and the Hindu priest seemed to be having a great time. Sandy wondered what it said about GIs that Weller, unlike most straights, got along far better with people on the question of religion than she did on most other topics. Han, Ogun and Khan sat nearby, waiting, as GIs did very well when required.

A woman in a dress suit came barefoot across the stone floor and greeted them, sitting cross-legged with a smile. "I heard you were here," she said. "I thought I'd come and say hello."

"Hi, Rashmi," said Sandy. Rashmi was a friend of Swami Ananda Ghosh, still a member of the Callayan Parliament, capitalising on Tanusha's proclivity to now and then elect eccentric spiritual oddballs to office. Sandy had become a friend of the Swami's by accident shortly after her arrival on Callay, and had been introduced to Rashmi through him. Technically she was a Hindu priestess, one of Callay's highest in the utterly unreliable way Callay's Hindus rated such things. More specifically she was a priestess of Durga, the eight-armed lady standing watch from the temple's far end with garlands about her stone carved neck, attended by a light but constant stream of worshippers. Rashmi's religious significance entitled her to a significant stipend and free accommodation, but she was a wealthy market analyst with no need for such trifles. Priestess was her other job.

"I didn't tell anyone you were here," Rashmi assured the GIs.

"I didn't ask," Sandy replied. "We'll be gone soon, it's just that this is one of the least monitored spaces in all Tanusha."

"I know, isn't it wonderful? I've love to uplink-shield it completely so people have a space where there's only one thing pressing on their mind, not a million like most of the time. But now we just have to settle for partial blocks."

Rashmi was middle aged, attractive yet with a face that might be stern, were she not so often smiling. Her hair was streaked with grey and she wore no jewellery or makeup. Sandy thought she looked very fit. Lots of Tanushan spirituals were fitness enthusiasts, like the surfing priests at the Shiva temple on Kuvalam Beach.

"Your firm doesn't mind you being away?" Han asked her.

"I'm a partner," said Rashmi with a smile.

"That means she's a part owner," Sandy explained to Han. Han hadn't been a civilian that long, so some of the terms escaped him. "She's her own boss, she can do what she likes."

"Plus of course it's very prestigious and fortunate," Rashmi added. "To have a priestess as a partner. The good publicity gets us lots of clients, so my fellow partners view my time off as an investment. You seem to be in some trouble."

"I've been in far worse," Sandy assured her.

"Durga Puja is next week, yes?" Weller asked Rashmi. Weller wore denim shorts and a T-shirt, hair tied in a short blonde ponytail. Han wore cargo shorts and a loud shirt, as did Ogun, though Khan's shirt was more stylish, too much the dresser to stoop so low. They all carried small backpacks. The four of them looked like tourists, which was the intention. No one in Tanusha glanced twice at tourists.

"It is next week," Rashmi confirmed. "Would you like to come? We should have as many as half a million people just around this temple."

"If we're still alive, I'd love to come," said Weller.

Rashmi looked at Sandy with concern. "But you said it's not too serious."

"I never said that," Sandy said calmly. "I said I've been in worse."

"Cassandra, I cannot be a party to anything that may end in Callayan citizens being hurt. And you have made yourself my concern by sheltering in this temple."

Sandy shook her head. "The only Callayan citizens who may conceivably get hurt here are us." She nodded at the GIs. "We'll not fight back. We know we are guests here, even me, and it would be no way to repay that hospitality. But neither does that mean we shall simply sit and watch as terrible things happen elsewhere that we might be able to prevent."

Rashmi nodded slowly. "You won't tell me what, precisely?"

Sandy shook her head again. "I can't. But you may guess."

"I think so. Ibrahim is adamant it is none of Callay or the Federation's business?"

"Ibrahim perceives that my preferred action would lead to turbulence that would upset the peace, and thus the security of the Federation. He's almost certainly correct. But I maintain that if we abandon morality for security, we are eventually left with neither. Morality is the ultimate underpinning of security. Without it, we are none of us secure."

Rashmi smiled. Then sighed, and shook her head faintly, at some private humour. "Very well," she said. "What can I do to help?"

Han noticed someone familiar approaching. A young man, broad shouldered, dressed touristy like them all. "Poole!" he said with surprise. "You decided to come!"

Ibrahim was called from an important meeting. An aide followed in case of other orders, and Ibrahim leaned against the wall by the conference room doors and put on some shades to better access the uplink visuals.

"*Ibrahim,*" he formulated.

"*Director, we have eyes on the target Poole,*" came the operations coordinator. "*We've traced him to the Durga Temple at Patna. We think it may be a rendezvous. CSA Director Chandrasekar has given his approval to go in, but he'd like a final clearance from you.*"

It felt odd to only have a supervisory role in Callayan security affairs now. But in the meeting he'd just left, they were discussing the deployment of assets a hundred times larger than Chandrasekar had access to. It would take his brain a while to adjust to this new paradigm.

"*I give you my final clearance,*" he said. And hoped that Chandrasekar knew what the hell he was doing.

Ayako finalised tacnet alignment and moved, walking quickly along the downtown Patna pavement to the intersection opposite the Durga Temple. MoB walked with her, slower strides on longer legs.

"No guns Moby," she told him, watching as tacnet changed the traffic lights, and gave them a pedestrian green signal. "Keep your hands visible."

"We're supposed to bring them in unarmed?" MoB asked in disbelief. MoB didn't like being called Moby, but it was a department rule that in a city with this many Mohammeds, alternatives were preferable, even nicknames. And so Mohammed Bilal became MoB which—face it, Ayako had told him—

was cooler than the original. He was a big guy, tall enough for basketball, with angled sideburns and a diamond earstud.

"Use your brain," Ayako told him. "If they want to shoot, we're dead. I'm good, but two hundred of me couldn't take Kresnov, trust me. With her friends, even less chance."

"So what are we doing here?" MoB asked as they strode across the intersection, past rows of waiting traffic. "Committing suicide?"

"Asking them to surrender."

"We can't do that remotely?"

"The way these guys backward-hack transmissions? It's too risky with the new construct still so young. They could find a loose code thread and unravel the whole thing. Besides, this is about psychological pressure. they're already defying Ibrahim and Chandi simply by not coming to work. Directly evading arrest is another step up."

They trotted up the steps to the temple, its huge trapezoid tower soaring overhead, replete with rows of carved statues and decoration. Then up to the main floor, which was open to anyone, like most Tanushan temples. A forest of square pillars, endless rows above a smooth marble floor. Ayako and MoB moved quickly on the diagonal, peering down each long avenue between pillars. Down the far end there were quite a few people, offering garlands and incense to the main statue. Here to one side was a shrine to Lakshmi, surrounded by offerings, and a small queue of worshipers. Tanushan temples were more democratic than old world temples, with their inner sanctums where only Hindus could venture. Old timers and recent immigrants complained of the missing authenticity, while long time Tanushans retorted that the success of Hinduism across the human galaxy was down to its flexibility.

Ayako was a Kresnov fan, and always had been. What she was being asked to do now did not make her happy. But she was also a professional, and knew that Kresnov would not respect her if she refused these orders. Plus, she'd always loved the adrenaline. Despite her serious doubts that any of the GIs would use force against their employers, the mere possibility had her heart thumping, eyes darting to every movement. Kresnov was not only deadly, she was smart. What was she thinking?

"We're sure she came in here?" someone asked on tacnet. Ayako could see the other figures, marked on a temple layout. Ten in all, all CSA Investigations.

Not much firepower against GIs, but like she'd said, if they'd all been SWAT in full armour, it wouldn't have made much difference.

"*Keep your eyes open,*" she replied. The circle on tacnet was closing. "*We know Poole came in here, and he didn't leave. Poole hardly ever goes anywhere away from his piano.*"

She passed another statue, trailing fingers upon the cool stone as she peered about a corner. Nothing down the next avenue between pillars, just some wandering locals, clearly not GIs. At the next corner were two more agents, she could see them on tacnet, so there wasn't much space left in between. Would the GIs really be hiding? If so, it spoke of ambush. Were their intentions really peaceful? What if they were more desperate than anyone realised?

She leaned around the next corner to gesture to the two agents . . . and found a couple of old folks instead, arranging garlands and incense sticks. Ayako blinked. Tacnet showed two agents here, and ten in total, but what the hell was this . . . ?

"*Mark One!*" she announced, the agency code no one ever wanted to hear. "*Mark One, we have been compromised! Tacnet is compromised, reform in temple center for a headcount!*"

But she hadn't seen any of the icons shift or disappear, she thought as she ran through the pillars to the central, open space. Here was a water feature in a square pool, the space surrounding filled with people relaxing, old folks retired on this workday, some parents with kids splashing in the pool. CSA Agents ran in . . . ten agents, but only five dots. Even now, as they watched, on tacnet the other five dots not gathered in the temple's center disappeared. They stared at each other.

"How the fuck did they do that?" one exclaimed. "Did anyone see the shift?"

"We're missing five markers," MoB observed, "and we're chasing five GIs. That's just great."

Ayako couldn't restrain a smile. "That's incredible. Has to be Kresnov. She's amazing."

"So let's get after them!" another agent pressed. "Where did they go?"

"We're not going to find them," Ayako sighed. "I don't know how she broke through tacnet barriers so quickly, but once she can do that, we can't trust any of our systems. She could pretend to be anyone, tell us anything . . ."

She didn't need to say more. This was why Ibrahim had rebooted the entire CSA and FSA constructs in the first place, because Kresnov and friends knew every code and could make fools of them. This shouldn't have been possible. Ibrahim had been assured the new system was water tight, unseen by anyone save a few elite network techs. And even then, much of the code had been randomised, changing itself unpredictably until the moment of propagation. How the hell had she done it?

"If I were you," said a female voice behind them, "I'd let her go." They turned to look, and found an Indian woman in a business suit leaning against a nearby pillar.

"Who are you?" Ayako asked, snap-freezing an image of her face and sending it to network scans.

"Rashmi Chakraborty," said the woman, a moment before the network replied to Ayako's query, telling her just the same thing. "I'm the priestess here."

"You're a friend of hers?"

Rashmi smiled, and walked closer. "Let me tell you this," she said, as though she were doing Ayako a favour. "Only fools and demons pick fights with Durgaji. You would be wise to be neither."

"She's not a Goddess," MoB snorted. "She's an artificial person, and a self important bitch."

"Durgaji is described the same way by her enemies," said Rashmi. "You may not see it, but I swear she is the avatar herself. Pray that you do not meet her darker face."

Hindus and Buddhists had always had fewer problems with GIs than the monotheistic faiths, believing that eternal souls could change vessels and that the vessel's composition was not especially important. The avatar, Rashmi said? A manifestation of Durga then, if not the real thing. Ayako could see how some Hindus might see that in Kresnov.

And her "darker face" would be Kali. Most frequently seen adorned with a necklace of skulls, blades dripping blood in each of her eight hands. Ayako could see how some might see that in Kresnov, too.

Ibrahim strode to the landing platform on the HQ rooftop in the darkening evening. "Reschedule my late appointments," he told the aide following him. "And tell the technical staff that I want plans B and C before my eyes as soon as they have them."

"Yes Director. Do you want me to call your wife and say you won't be home?"

"No," said Ibrahim as the cruiser appeared in the near sky, growing larger against the orange glow of sunset and the silhouettes of a hundred near and distant towers. "That I always do myself."

President Singh demanded to see him. Normally the head of a Federal agency could refuse the Callayan president anything, but this time, as so many times of late, local Callayan security and Federal security were overlapping. With the CSA leading, the FSA were dragged into it whether they liked it or not, and after a day of stalling, President Singh had finally twisted Chandi's arm hard enough to force Ibrahim's compliance as well, if just to keep Chandi's arm in its socket.

The cruiser landed and Ibrahim got in. Immediately it lifted, heading for the Callayan Parliament, some ten minutes flight time through heavy evening traffic. Lost in thought, he barely noticed the agent alongside, in the backseat, turn to look at him. He returned a glance . . . and was almost unsurprised to find Cassandra Kresnov barely an arm's breadth away. Almost.

He nearly laughed. "Oh Cassandra," he sighed. "How in the world, I almost don't want to ask."

"But you will anyway," said Cassandra. "Because you're you."

"Where are the cruiser's crew?"

"I imagine they're fine. This isn't your cruiser, it's an identical one we picked up. You've been compromised, and nothing is safe. Not cruiser transponders, not identification codes, not basic communications. We gave your real cruiser a false message and placed a com bubble around them. They won't realise all their incoming traffic is false for a while yet."

Ibrahim tilted his head back to stare at the roof for a moment in exasperation. "The FSA's systems are in that bad shape?"

"No," said Cassandra, mildly. She was wearing a CSA agent's suit with a pronounced female cut to it. She wore it well. "Your systems are actually quite good. Especially this new reboot, first class stuff. Unfortunately, I'm quite good at sequencing widely dispersed pattern encoding. I've been with you guys for a long time now."

Ibrahim frowned. Network systems weren't his specialty, but he knew enough. "There's not enough pattern repetition in our systems for you to find any security variable in the new reboot. I was assured of it. The statistical likelihood against it was in the trillions."

Cassandra pursed her lips. Nodded. "Thing with statistical predictions is they're based on models, and your models are only as good as what you know. You guys don't really know me that well."

"You hacked in." Her blue eyes just gazed at him. "In a few hours? That's impossible."

"Said the caveman to the simtech." Something about her expression bothered him. Not alarming, just disconcerting. Utterly calm, yet faintly amused. Like a scientist studying a rat in a cage, wondering what it would do. "There's a lot of things I haven't been allowed to do, working for the CSA and FSA. I'm not feeling so restrained right now. In seven years a girl can accumulate a lot of experimental ideas. I've been working on coding routines of dubious legality for a while. Naidu's seen a few of them."

Ibrahim remembered. Naidu discussing with some incredulity the latest surveillance routines that Cassandra had introduced to CSA Investigations as a point of conversation, she insisted, nothing more. That conversation had become a full on controversy, ethics and lawyers all scratching their heads well into the night. Those routines had run stress patterns over vulnerable construct segments, measured results and compiled them in way that allowed a user to run what were effectively psychological profiles on the creator of any significantly large network software, like reading a novel to determine a psychological profile on the author, only far more accurate. Statistically, alarmingly accurate, it turned out.

Even Ariel Ruben had called it "crazy voodoo shit," and found the implications a little scary, in the hands of security agencies. That particular routine still languished in the too hard basket. Cassandra had just shrugged, expressing unconcern either way. Ibrahim had found that concerning, that the ethical issues hadn't seemed to alarm her, when she was usually so careful. Or perhaps, he thought now, she'd merely been testing them. She had that look now. The look of an interrogator, judging his every reaction.

Ibrahim looked to the driver's seat. "Is that Han up there?"

Han waved without looking back. "Hello, Director. I hope this won't count against me in my performance review."

"Goodness, no, you've just kidnapped the FSA Director," Ibrahim said with mild exasperation. "Why should that count against you?"

"We've done no such thing," said Cassandra. "We're just giving you a ride to the Parliament. When we get there, you're free to carry on your business. I just wanted to talk, face to face."

"Cassandra," said Ibrahim with a frown, "you know very well that had you wished to arrange it, I would have allowed that at any time. You're like a daughter to me. We currently find ourselves at odds, but should you wish to meet under a flag of truce, I would have come alone."

"You know I don't work that way."

"No, you seek every advantage. It's what makes you formidable." The cruiser banked through darkening skies, towers passing, lights just now brightening their soaring glass facades. "Cassandra, whatever my affection for you, I cannot stress enough my disappointment. I feel you've taken advantage of our relationship, and taken your duties lightly. This is effectively a coup. A coup against Federal security policy. I cannot on principle allow it to succeed. And as such, you cannot hope to win this struggle, for you know that even should you do me harm, I would never change my position."

Cassandra looked for a moment out the windows, at the sprawling, endless city. As though sighting something far distant, that no one else could see.

"I'm sorry for all of this," she said quietly. "Lately I've been wondering if my emotions are the same as those of normal humans . . . I mean, when I say 'love.' and you say 'love,' do we truly mean the same thing? And how would we know, without personal experience of exactly what the other person is feeling?"

"Not merely a problem between synthetic and organic," Ibrahim agreed. "A problem between all human beings, and that surely includes you."

That seemed to touch her. For all her control, Ibrahim knew her to be actually quite bad at hiding her emotions. She expressed them calmly, almost placidly at times, but when they shone, they shone bright.

"Well whatever I or you might call it, I love you," she said simply. "But you're killing me. You're killing all of us. Every time GI technology advances, it finds us. And we're easy to find, here on Callay, center of the Federation. Jane came to find me. Mustafa did. Eduardo. Even these, my friends. They all come to find me eventually. The new generation from New Torah will come too, eventually, because in my position I'm a threat. And this time I'm not just going to sit here and wait."

"That may be your choice," Ibrahim replied, forcing his tone to calm. Her words made sense, but did not change what needed to be done. "But you do not have the right to drag the rest of the Federation into your personal war, however much I or others may sympathise. Please understand, Cassandra, that if this were up to me personally, and what I believe in my heart to be right and good, I would have us committed to solving the New Torah problem in an instant. But my heart is not in consideration here. It is my head that must rule these decisions. And my head says that whatever New Torah's potential threat, the League has demonstrated that it views any preemptive action against New Torah as verging upon a new declaration of war. Considering what the last war cost us all, that is too high a price, and the price is not mine to pay."

"Do you understand why I'm a threat?" She gazed at him closely. Those pale blue eyes were so full of life.

"You have insight into GI development that has already influenced myself and others to move heavily against New Torah," Ibrahim replied. "But we lost that battle, Cassandra . . ."

"We did not. You conceded it."

"Given my position, your distinction is meaningless."

"I don't think so," she said softly.

"Cassandra." The cruiser was beginning its approach toward the Parliament building now, a gentle turn and descend. "I know that you respect democracy. I know that you do not believe that your voice alone should carry a greater weight than any person's. Yet your actions do not demonstrate it."

"We work in security," said Cassandra. "The common people have no say in our decisions either way, yours or mine. Or did you consult them before arriving at your current position?"

"I am just now about to consult with their elected representative," Ibrahim said sternly. "As I have been in constant consultation with the Federal representatives. They can overrule me if they wish."

"They are not in possession of all the facts."

Ibrahim sighed. He'd expected better from her. "And you are?" he suggested.

"More than you."

"And yet I remain unconvinced."

Cassandra smiled.

The cruiser disappeared. Ibrahim was seated on an open floor before grand Corinthian pillars, overlooking an old city. Rome, he recognised immediately. Ancient Rome, with all its sights and smells. It took several moments to overcome the disorientation. This was VR. It was very, very impressive VR. He could feel the old chair's hard edges digging into his thighs, hard leather against his back. The immediate smell was incense, but more distantly there came animal manure. Hooves clopped down nearby streets, and a rattle of passing carts.

"Cassandra?" Ibrahim asked cautiously. He'd been barrier hacked before, but only as a demonstration. This was his first time without warning. As FSA Director, he was supposed to be far too well equipped for it to happen. "Cassandra, this is a very nice trick, but you insisted this was not a kidnapping. I fear that legally it may have just become one."

Brain napping, the media called it. It required ridiculous amounts of rapid processing power, an overwhelmingly large containment matrix, and a real-time map of every integrated network function his nervous system had been upgraded with. Regular humans couldn't do it, it needed AIs, and most AIs were far too civilised to engage in something like this. GIs, evidently, were different. Or this one was.

"I didn't know you could do this," he admitted, looking around him. If he'd had no memory of how he'd arrived here, he'd have sworn it was real. He stood up. Even that felt real.

"Neither did I," said Cassandra. She swept before him, now wearing a lacy Roman gown, white with gold trim. And provocative, slit up one leg and entirely bare at the back. Her previously mid-length hair was now curled and swept with combs, and threaded with braid. "But as I said, I've been experimenting. I was designed with this in mind as much as anything else, yet my network abilities remain the most under explored capabilities I have, thanks to my usual operating restrictions."

Ibrahim did not know what to think of the gown. It was so unlike her—not that she objected to such styles, just that she knew what she was, and it was not this. But here on the network, of course, she could dress any way she chose and not compromise her safety, or her nature. Partly, Ibrahim suspected, it was playful provocation. Any heterosexual man would notice her, dressed like this. That he was devout, and loved his wife, she would never doubt. And so he found the dress . . . frustrating. Perhaps even faintly angering. It showed a lack of respect for the relationship they had, teasing him with the promise of something unwanted and disruptive.

"Why here?" he asked her.

"To show you," she said simply. She beckoned for him to walk to the view. He followed, and her hips sauntered. So much she'd learned in her seven years as a civilian. "It's not possible, you know. Not against your will, not even for most GIs."

"This is a 150 Tigs construct at least," Ibrahim affirmed, looking around.

"Two hundred and ten," Cassandra corrected, showing him the view. "To bring the FSA Director here against his will took some doing. To hold him here in such a state requires some new tricks."

"Which new tricks?" Getting angry at her would achieve nothing. She controlled this space, and even if he could lay a finger on her, this was of course not real, and she could not be harmed. And probably her combat skills translated to this place, anyway.

"As I said, I've been experimenting. We evolve, you know. I've evolved, and not merely as a person. Technologically, up here." She tapped the side of her head, behind the ear—the traditional location of uplinks. "The next generation shall be even more advanced, and they'll learn better tricks than mine."

"A regular human mind is more susceptible to VR simulations than a GI's," said Ibrahim. "I hadn't thought you could even experience this environment."

"Until recently, neither did I. But technology moves on. Here, let me show you this."

Ancient Rome vanished, and they were standing in a narrow, crowded lane. It was hot, but the walls provided shade. Everything was commotion, people walking, carrying things, hawkers shouting, mules hauling loads. From the people's look and dress, Ibrahim guessed North India. Again, it was very pretechnological.

"Come," said Cassandra. Now she wore a lehenga choli in the traditional embroidered style, a pleated skirt and short bra top, even more provocative than the Roman dress, it left her entire middle bare. She moved down the lane and Ibrahim followed. It was a busy market lane, crowds, sellers and buyers on all sides. Spices assaulted the nostrils, flames from passing cookeries glared upon the skin. Here were fabrics of kaleidoscopic colours, and there jewellery, rows and rows of gold and silver bangles. There were Sikhs and Rajputs in turbans, Muslims in skullcaps, arguments and hawkers' cries in Hindustani, Urdu, Persian, Punjabi, Kashmiri. No English, so this was pre-Raj.

Men bumped him in passing, and his arm felt the impact. He did not wish to test the very realistic cow shit in the lane by stepping in it. Now he was truly amazed. This was the hardest thing to animate in VR—people. More than people, these were crowds, doing all those things that crowds did, with sounds, smells and colours almost overwhelming. In fact, if one wished to show off the technological prowess of one's VR matrix, an ancient Indian marketplace would be just about the most complicated thing to animate. Even the very modern markets here in Tanusha were approaching sensory overload, but this old-fashioned chaos was something else again.

"Well, now I am very impressed," he admitted, following Cassandra about a corner. The surest sign that the scene was not real—Cassandra was the only woman in sight, and yet all these rough and moustachioed men did not turn to stare, as the lehenga choli revealed curves and her blonde hair flashed in the occasional splash of sunlight between buildings. "What period are we?"

"A few more corners and you will see," she returned past her shoulder. They walked some more, turning corners and lanes, and Ibrahim reflected that the absence of wandering cows probably meant the Mughal period . . . and then the lanes ended and a grand space opened before them.

Here was a mosque, huge and wide, with great walls and minarets. Its three enormous teardrop domes remained in the final stages of construction, surrounded by scaffolding.

"Jama Masjid," Ibrahim murmured. "We are in Delhi, 1656." And what they'd been walking through was the Chawri Bazar. "The time of Shah Jahan."

"One of your ancestors," Cassandra suggested.

Ibrahim shrugged. "Perhaps. Most of India's invaders came through Afghanistan at some point." He looked about. The wide scene was now suddenly vast with open space, yet about them people still crowded. For the VR to be processing at once vast spaces and market crowds . . . "I can't imagine how many Tigs this takes to generate."

"Thousands," said Cassandra.

"That's not possible," said Ibrahim. "The technology does not exist."

"For integration with the human brain, no," said Cassandra. "But as I said, you don't know me very well."

Jama Masjid and old Delhi abruptly vanished. Now they stood in a room. It was the president's room in the Parliament building. Here were the old familiar furnishings, the desk behind which Katia Neiland had once sat. Now the space was occupied by President Singh, gazing into space. Also present in various chairs were senior advisors, several cabinet ministers, and some security men, some standing, a few sitting. None of them moved.

"This scene is not so challenging," said Ibrahim. "Twenty Tigs at most."

Cassandra was wearing her CSA suit now. She sat on the president's desk, right before his vacant gaze. "Zero Tigs," she said.

Ibrahim blinked. Then stared about. The main difference between this scene and those previous was that in this one, the people did not move. He knelt abruptly and ran his hand over the floor rug. It bristled against his hand in the way that only true texture could.

He stared up at Cassandra, as she drew up her legs and sat fully cross-legged on the desk. "This is real?" he breathed. Cassandra nodded. The look was back, the lab rat was being watched.

Why were the people not moving? Ibrahim walked to the nearest—Communications Minister Petrov. She stood easily enough, all motor functions operational; she blinked and breathed and showed every sign of neurological health. Save that she did not move, nor seem to react to anything around her. None of them did.

Leaning against a far wall, he spotted a face familiar from security briefings—Poole, he recalled the GI's name. Arms folded and watching him, expression not unlike Cassandra's. Against another wall, Han, more familiar. And Ogun, by the door. Only the regular humans were immobilised.

"You hacked them all?" It wasn't possible. It was so far beyond impossible it lay outside comprehension. Cassandra just looked at him, with cross-legged insolence on the president's desk. Ibrahim put both hands to his face. "What have you done?"

"Scratched the surface," said Cassandra. "I haven't had cause to explore it before. But GIs were made from inception to process information. Tacnet was the greatest innovation of infantry combat since the firearm, and information processing creates situational awareness. I process at seventeen times beyond what any regular human can, as you know.

"But you don't know what that means. I didn't, until recently. Many high-designation GIs, coordinating together, can maintain containment matrixes for high level VR functions that increase exponentially in power. I came across it practising for Pyeongwha—we tried all sorts of new stuff there. GIs are made to operate in an information environment, and here in a civilian city, with all these open and hackable networks, we just process so much faster than anyone else. Doubtless the defensive writers will find counter codes to this once they realise the risk, and then begins the usual arms race of offensive and defensive software, but I'm starting to write the stuff myself again now, and I know so much more than I did. It turns out I'm better at that than the very best regular human programmers. I'm built for it. And with friends helping, I could go even faster."

The walk through Chawri Bazar, Ibrahim realised. She'd been navigating him through the halls of the Parliament building. He'd actually been walking, for real, like a zombie, thinking he was time-frozen in the cruiser. But she'd let immersion time run real-time, and Allah knew how she'd managed that. Time was supposed to run much slower in full immersion VR. What had happened to all the people they'd surely passed along the way? Had they been hacked, too? Was the whole Parliament building network down?

"This VR stuff is an amazing thing," she said, leaning forward slightly in her cross-legged pose, as though to make a point. "Regular human brains are fooled by it. I'm not. If I get it set up well like this, in systems I'm familiar with, I can just turn you off. All of you."

Now Ibrahim was properly alarmed. "Cassandra," he said, "this is not ethical. You release these people at once."

"You're damn right it's not ethical," Cassandra replied, her eyes narrowing. "I'm not built to be ethical. I'm built to dominate. I'm unequal. Understand what that means. It means that the worst fears of all the GI-haters out there are right. I could be the death of you all, should I choose, and should my friends choose with me. I could end this civilisation."

Ibrahim stared at her.

"Now imagine that there's a place out there in League space that is trying to improve on me, using unsafe technologies that could turn the next generation of GIs into psychopathic monsters. And understand that if they succeed, then not only is Callay not safe, but none of us are. I think it's possible that what you see me do here, is just the tip of the iceberg. If I'm right, then even I can't protect you from that next wave. They'll take me out first, and that'll be it. It—do you understand me? No more. No more any of this, this wonderful, free civilisation, filled with wonderful people whom I've grown to love so much.

"Now, I'm sorry I've had to make this demonstration, but understand you've only seen the tip of what I can do, because I've only seen the tip. I'm still learning. Pray that whatever comes next from New Torah does not know more and learn faster. Now, while you're here, will you please discuss with this damn fool of a president why we need to go hard after New Torah, irrespective of whatever threats the League makes? Or do I have to wake him up and do it myself?"

CHAPTER FOURTEEN

Two months later, Vanessa was having a day off at the Tanusha Zoo when she received a message from Justice Rosa, asking if he could come and talk with her briefly. "About our mutual friend," he said.

Vanessa agreed. They'd spoken a few times, always about their "mutual friend," sometimes to get a second perspective on events, and also as a character reference. Vanessa assured him that he had no chance of getting an objective opinion from her, but Justice didn't mind. "You can tell as much about a person by their friends and enemies as you can from the person themselves," he'd replied.

Tanusha Zoo was amazing, with one of the biggest collections of xeno-biology anywhere in the Federation. She walked the enclosures and displays with Phillippe, Rhian, Rakesh, Salman and the twins. The jungle enclosures were huge and lush, populated by amazing, multi-legged creatures that howled and whooped, and lizards that flew, and birds that changed colour before your eyes. The marine section was also superb, with great underwater viewing windows to see huge, multi-finned predators from various watery worlds, and aquapods that were like great winged squid, moving with water jet propulsion, and communicated in complex codes with electric body flashes that could be seen in dark water.

But everyone loved the methane breathers best. Those enclosures were underground, and though viewing was restricted behind heavy glass and in atmosphere thick like soup, the creatures here were utterly alien, from ground hugging, multi-legged scuttlers to hive writhers that looked like a giant mass of snakes writhing together, but were actually just one creature. Salman stared goggle-eyed like all boys his age, and Sunita, one of the twins, got scared and began crying. Phillippe loved it every bit as much as Salman, and explained to him what crazy conditions existed on many of the worlds where these creatures lived, and how that had affected their evolution.

"He's good with kids, yeah?" Rakesh said suggestively to Vanessa near the enclosure for bubbleskinks, which could inflate like a giant ball, and in the low gravity of its home world, float away on updrafts. Here, giant fans were simulating the drafts and low gravity.

"I'm sorry he's borrowed your son," Vanessa said diplomatically. "I promise he'll return him undamaged when he's finished."

"He's welcome, I've got my hands full." Rakesh had Sunita in one arm, offering a broad chest she could press her face into when she didn't want to look at any of the scary animals. Maria, less timid than her sister, was with Rhian, face pressed to the glass. "But maybe he wants a boy of his own?"

Vanessa shook her head. "We've got a girls' club, it'll be a girl."

And that made her sad, because the girls' club was incomplete at the moment. Sandy loved the zoo, and loved spending casual time with her best friends. Vanessa missed her terribly.

Justice contacted again to say he'd arrived, and Vanessa directed him to the methane breathers' enclosure exit. He was waiting there when they came out, blinking in the sunshine. Vanessa suggested the others grab an ice cream with the kids, but Phillippe recognised the tall man in the cycle shorts, leaning on his twenty-four speed road bike.

"That's Justice Rosa!" he exclaimed. "Is that who you're meeting?"

"He's writing a book on Sandy, remember?" Like a lot of brilliant people, Phillippe was occasionally forgetful. "I've spoken with him a few times."

"Well I want to meet him," Phillippe insisted. And put a finger to her lips before she could think of a reason otherwise. "Come, I've read everything he's written. You can't have all the interesting life to yourself, you know."

"Yeah, like your superstar musician's life is so boring," Vanessa retorted as Phillippe led her over. "Pretty girls fawning over you at every expensive function."

"I know, isn't it a drag? Sometimes I even have to marry them." Vanessa laughed, and elbowed him.

Certainly her husband was no shrinking violet. "Hello!" he said brightly, with an outstretched hand to Justice. "I'm Phillippe Hurot, Vanessa's husband. You're one of my favorite writers, I'm very pleased to meet you."

"And likewise," said Justice. "I was at your concert two weeks ago, the Vivaldi one. Just marvellous."

Phillippe beamed, and they talked music and writing for a little. Not for the first time, Vanessa found herself wondering how a SWAT grunt had come to move in such circles. When she'd entered the business world out of college, she'd imagined climbing the great heights of Tanushan society, and meeting people like these at expensive parties. When she'd abandoned that world for the CSA, she'd thought she was abandoning all of those high society dreams in the process. But the universe played funny games sometimes.

"Well," said Justice, sipping at his bicycle's water bottle, "I don't have news on Sandy, exactly." Vanessa wasn't certain when Justice had begun referring to Sandy by her nickname. She hoped it was a sign of affection, and that his book would reflect it. "But I was just at the Ahimsa Hotel, meeting with the League Under Secretary of Trade, who's in town at the moment."

"I know," said Vanessa. "His security plan's a pain. Lots of unreasonable demands. You'd think he's never been somewhere where people would like to kill him before."

"Given he's from the League, that does seem unlikely," Justice agreed. "Anyhow, I was asked a lot of questions about Sandy. Too many questions. It seems the League have heard about my book."

"Our protection offer remains open," Vanessa said flatly. "You've been told it could be trouble, we weren't kidding."

"I'm thinking on it," Justice admitted. Vanessa was surprised. She'd expected Justice to continue to refuse CSA protection outright.

"You don't think . . . ?" Phillippe began, concerned and puzzled. "Why would the League want to threaten a writer writing a book?"

"Sandy knows things she hasn't spoken of yet that the League will find embarrassing," Vanessa explained patiently. "And they might just want to find out what she knows, for which a writer is a far easier target than she is."

"There were questions in particular about the President's Office incident," Justice added.

"The what incident?" asked Phillippe.

"Oh, great," Vanessa sighed. "You're not supposed to hear that. I'm going to have to take you to our lab and have your brain erased."

"You wouldn't," said Phillippe. Then looked at Justice, amusement fading. "She can't, can she? I mean, they don't have any technology like that?"

"Oh, it exists," Justice assured him. "In a mild form. Whether they actually use it is another matter."

"Please stop corrupting my husband," Vanessa said sternly.

"But you know I like to be corrupted," her husband teased. "What's the President's Office incident?"

Vanessa just looked at him. She wasn't amused at all. They'd had this discussion before, and he'd agreed—he wouldn't ask questions where she judged it could cause trouble, for both of them. But Phillippe was born curious.

He saw her look, and sighed. "Okay. Very well." And his face just kind of . . . closed off. That upset her. She loved Phillippe for his enthusiasm and love of life. Now she had to step on that enthusiasm, and it hurt like a physical pain.

"They know rather a lot," said Justice. "More than I do."

Vanessa didn't bother asking where Justice got his sources. Intel was of the opinion that he was safe enough, for as long as he saw personal profit in maintaining exclusivity. Plus he had a reputation for integrity, but Intel was full of suspicious characters who didn't trust that kind of thing.

"What did you tell them?" she asked.

"Nothing. I smiled politely and changed the subject."

"Did they ask where Sandy is now?"

"Oh, I think they know. They're not stupid. And why else would they be asking about the President's Office incident?" He sipped his water bottle. "They're still there. The Ahimsa Hotel. They've set up a bear pit on the lower business level, I got the impression they'd be there all day. I saw various important officials calling in, some government, some private. League officials are very popular these days."

Phillippe's downcast mood only lasted until Justice had pedalled off. "You want to go to the hotel, yes?"

"I won't get authorisation," said Vanessa, thinking hard as they walked toward the refreshment outlet. Somewhere in the crowd of visitors were Rhian, Rakesh and the kids. "It's an Intel job, not for SWAT."

"But Intel will already be there, yes? They will not miss an opportunity to poke around the League delegation and see what questions they are asking?"

Vanessa gave him a sideways look. Not stupid, her husband, and reading lots of spy novels actually could give someone a few ideas of how these things worked. A lot of those authors were retired agents and pretty good; she'd read a few herself.

"I'm worried they'll miss something." She stopped, gnawing at her lip. Phillippe stopped with her. "Obviously the League knows Sandy's gone to New Torah, which means they know FSA and CSA are lying to them. So now they send a high level delegation and ask questions of everyone except the FSA and CSA. It's pretty fucking brazen."

"Maybe they know how tight security is for them now," Phillippe offered. "Maybe it's easier to operate in plain sight than to try and sneak around."

Not stupid at all. Phillippe didn't know much about Mustafa and the ISO, who were even now helping with whatever Sandy was doing in New Torah. But unwittingly he was right—without the ISO's help, any non-ISO League operatives would find it very hard to move around Tanusha quietly. And to the best of anyone's knowledge, the ISO and the current League administration were still not on speaking terms.

"Look," said Phillippe, eyes lighting up, "how about we go and talk to them?"

"Phillippe," she began.

"No!" he cut her off, all animation. "I'm the superstar famous musician, yes?" Vanessa raised an eyebrow. "I go and say that my friend Justice was just here and said that the League Minister of Trade would like to meet with me . . ."

"Under Secretary of Trade," Vanessa corrected.

"Exactly, yes, that he would like to meet with me, and you can make with me a tacnet link, and I can get you preliminary intelligence, yes? Scout out the hotel, because of course they have your face on record, but not mine . . ."

"But a simple net search will show you're my husband."

"And so what?" His hands spread wide. "You will be outside somewhere! Maybe they suspect I'm spying, but I am an inexperienced agent, they are experienced agents, maybe they think I'm out of my depth . . ."

"With reason."

"Yes, but you can monitor me, and the moment there is anything you don't like, you say leave and I leave. I'll make them tasty bait though, if they think they can trick me into saying things, you know, the inexperienced agent recruit who knows too much?"

Too many spy novels indeed. God help her, it was actually not a bad plan. Agencies did this sort of thing all the time, recruiting non-agents as intelligence sources. This was very safe ground, in a big public hotel in Tanusha— lots of security around, them knowing they were being watched every second . . . and yes, knowing he was the husband of Tanusha's senior-most SWAT agent was a very tasty opportunity for them, because he knew things that might be valuable, yet lacked the training to defend what he knew.

Vanessa pulled at her face with a hand, thinking. Phillippe waited with puppy dog excitement. She couldn't tread on his enthusiasm again. The long term view of what would happen to their marriage if she made a habit of it was not something she enjoyed looking at.

He read her face. "Yes?" Vanessa sighed, glumly. "Yes, yes, yes!" He hugged her. "Come on, we can do this together. Very romantic."

"Babe," she warned him, "I stopped thinking this was romantic the first time I saw an Intel operative get plugged between the eyes when the operation went bad."

"Yes," he said, sobering fast. "Okay. Very serious, I understand."

Vanessa didn't believe a word of it. Though if she thought for a second that it might be genuinely dangerous, she'd never have said yes. This was a government delegation, as physically harmless as they came. And they knew that these days, Callay's temper with all visiting potential troublemakers was short.

Intel had several people in the Ahimsa Hotel, and were worried that they didn't have enough bases covered. Plenty of shooters and snoops, Chandi told her, but not enough bait. Phillippe fit their needs perfectly.

"Okay, you've been greenlit," she told him as the maglev zoomed over Tanushan suburbs. Phillippe beamed, and tugged his nice, open collar jacket down neatly. "Chandi says nothing stupid, they've got the whole place watched, don't ask silly suspicious questions, just be yourself and make small talk."

"You know, darling, I'm very good at small talk." He kissed her.

"I know." It would be just like one of those soirees that Vanessa mostly disliked, and Phillippe excelled at. Truthfully, he got tired of them also, but that didn't mean he wasn't good at them. "Remember who you are, you're a famous musician, your curiosity was sparked by your friend Justice Rosa, and of course your other friends Cassandra Kresnov and Rhian Chu . . ."

". . . and I'm interested in the music scene in the League," Phillippe continued, "because maybe I could even do some concerts there one day, and the possibilities for travel arrangements and visas, maybe something to do with these peace and reconciliation tours the Federation Department of Arts is always arranging. And I'll also be interested in the humanitarian concerns about the League's GIs, since my friend Cassandra is obviously upset about it, so naturally I am too."

"Yes," Vanessa affirmed. "Perfect. Don't show interest in anything you can't explain your interest in. Another thing—the President's Office incident."

Phillippe looked surprised. "Yes?"

"I'm authorised to tell you, since they're already asking questions. It's something Sandy did, with a few GI friends. No one knows exactly what, but evidently it changed Ibrahim and Chandi's minds about New Torah, and that's why Sandy's out there now with full support."

"Something happened in the President's Office?"

Vanessa nodded. "No one involved will say. Whatever she did, it scared the shit out of them."

"No one knows what?" he asked. Vanessa shook her head. "A demonstration maybe? Of what?"

"I think I know," Vanessa said grimly. "But that, dearest, is a GFS."

A Genuine Fucking Secret. It was their own personal acronym, and Phillippe held up his hands, conceding with a smile. "That's okay. I don't need to know that." He grasped her hand. "Sandy will be all right. You know how tough she is. She can survive anything. She will be back shortly and she'll be fine, I promise."

He meant it as reassurance, and that was nice. But he couldn't promise anything of the sort, and Vanessa only smiled, wanly, and gazed out the window.

Vanessa went and got a coffee in the groovy establishment across the road from Ahimsa Hotel. It had an upstairs section with tables, and big windows with a view across a crowded city road. This was downtown Subianto, big towers and crowds everywhere, it made surveillance and security operations tricky.

Internal vision showed tacnet, and Phillippe entering the upstairs lobby and talking to people. There was a big cocktail set here, cordoned off by ropes, manned by local hotel security—nothing official from either side here, that she could see through Phillippe's eyes. Frustratingly, he only had standard civvie uplinks, the kind you could get installed in an hour at a local clinic, then leave to propagate over perhaps a month and monitored by a network overseer. It meant his processing speeds were slower, and the vision feed kept fuzzing, starved of pixels. There were times she'd realised that he didn't really understand how much more advanced her systems were, especially after recent upgrades. CSA neuroscientists did papers on her, she was one of the best integrators they'd ever seen. She'd seen graphic modelling of her brain lately, showing synaptic increase of up to forty percent in high-traffic regions—an entirely natural phenomenon to deal with increased traffic. Brains weren't so different from muscles—exercise them frequently, and they would grow.

Phillippe talked his way sweetly past the hotel security admitting people into the bearpit, as CSA called such VIP hotel gatherings.

"*Good,*" Vanessa formulated, sipping coffee. "*Someone will scan you pretty soon, they'll check your face and net-trace. Go to the bar, someone will come to you.*"

He did that. She looked about her establishment, refocusing past net vision. Lots of people, mostly office workers out early, doing afternoon errands, working on portables. In another hour the rush would start, then it would get really crowded. Quite possible that someone's security was here with her, friendly or otherwise—this place had a good view. CSA control had the whole region's network locked down, and any odd transmissions would be spotted. The bad guys didn't have that luxury.

Phillippe's feed showed a woman in a low cut dress, smiling and shaking Phillippe's hand. Pretty, blonde, European. Sophisticated. Big tits, once again.

"*Steady, boy,*" said Vanessa. "*You do realise this feed is following your vision?*" With adjustments for wobble and rapid movement, of course, or she'd get motion sick. The blonde girl finished introductions, and led Phillippe away from the bar and through the crowd. Backless dress. Nice ass. Swaying, back and forth, back and forth . . . Vanessa grinned. "*You and me are going to have a little talk when this is over.*"

She wasn't going to get a reply from him. He wasn't as good at internal formulation; it took practise and higher level upgrades than he possessed. She'd only hear him when he spoke. The girl made an introduction to someone . . . audio wasn't great either, but Vanessa heard "Assistant Secretary to the Under Secretary," which was good. Phillippe was making progress. Soon he'd be passed up the chain. Already, some higher League spook would be receiving notification and putting Phillippe on his schedule. A drink was pressed into his hand, and small talk ensued.

Vanessa passed time scanning the hotel network. She was nowhere near as fast at this kind of thing as Ari, to say nothing of Sandy, but as she made her leisurely way around the complex bundles of pulsating lines and graphical representations, she could clearly see how the CSA's constructs had integrated themselves into the hotel's information matrix. There was a lot of traffic going in all directions, of course, most of it oblivious—lots of business travellers doing their work, tourists relaxing on high-end VR, complex webs of information branching like micro-roots off a tree, spreading into the surrounding maze.

CSA tacnet had a useful function, tracking all hotel in and outflows, so she used it, seeking a couple of useful parameters she was familiar with from spending so much time with GIs lately. Almost immediately she had a hit, zoomed on it, and became concerned.

"Central, what is this? Is this a GI signature?"

It was always the worry, with League operatives. League GIs weren't allowed off embassy grounds without special clearance. Mustafa had one, but Mustafa was ISO, and ISO weren't on good terms with this party at the Ahimsa Hotel. Not all League GIs were ISO, of course—in fact, Mustafa was quite rare. But not many of the rest were cleared for this kind of intel work.

The signature disappeared. Vanessa frowned, searching fast.

"I'm sorry Jailbait, repeat that last?" came Central's reply.

"Someone's processing seriously fast in there," said Vanessa. *"Third floor, room by the elevators."*

"We'll have someone check it out."

Vanessa had no doubt they would, but it gave her a bad feeling. League software. Sandy occasionally pulled out some nasty tricks that had the best Federation people shaking their heads in disbelief. Not so much superior software as different, as all League and Federation infotech had diverged over the many decades and light years of estrangement. Like two separate species of the same animal evolving on separate continents, given enough time they wouldn't look too similar at all. The best Federation work, particularly Tanushan work, gave League specialists the shits, as they had nothing to counter it with. Ditto League functions in Tanusha.

She set up an analysis function and began entering parameters. Full VR would have been faster for input, but she didn't want to be seen typing the empty air at her table before the windows. Sandy would do this in a microsecond, she thought with exasperation. Phillippe's group had been joined by someone else—a woman, older. More handshakes. Personal assistant to the Under Secretary, no less. Big fan of European classical, had no idea it was so popular on Callay given the preference for South Asian classical.

Vanessa would have bet her eyeteeth this was an agent. Personal assistant was an ideal position—a multi-purpose organiser with contacts everywhere. But she didn't want to make Phillippe anxious, so she said nothing.

She finished with the parameters, and activated. Scans ran for a few seconds, then a reply. Fuck. Her eyes widened. Was something wrong with the system?

"Central, I just ran a scan on the hotel's intra-networks. Inputs and outputs don't match."

Pause from Central. *"Hello Jailbait, please explain?"* He didn't sound very interested, the usual way with Intel network specialists dealing with SWAT grunts. Although her call sign probably didn't help. It was an internal joke in SWAT: small and cute, she was 42 years old but was still asked for ID at clubs.

"Network inputs and outputs in a closed building system have to match, right? These don't match, it's like they're running a much larger, enclosed system in there somewhere."

"Jailbait give me the parameters of your scan, I'll double check it." No doubt thinking the SWAT grunt had stuffed it up. Vanessa sent, and waited. Pause. *"That's very interesting,"* said Central. Puzzled. Puzzled wasn't good. *"Someone should check that out."*

Vanessa walked in. She bypassed the bearpit completely, with its well dressed crowds and awful lobby music, and headed straight for the elevators. She was armed, of course, as she was every day now, on duty or otherwise. These days, you just never knew when you were going to need it, and she felt nearly naked without the pistol weight against her ribs.

She went up to the third floor, the first major floor above the high ceiling of the lobby. There was a sky bridge here across the side of the lobby, and she walked straight, heading for convention rooms on the far side, where hotel staff were setting up chairs and refreshments for some later function. A few of them glanced at her. Probably there were League security disguised here somewhere, but Vanessa didn't care. They knew they were being watched, and she didn't care if they knew. Someone might vis-scan her face and connect it to her husband downstairs, but fuck it. Sandy had long ago taught her that nervous enemies were preferable to confident ones.

She walked through convention rooms, then into a new hallway. Nothing. She headed for the bathrooms off the hallway. Where would you set up some kind of separate matrix? Not from the guest rooms, those had too many points of ingress for back hacking. One of these lower rooms then. Internal vision showed Phillippe being led to a smaller back room. Plenty of people around, and the new room looked to have better drinks, and food. And here was the Under Secretary himself, a cheerful black guy delighted to make Phillippe's acquaintance.

Great way to meet everyone in Tanusha, Vanessa reflected as she checked first the men's, then the women's bathrooms. Set up in a big hotel for a day or two, and let everyone come to you in informal circumstances. Chaotic security environment, hard to keep track of everything, not like these one-on-one meetings they usually did that were so easy to spy on.

She headed on to the gymnasium, then the swimming pool, then the outer patio deck overlooking crowded Patna streets. Nothing.

Tacnet showed her an agent was coming to help her. Good, they'd cover more ground more quickly together. She walked to the hallway junction and sure enough, there was one of the hotel staff who'd been helping arrange the banquet in the other rooms. They made eye contact on approach. Obviously it was a CSA Agent—an attractive woman, slenderish, dark hair tied back in a serviceable bun, wearing hotel uniform. And her stride was . . .

Vanessa went for her gun—they both did—then flung herself sideways, shooting and rolling, coming up in a crouch beside the wall still shooting, somehow still alive as the GI took bullet after bullet, slumping against the wall, weapon sliding from her hand. Vanessa got up, walked forward, and unloaded the rest of her magazine into the GI's head point blank. Her pistol was large caliber, for precisely this purpose, and made a real mess.

Then it hit her. Holy fuck I went head to head with a GI and lived. It must have been a Reg.

"Red, Red, Red!" she was yelling on open channel even as the thoughts occurred to her. "Full Red, come in shooting, we've got GIs!"

She sprinted down the hallway, exchanging magazines, then slid into cover alongside the next corner and peeked around. Bullets sent her ducking back, too inaccurate to be another GI . . . she back handed her pistol low around the corner, armscomp gave her an internal-vision flash of the target and she fired, sending him ducking and running. She saw other hotel workers running, at least one might have been League, but her husband was downstairs in this and she wasn't waiting.

She did what Sandy would have done, and went straight at them, only slower, shooting as she came. One tried to hit her and died, others dove behind tables as glasses and plates exploded, and those who didn't shoot back really were hotel staff, she figured, and shot the woman leaning about a table for an angle. No GIs, these; they died quickly.

She took off again, past panicked and screaming staff, straight for the balcony level overlooking the lobby below and the bearpit party. Without looking, she hurdled the side and fell seven meters through the air. Someone half broke her fall and went flying as she rebounded backward and rolled through an impact that might have killed her, unaugmented. Phillippe had been taken to the back rooms, she recalled . . . this way.

She charged through the pandemonium of shouting, running, huddling guests, straight arming anyone who got in her way like a footballer breaking tackles, bowling them over. Someone in a tuxedo took a shot at her, missed, and she blew half his head off. Not a GI either.

Hotel security wisely ran away rather than confront her, and she charged into a hallway to the adjoining rooms and kicked open the first doorway she saw. Ducked back, but drew no fire, and slipped quickly inside.

Here were several people in reclining chairs. Lying still and silent. About their necks were VR collars, plugging them in. Bearpit guests. Serious VR. GIs in the hotel, running some massive-depth VR matrix as only GIs could from a mobile setup without hardwire support. It all hit her fast and hard, what the League was pulling here, right under everyone's nose. Data retrieval, big time. Brain jacking. Something like what Sandy had pulled in the President's Office, only bigger, chasing after people who knew anything about what Sandy and the FSA/CSA combine might be up to on New Torah.

None of these people were Phillippe. Someone appeared in the doorway and nearly died for it, but it was just a terrified guest, looking for safety.

Vanessa tore past him, into the hallway, and kicked in the next set of doors, spinning aside as this time she did draw fire. She wasn't in the habit of carrying flash-bangs on her day off so she improvised, angling her pistol around the corner, unable to get an angle on the shooter but looking up. Armscomp vision sighted nicely on the silly hotel chandelier, which she blew from its base. It fell with a crash, possibly hitting someone, as she ducked and rolled in, shot the shooter twice, then swept the rest of the room as she came in properly.

Here were two more guests unconscious in reclining chairs, and Phillippe, dazed and blinking. "Vanessa?" He stared up at her, bewildered. "What's going on?" Then he saw the body on the floor, and paled.

"Fuck it," Vanessa muttered, crouching to peer into his eyes, checking pupil dilation, reaction. "You're in pre-immersion hypnosis, somehow they cracked these fucking barriers, it shouldn't be possible."

There was shooting out in the lobby now, agents were busting in, removing obstacles the easy way. Shouting nearby, and running footsteps. They'd try to retrieve the data, transmit to the network before the CSA arrived.

"We have to get out of here!" Vanessa snapped. "Move, move!" She grabbed him and tried to haul him to the second entry doorways to this room, but Phillippe was dazed and stumbling. Movement in the first doorway; Vanessa threw him flat and shot through the door at the first man, who barely ducked away in time. She crouched low as return fire came past the doorframe, emptying her second magazine as she slithered sideways toward her husband, shoving him towards the second doors again as bullets cracked and fizzed about.

She reloaded as Phillippe made a dash for the doors, got one open, which she sprang through and past him to clear the hallway beyond. Someone peered around a corner ahead, and she blasted the walls to dissuade him. Bracing against the doors on the opposite hallway wall gave her a better angle, but then one of those doors shoved abruptly open, sending her sprawling. Phillippe leaped at the new arrival, who knocked him aside, only to be hit by Vanessa in an eye blurring co-mingle of interlocking limbs, bodies twisting for leverage as they spun about, and then something abruptly broke, with a horrid snap louder than a branch breaking.

Bodies fell to the ground, Vanessa shoving the oddly right-angled torso off her and coming up shooting to keep the man at the hallway corner back.

"Yeah that's right, you piece of shit!" she yelled at him. "Come and get some!"

Someone shot him from further up the adjoining hallway, and he stumbled into Vanessa's field of fire. Vanessa took his legs, he fell, screaming, and writhed.

"Commander Rice!" she yelled at the footsteps of approaching agents coming up the adjoining hall. "Me and one friendly, but this hallway is not secure!"

They peered at her, fast and professional in suits with handguns, then rushed on to secure the rest of the floor. No one was trusting tacnet; everything had to be checked visually.

Phillippe was staring at her, slumped against the hallway wall. Vanessa realised the moisture on her cheek was blood, not hers.

"Are you okay?" she asked him, suddenly worried that his pale expression might betray some injury.

"Fine," he said hoarsely. "I'm fine." His eyes strayed to the big man she'd nearly broken in half, clinging to his back like a jockey on a horse. The man was still alive, trying to breathe through a shattered diaphragm. The look on his face as he died was beyond horrifying. "Oh, God. Should we help him?"

"Sure," said Vanessa, and shot him.

She didn't need to. The guy had maybe thirty seconds left, if that. She wasn't sure why she did it, so cold and brutal. More CSA agents rushed past, checking their hallway, moving on to the next. Their shouts and calls filled the air as they cleared one space after another with reassuring speed.

Phillippe stared at the body, eyes filling with tears. He looked at her, and reached for her hand.

"Vanessa, I'm so sorry," he said. "I put you in danger. I was stupid, I thought it was a game. Oh, God, I'm sorry, I nearly got you killed. Look what you had to do to save me."

That was what bothered him, not the blood, not the dead man. The fact that he'd been trapped in enemy hands, and she'd had to charge through them to get to him.

Now she was tearing up. "I'd do it again. I love you."

"You won't have to," he told her, with firm earnest. "No more silly hero stuff from me. I'm out. You're the professional, I'll do whatever you say."

Vanessa took a deep breath. Phillippe might come to regret that decision too, she thought.

SWAT One's flyer picked Vanessa up from the Ahimsa Hotel rooftop. It was a relief to get away from the place, the swarming agents, police and media, the many people requesting directions and information she was neither prepared nor willing to give.

"Sitrep," she said whilst stripping to her underclothes before her team of assembled grunts. Visuals came in on her headset visor: displays of Tanusha, the location of all SWAT units, some known League targets, some others located only by guesswork.

"*Everyone's up,*" came Captain Arvid Singh's voice. "*Twelve teams, three more on standby. We've got two hundred and forty-six confirmed League entities we want detained, forty of them are possible hostiles. The cops are taking the lead and our ground guys are going after the more significant ones. And we're closing down the League Embassy, all power and communications. SWAT Three and Nine are taking up perimeter positions now.*"

So that was two of her teams pinned down at the Embassy, Vanessa noted as she stepped into her armour suit in its rack, and began buttoning up. The others were all airborne save for the three standbys, which usually meant they were having trouble recalling troops on leave, and hadn't gotten off the ground yet.

"Copy Arvid, give me two minutes to soak this up, then I'll take command."

"*Copy Ricey, two minutes then you have command.*" It was her procedure. Stupid to have a commander issuing orders straight from the first second when she hadn't had time to absorb the scale of this yet. If anything happened in the next two minutes, Arvid would make the call.

An important message light was flashing, and she opened it. "*Why did they shoot at you?*" came Director Chandrasekar's voice. "*A high risk intel operation is one thing, but why defend it with force?*" Given the consequences for Federation-League relations, he meant.

"Buying time, I'd guess," said Vanessa, as the armour's leg seals hissed and clicked into place. "Assimilating that kind of data takes a little while. They had to package and encrypt it before they could shoot it off to where ever it went. So whatever it was, they valued it a lot."

"*The clear pattern is anyone who knew anything about our activities on New Torah, even those peripherally connected.*"

Something occurred to Vanessa. "Shit, so they got Justice Rosa."

"*We're pretty sure. We're reviewing him now, but it looks like he was in their web before he went to you. And had no idea what had happened to him, he thought he'd just been at a party, no memory at all.*"

"So they'll know everything he knows about Sandy and New Torah."

"We're not certain how good their technology's recall is. We'll have to study it now we've captured some, though they destroyed a lot before we could grab it. They might not have that much, and Justice didn't know very much anyway."

"He knew that Sandy was 'going away' for a while, so they couldn't continue their interviews. He's not dumb, he knows what that means." She wriggled into the torso harness, felt it tighten around her with a familiar, gripping embrace. "So we're taking their Callayan access away from them?"

"No choice; this is very nearly an act of war. We can't set foot on the embassy grounds, but we can sure as hell cut it off. All of their personnel or League-associated people we're collecting now. At least a few of them might try and escape, maybe shoot back. I'm not taking any chances." Chandi spoke quickly off-mike—he'd be doing about five things at once at the moment, and briefing his SWAT Commander was just one of them. *"Intel tells me you took out a GI."*

"Yeah. She must have been one of the ones making that VR matrix work. Sandy's only just discovered how good she is at that. It figures that the League would have known about it for a while longer."

"Intel found two more GIs at the hotel, both non-combat designations. They tell me the one you shot was very much a combat designation. A 39."

Vanessa blinked. She really shouldn't be alive. Thirty nine was Rhian's designation, and Rhian was deadly. Not as deadly as Sandy, but that was an unfair measure. "It's the way they walk," she explained. "Combat pre-tension. Their muscles tense up as combat reflex kicks in, I've seen it in Sandy and others. It changes their stride just a little, I got the jump on her."

"Yeah, well 'getting the jump' on a GI of that designation should only give you point zero five of a second head start, which for most people will not be enough. Given you're still here and she's not, I think you did a bit more than just 'get the jump' on her. I think you may have just made human augmentation history."

He disconnected. Crap, thought Vanessa. That made her sound like a lab rat. Which was always going to happen, she supposed further, as soon as she'd made the decision to get the latest upgrades done. And it sure beat being dead.

She got her arms in, then mated the two armour halves together with a hard seal, and suddenly the deadweight suit sprang to life. Power cells hummed and artificial muscles flexed and sprung. She left the helmet on its hook at the back of her collar, and strode up the narrow aisle between armoured soldiers to her command chair at the front.

There she took command from Arvid, and set the various airbourne units into wide holding patterns over various parts of the city, heavily armed backup for ongoing operations on the ground. Calls came in quickly enough. Cops chased one running suspect into a tall building and given that the target was suspected spec-ops and high value, asked for support. Vanessa put SWAT Eleven down on the building rooftop to trap him.

Some more high-risk targets made rendezvous in a park. She sent in one of the combat flyers to get a heavy weapons lock on them. They surrendered to local police, with expressions that suggested they thought such tactics were a little unfair. Barely an hour into the operation, three quarters of all targets were accounted for. Vanessa thought back to seven years ago, when Sandy had first arrived on Callay and all this mess had started, and tried to imagine any security task this complicated being done in so little time with no casualties so far. It was unimaginable.

The League Ambassador tried to go on local news nets to protest this action by the heavy handed CSA and FSA, but the feed mysteriously cut out before he could get to the good bit where he'd start threatening League-Federation relations with "instability." News nets protested to Chandrasekar directly, asking if the CSA had cut the League Ambassador off, and if so, what had happened to free speech? Chandrasekar issued a statement through a spokesperson replying that the League Embassy was implicated in large scale security violation in Ahimsa Hotel, which had been broken up by CSA Agents with a number of casualties (which the media already knew), and that CSA policy was to disallow any figures actively involved in the violation of Callayan security from making public statements that would do no more than further their cause.

Vanessa thought it was quite well played, and listened a little to the media back and forth as they circled into the Tanushan evening. They monitored the apprehension of the remaining League citizens and subjects of interest across the city. Some media commentators wondered if this meant the war was back on. More sensible folks said that was stupid, and wondered what the hell the League had been doing at the Ahimsa Hotel that had led to a shootout. Thankfully, they had little evident clue of the answer.

In the early evening they landed at a public flyer port atop a mid-level tower for refueling. She let her troops out to stretch their legs—it got deadly boring after a while, sitting in the rear in full armour, watching visor displays and not actually doing anything. Such was the lot of a SWAT grunt. Sometimes you got to go in, and sometimes you didn't.

Rhian called. *"They're after Sandy, aren't they? They're trying to find out where she is."*

Vanessa stood on the landing platform beside the flyer's rear ramp, as engines whined and refueling pumps hummed. Before her, the lights of Tanusha glowed in their millions against the gathering dark, as the flyer's landing lights strobed the pad orange. "Oh, I think they know where she is. They want to know what she's doing, and probably what Mustafa's doing to help her."

"I notice none of our targets are ISO."

"Yeah. That ought to make relations between League government and ISO even worse."

"Vanessa, what if the League intervene in New Torah themselves? I mean, not to stop the New Torah administration, just to stop the ISO and Sandy?"

Vanessa gazed across the cityscape horizon. Techs manning the fuel pumps gesticulated to each other above the noise. "Let's find out what they know first. Then we'll start worrying."

"What if they know a lot?" Rhian sounded worried already. Rhian was usually so optimistic, it wasn't like her. *"I mean, if Sandy's about to get trapped out there . . . what do we do?"*

"I don't know, Rhi." Vanessa forced herself to calm. "Like I said, let's wait and find out what we can find out first, okay?"

She knew damn well what she'd do. But doing so was going to make a real mess.

"Okay," Rhian said quietly. As far as she'd come as a person, Rhian would never be a commander. In some things, she'd always need to be told what to do. Thankfully, her judgment in who she'd listen to was pretty good. *"I heard you got a high-designation GI just now."*

"Yeah. Your designation, actually."

"Now yours, too," said Rhian, with a faint smile in her voice, and disconnected. And left Vanessa, slightly stunned, to ponder that.

CHAPTER FIFTEEN

Danya awoke, and peered through the hole in the wall. Dim sunlight, a yellow glow. Still, it was very cold. He took a breath from his puffer.

"Svet." He put a hand on her shoulder. "Svetochka. Wake up, it's morning." She complained, as she always did, and burrowed more deeply into the coat she used as a pillow.

On Danya's other side, little Kiril was already awake, sitting up without complaint and taking his puffer in both gloved hands. Danya stretched, and adjusted his woolen cap. It had slipped up on one side during the night, and his ear was numb with cold. There was no heating in their little hidey, just room on the floor for three, with holes in walls that let in the chill. He'd tried to plug them, but any material good for plugging was good for bedding and blankets too, and better used for that. Within their little nest, three bodies lying close could keep warm enough, even on Droze nights.

Danya reached into his side of the nest, pulling out his coat and struggling into it. That movement upset the big cover over smaller blankets, and Svetlana complained as the cold got in. Danya slipped out of the covers entirely and pulled on his heavy pants over the light leggings. A fresh pair of socks, because the old ones were becoming truly ripe. He could get their stuff cleaned, but it cost coin he'd rather spend on food. Sometimes Henrietta who worked at the laundromat would smuggle a bag of their bad clothes in and wash them for a trade. Trade got you more than coin did, lately. Danya was good at trade. He'd had to be.

He crawled over his sister and cracked the door a little. Never a lot—with the UAVs around, it was never smart to make a lot of movement on the upper floors. He peered out. This was the fifth and top floor of what had been an office building. Beyond the hidey, the floor was scorched and blackened. That had happened during the crash. No one really knew why this building had been targetted, and anyone who'd witnessed it was likely dead in the witnessing. Anything of value was long ago taken, all that remained were bits of charred and melted furniture, even the walls stripped of wiring, surviving panes of glass and fittings. An outer wall and much of the ceiling were entirely missing, exposed to the yellow morning sky.

Beyond that, Rimtown, a frontier sprawl of low-rise buildings along gridwork streets, smudged with ever-present dust. In the distance, the corporate zones, clusters of high-rise buildings, unreachable behind their defensive walls. From outside came morning noise, generators whining, a few vehicles. The water crier, trundling his barrow. The snorts of luozi, hauling loads.

The need to use the bathroom finally got Svetlana up, as the only working facility was downstairs, and she hated to pee in a bucket. Danya made certain Kiril had his scarf, gloves and goggles, because the pirate frequency last night had said it would storm today. Svetlana double-checked him, because Kiril was forgetful, and they went down the short hall to the stairwell, where Danya took the big padlock off the door.

They descended the echoing concrete stairwell together. Danya was always cautious doing that, and insisted Svetlana and Kiril should not do it without him. They were not the building's only tenants, and some of those below them, who also used the stairwell, made him nervous. He had a big knife in his coat pocket and knew how to use it. Sometimes he thought of upgrading it to a gun, but the corporations' penalty for NCPs carrying guns was death. That didn't stop lots of folks from doing it, but then, lots of folks ended up dead, while he and his siblings were still alive. Danya's sole mission in life was to keep things that way.

Downstairs had once been a floor of offices like all the others. Now it was a tavern of sorts, all the partitions cleared out leaving only open space and ceiling supports, like an empty shell. Against one wall was a bar and behind that, the kitchen, adjoining Treska's office. Opposite that was storage, boxes and trunks and spare junk, all Treska's stuff. Generator engines and fuel, the place always smelled of fumes. Elsewhere about the floor were trestles and tables for patrons, a small stage that could be used for music, and some pool tables.

Danya tried the switch and the lights came up. "Power's on!" he told the other two. It was always good to start the day with good news. "Svet, you can make us some coffee, the machine will be working."

"I don't like that coffee," Svetlana complained, leading Kiril to the rear bathroom, behind Treska's office. "It smells of juno piss."

"That's probably because some juno pissed in it," Danya explained.

"Ew!" said Svetlana.

"Yuck!" added Kiril, cheerfully.

Danya set about making up the tables, pulling table cloths from their trunk by the wall, and cutlery from the box beside it. Treska kept their rent low and let them have breakfast if they set up every morning. Treska lived on the floor above, where it was rumoured he used banned communications to do business. Danya didn't ask what, though he could guess.

He was making up some tables near the front door when he noticed one of the locks securing the big steel shutter across a window was broken. He froze. The shutters were heavily secured; breaking one wasn't easy. Had it been opened from the inside? But how could it have been, when anyone sleeping inside could have just left through the door?

He heard the bathroom flush for a second time. Svetlana was already in the kitchen, clashing pots and pans. Danya examined the big, heavy window shutter. It was open, all right, the locks sheared right off. Had it been open like that all night? That was an unpleasant thought. There were some things out in the night you didn't leave a window open for.

"Danya!" It was Svetlana's voice, shocked and frightened. His heart stopped, and he spun. Svetlana stood in the kitchen door, frozen, staring at something behind the bar. "Danya, there's someone in here!"

Danya ran, hands fumbling for the knife in his coat. Around the edge of the bar he saw her—a blonde woman, lying as though unconscious on the floor.

"Is she dead?" asked Svetlana, hopefully. Dead people were a nuisance that could be disposed of. The live ones could be trouble.

"I don't know," said Danya, warily. "I don't want to check, she might be a GI."

Svetlana's eyes widened, and she backed up a step. "A GI, really? Why?"

"The front shutter's been broken. It looks like someone just forced it open."

"Is that a GI?" came Kiril's voice from the kitchen. He peered past his sister in the doorway. "Is she alive, Danya?"

"I don't know, Kiri." Danya crouched just short of her feet, peering to try and get a better look. She wore a heavy black coat, which made it hard to see if she was breathing. He thought hard. A GI could be trouble. There was no telling whose side she'd be on, or who she worked for. Though she could be a privateer. That would be even worse—the companies took a hard line with privateers. "I have to tell Treska."

"No, Danya, don't leave us here with the GI!" Svetlana protested. "I'll go and tell Treska!"

Danya shook his head firmly. "I've told you, Svet, I don't like you alone with him."

"I'll be fine," she retorted, "better Treska than a GI!"

"I don't even know if she is a GI. She might just be augmented, that could be enough to break the shutter." There was blood on her clothes, he saw. Whether or not it was hers, there was no way to tell.

"I'm not scared of GIs," said Kiril.

"Kiri," Danya warned, "you listen to me. They're not all friendly like Gunter, do you hear me? Some of them work for the companies, and they're very dangerous. You stay well away from them, understand?" Kiril nodded, gazing at the unconscious woman. "Now, I'm going to go and get Treska. If she wakes up, be very polite and stay out of her way. She won't hurt you if you don't give her any reason to, okay? GIs don't hurt people for no reason. But don't you go near her, or you might give her a reason, understand?"

Danya left for the stairs. He couldn't check for a pulse, anyway, because GIs didn't have a jugular vein, everyone knew that. He really didn't want to leave Svetlana and Kiril alone with the maybe-GI. But also, he didn't want to be slow to tell Treska, and make Treska upset. If Treska got upset with them, they'd have no place to sleep, and no breakfasts.

He climbed the stairs back up to the first floor. Treska's door was sealed with steel hinges, with an electronic peep hole in the middle. Danya hit the doorbell. That would make a noise inside the apartment, though Danya couldn't hear it. He waited. There was no telling if he'd been heard or not, and no way of hearing if someone was coming. He hit the doorbell again. Sometimes he thought Treska had set it up like this just to be disconcerting. It worked.

After what he figured was a fair time waiting, he turned and went back down the stairs. Treska could hardly claim he hadn't tried to tell him. Down in the tavern he could see Svetlana hustling over a stove, through windows in the kitchen's prefab walls that closed it off from the rest of the floor. And behind the open bar . . . his heart nearly stopped for a second time. Little Kiril was helping the blonde woman to sit on several storage kegs behind the bar.

He couldn't yell—a sudden noise might scare her, and if she was a GI, he couldn't scare her. He walked forward, hands balled to fists, willing himself to calm. The woman was awake, though moving very gingerly. She was having trouble standing on her own.

"Kiri," he said in measured tones, and leaned on the bar. "I think you should move away from there."

The woman slumped back against the wall, head lolled, and looked at him. Pale blue eyes, shortish hair, all messed up. Beautiful, if she didn't look so awful.

"She's okay, Danya," said Kiril, supporting her to make sure she didn't slide over. "I think she's sick."

The woman seemed to note Danya's alarm. Her hand on Kiril's shoulder lifted, a pronounced gesture. Almost an apology. She seemed to have difficulty breathing.

Svetlana emerged from the kitchen with a glass of water. Danya glared at her—she should have been watching Kiril. Svetlana made a snotty mimicry of his glare and handed the woman the glass. Her hand shook. Kiril moved to try to help her drink it.

"Kiril!" Danya commanded, and he stopped, looking confused. Kiril was such a nice boy, he thought everyone might be his friend. Danya worried about him constantly.

The woman spilled a lot of the water on her chin. It trickled onto the pullover under her coat. When the glass was empty, she handed it to Svetlana, who took it before she could drop it.

"Hello?" Danya tried. "What is your name? What happened to you?" The woman said nothing. Whether that was because she would not tell, or could not, Danya didn't know. "We don't own this place, do you understand me? We pay rent. The landlord is upstairs, I tried to reach him but he didn't answer the door. Either you tell us, or you tell him. He's not always a very nice man."

The woman slumped her head back against the wall, and closed her eyes.

"Who are you?" Danya tried again. "Are you a GI?"

A faint nod. Svetlana grabbed Kiril's shoulder and pulled him back a little. Danya could have smacked her on the head. *Now you're worried?*

"Who do you work for? What designation are you?" Nothing. "A high designation, or low?"

"Very high," she croaked.

So she could speak. "Do you work for a corporation?"

"No," she said. "I got hit with . . . tranquilizer. GI specific. Can you get . . . bipofalzin?"

"Drugs?" Now Danya was very wary. "Is it expensive?"

"Don't know," she gasped. "Maybe."

Danya spread his hands in exasperation. "Lady, we've barely got enough to eat. Thieves get killed. Either this bipofaz . . ."

"Bipofalzin."

" . . . either it's easy to get, or I can't get it. I'm sorry. I don't even know if you can stay here, once Treska finds out." Pity she's a GI, he thought. If she weren't, with looks like hers, Treska would have let her make payment in other ways. But no one was crazy enough to offer that with a GI.

"The tranq shuts down my systems," she said. "If I don't get it, I'm dead. Forty-eight hours, max." She had a funny accent. At first Danya had thought it was just her condition. But now that her voice was loosening up, it was undeniably an accent. Which was odd, because old people had accents, those that had come from other places. No younger people did, and never any GIs. How did a GI get an accent? Where was she from?

"I'm sorry, lady," Danya repeated. "But this is Droze, people die all the time. I have to look after my brother and sister. They're all I have."

The woman looked across the room, gathering thought as she tried to gather air, one deep gasp at a time.

"You're fifteen?" she asked, looking back at him.

"Thirteen," he said, a little self-consciously.

"So you were seven in the crash." Her eyes rolled across to Kiril and Svetlana. "And these two . . . the little one might not have been born."

"He was a baby," Danya confirmed. "Svet was four."

"So this is all you've known. Do you like it here?"

Danya frowned. What kind of a question was that? "What difference does it make?" he retorted. "Here is all there is."

"No." She shook her head, with slow effort. "I'm Federation. Tanusha, on Callay."

"Don't be stupid," said Danya. "The Federation doesn't make GIs, everyone knows that."

"I came from the League," she replied. "But I left. I emigrated. Became a Federation citizen."

Danya was unconvinced. "Danya, I heard about this," Svetlana cut him off, eyes wide, before he could ridicule the GI further. "People say some GIs went to the Federation. To Callay."

"Which people said that?"

"News feeds," Svetlana insisted. "I read them, Danya. How does she have an accent if she's not from the Federation?"

"She could be League," said Danya, coldly. "All offworlders have accents."

"But that would be suicide!" Svetlana insisted. "Everyone hates the League!" Danya was uncertain. Svetlana was a dreamer, and too often she wanted things to be true that weren't. But she did read the news feeds, and all kinds of things Danya never found useful. If she said she'd read that GIs had gone to the Federation, it was probably true. But that didn't mean this one was telling the truth.

"If you're from the Federation, why are you here?" he asked suspiciously.

"Can't say. It's secret. But I'm not supposed to be here. My group were ambushed. I think betrayed." She stopped for a moment. It might have just been the tranquilizer, but she seemed to be struggling with emotion. If so, that would mean she was a very high designation. "Some of my people were killed. I escaped. Ended up here. Kid. Your name's Danya?"

"Danil. Same thing."

"Right. Russian nickname. You know it's a girl's name in Hebrew? Means 'God is my judge.'" She rolled her eyes to Svetlana. "You're Svetochka. From Svetlana. That means 'light.'" Svetlana blinked. "I'm Kresnov. But never Kresnova. GIs don't have families like that. The feminine stuff doesn't work."

Danya and Svetlana looked at each other. GIs never talked like that, didn't know this kind of stuff. Very high designation? Or foreign? Or both?

"Danya, the Federation is interested not just in Droze. We're interested in New Torah. We're trying to help, you understand? I can help you. Maybe get you out of here, somewhere nice. But I can't do that if you don't get me bipofalzin. Fast."

"So, what does Kiril mean?" Kiril asked as Danya led them into the cold morning light.

"I don't know, Kiri," said Danya, distractedly. "Mama never said. Maybe Kresnov knows."

The street was cold and dusty, though the glare was not yet bright enough for goggles. Most of the traffic was pedestrian, but there were a few vehicles, driven by home-built combustion engines—ancient things that rattled and clanked. Labs made various combustible fuels, the only thing available for the purpose as the companies jealously guarded the electrical grid, which in turn deprived any working lab of the power required to generate hydrogen or other, more modern fuels in sufficient quantities to power vehicles. Company workers still flew in aircars or flyers, sometimes one could be seen far overhead, beyond small-arms range. Adults told tales of a time when such vehicles had been everywhere. Danya remembered a little of that time himself, but those memories were fading fast. He was too busy with the present to waste time mooning about the past.

They'd left Kresnov in their upstairs hidey, with a key to lock the door. She wasn't able to do much more than lie there—he and Svetlana had had to carry her most of the way up the stairs. Danya hadn't told Treska. He had no idea if Treska would even open the door if he tried again. Danya wasn't sure if it would be smarter to just dump her—obviously, nasty people were after her. But that wasn't so uncommon in these parts of Rimtown, and if he became known on the street as unreliable, he couldn't expect much help when trouble came for him or the kids.

Besides which, there was her offer. Danya didn't really believe it. The Federation was an awful long way away. But now Svetlana had gone from wishing Kresnov dead to mooning about that far-off land of wealth and plenty, like some tale on a story reader, with fairies and talking animals. And Kiril, of course, was the same. That was expected from a six-year-old, but Danya was disappointed in Svetlana—she was ten now, and was supposed to be more grown up.

"So, are you going to get this bipofalzin?" Svetlana asked as they walked. Storefronts were opening, big metal rollers grinding up. Atop building balconies, solar panels were unfurled, rigged to multi-purpose batteries.

"I don't know," said Danya. "I'll look. But I have to be careful, I can't just ask around. If it's a banned drug, or something only for GIs, people might get suspicious that I'm asking. I have to find out what happened to Kresnov and who is after her."

"I don't care who's after her," said Svetlana. "We should help her."

It wasn't altruism on Svetlana's part, Danya knew too well. He loved her and Kiril more than his own life, but it was his objectivity that kept them alive, and on his siblings he was most objective of all. Of the three of them, Svetlana was the most ruthless. She wanted what she wanted, and cared little for anyone or anything beyond their little circle. If she wanted to take risks on Kresnov's behalf, it was because Svetlana thought something good for herself and her brothers might come of it. Kresnov herself was just a shiny bauble, a ticket to better things.

"I think we should help her, too," said Kiril. "I want to go to Callay."

"Yes well, now you're going to school," said Danya.

School was Abraham's Mosque on the outskirts of town. In an open square it sat, a simple structure of clay bricks, seeming to have risen from the desert sand. Luozi were tethered by a water trough, long ears drooping as they drank. Kiril patted one in passing, and then they entered the building, a simple earth floor and bare walls, the ceiling held up by symmetrical concrete pillars.

Abraham was a tall man in robes. Some folks called him the Bedouin, but he'd actually been a company man before the crash. He'd seen things, people said, that had caused him to cast off his suit and tie, and build this little mosque from nothing. Today there were perhaps forty children present, of varying ages, reading and doing sums. Abraham would teach them reading and maths and history. Sometimes he'd talk to them about Allah too, but no one minded that, so long as the kids learned the important stuff.

"Young Danya," said Abraham, as Svetlana joined Kiril on the floor with a slate and read with him. "You should come and learn more often. Your own reading could improve."

"I have to work," said Danya.

"At least let Svetlana stay for an hour." His manner was very kindly. Danya had learned to be wary of some adults who professed their love of children, but he'd never heard a bad word said of Abraham, save for a few who muttered he was crazy. "Danya, we do not have the luxury of tape teach like the company children do, so learning takes more time. It's very important for children to learn."

"Will you feed us if we don't work?" Danya asked. Abraham sighed. "So stop asking. What do you know about drugs?"

Abraham frowned. "What kind of drugs?"

"The kind that fetch a good price. I'm not interested in taking them, I just want to know some prices."

Abraham nodded slowly. He always refused to say exactly what he'd done in the corporations, but some rumoured he'd been quite senior. That meant he knew a lot. "Which drugs?"

"GI drugs."

"There are quite a few of those. Most of them are expensive. Have you come across some?"

Danya shrugged. "I might have. What do you know about bipofalzin?"

"That's an anti-toxin. There was a lot of Federation research during the war into how to kill GIs with chemicals. The League did a lot of counter-research to make drugs that cure those effects. Bipofalzin is one of them."

"Do the companies make it here?"

"Probably," said Abraham. "Drugs are quite simple to make. But they won't make very much of it, because who fights GIs with chemicals here?"

That's a good question, thought Danya.

"Danya, Danya," Abraham sighed, and put a hand on his shoulder. "Sometimes you sound so much like a man, I forget that you're a boy."

"I am a man," Danya said stubbornly, removing Abraham's hand. "I don't have a choice."

"And Allah loves you for it," Abraham assured him with a smile. "It is his strength that makes you a man, so that you can protect your sister and brother. But some things a man knows that a boy cannot, no matter how wise before his time. Things like when to take a risk. Do not play around with dangerous things, Danya. It can be tempting, when there are riches on offer, but riches on Droze are a mirage. It was that realisation that brought me here, to serve Allah."

"He doesn't know about the teacher, does he?" Svetlana asked as they walked up Grande Road toward Steel City.

"I don't think so," said Danya. "He still doesn't think you read very well, though. You should practise more."

"I practise plenty," Svetlana snorted. "We need to buy a new card, that old one gets boring. And some more pills."

"Svetlana," Danya told her for the thousandth time, "we have no money for that."

Svetlana made a face. A tractor bus trundled past, its open tray bouncing on the potholed road. The people sitting in the back bounced with it. It was going their way, but even that small fee was pointless, and walking was good for you. Danya had had a bicycle a year ago and that had been wonderful, easy to keep and cheap to run, but it had been stolen, despite his best efforts at keeping it safe. Everything useful got stolen eventually.

They passed the Kasperwitz Tavern on a corner, music booming out, gaming lights flashing. Armed guards at the door with big rifles, one of them cybernetic, the other certainly augmented—corporations didn't mind NCP business guards being armed; some rumoured they did deals with small businesses beyond the security zone to keep them sweet. These would be registered. Svetlana peered yearningly for the doorway as they passed, as though hoping to catch a glimpse of the riches inside. They weren't real riches, Danya had told her firmly, plenty of times. Only the tavern ever really got rich. And people who won too often had a way of getting hurt, or worse.

Next to the tavern was the brothel, one of the only good looking buildings in town, with a railed balcony and fancy French doors with lacy curtains. That told a story of who the profitable businesses were. There were guards here too, sitting and playing backgammon on the balcony, big rifles nearby, and more inside. Danya had been in a few times, strictly on business, running errands for the Kasperwitz family who owned both it and the tavern, and a few other establishments in the neighbourhood.

The Kasperwitzes were fair and paid well, but he refused to let Svetlana ever go inside for fear that they'd see her and get ideas. Svetlana had blue eyes, dark hair and fine, pale features. At this age she was only going to get prettier, and a few of the girls in the brothel couldn't have been older than fifteen. For now she kept her hair cut short under a floppy hat, but that wasn't going to hide her forever. There were even days when he thought that the brothel wouldn't be the worst thing. At least she'd get fed there, and protected from the meaner clients by well-paid and heavily armed men. And then he'd hate himself for even thinking it.

"Maybe we should get a new card for Kiril," Danya thought aloud, as traffic got heavier and the air thicker with dust from the tires. Vehicle workshops lined the road, from which came the sound of lots of hammering and machine tools. "He's so smart, I don't want his learning to fall behind. Especially his maths, he could get a good job with maths."

"My maths stink," said Svetlana. "I'll never have a good job."

"You could if you practised more."

"I'm not good at maths!" She kicked at the dust. "How are you going to afford a new card?"

"We," Danya corrected. "How are we going to afford a new card. We're a team."

Svetlana was hurt. "I know."

"I'll think of something." He grimaced. Thinking on it was frustrating.

"Danya," said Svetlana, holding his arm with urgency. "Bipofalzin."

"Svet, if we can't even afford a teacher card . . ."

"How many lucky breaks have we ever had?" Svetlana pleaded. "Kresnov could be a lucky break."

"She's more likely going to get us killed," Danya muttered. But she looked so hopeful, looking up at him with her big eyes beneath her floppy hat. Danya sighed, and put his arm around her. "I know, Svetochka. I'd like to help her, too. I'll ask Gunter."

Gunter didn't know anything about bipofalzin. "Just because I'm a GI," he explained, "that doesn't mean I've heard of all this stuff."

Gunter worked security at the Ting Yard. Blond and muscular, he was an okay designation who'd been part of the security detail the League had left on Droze before the crash. When the League pulled out, they'd had seats only for organic humans, and a lot of GIs had been left behind without employers. A few had found work with the corporations, but the corporations didn't trust formerly League-employed GIs, especially the higher designations, and most of those they did employ were regs. Gunter had chosen to work for Mr Ting, to Mr Ting's good fortune. A lot of GIs in Droze were quite rich. A company or business family with a GI employed was relatively safe, while their potential opponents were not. Wealth flocked to safe investment, and the Tings now owned one of the biggest scrap and recycling yards in Steel Town.

"He's not very smart, though," Svetlana reasoned as they worked, after Gunter had strolled away. This time the crate was full of broken home appliances. Danya and Svetlana would take them out and disassemble them, tossing any still-useful bits into various trays for reuse. Mostly they looked for chips, the only parts of real reusable value—the technology was old and crappy, as frontier technology usually was, but old chips were more reusable than new ones. "Just because he doesn't know about bipofalzin doesn't mean it's not available."

She grimaced as she reached into the mechanism of what had been a food processor. She wasn't as young and slim as she had been, but her fingers were still more nimble than Danya's, better for tight spaces. The yard itself was an old rusting factory space, its floor completely crowded with junk. Machinery echoed and whined beneath the high roof, as heavier equipment moved larger items of junk, or tore them apart. Kids worked on smaller things, with a hope to graduate up as they grew older—there were eleven others on this part of the yard floor, working at their benches.

"Abraham said there weren't many people on Droze who used chemicals to fight GIs," said Danya. "Those are the people who'd have bipofalzin, though."

"But only people who employed GIs, themselves," Svetlana reasoned, digging out the chip and tossing it in its tray. "The big families would have some, I bet."

"Yeah, but a lot of the GIs won't fight each other," Danya replied. "So the big families like the Tings who employ GIs can't really fight other families, at least not using their own GIs. They all used to serve together in the League, a lot of them are still friends."

"Not the regs. Regs don't have friends."

"And most of them are working for the companies. The companies don't like GIs with loyalties." He wasn't working as hard as he should be, he was too distracted. But they weren't paid by the hour, only by the value of the junk that they salvaged.

Svetlana dug out some wiring, disconnected a chip, and tossed both in a salvage tray. "I'm going to talk to Pedro."

"Why?"

"He works in stores," she reasoned. "He'll know if the Tings have bipofalzin. I bet they do, Gunter's the most valuable thing they have."

"The Tings don't own Gunter, Svet, he works here 'cause he chooses to."

"Same thing."

"And how would the Tings have bipofalzin if Gunter doesn't know himself?"

Svetlana rolled her eyes. "Danya," she complained, "how will we ever know if we don't ask? Pedro will know, he likes me. And seriously, if you were the Tings, and you employed Gunter, would you tell him everything? I mean, what if they've got drugs that kill GIs as well as drugs that fix them? Would you want Gunter to know that too?"

Danya thought about it. Sometimes, he reflected, Svetlana made a lot of sense. But only sometimes. "You be careful with Pedro, Svet. He may like you, but he likes his job more."

Svetlana made a face. "You worry about getting the D-chips out of that vacuum bot, I'll worry about Pedro."

CHAPTER SIXTEEN

Sandy awoke. She felt horrible. Well, she supposed, that made sense, given that she was dying.

She tried to recall where she was. Droze, on Pantala; her memory wasn't that far gone. But the details were hazy. Time, place, the sequence of events, all overlapped in her head. Breathing was hard, and her limbs ached. She should open her eyes, she supposed. Not yet. Try to remember, where were her friends?

Dead, she was fairly sure. Han, Khan, Weller, Ogun, Poole. Aristide's had been a safe location, supposedly. An ISO plant in Mid-East. The ISO had others, isolated, not knowing each other's names or locations. But Aristide was an ISO agent, fully trained and bred, horrified by what had happened to Droze since the crash. Surely he hadn't turned for money or threats, not to the corporations he despised. So, how?

It had come in through the air conditioning, a strange mist. Sandy had secured that, three times over . . . someone had to have betrayed them to get synthetic nerve toxin into the aircon while they slept. Even then, she'd woken fast, alerted the others . . . but then the attack, and it had all been so fast, the perimeter already breached, the alarms silent, their reflexes slowed just a little by inhaling the pervasive mist. GIs. She remembered targets flashing, explosions, professional assault tactics, deadly fast and high-designation. Hard to fight with your head swimming, the attackers all wore breathers. Still she'd killed a bunch, she couldn't remember how many, but she'd been hit too, a few bullets, a few tranq rounds. They hadn't been trying to kill her, only capture. But Khan she'd seen dead, a horrid, messy memory . . . Weller, too. They'd known who she was. They'd known where she slept. They'd been non-lethal against her, even knowing how hard she was to take down with any method. Why?

Too many thoughts. Bad ones. She opened her eyes, and her vision was a blur. Tranq relaxed the muscles, even in her eyes. Vision focus became difficult. But her hearing remained.

Men were talking. How was that possible? She was in the kids' hidey on the top floor, and there had been no one else there. Only, the light here was different, dimmer, artificial. The kids' hidey had holes in the walls that let in natural sunlight. Had she been moved while unconscious?

Footsteps across the floor. Moving past, not toward. Then a new voice to the conversation—someone else had arrived. Exclamations of amusement, incredulity.

" . . . so they don't know I have the ground floor monitored, right?" a male voice was explaining. "So I'm listening in, and the boy comes up to knock on my door, but I pretend I'm still asleep or not here or something, I want to listen. And the girl says she's a GI. Federation, can you believe that?"

"Oh, perfect," said another. "I mean, no one will miss her."

"Exactly!" said the first man. "If she were some corporate skinjob, they'd send folks to look for her—I mean, those things are valuable. But the fucking Federation's got sand in their heads if they think they can do covert ops on Pantala. They wouldn't survive a week."

Well he was nearly right about that, Sandy thought tiredly. They'd been just short of three weeks downworld, after a month in-system but offworld, preparing.

"Anyhow," the first man resumed, "she said she needed bipofalzin or she'd die. So I called around, found a batch and injected her." Sandy took a moment to process that. She was going to live? "Had to get a special industrial needle, fucking impossible to get the thing in otherwise. Gave her a shot of some alfadox too . . . Gomez gave me the formula, right here. You get the proportions right, keep the bipofalzin to minimum while countering with the alfadox, you can keep her in a zombie state for weeks. Months maybe."

Sandy exhaled with difficulty. She could have guessed it wasn't going to be that easy. She tried to move, and her muscles just wouldn't cooperate. Alfadox was another form of tranquilizer, close to what the CSA had dosed her with upon her first arrival on Callay seven years ago. It kept her muscles from consolidating beyond the critical mass required to break out of basic restraints. Alfadox was a slightly more aggressive version, dangerous if misused by even a small margin. If she'd been injected with that, plus the remnants of the original lethal tranq, then bipofalzin or not, it was no wonder she felt like shit.

"So come and look, come and look," the man continued, all enthusiasm. Footsteps approached. "I mean, think what you like about skinjobs, there's some damn fine engineering that goes into making the girls hot. And this one's pretty damn nice, if you like the athletic look."

Footsteps came right over. Then someone was grabbing her face, turning her head, like a farmer examining some livestock. She couldn't see much more than a blur, but she could smell his breath, and it was stale.

"Nice," he said. One of the other two men . . . or she thought there were two, three in total. "Real fucking nice." His hands moved down, pulling up her shirt. And doing other things. Sandy was half-relieved she couldn't feel very much, the tranq doing strange things to the sensation of contact on skin. It felt like it was someone else's body, that she was only borrowing it for a while. "Yeah, she's not real skinny, is she?"

"I like curves on a woman, myself."

"Hard as a rock. Don't like athletic girls myself. Soft and squishy's my thing."

"Sure, and how many sluts do you have in that whorehouse who look better than her?" That was the first man again.

The whole thing was surreal. Sandy had wondered a few times if, being what she was, she would be less psychologically damaged by rape than most women. For one thing, the very concept was mostly unthinkable. Most men weren't suicidal, and GIs never did it to each other, as far as she knew. She'd never thought she'd have to find out for real. Still it didn't seem right to get too upset about it. Largely that was the drugs, she knew, screwing with her head. But also, she was responsible for hundreds of deaths in her life, and regardless of how many of them had deserved it, it didn't seem that she was in any moral position to complain when bad things happened to her. She would deal with it, like she always did, and hope that karma sorted itself out in the end.

"I think about thirty chits," said one of the other men.

"Forty," said the first man. "The ropes only make it more kinky, I know some of your regulars are real perverts. They'll like that."

She was tied up? Sandy could barely move enough to feel the tug of restraint. But maybe it was just that her reduced sense of touch wasn't allowing her to feel the ropes. Maybe what felt like a lack of mobility was actually ropes tying her up? In that case, maybe the drugs weren't affecting her as badly as she thought, and she'd move okay if untied.

She strained her vision. The blur shifted, overlapping outlines coming together, resolving into two men. They were still fuzzy, but she could make out basic features. One was black, grey streaked, weathered. Another was big, Caucasian, moustachioed. The third man she couldn't see.

"Thirty-five," said the black man. "It's a trek for my customers to come across here, unless you want to move her, and she can't come to the brothel. My girls won't like it."

"Hard to do without being seen," said the third, invisible man.

"Thirty-five," the big, moustachioed man agreed, reluctantly.

"Fifteen for me," said the black man—a brothel owner, it seemed. "Twenty for you. Deal?"

"Deal." They shook hands. Perhaps the moustachioed man saw her looking, unfocused though her drug-addled stare was. He leaned down close to her, and beamed. "You should be flattered. Whorehouse girls don't go for more than ten, usually."

Danya was washing his hands in the bathroom, splashing some water on his face, when Svetlana came in. She looked anxious, hands thrust deep in jacket pockets, hat pulled down low over her head like she didn't want to be recognised.

"So, what did Pedro say?" She'd been gone a while, he'd been starting to worry. She grabbed his arm and pulled at him. "What's the matter?"

"Pedro said yes," she said, hushed and agitated. "I got this." She pulled a vial from her pocket. Within was a small quantity of clear liquid. Danya stared at it. "Bipofalzin. Danya, let's go!"

"Wait." He grabbed her wrist. "Svet, where did you get that?"

"It doesn't matter, let's go!"

"Go where? Svet, where did you get bipofalzin?"

"I took it from the Tings' private storeroom, okay?" she hissed. "Now let's go back home and help Kresnov!"

"You stole from them?" Danya was horrified. "Svet, you know what they do to thieves?"

"Let's go!" she urged him. Danya followed to the bathroom doorway and peered out . . . sure enough, there were yard bosses walking the floor like they were searching for something, with lots of finger pointing and shouts. One of them was coming toward the bathroom.

Danya ducked back and swore. "They're coming. Out the window." He pulled her over and boosted her up. She got a boot on the pipe to the urinal and scrambled up to the window sill, then slid out. Danya followed, more athletic than his sister but not quite as nimble, and the window was a tighter squeeze. Below was a long drop to the top of a storage tank, Svetlana already clambering down to the ground with all the dexterity of a Droze street kid. The window wasn't wide enough to allow Danya to get his feet under him, so he went out headfirst, caught the rim to swing around as he fell, overcooked it and hit hard on his chest. Then up and after Svetlana, shimmying down a pipe, then running along the alley at the back of the yard.

Svetlana took a right, rather than join the main road directly, and disappeared like a juno up a drain. The wind knocked out of him, Danya struggled to keep up. This alley was narrower, filled with junk and dust, and bad smells from the workshops in dilapidated neighbouring buildings. Svetlana paused to look up one alley, but passed as it was too narrow even for her. Then another, which she took, then a quick turn back to the left. Here the alley was a little wider and clearer, enabling Danya to start running properly and catch up. Until a dark shape dropped from the sky and landed with an athletic thud before Svetlana, and she skidded to a halt.

It was Gunter, broad and blond, and doubtless armed in one of his many pockets. Svetlana tried to back up, but Danya caught her and held her steady. You couldn't run from GIs, not when they were this close.

Gunter walked forward. "Did you steal from the Tings?" he asked Svetlana. She shook her head, fearfully.

"Svet, tell the truth," said Danya. He didn't see any other choice. "Gunter, she took bipofalzin," he tried, desperately. "It's that drug we asked you about. It's for GIs. We met a GI, she was nearly dead, we were trying to get her bipofalzin so she would live. If you don't let us go, she will die."

"Are you telling the truth?" His jaw was square, blue eyes hard and impossibly handsome. Like some beautiful god, out of place amidst the squalor of Steel Town.

"Why would I lie?" Danya retorted. "And why would she steal just one vial of bipofalzin, when there are so many more valuable things she could have stolen? Show him, Svet."

Svetlana reached into her pocket and produced the vial. Her hand, Danya noted, was not shaking. He wanted to spank her, but damn she was tough. Gunter looked at the vial. GIs could zoom in with their vision, Danya knew.

"Where is this GI from?" Gunter asked.

Danya decided to take a big chance. "She's an offworlder. Like you."

Gunter gazed at him. Not very smart, Svetlana had said. Danya didn't know about that, they'd never talked for long enough. But he'd never been mean, and had often shown small kindnesses to yard workers—a gift of food here, and kind word on one's behalf to a supervisor there. Mostly his job at the yard was as deterrent, to stop major theft or attack through the simple fear of his presence.

"A League GI," said Gunter.

"She was from the League, yes," Danya answered. Technically it wasn't a lie. Gunter had been League before the League had left him behind, six years ago. Kresnov had been League, until she'd gone to the Federation. A lot of corporate GIs these days were locally made, and every year the number grew. Danya had often gained the impression that a lot of formerly-League GIs weren't impressed with the local newcomers. "I can introduce you to her, if you'd like to meet her. Once she gets better."

"She arrived recently?" Gunter asked.

"Yes. Gunter, we have to go!"

Gunter nodded. "Tell her to come and say hello if she'd like. I'll tell the Tings you went another way."

He leapt vertically, straight up, and onto the rim of a factory wall overhead. And disappeared.

Danya headed not to Treska's, but to Abraham's Mosque. They took a back way, which took longer but would keep them away from anyone reporting to the Tings, through Buckethead Market with its crowds and commotion, under the wary eye of stall owners naturally suspicious of lurking street kids. But the merchants had little to do with Steel Town owners like the Tings, and street kids were common everywhere through Droze, for the most part they were invisible.

"Great," Danya muttered as they walked fast, "well, we've lost that job for good. And any other job in Steel Town, no one will take us now. Where are we going to get money, Svet?"

He felt a rising sense of panic. They'd been doing quite well lately. Not like before. Svetlana had already forgotten a lot, in the years immediately after the crash. She'd been four, barely old enough to do more than sit in whichever derelict hideout he'd found for them, and look after baby Kiril, sometimes with the help of other street kids, sometimes not. She'd cried a lot, skinny, bedraggled urchin that she'd been then. And when they'd really begun starving, she'd stopped crying, from sheer exhaustion.

Danya remembered long days and nights scavenging for scraps, coming home to share whatever he'd managed to find, and the horror at seeing his little sister and baby brother so thin and sickly, ribs showing, eyes hollow. He'd given them portions of his share too, until he'd been weak and stumbling from hunger. They'd joined a gang of other street kids then, which had probably saved their lives, because the scavenging became more coordinated, and food improved.

But the gang had fought and split up, as gangs tended to do. For a while they'd run with Peng and Kumetz, but Kumetz had disappeared one night and never resurfaced, while Peng got caught on a security fence and bled to death before Danya could get him to help. Of the sixteen members of that original gang, Danya knew of only seven, excluding themselves, who were still accounted for. Some of the rest might still be alive, but given the tales that were told about some kids who were taken, it was probably better if they weren't.

Those first two years had been the worst. Then Droze had begun to recover a little, businesses had emerged from the chaos, survivors began to organise and form some semblance of a livelihood. Suddenly there was a little money around, and clean water, food and meds. Scavenging had become easier, and a few little charities sprung up, mostly run by religious folk like Abraham, who frightened or guilt-tripped the faithful into contributions that they'd spend on providing for street kids.

Also, Svetlana had turned six, at which age she'd proven a truly exceptional pickpocket and general thief. So exceptional that Danya had forbidden her from using her talent unless absolutely necessary, for fear she'd get cocky one time too many. Like this time.

"Why aren't we going back to Treska's?" she asked him now, knowing better than to argue the point.

"Because we have to go to Abraham's and get Kiril," said Danya, walking a little faster up the narrow, crowded street.

"But why not let Abraham look after Kiril for a little bit longer?" Svetlana complained. "He's just a baby, he'll get in the way . . ."

"Svet," said Danya in frustration, "you don't know what you've done. If you steal from someone in Droze, they know who you are. They know who we are, all of us."

"Oh, they won't come after Kiril!" Svetlana said scornfully. But her voice was tinged with fear. "It's just one vial, he's got nothing to do with it!"

"He's got everything to do with it," Danya retorted. "You don't know how they think. And you don't know how they think because you never fucking listen!"

He wanted to run, but that would attract attention. Svetlana walked fast at his heels, head down, all pouting, rebellious and frightened at the same time.

Danya could see something was wrong before they even got near Abraham's Mosque. People were running, shouting alarm, others were emerging from shop fronts to see what was going on. Some shop fronts were closing, big rollers hauled down, windows shuttered and barred.

Danya ran behind a truck loaded with bags of fertiliser, and peered toward the courtyard where the Mosque was. There was dust everywhere, big clouds of it, and more people running. Someone was being carried by others, obviously hurt.

"A flyer!" someone was shouting to a neighbour. "It came down by the Mosque! Lots of men with guns, they went inside!"

"They shoot anyone?" came the incredulous reply.

"Didn't hear any shooting."

"What's anyone want with Abraham?"

Svetlana ran out, but Danya dragged her back.

"We have to find Kiril!" Svetlana shouted, eyes filled with tears. "This is my fault, they came for Kiril because of me . . ."

"Svet, calm down." Danya pulled her down, and they crouched together, watching the commotion. "There's no way this has anything to do with you. The Tings couldn't afford a flyer. Men with guns in flyers means corporations. The Tings don't have anything to do with corporations."

Or at least, nothing important. A wind blew the dust toward them; Danya pulled up his goggles to keep it from his eyes. He could see Abraham now, tall in robes, discussing with neighbours, describing what had happened. No sign of any kids. Probably they were being kept safe inside.

Someone joined them behind the truck. "Danya," said the new arrival, "was Kiril in there?"

Danya looked—it was Modeg, a slim black guy in a heavy jacket. He was Rimtown district Home Guard, which meant he was probably armed. Home Guard wore no uniforms least the corporations just pick them off with snipers. Only locals knew their identities.

Danya nodded. "He was in there. I want to see if he's okay, but there's some people after us and I don't want to put them onto Kiril." Modeg could be trusted . . . which wasn't to say that he was a friend. The Home Guard fought the corporations. They were leftovers from the crash; the only remnant of organised armed resistance the neighbourhoods had left. But the Home Guard knew street kids were excellent reconnaissance, and made it a point to know them all. Modeg's only interest was in resisting the corporations, not in befriending street kids, but sometimes those two things were the same.

Modeg thought about it. "You'd better come with me," he said. "We've got someone over there. They'll come with information on what happened and if anyone's missing."

Danya and Svetlana followed Modeg down a narrow alley between shop fronts, then up a small rear stairway. A doorway led into a small back room with other rooms adjoining, all cluttered with close living. A woman sat before some small display screens, a short machinegun over her shoulder. There were posters on the walls, all political stuff. Some of them denounced corporations. Others were famous photographs from the crash, masses of people running down streets pursued by AMAPS and aerial vehicles. A bloody resistance soldier, badly wounded, raising his fingers in a defiant victory sign to the camera. And one photo from the Dawn Theatre, its seats smouldering, bodies carpeting the floors. Everyone knew that photo, the random limbs protruding amongst the seats.

"Who were they?" Danya asked. Modeg opened a small fridge and offered them a choice of a fresh pear each, or a chocolate bar. Both kids grabbed the pears, and ate.

"Chancelry," said Modeg. "We think. First got an idea they were coming when the jamming started—they do it with UAVs, circling high above. All our coms went dead."

"How long ago was that?" Danya asked, careful not to let any pear juice go to waste.

"Just ten minutes ago. We might have taken a rocket shot at this bastard, but we didn't have anything close enough to where he came down."

Svetlana peered at the display screens, which showed the Mosque from several angles. Luozi ran through the dust, panicked and bleating.

"We have to randomise the transmissions," the woman watching the displays explained to Svetlana. "Otherwise the corporations can track airbourne signals back to their source. They could put a rocket right on our heads."

Once upon a time, Danya knew, quite a few Droze citizens had had inbuilt uplinks. Some of those still remained, but a lot had been killed. The corporations tracked such people down, gave jobs to some useful ones, and killed the rest. Uplinks were a threat, and now the technology for surveillance and communications was several centuries behind what existed on other worlds. Outside of the corporations, anyhow.

Soon several more people came up the stairs. One was an older black man with a pointy beard. "Danya and Svetlana," he said, not very surprised to see them here. He pulled up his goggles and brushed dust from his face and clothes. "They took ten children. Education purposes, Abraham was told. Said they'd raise the kids properly. An act of charity. Kiril was one of them."

Danya stared at him. He didn't know what to say. If it was true, Kiril was lucky. He should be happy for him. But Kiril was his brother, and if Chancelry Corporation had taken him, most likely he'd never see him again. Or if he did, it would be years from now and they'd be strangers, on opposite sides of the Corporate-NCP divide.

"No!" Svetlana screamed. "No, no, no!" And broke down sobbing. Danya held her.

"Did they say why?" he asked the new arrival—Duage was his name. Danya knew him well enough, he was the regional Home Guard commander. Modeg was his son. "Why here, why these kids?"

Duage shook his head. "I wanted to ask you. They've always left Abraham alone, so this is an unusual step. Can you think of any reason you might have drawn the attention of the Chancelry Corporation lately?"

Danya thought. He could. She was lying upstairs in their hidey, awaiting a lifesaving injection. Tell Duage about her? Duage would then have to tell the rest of the Home Guard, possibly all the way to the top. They might want to take Kresnov themselves. If Kiril were captive, Danya wanted to find out if he was truly safe. If not, he was going to need some serious muscle to help get him out. The Home Guard couldn't do it; they were completely defensive. Danya couldn't remember the last time they'd ever attacked a corporation directly—they just skulked around the neighbourhoods and took occasional potshots at passing flyers. But a high-designation GI from the Federation . . .

"No," he said. "No I can't . . . well, I mean, we upset the Tings just today, but that was less than an hour ago. Chancelry Corporation don't care about the Tings."

Duage accepted that, and talked with Modeg and one of the others who'd come in. Danya thought he'd played that well enough—Duage would hear the Tings were looking for him and Svetlana, and wonder perhaps if he'd lied, unless Danya admitted it first. Now it wasn't suspicious.

Svetlana clung to him and said nothing. She'd trusted him with her life for all her life. Now she continued to, and with Kiril's also. Even if Chancelry treated him well, Kiril would still be terrified.

"Don't worry, Svet," he murmured. "We'll get him back."

They entered Treska's place shortly after, past several patrons who were at the tables, nursing drinks, playing games, watching a vid. No one paid two kids any mind. They took the stairs fast, then unlocked their door at the top of the stairwell.

Kresnov was no longer in the hidey. Svetlana nearly freaked out again, but Danya wasn't buying it.

"Svet, Svet, calm down. It's Treska, it had to be."

Svetlana stared up at him with teary eyes. "You think Treska took her?"

"He had to. You know how I was saying I think he might have some surveillance in the building? I think maybe he has some downstairs. Our locks are still on the doors Svet, all of them. None of them are broken. Some thief getting in here would have had to break some locks, but of course Treska has a key. He's the only other person who does."

"But . . ." Svetlana was confused. "Why would Treska want her? I mean, she's trouble. Treska doesn't like trouble."

"Yes, but Treska likes pretty girls. You know who he runs with."

"Donogle," said Svetlana, distastefully. "You think he'd really risk that with a GI?"

"Treska's gotten into trouble over pretty girls before," Danya reminded her, heading out of the hidey and across the corridor, into what had once been an office. Now it was bare, stripped of everything. Svetlana followed. "He's collected them for Donogle before."

"That's disgusting," said Svetlana. Danya stuck his head into a part of the wall where a display screen had once been. Now the wall cavity was filled with debris. Danya pulled a bit of boarding aside and pulled out their backpacks.

"Yes it is," he agreed. "But it makes him a lot of money on the side." Inside the backpacks were all their useful items—the teacher, bound up carefully in cloths and plastic. Ropes and clips, for climbing. Several good knives. A makeshift first aid kit. A couple of electronic gadgets they hadn't yet discovered the use of, and a bunch of other odds and ends. Street kids were hoarders; you never knew when something you'd found would be useful, or valuable to someone else. Now he pulled out the rope and examined their clips.

"You're going to climb down the shaft?" Svetlana asked dubiously.

Danya nodded. "If I take the crowbar, I bet I can get the elevator doors open from the inside."

"Danya, that's stupid. I'm a much better climber and I've climbed that shaft before."

Danya stared at her. "You have? Without me?"

"Yes, without you. I'm the sneaky one, remember? I'm good at climbing and stealing and it's my job, because we're a team, like you said. This is my special skill. So I climbed the shaft a few times when you were out, just to see where everything is in case we needed it. Treska's got some sensors in there. They're not very good though, just laser triggers. I think he made them himself. I can get past them, but you'll trip them and then we'll be fucked."

Danya blinked. "Why didn't you tell me?"

"Because I knew you'd be mad!" she said impatiently, taking the ropes off him and putting them back in the backpack. "And I don't need these. They'll just swing and trigger the lasers. You go down and wait by the door, and I'll let you in, okay?"

Svetlana climbed. She liked climbing. She liked the freedom it gave her, and the sense of power. It was only a little power—the power to choose where she wanted to go, and the power to overcome obstacles other people had put in her way—but to a street kid, even a little power was an exciting thing.

The elevator shaft was completely black, so she climbed with a flashlight in her teeth. That was awkward, but she'd found that if she wrapped the hard plastic first in a little cloth, her teeth got a better purchase and it hurt less. Besides, it was only four stories, and she hadn't been kidding with Danya—she really was good at this. It pleased her to have something she was better at than Danya, not because she wanted to be better than him, but because it meant she could be genuinely useful to him. She'd have died for Danya. Killed for him, certainly. She hated to be a burden on him, as she knew he sometimes found her to be. This was her chance to give something back.

Finally she got down to Treska's level, and balanced on the narrow ledge. Shrugging off the backpack, she reached inside and pulled out the crowbar. The elevator shaft hadn't worked since the crash, it was said. But she'd tried the doors on their own level, and found the crowbar worked well enough to get them open. Treska had had the ones on the ground floor welded shut, so no one could access the shaft from there. She was hoping he hadn't anticipated that one of his tenants on higher floors might use the shaft themselves. Probably not, given how useful it was as a second escape route . . . particularly for Treska, one floor above the ground and at no risk of a long fall.

Sure enough, the doors came open when she pried hard enough. Svetlana slipped through, then pulled the backpack after her.

She was in what had once been a hallway outside this floor's offices. On the opposite wall there were plaques with company names on them. They hadn't been polished in a long time.

Her flashlight off, Svetlana slipped silently down the hall, then peered in a doorway. She knew she should go to the door and let Danya in, but she had to scout first. Treska had not been downstairs at the bar or in his office, where he often was. That meant he was either here, or he'd gone out.

Immediately she could hear voices, coming from the far side of the floor. Treska used that part as his kitchen and bedroom. Here between were larger living quarters—she'd never been in them herself, but Danya had described them to her. It sounded like at least two people were in the kitchen, one of them Treska.

Svetlana considered her options. Treska's door had lots of locks on it. She didn't need a key to open them from this side—Danya had taken note of that, also. But it would be noisy, and much closer to the kitchen. Someone could hear or notice, or could simply be going to the door. And getting Danya inside would achieve . . . what? He was quite a bit bigger and stronger than her, sure, but bigger and stronger than Treska? Not a chance. Treska was a big man who lifted weights, Danya was a thirteen year old boy.

She would move faster alone, and didn't want to put Danya in unnecessary danger. He'd risked his neck so often for her and Kiril. This was her turn.

She slid into the living room. There, as Danya had suspected, she saw a pair of black boots hanging over the edge of a sofa. Kresnov had worn black boots. Svetlana moved quickly, and came around the edge of the sofa . . . and got a shock, to see Kresnov's blue eyes staring straight up at her. She was tied up, thick synthetic ropes with heavy knots. Normally a GI could have broken them, no problem.

"Here," she whispered. "I've got some bipofalzin, and I've got a syringe. How much do you need?"

Something was odd, because Kresnov's blue eyes were following her. She looked more alert than she had. But there was a handkerchief tied around her mouth for a gag, she realised. Quickly she pulled it off.

Kresnov wiggled her jaw, and yawned. "Don't need the drug," she murmured in reply. "The big guy already gave me some." Svetlana blinked. "Wants me alive for a while, apparently."

Svetlana could have smacked herself on the head. Neither she nor Danya had thought of that. "So you can break free?"

"No. He gave me another drug, muscle relaxant. Not strong enough. Got a knife?"

Svetlana produced one. Kresnov smiled up at her. She was very pretty when she did that. Svetlana smiled back, and began cutting. "Good girl," said Kresnov.

The knife wasn't very big, and the ropes were thick and tough. "My little brother Kiril was taken by a corporation flyer just now," Svetlana whispered as she worked. "Danya thinks it might have something to do with us helping you. You have to promise you'll help get him back."

Kresnov frowned a little. "But how could they know? If they knew where I was, they'd have come here already and grabbed me."

So she did have enemies amongst the corporations. Danya had thought as much. "Treska has some illegal communications gear," she offered. "He talks on it sometimes."

"Ah," said Kresnov. "If they overheard him talking about me, and you, that could be it. They couldn't trace it, but they'd know who you are."

Wow, thought Svetlana. Maybe she'd gotten out of the Tings' yard just in time after all. A rope snapped, but there were plenty more. She kept sawing.

"Promise you'll help get him back," she persisted. Kresnov said nothing. Svetlana stopped cutting. "Promise!"

"I promise," Kresnov murmured. "Cross my heart and hope to die."

"What?"

"It's just something they say in the Federation. My name's Cassandra, by the way. Cassandra Kresnov. You can call me Sandy." Suddenly the voices were getting louder. Footsteps approached. "Quick, give me the knife. I'll keep cutting, you hide. Oh, and put this gag back in."

Svetlana pressed the small knife into her hand. She could hide it there under a heavily knotted rope and cut, not easily seen unless you were really close. She retied the gag, then scampered for the doorway and hid by the frame.

"So what do you think?" she heard Treska's voice in the room she'd just left.

"Oh, pretty hot." She didn't recognise the other man's voice. A customer? "Blonde, I do like 'em blonde. Pity she doesn't look a bit younger, though. She looks, what? Twenty-five?"

"It's all cosmetics with GIs, my friend," said Treska. "She could be anything. Though, if you like 'em real young, there's a fine little piece who lives on the top floor here, cute little brunette. Ten years old as of now."

"Bit young. Wait a few years."

"That was my thinking. A few years' time, I take her to Donogle . . . her brother's a bit protective, might have to do for him first. Shouldn't be too hard, who'll miss another street kid?"

They were talking about her, Svetlana realised. Her and Danya. She was surprised at how little surprised or shocked she was. She'd known Treska was a bad man, but they'd needed a place to stay, and this place was perfect. It had seemed worth the risk. Although in truth, it had been Danya who'd been most worried by and suspicious of Treska, especially where she was concerned. Her big brother was right again.

"You can have a turn now if you'd like?" Treska offered to the man. "You can be the first, break her in."

"Don't mind if I do," said the other man, with eagerness.

"I'll close the door," Treska said cheerfully. "Just make sure you don't let that gag off her. She might still be strong enough to bite your ear off."

He left, and there came the sound of a door closing. The rattle of a belt coming loose. Clothes removed. Svetlana peered around the doorframe. The man was disrobing, sure enough.

Should she wait, Svetlana wondered? She didn't know what she could do. The man was much bigger than her, and Sandy had her knife. How many ropes had she cut through? What if she hadn't cut through enough? What if there was no choice but to stand here and wait for this horrible man to finish his business? But if she waited, surely he'd discover the knife?

The man was now climbing onto the sofa, on top of Sandy. There came the sound of mutterings, of dirty talk. Svetlana had heard that a few times, and had no idea why people did it. The other thing, she was coming to have some idea. But not like this.

Something went pop! The dirty talk ended. Then a thud, as the man's body hit the floor. Svetlana ran into the room in alarm, rounded the sofa, and stared.

Sandy was sitting up, pulling severed ropes off her arms. The man lay on his side, eyes wide, tongue out. Unmoving.

"Is he dead?" Svetlana whispered.

"What do you think?" said Sandy, now pulling at the knots that bound her ankles. She was naked from the waist down. Svetlana hadn't seen before, beneath Sandy's long coat. The man had been trying to roll her onto her stomach. Her fingers didn't seem to be working properly, and she gave up the knots and resumed cutting instead.

Treska's voice came from the other room. "Amdo? Are you okay?"

Svetlana knew she should have hidden once more, but she was tired of hiding. The door opened, and there was Treska, in singlet and pants, his gut bulging, a cup of coffee held to his moustachioed mouth. Staring at the GI sawing through her last restraints, and the little girl who'd set her free.

"You little BITCH!" he roared, and charged at her.

"Dodge," Sandy instructed, still sawing determinedly.

Svetlana dodged one way around the sofa, then the other, as Treska thundered after her, sliding on the floor on socked feet. He could have barged straight over the sofa, but on it sat Sandy, still sawing. She snatched at him as he came close, one-handed, and missed.

Svetlana was further surprised at how little frightened she was. Treska would kill her, she knew. But Sandy had her arms free, and even with the drugs, those arms were nothing Treska could survive if they got hold of him. She just needed to stay close to Sandy, and Treska couldn't touch her. And Sandy's ropes were being cut, one by one.

Treska seemed to realise the situation as she did, and ran cursing for the next room. The last of Sandy's ropes came off and she stood . . . and nearly fell. Svetlana dashed to her side and held her up. Sandy accepted that balance, and lurched awkwardly toward the door that Treska had gone through.

"Stay back," she warned Svetlana, and pushed through the door. But again she nearly fell, and Svetlana went with her, holding her up. The kitchen was empty, and beyond was the bedroom. Sandy went for it, Svetlana with her.

There on the bed was a crossbow—a favoured weapon of establishment owners. Corporation spies sometimes reported firearms, but crossbows were not illegal. Treska was loading it.

"Back!" Sandy warned Svetlana, who ducked behind the doorframe, but peered about to see Treska pick up the weapon and fire. Sandy snatched at the bolt, her hand a blur . . . and missed. It struck her in the throat, and she staggered back a step. Frowned, and pulled the bolt out. A single droplet of blood followed. No jugular vein on GIs, Svetlana recalled hearing. The veins went through the spinal column instead.

Sandy ran at Treska, who fled through the adjoining door. Svetlana followed, as Sandy collided with the doorframe, and Treska tripped in the room beyond, scrambling back to his feet. Sandy came after him, like something from a zombie vid, and Treska swung at her with a big right fist, and connected with a loud crack that would have laid most men out cold. Sandy's head jolted back, but only a little. Treska, however, screamed with pain and clutched his hand.

He'd probably broken it, Svetlana realised. Smarter to punch a steel wall than a GI. Sandy stumbled forward, grabbed him by the neck, and drove him against a wall. And pinned him there, as Svetlana scrambled around to watch. Sandy's fist tightened, and Treska's eyes bulged.

"Fast or slow?" Sandy snarled. Only it wasn't quite a snarl. It was too cold, too simple and straightforward for that. It was hatred, but controlled, almost calm. Svetlana stared, utterly mesmerised.

Treska wailed obscenities and whacked at her with his one good hand. His pants darkened in colour, and the air suddenly smelt bad.

Sandy looked at Svetlana. "Turn around," she said. Svetlana shook her head, eyes wide. Sandy snorted. "Fine. Fast, then."

Her arm jerked, and there was another loud pop! Treska's head flopped like something no longer connected to his body. Sandy dropped him, and his limbs bounced. Then nothing.

"Of all the fucking stupid things," Sandy muttered, looking about with distaste. "I want my pants."

CHAPTER SEVENTEEN

Her pants were ripped and unwearable, so she took some of Treska's instead, and tied them with some of the kids' rope since the tailoring fit her so badly. The kids, enterprising as always, ransacked the apartment for all sorts of useful things before leaving.

Danya knew a back way that didn't involve passing through the tavern downstairs. They went into a back alley, then through several zigzags, Danya and Svetlana scoping their surroundings with all the professional poise of special forces recon. They seemed to think someone else might be after them, people called Tings, but Sandy's head wasn't working well enough to process it further. Svetlana walked at her side, providing support in case she needed it, which she occasionally did. Her balance came and went. One minute she could be fine, the next flailing up against some wall.

A sandstorm was kicking up dust, and the kids fastened on their goggles. Everyone on Droze had them, save Sandy. Sandy squinted; even GIs could get sand in their eyes. Danya rummaged in his pack and found a pair of old shades, not proper goggles. They were scratched, but better than nothing.

"Where to?" Sandy asked. Sand darkened the yellow sky to brown, and even now the temperature was plunging. Static lightning crackled, an electric blue flash, almost industrial. The thunder that followed was high pitched and short, not deep and booming like she was used to. It was sandstorm weather, one of Pantala's more interesting atmospheric features. But the novelty soon wore off.

"How about Cheung?" Svetlana asked, voice raised above the wind.

"We owe him money," Danya reminded her. "Maybe Turner?"

Svetlana made a face, pulling her collar up higher to keep stinging sand off her neck. "She doesn't like us."

"I think she's okay."

"She accused me of stealing last week. I called her a lying bitch."

"Were you stealing?" Danya wondered.

"It was just an apple!"

"Okay, not Turner. Svet, you've got to stop making enemies of our friends."

Svetlana scowled. Visibility on the road was down to dark shadows against yellow gloom. Sand showered against metal shop fronts, their roller doors descending even now. Vehicles roared by with their lights on. Sandy reckoned it would have been painful against exposed skin, for a regular human, but the kids were well covered up, save for their faces.

They turned a corner. This street was narrower, giving more protection. People darted into shop fronts and lobbies through side doors . . . business was still open, Sandy saw, the shutters were just down to keep the weather out. She yawned to keep her ears equalised—the drop in temperature was actually a drop in air pressure as well, one of the stranger local meteorological phenomenons. Pantala's air pressure was only eighty percent the preferred human standard, and in some bad storms, people caught outside had been known to suffocate.

"We're being followed," said Danya. "Vehicle behind us, lights off."

Svetlana swore, but didn't look back.

"What kind of vehicle?" Sandy asked.

"Belcher," said Danya. A combustion engine, in local slang. "Old thing, not like your enemies would drive."

"Tings," said Svetlana. "Can you run?"

"Not really. No balance, weak legs."

"Well, if we just keep walking, they'll coordinate some ambush," said Danya, scanning the road ahead. With the drugs affecting her vision, and now the sandstorm, Sandy wasn't confident she could see any better than him.

"What did you do to these Tings?" asked Sandy.

"Stole some bipofalzin from them," said Danya. "Or Svetlana did."

"Oh gee, thanks," said Svetlana. "Blame it all on me."

Sandy gave her shoulder a squeeze. "Thanks. Let me deal with it. They likely to be armed?"

"Yes, but not heavily," said Danya, uncertain if this was a good idea. "Better not to kill them if you can help it."

Svetlana made a face. "I wouldn't care."

Sandy couldn't quite believe she'd just received those two remarks from a couple of kids. "Keep walking," she said, and turned around.

The vehicle was indeed an old combustion engine design, with a pickup tray on the back and a four-person cabin. Very tough and easy to operate in a low tech environment where electricity was often more expensive than base-ment ethanol, high tech tended to grind in the fine sand, and hydrogen was just plain dangerous in an atmosphere with this much natural static charge.

The vehicle stopped. Doors opened, and two men got out. One sheltered behind the door and pulled a pistol on her, realising they were identified. "Stop right there!" he shouted.

Bad as she felt, Sandy didn't feel completely helpless. She pre-tensed her arm and shoulder muscles, dove and rolled for the cover of the car bonnet, then grabbed the front fender. She reckoned she had barely five percent of her usual power, so flipping it end over end was beyond her—she settled for going sideways, and the man on that side ran desperately as his car nearly rolled on top of him, and crashed on its roof.

In that confusion his friend recovered to try to shoot her, but she kept low, zigzagged, and came up under the gun, turned and threw him at the wall. He crashed off the roller door and slumped to the ground. Which left Sandy holding his pistol, and she checked the ammo. The first man was sheltering behind the overturned car, peering fearfully past a wheel, not stupid enough to engage now he saw what she was.

"Fuck off," Sandy told him, pointing back down the road. He ran. She slid in beneath the car, recalling what Danya had said about ambushes and some-what worried about snipers. There was another man in the car, who panicked as she came in a window, and scrambled out the other side. Footsteps receded fast, and Sandy searched the interior.

Inside was a Teller 9, bullpup assault rifle, compact and very recent tech. League special forces model; to say she was familiar with its utility was a severe understatement. There was also military webbing with extra ammo and kit.

"Outstanding," said Sandy, collecting all. She was due a few lucky breaks.

Through the cracked windscreen, she saw the street mysteriously deserted. Residents in Droze knew when to disappear. Then, into the middle of the street, dropped a man. A ten meter drop, and he didn't even bother to roll.

Sandy had him bull's-eyed through the windscreen with her new weapon before his boots had even hit, for he was clearly a GI . . . but dropping from a good vantage into an exposed street was a strange move for a guy doing an ambush. And then, stranger still, she saw him take his eyes off the overturned car, toward Danya . . . who was running from cover to talk to him. Svetlana, too. It had to be safe, then; the kids' instincts were far too good for them to do that if it weren't.

Sandy slid out, her rifle still targeting the GI's chest. She was half in combat mode, and it seemed to steady her hands and stop the world from spinning. The kids and the GI walked over. He carried a DV-6, longer than her Teller. Not strictly a sniper rifle, but as good as one in the hands of any GI better than a reg.

"Sandy!" said Svetlana, quite relieved and excited. "This is Gunter! He's our friend."

Gunter's apartment was in the attic of a big warehouse and workshop. Sandy barely made it up the stairs—combat reflex was fading, and her strength went with it—and Gunter had to half-carry her through the heavy steel door. He had big locks on it, too, and a good security setup, multi-level ID processing.

Within was a big, wide floor broken by ceiling supports, and small windows on the far wall. Furnishings were sparse and sensible, yet everything was clean and neat. By what she'd seen in this part of Droze so far, Sandy thought it luxurious.

Gunter helped her to lie on his bed . . .

. . . and then she woke up, feeling dazed. The window above her head was dark, occasionally rattling with some gust of wind. She rolled her head, and saw Danya and Svetlana sitting on the neighbouring bed, going through the various possessions from their backpacks. There was only dim light from various fittings, soft and blue.

"Is the power out?" she wondered.

Danya nodded. "The corporations do it to show us who's boss. They run fusion power plants. There's no shortage of power; they cut it on purpose."

"Kind of," said Gunter. He was cooking over in the kitchen, against the side wall. "They do have distribution problems. No one maintains the lines, and lots of people steal. Lots of lines were damaged in the crash, too, and no one actually pays for power, they just demand it. The problem with Droze is that everyone takes but no one gives back, so the lines don't get repaired."

"And whenever someone shoots at a corporation flyer," Danya said determinedly, "or lobs a mortar over the security walls, we lose power for days. If it's a big incident, we won't get it for a week."

"Yes," Gunter agreed. "That too."

Sandy couldn't see what he was cooking, but it smelt nice. She struggled to sit up on the bed, and get a pillow behind her. She felt weak, but her head was clearer. She couldn't have been out for more than a few hours.

"You live here alone?" she asked Gunter.

"Yes. I work for the Tings. Svetlana stole from them."

"But for a very good cause!" Svetlana retorted, not seeming particularly worried.

Gunter smiled, still cooking. "Yes," he agreed. He had that very straightforward manner of a mid-designation GI. Perhaps a high-30. Though, Rhian was a 39, and she'd been a bit like that once. No longer. "I think so, too. The Tings wanted me to help them ambush someone. They didn't say it was you, though I suspected. I wouldn't have let them. But then I saw you overturn that car, and I knew Danya and Svetlana had been telling me the truth about why they needed bipofalzin."

"Thanks for helping us," said Sandy. "We really appreciate it."

Gunter nodded. "We GIs should stick together," he said.

Sandy blinked. She'd heard that sentiment a few times on Callay, among newly arrived escapees from the League. She'd never been aware it existed anywhere else.

"Any chance they'll suspect you and come here?" she asked.

"Maybe," said Gunter. "Though I don't think anyone saw us. Visibility was bad."

"It's Rimtown," said Danya, checking and re-winding up his precious rope. "Someone always sees."

"If they did," said Gunter, "they won't come here. There's only one way in, and they're not GIs." There was a gun on the bench beside him. And being a GI, he had other ways out, like the windows. "The Tings only set an example against people who steal. They don't mind killing, but not if it means a few of them dying."

"Besides, you're too important to them," said Danya. "You make them a big deal in Steel Town. I don't think they're paying you enough."

Gunter seemed to like that. Clever Danya, Sandy thought with admiration. He seemed so relaxed here, where it was safe, but his brain never stopped working.

Sandy got Svetlana to help finally take the slug that had been bothering her out of her thigh. That was a bit icky, because the wound had inflamed and pus came out, but the kids' bag of tricks included tweezers, and Svetlana had the most nimble fingers. The bullet had hit her thigh on an angle, so it had only strained her quadricep a little, barely even causing a limp. Otherwise she had a scar on her elbow, and another on the hard muscle at the side of her neck, where bullets had just ricocheted away.

Gunter offered them all the shower, and Sandy went first while she was still clear headed. The shower was just one corner of the open floor, but Gunter had put up a big curtain for privacy, inside of which the floors and walls were tastefully tiled, with a fluffy rug on the floor to soak up extra water. There was even a little green plant, thriving in the humidity of many showers—a rare sight in Droze, with so little native vegetation. Gunter's decoration would hardly win any interior design awards, but it was real, and heartfelt. Sandy had seen many astonishingly pretty places in Tanusha, yet somehow none had touched her the way that her soldiers' bunks had been decorated in Dark Star—little photos of places they'd never seen, a favorite animal, a beautiful cityscape. The faces of friends who'd died. What else would GIs, with no family or pets waiting for them on some far distant home, decorate their personal spaces with? Gunter's apartment reminded her of that. It made her unutterably sad. She thought of her own friends who'd just recently died, and felt sadder still.

Dinner was sausages, and various cooked vegetables Sandy couldn't identify. The sausages even tasted like real meat—probably vat-grown like most meat these days, but that was "real," and tasty. Danya and Svetlana were impressed, and as ravenous as Sandy had expected.

"If you're from the Federation," Gunter said as they ate, seated on low stools about the chest that doubled as a table, "why are you here?"

"Why do you think?" Sandy asked.

"It was Chancelry Corporation that took Kiril," said Gunter. "If they'd found out Danya and Svetlana were helping you, that could be a warning. Or leverage."

Sandy had no way of knowing what he'd think, or where his loyalties would lie. In the worst case scenario . . . well, he was a lower designation than her. And she'd be back close to top shape by the morning. She hoped.

"What do you know about Chancelry?" she asked.

"They make GIs," said Gunter. "Lots of experimental stuff. They've had the technology since the war. They didn't make me, though, I was here before the crash. I was a League soldier, but the League left me behind."

"The League make a habit of that," Sandy agreed. She sipped some juice from a chipped mug. It was quite good. Gunter's money gave him access to good stuff.

"I know the other corporations don't like Chancelry much," Gunter continued. "GIs are a good weapon. They can do damage without destroying infrastructure, like heavier weapons do. Corporations can afford to kill people, but they can't afford to destroy infrastructure that keeps everyone alive."

"That was why we were so useful in space warfare," Sandy agreed.

Gunter looked troubled, and frowned as he cut his sausages. Sandy waited for whatever was on his mind to surface, still eating. Danya and Svetlana watched this exchange between GIs with intrigue.

"We find them sometimes," Gunter said finally. "Projects. That's what we call them. GIs from Chancelry. Not many of them get away, but you know, GIs sometimes are hard to stop."

Sandy nodded. She'd heard this before, but still she felt cold. "Go on."

Gunter looked up at her, with bothered blue eyes. "One I found was insane. I mean really. His mouth foamed, and he spat, and made sounds like he was trying to talk, but couldn't. We looked after him for a few days, but he died. His heart just stopped."

Sandy wanted to ask who "we" were, but didn't want to change the subject. "Go on," she repeated.

"There was another. She lasted a week. She wasn't so bad, but she shot herself. Twice, because she messed it up the first time."

There it was. Sandy felt it, like a hard core in her soul. She'd been too dazed, befuddled and desperate, the last crazy day, to wonder where it had gone. But it was back now, and she welcomed it like an old friend. It was rage. Murderous rage.

"Chancelry's working on new GI technology," she affirmed. "It doesn't always work. Sometimes they get out."

"You were going to hit them, weren't you." It was a statement, not a question. Sandy just gazed at him. Wondering if she dared to trust. "The Federation never liked GIs."

"I'm a GI," said Sandy. "I'm Federation. The Federation doesn't like the idea of people made and used as slaves. I went to the Federation to be free. Now I'm back. I'd like to spread that freedom. What about you?"

Gunter considered her for a moment. All eating at the table had stopped. With appetites like Danya's and Svetlana's, Sandy hadn't thought that possible. "You're Dark Star, aren't you?" said Gunter.

Sandy nodded. "Former. I left."

"Designation?"

"The highest. Ever."

Gunter nodded slowly. "I've heard of you. You're the one who defected, and made the League upset."

Sandy nodded again. "I rose high and I have lots of friends there. A lot of them don't like GIs, but a lot of them do like me. That's the difference. In the Federation, they accept that I can be just me. That GIs are people, like any other people. Here, in the League, we'll always be GIs first and foremost, however much they claim to love us."

"But we're never really just us, are we?" Gunter replied. "We're different. We might want to hide it, but we can't. I mean, look at me, in this place. If I weren't a GI, I'd have nothing. We change things, just by being what we are."

Sandy nodded thoughtfully. Far from some mindless drone, this one. "What designation are you?" she asked.

"3801-S1." Less advanced than most of her high-des friends, then; the gap even between 38s and 39s was steep. But if he'd been here since the crash, he might be quite old, by GI standards. Age made a big difference. She was proof of that. "You?"

"5074J-HK."

Gunter blinked. "A lot of people would say that's not possible. That the technology's not able to go up that high."

"There's a number of different strands of neural growth tech. I'm an unusual branch. They didn't make many; apparently we're unstable. And when fully grown, prone to think for ourselves."

Gunter smiled a little at the humour. You had to be a GI to find that funny.

Svetlana leaned forward in amazement. "You mean they made you in experimental labs like in Chancelry?"

"No," said Sandy. "League space, a long way from here. But yes, highly experimental."

"Recruitment Department," Gunter added. "The government agency in the League responsible for making GIs. They had experimental divisions."

"But, I mean, what about the Projects?" Svetlana pressed. "These GIs Gunter found who had things wrong with their heads? What if they had to do that to make you? Go through hundreds and hundreds of failures until they got it right?"

Sandy swallowed, and looked at the tabletop.

"Svetlana," Danya muttered, and put a hand on her shoulder. "Enough."

Sandy took a deep breath and looked at the kids. Danya looked cautious as ever. And Svetlana now a little anxious, as though wondering if she'd really stepped in it.

Sandy managed a weak smile. "Don't ever be scared of me," she told them. "I'll never hurt you. Svetlana asked a good question. The answer is that I don't know. I don't think there were that many failures, at least not that went to full commission. We have good enough intelligence on how Recruitment's high-designation programs went to know that. But not precise intelligence. There probably were a few commissioned failures, at least, before me. I can only hope it wasn't very many."

"I'm sorry," said Svetlana, and reached for her hand. Sandy took it. The hand was half the size of her own. Children *grew*. It was hard to get her head around that fact, sometimes. It made the gulf between herself and regular humans just seem enormous. "You don't like Chancelry very much, do you?"

"It's not a matter of not liking them," Sandy replied, gently clasping the girl's hand with some intrigue. "That kind of GI development left unchecked is against the Federation's interests. It's my job to safeguard those interests."

"Sure," Svetlana said drily, with wisdom beyond her years. "But you really don't like them, do you?"

"No," Sandy admitted. And released her hand, reluctantly.

"What were you planning, before you got hit?" Danya asked, resuming his meal.

It was all highly classified, of course. But now, there wasn't much left to classify. The only reason not to tell them was to keep them out of danger, but Danya and Svetlana were already in danger, to say nothing of Kiril. She was really lost in the woods here, and these two children, and this one rogue GI, were all she had for support.

"Our contact was a local tech," she said, resuming her meal as well. "He'd done some probing of Chancelry's systems. He had contacts in other corporations who fed him details, codes, possible ways in. He thought he'd found a central command node in Chancelry's secure network."

Danya looked a little blank. "What secure network?"

"Every corporation has a secure communication network. You have to understand, in modern cities, the networks are enormous. Droze is a long way behind. There are very few uplinks or even working computer systems outside of the corporations themselves, and everything's shielded.

"Now, all the GIs are plugged into that network." She looked about at them. Without knowing what she knew about neural cluster technology, they'd probably not understand why that was significant. "All the Chancelry new GIs included. These new GIs, these Projects, their brains are different. They use a different kind of neural growth technology. We thought this central command node might be the key to controlling the GIs brains."

"You think it's a hive mind?" Gunter asked.

"I'm not sure. We were trying to hit a building on the edge of the Chancelry secure zone; we thought it could get us some information on the command node."

"But they'd have known it was some outside operation," Gunter countered. "No one else in Droze has the ability to do a precision military hit like that, except for another corporation. And they're all trying to make peace at the moment."

Sandy nodded, and swallowed a mouthful. "We're not here to destroy the whole system, Gunter. We were just a few operatives on a recce mission. The idea was to gather intelligence and take it back. We'd figure out what to do about it after that."

Gunter paused to think about that.

Danya saw his chance. "How do we get Kiril back? You said you'd help."

"I'll think of something," Sandy promised. Exactly what she was promising, she didn't know. "I need information first. Any contact any of you have that could help, I want. If you want to help, that is?"

She gazed at Gunter.

Gunter still thought about it. "Going up against Chancelry's a good way to get dead," he said. "They have an army. All the corporations do. It's quite advanced, even by Federation standards. They'll be looking for you right now."

"Probably," Sandy agreed. "But this is hostile land for them. I know what they do to corporation spies around here."

"That's just the Home Guard," Danya warned. "Lots of people would sell you to Chancelry for money. Home Guard are the only ones who hate the corporations enough to kill traitors. Everyone else is just trying to get by."

"Maybe we should tell Duage?" Svetlana wondered. "He hates the corporations, he'd help."

"Duage?" Sandy asked.

"He's leader of the local Home Guard division," Danya explained. "And he doesn't like the Federation either—I don't think it's a good idea."

"Capabilities?" Sandy asked. She'd been briefed, but you could never have too much local intel.

"Very little," said Gunter, shaking his head. "Most of the real fighters died in the crash. They're very outgunned."

"I sometimes wonder why the corporations let any of us live at all," said Danya. "None of us like them, they get nothing but trouble from us."

"They have dreams of building New Torah up to be a power one day," said Sandy. "They'll need a local population for that. An economy, to buy and sell things, and to make things. Besides which, I hear they take talent when they need it, to fill manpower shortages."

There was a silence. It was the wrong thing to say, because now they were all thinking of Kiril again. Svetlana started to cry. It wasn't a little girl's crying, all weak and helpless. It was just pain. Real pain, in Sandy's experience, looked much the same on anyone, no matter the age, gender or physiological makeup.

Danya pulled her close and kissed her head. Svetlana clung to him. In Tanusha, Sandy had seen siblings who were close, but nothing like this. Closeness amongst siblings in civilised places was a luxury. Here, it was survival, and these two kids were permanently grafted to each other's souls. As was the third, and losing him hurt like losing an arm.

But not quite like losing an arm, because Kiril was still alive and almost certainly well looked after, the corporations needing manpower, as Sandy had said . . . plus, if they wanted him for leverage, that only worked if he lived. And so Danya and Svetlana took turns using the shower, as Gunter monitored local net traffic with the help of some shades to block out the light, and Sandy sat on Gunter's bed and refamiliarised herself with the Teller 9.

Gunter had shampoo, and mouthwash, and other amazing things that Svetlana was desperate to try. Gunter let them. Then Svetlana discovered the hair drier, and much amusement followed. Sandy could even hear Danya laughing, as his sister tried to dry his wet hair into a new style, and lots of protests and arguing. It was a nice sound. Kids were amazing, Sandy decided. So resilient, tormented one moment, laughing the next.

They came out in their clothes, and Sandy reflected that she'd never heard tell of any brother and sister who'd comfortably get changed together at that age. But then, as she knew from personal experience, when you'd seen the big horrors the world had to offer, the little ones just stopped mattering as much.

Svetlana came to Sandy and sat on the bed opposite, looking at the rifle. "Wow," she said, wide eyed. "That looks dangerous."

Sandy recalled what Rhian had told Salman one day, when Salman had spotted her pistol. "Do you want to see the most important thing on this rifle?" she asked. Svetlana nodded vigorously. "This switch here." She pointed. "This is the safety. If you see this weapon unsecured, put this switch on, like this. Don't touch anything else, just this."

"What else does it do?" Svetlana asked eagerly. "Aside from fire bullets I mean."

Sandy glanced at Danya. He gave them a wary look from the second bed, looking through his things again. Normally Sandy would have stopped the lesson with the safety. Kids shouldn't need to know about guns like this one. But then, kids shouldn't have needed to be hungry, scared and in danger either, and wishing it otherwise changed nothing.

"Interface," she said, tapping the small CPU in the stock. "I'm running an interface on my uplinks, connecting me into the weapon. Once I'm in I'll feel its balance from the internal gyros, I can measure the speed of its movement from its accelerometers, it'll be like it's an extension of my arm. I'll feel that feedback directly into my brain. And of course it has armscomp, so I see from its targeting here," and she tapped the pinhole camera/laser on the muzzle, "and it also sees what I see, and it shares calculation with my own armscomp."

Svetlana stared. "You have armscomp built directly into your brain?"

"All GIs do. Ever wonder how all humans can recognise faces? I mean, faces are all so similar, you'd never recognise a hundred arms or legs and know whose were whose. But a hundred faces, most people can do that easy, with people we know. A thousand even."

"Yeah I know, humans have a part of their brain just for recognising faces," Svetlana said with faint impatience at being thought dim. "I learned that, I'm not uneducated."

"Not *entirely* uneducated," Danya corrected from the other bed. Svetlana made a face at him.

Sandy smiled. "So that's what GIs have, big parts of their brains just for calculating trajectories. Interconnect them with uplinks for external information feeds, and we're actually faster than AIs. We have the same thing with coordination and movement, too. It's not too different from regular humans, we just process more information, more efficiently."

"I bet you're not so fast right now, though," said Svetlana. "Here." She put out her hands, palms pressed together, fingers pointing at Sandy. "Do you know this game? Hands like this, and try to slap mine."

They played for a while. Even light headed and with her muscles slowed, Sandy found it utterly unchallenging. And yet, she enjoyed it immensely. Aside from her few unsatisfying forays into sport, she couldn't recall ever having played before, as children played. And Svetlana of course found it very challenging, though Sandy made it much easier by keeping her hands slow. Which Svetlana knew, and a few times accused her of not trying hard enough . . . but that was the point of play, Sandy supposed. It wasn't supposed to be about fair contests or challenging matchups, it was just supposed to be fun.

Though it wasn't entirely true that she'd never played before, Sandy reconsidered. Combat training had been a substitute back in the League. And entertainments, of course, her never ending search through net libraries for books, music or films. And then of course there was sex. But all of those were selfish to varying degrees. Child's play wasn't, when shared. She began to see what Rhian saw in it.

Soon Svetlana's eyelids were drooping. Gunter insisted his visitors take the beds for tonight, he'd sleep on the couch. Danya came to escort his sister to her sleep, and she protested, but her heart wasn't in it. Sandy gave her a kiss and a hug before she went.

"Thank you for saving me," she said, and meant it.

"You're welcome," said Svetlana with a sleepy smile, and hugged her back, and went to bed.

Danya sat in her place for a moment, and watched as Sandy finished with the rifle, slapped the magazine in and chambered a round. The interface felt good, a solid presence in her mind. It was good to have something to interface with, so long it had been since she'd used uplinks in a meaningful way on this network-barren world.

"Won't it give you away?" Danya asked, nodding at the rifle. "If you have to move stealthy, won't sensors pick up the rifle transmissions when you interface?"

Sandy nodded. "It's a danger. These are real short range. I lose contact more than two meters out of reach; the transmissions don't penetrate walls and such. When I'm fully armoured the interface goes through the glove to the handle sensor patches, so no transmission at all. But on a stealth mission I'll turn it off. Don't need it much, really. It's just nice to have if I do."

"She likes you," said Danya, nodding at his sister, crawling beneath the covers of the nearby bed. He spoke in a low voice, but Sandy suspected he didn't really care if she overheard a little. These two had almost no secrets at all. "She thinks you're going to save us, and bring us a better life."

"I'll try Danya. I honestly will."

"Svetlana, you know." Danya shrugged. "She hopes for things. I can't hope for things. Things don't happen because you hope for them. You know?"

"I've been a commander in war," Sandy agreed. "I know that better than anyone. You remind me of good commanders I've known." Danya nodded, arms around drawn up knees, looking anxious but hiding it well. A slim nose, but the beginnings of a strong jaw. Intelligent, somber eyes. "But a good commander also knows when to take an opportunity."

"And when to avoid a trap," said Danya.

"Do you think I'm a trap?"

"Not you personally. But I once knew this kid. Haral. I was only ten then, he was fourteen. Said he knew a way through the Caltier Pocket security wall, to a warehouse where there was food and tech and other stuff. I knew that part of the wall pretty well, I told him sometimes they move the auto patrols, sometimes they try to lure people in—it's a learning grid, an interactive defence, it doesn't just sit there and wait for people to figure out how to get around it, it makes mistakes on purpose as a lure. That way it learns how people will try to beat it."

Sandy nodded. "That's exactly what they call it. An interactive defence grid." She'd known adults who'd had trouble understanding it when explained to them. Danya explained it perfectly, just from observation.

"Anyway," Danya continued, "Svetlana thought Haral's idea was great, she was only seven then but all she heard was 'more food, more good stuff,' you know? I said no. I tried to tell Haral and some of the other kids he talked to that you don't fuck around with the security wall. They didn't listen. Svetlana was so upset we didn't go with them. She cried. And then, when none of them came back . . ." He looked at Sandy, with eyes that had nothing of "child" in them. "That was the last time she ever really argued with me when I decided something. On big things, anyway."

"Haral didn't mean to be a trap," Sandy said somberly. "But he was one without knowing it." Danya nodded. "But we all might be. Danya, I can't promise anything. But you want Kiril back. You're usually the most cautious, conservative guy there is, but if you were ever going to do something stupid, it would be for Kiril. Or Svetlana."

Danya didn't reply. But his silence said volumes.

"But you have options now, besides doing something stupid. I'm doing recon. That's what I came here to do, and it's what I'll keep doing now. I want to find out what happened to all of my team. I want to find out who did it. And I have to follow up on our information on Chancelry. If I'm doing recon on that, I can do recon on Kiril, too.

"But there's another option. Chancelry might try to contact you, and promise you Kiril's life in exchange for betraying me." He'd thought about it. She could see immediately that he had. "And I think you'd probably do it." She put a hand on his arm. "Don't worry. I wouldn't even be upset. Kiril's your brother, you'd do anything for him, and I respect that.

"But think. Chancelry don't like loose ends. Kiril's seen the insides of Chancelry by now. They won't like giving him back to you, wandering on the outside, with that knowledge in his head. They won't like anyone out here getting the idea in their heads that once Chancelry grabs you, they might let you go.

"So maybe they'd offer to take you and Svetlana as well. Give you a new life in the corporation. It's real fancy in there, trust me. Much more comfortable than out here. But you know they like to grab their kids young. Kiril's the perfect age, he'll miss you for a while, but young kids are adaptable. He'll adapt to his new situation, and in a few years he'll be a corporation kid—that's no offence to him and how much he loves you, it's just how kids his age are. But you and Svet . . . you'll always be street kids. You'll always be suspicious of them, always remembering your friends out here. Always questioning Chancelry policy when it comes to exterminating troublemakers."

Danya just absorbed, unblinking and unshockable. He gave away very little.

"What do you think the easiest option would be?" Sandy asked. "For a big corporation like Chancelry, with so much at stake? Take a risk on you guys? Or use three bullets and be done with it?"

Danya thought about it, looking at Svetlana, settling to sleep beneath the covers. Whether she heard any of their low conversation, she gave no sign.

Then he looked back. "You really are a high designation, aren't you?" With a faint trace of humour.

"I'm smart enough to be stupid and sentimental with kids like you," said Sandy. "I know you don't trust easily. You're right not to. And in any other circumstance, I'd tell you to go back to your lives here, and forget about me. But I'm not going to watch you get killed doing something stupid for Kiril. I got you into this, I'll do what I can to get you out. But you don't need me to give you any odds on success, because you're too smart to believe me anyway."

Danya nodded. Then looked like he wanted to ask her something, but didn't know if he should. Sandy waited. "What's Callay like?"

"Callay's very beautiful," said Sandy. "There's lots of wilderness, the population isn't very big and nearly half of them live in Tanusha, so you can go from one of the biggest and most amazing cities in the history of human civilisation, to beautiful wilderness, in just an hour. I like to surf."

Danya blinked. "On ocean waves?" Sandy nodded. "I can't imagine an ocean. How do children live in Tanusha?"

"Safely. They go to school, they play sports, they learn arts. There's a lot of community programs. Kids are encouraged to get involved through their schools, not just sit in classrooms. Schools aren't just used as places to do dull lessons, they're places where children learn about their society and their place in it. They're never hungry. I recall one murder a few years ago, an adult killed a child. The whole city was horrified. It was all over the media. Thousands came to the funeral. That's how rare it is."

"There's no crime in Tanusha?"

"Oh there's lots of crime. Crime's a constant in human societies. But it rarely touches children. Children are protected. Some say they're too protected, that they're getting soft."

Danya smirked. "Hell of a problem to have."

Sandy smiled sadly. "Yeah. Hell of a problem."

Danya sat for a moment on her bed, thinking. Wondering if he dared to dream. Sandy felt a lump in her throat, watching him. She wanted to hug him, but respected him too much. He'd resent it, she was sure.

Finally he nodded. Took a deep breath. "Interesting," he said. "Good night."

"Good night, Danya."

CHAPTER EIGHTEEN

Vanessa awoke with a start, a sensation like she was falling. To find that her body was trying to elevate off the bed didn't help. A strap pulled tight, and she recalled the approach plan went weightless an hour out from station, the habitation cylinder no longer rotating in preparation for dock. Crap, she'd slept longer than she'd meant to.

She unclipped the straps and swung from the bed, pulling the webbing across behind her to stop the covers floating away. Then she grabbed her pre-packed bag and gear, secured to the bunk's underside, and pushed off for the door. She spent so much time in 3-D tacnet spaces these days, the abrupt loss of 2-D orientation didn't bother her much. The door whined open and she squeezed through, along the corridor to the neighbouring chambers.

Here was a tiny galley, as everything was tiny on the *Farseeker*, an independent, League-registered freighter bound for Antibe Station via several smaller jump points that wouldn't have been profitable to a larger vessel, and were barely profitable for this one. The galley was larger than she recalled, her brain struggling to comprehend how the room had looked before, only now the wash basin was upside down and her brain kept trying to insist that the ceiling was the floor.

Rhian was already here, floating comfortably, strapping on a thigh holster, a similar one for a knife already on her forearm. She had her pants down to do it, but Ari wasn't noticing, holding his own gear bag, looking pale and unhappy.

"I told you an upload wouldn't cure space sickness," Vanessa told him, floating in and flipping to wedge herself between fixed tabletop and floor, so she could stay in one spot while preparing.

"Your prediction is noted," Ari grumbled. "Yay you."

"How far out are we?"

"Twenty minutes," said Rhian, testing the release on her holster, all business. About her floated various other weapons she'd not yet secured. "We'll have an hour after we dock, no rush."

"Fucking dead system even this far out," said Ari. "You get this close to Callay you get all kinds of transmission traffic, but there's nothing here."

"Enough weapons, Rhi?" Vanessa asked, eyeing her assortment.

"Barely," said Rhian. Vanessa hadn't wanted her to come. Had been privately relieved when she'd come anyway, overruling Vanessa's protestations, but even so, she was a mum now. Rhian had thought Pyeongwha would be a simple thing, you go and do the job, then you come back, but even that had been harder than she'd thought. Kids grew when you weren't there, and missed you, and asked where you were. This time, at the prospect of her going away again, this time for longer, they'd been upset. Rhian had been upset, too. Vanessa had never actually seen Rhian cry before, or look generally miserable, but so far on this journey she'd been both. But under it all was steely determination, because if Sandy was ever in trouble, Rhian would be there, and that was that. One day, she insisted, her kids would understand that, too.

Sandy wouldn't, Vanessa was pretty damn sure. Sandy was going to be mad as hell she'd let Rhian come, had been very determined that Rhian wouldn't come in the initial mission with Han, Weller, Khan and Ogun. Rhian was Sandy's big success, the one GI who'd transitioned from combat vet to happy motherhood, and Vanessa knew it was more than just love for an old friend that caused Sandy to be protective. Rhian was proof that it could work, that the fate of synthetic humanity wasn't always bound to be tragic, and Sandy would happily wrap Rhian in cotton wool and forbid her from ever facing danger again, if she could. But that wasn't up to her, and neither was it up to Vanessa, because ultimately, what Sandy had fought for herself and Rhian to have was freedom. And Rhian, being free, chose to come.

Vanessa dressed in her own civvies, functional and heavy duty, good for station wear with lots of pockets. Not so many weapons as Rhian, but Rhian had her own ideas of what worked, and was experienced enough at civvie security duty that Vanessa wasn't about to tell her otherwise.

Geared up, she returned to the corridor and made her way carefully toward the bridge. She wasn't as graceful as Rhian up here; Rhian was an experienced spacer. Sometimes she forgot that most of Sandy and Rhian's early life had been in places like this, ship corridors and cramped quarters, bulkheads, stations, snap-frozen rations. No wonder Sandy loved the outdoors so much.

Procedures and security were pretty lax on a small freighter, and there was no one to stop her drifting onto the bridge. It had only five stations, chairs stuffed into small spaces amidst a crowd of automation, life support and wrap-around scans. A lot of it required a direct uplink to look at, but Helm's primary scan was simple enough to read, and showed the station ahead as a small dot moving across Pantala's wide surface on a fixed trajectory line, surrounded by a clutter of smaller dots. Some of those would be debris, some small vessels, some atmospheric shuttles on ascent or descent. Probably none were starships, not at Antibe Station; they couldn't get many more than one a day, if that. Not only weren't the routes economically viable to most, they weren't safe either. And the corporations didn't trust big League liners, and only traded with independents these days.

"Not on a very high orbit, are they?" she volunteered. Scan read them at 320 kilometers altitude.

"Magnetic field's a bit weak, sun can get lively," said Captain Ocha, eyes hidden behind his wrap-around visor. "Safer down lower. Plus less fuel from the surface—they do more up and down traffic these days than side to side."

Ocha had a good working relationship with the FSA, and it made him enough money that he could keep his head above water, not always easy for a privateer in these lean, post-war years. Mostly he just gathered intel, and told them what he saw. Sometimes he smuggled FSA operatives or equipment through League space. Privateers weren't reliable, of course, but Ocha's daughter had been press-ganged onto a League cruiser in the dying years of the war, forced into Fleet uniform at gunpoint, so desperately short of good spacers the League had been. That cruiser had died in one of the many small exchanges across the contested systems, a cold and lonely death at some forgotten mass point that barely made a dot on the official charts. FSA folks Ari trusted, and there weren't many of those, said Ocha was no friend of anyone officially League, and New Torah even less.

"Can we see who their guests are?"

"Wait five minutes," said Ocha. "We're on the wrong side, we'll make a burn in three to bring us around."

Helm brought up a forward image on one screen so Vanessa could see. Antibe Station was a big, round wheel, like stations everywhere. But unlike stations everywhere, this one was massive, a big export hub through which a large portion of the League's grounded war machine had passed at one time. Now it sat lonely and bloated on Pantala's horizon, with barely more than a skeleton crew to keep it operational.

Com was talking to station. Vanessa overheard discussions of cargo and prices. They were transmitting manifests, checking the board as they called it, to see how the prices were moving. Lots of perishables, Vanessa guessed; Pantala didn't grow much. Most of the population wasn't rich enough to trade, but the corporations still had money. Luxury items for the suits, while the masses scavenged.

"Look at this," said Scan, and put a visual on a screen. It showed a ship, a big steel spine and modular tanks, small habitation circle, no jump engines visible to Vanessa's less-than-expert eye. The engines were glowing.

"System runner," said Ocha. "She's leaving?"

"Yeah, heading 258, that's Anak."

"The shipyards?" Vanessa asked. They were out in orbit around the Pantala system's third planet, where the asteroid belts made good ore bodies for mining.

"Nothing else out there," said Ocha. "Big, isn't she? Acceleration gradient?"

"Um . . ." said Scan, analysing the runner's track. "Yeah, she's loaded. At that thrust she's maybe forty percent slower than empty; those holds are full."

"With what?" Helm wondered. "Anak yards are pretty complete. There's not much industry around there they'd need."

Ocha made a face. "Everything deteriorates, Anak's a rough orbit, they get micro impacts all the time, they'll need to replace things."

"Great," Vanessa muttered. "They're expanding."

"Too early to tell," said Ocha, entering control adjustments for the upcoming burn. "Let's get a look at this station." He flipped the shipboard microphone. "Everyone take hold, burn in ten."

No one told her to strap in, so Vanessa guessed it wouldn't be hard, and grabbed a support. Then a rumble, which grew to a gentle roar, and everything tilted. Suddenly "back" was "down," and she was dangling from the support at a third of a G. She hooked a leg around the support and watched Helm's screen as Scan's station visual shifted perspective.

A minute later the burn ended. The station was passing elliptical, its docking face becoming visible for the first time. A blaze of sunlight momentarily blinded the feed, then a darkening adjustment.

"What the fuck is that?" said Scan.

Vanessa could see five ships, locked in amidst the mass of docking supports and heavy duty frameworks about the station rim. Some of those were bigger than the ships at dock, having to support thousands of tonnes of weight at the station's full one-G. But worth it, from station's point of view, because there was space on the rim, and very little at the non-rotating hub.

"That's . . ." said Ocha, peering at the feed. "That's a big fat ass on that thing."

"Which one?" asked Vanessa.

"Berth 12. The big one, far side, just coming toward us down below."

Vanessa could see it now, and it was tail heavy, even to an untrained eye.

"Computer says cruiser size, but that's no cruiser," said Scan. "I don't see any cargo; that fucker's all engines."

"Not a civvie," said Ocha, and Helm muttered something under his breath.

"It's a warship?" Vanessa asked. "League Fleet?"

"Yeah, but nothing line. I'd recognise it." He was squinting at the picture, a weathered, bearded face, a man who had run this ship all through thirty years of League-Federation war and had seen most things. "That's a ghostie."

"Yeah," said Scan, reluctantly. "Yeah, the displacement's all wrong for a cruiser. I mean, you can't be all engines. You need some midships. That thing's fast."

"Ghostie?" asked Vanessa.

"Rim recon. Long jump range, can come in way further out from an anchor mass than most of us, sits out on the rim all silent and watches."

"Don't come into station very often," Ocha added. "Or not the open traders. Dark facilities mostly, I've been doing this all my life, this is oh . . . the fourth I've ever seen?"

"Cool," said Helm, turning to grin at his fellow crew. "How many Talee you think this guy's seen?" Skeptical looks came back. "Oh, come on. What else is he doing out this far?"

"I've got a better question," said Ocha. "Why the hell does New Torah allow a League warship to dock at Pantala? And why would League want to?"

Outer collar dock was cold. Vanessa huddled in her heavy coat, arms folded as Rhian manned the inner airlock door. Ari looked better for the return of gravity here at dock, but worse again for the deep freeze, his face pale beneath his newly grown black beard.

A crash from the outer airlock, grapples attaching. Rhian pressed some controls and exchanged words on the mike, watching a vid feed. She'd done this before, which made her the lead on this op. Vanessa was comfortable enough in command—she had led the attack to liberate Nehru Station from Fifth Fleet five years ago, so orbital operations weren't completely strange to her—but her everyday experience in mundane things like how to operate a collar dock was well below that of Rhian's. Which left Ari, with his dislike of all things offworld, but probably the most important of the three.

After some minutes of securing, the outer lock opened, and someone in a station worker's jumpsuit appeared. Rhian saw the pressures were equalised, and popped the inner doors as well.

"Who won the Callayan football grand final?" asked the heavy set man in the airlock.

"Subianto Dragons," said Vanessa. "Eighty-nine to sixty, pretty disappointing match."

The man extended his hand. "Tung," he said. "Wait ten minutes, I have to make a crew inspection, then we'll load this stuff and leave." He strode past the crates and boxes waiting in the corridor, and headed for the bridge.

The three new arrivals exchanged looks. They'd gone over how this should work too many times to start discussing it again now.

Tung returned in ten minutes, and they helped him load the airtight transport crates into the runner, lashing them down in the cargo space behind the seats. Then they followed him into the cold, cramped interior, found various seats and strapped themselves in. Tung's pilot fired up the engines, then released grapples, pulling them clear. And then, with a startling silence, cut engines. Weightlessness returned, as the station's spin carried them out and away. The pilot's touch on the control stick kept them oriented, with a huge view of Antibe Station's curving expanse outside the forward windows. Real windows, Vanessa marvelled, gazing out at the extraordinary view. She'd missed them; starships of course had none.

Once clear of the station's dangerous rotation, the runner fired up engines once more and headed slowly for the station hub. Everyone stared out, even Ari, for the station at this range was quite a spectacle—a good three kilometers wide, it was said by some to exert its own minor gravitational pull. Bullshit really, most of that width was empty space between spoke arms, but to look at it, it seemed it might be true.

"That's a Fleet ship?" Vanessa asked Tung, pointing to the ghostie where it nestled amidst a tangle of supporting gantries, like a bird caught in the vines of some carnivorous plant.

"U-huh," said Tung. "No idea what, they won't let us near it. Used their own docking crew and everything."

"A year ago that might have been an act of war."

Tung shrugged. "Torah doesn't have its own navy, not much we can do."

Which was a bullshit answer, because you didn't need a navy to stop uninvited vessels from doing what they wanted in your space. Callay hadn't abandoned its independent anti-shipping defences it had acquired five years ago during the troubles with Fifth Fleet. Modern guided missiles could make life this close to a planet extremely dangerous for any League ship, and Pantala was an arms factory world. You didn't need an FSA briefing to figure that one out.

So who in the corporations had given this one permission to dock? And to what purpose?

Station hub had a pair of huge docking funnels, like an axle running through the rotating wheel. Huge mechanisms ran the funnels counter-spin so they didn't rotate as fast, making for an easy docking. Various vessels were clamped to the outside, like barnacles latched onto a bridge pylon. Suddenly station orbit brought them into Pantala's night side, and huge station lights glared as darkness abruptly fell, with a smattering of smaller lights from each docked vessel.

Tung piloted them into the end of the docking funnel, and Vanessa felt like some character from a story book, being swallowed by a giant monster. Within were more ships, several big in-system runners like the one that had just departed, numerous orbital service vehicles, and a bunch of atmospheric shuttles. Everything was lit like the interior of huge factory floor, metal ribbing everywhere, ships pressed comfortably to the funnel's outer rim by the gentle rotation. Vanessa counted fourteen orbital shuttles, five of them big VTOL assault shuttles, no wings and all armour, for rapid ascents and descents. Pantala industries made them, too. Were they still making them? Where did the money come from, in a collapsed economy?

She glanced at Ari, and found he had quite casually commandeered a display panel by his seat and had plugged in. Neither Tung nor his pilot had noticed. That was sloppy. Ari would have every security system internalised by the time they docked. Ari saw her looking, quite calmly, and looked much happier in zero-G with something else to think about.

"Is this a standard traffic day?" she asked Tung, to keep his attention.

"Quiet," said Tung. "You should have seen it before the crash, it was something." Most of the funnel berths were empty, Vanessa supposed. She imagined it with most of them occupied, and saw what Tung meant. "Station capacity's nearly half a million, but there's barely ten thousand living here now. Two thirds of it are shut down to save power."

They docked at a vacant berth with a crash of grapples, then some waiting as the tube was positioned, Tung talking to someone on the other side. Tung gestured for them to unleash the cartons behind the seats, which they did, then drifted them across the cabin. The airlock finally opened with a hiss and pop of escaping air, and everyone yawned to equalise. Tung pushed several cartons ahead of him up the tube, then gestured back for more. Vanessa sent the whole lot over, still lashed together.

Tung disappeared around a bend in the tube. They heard talking, and laughter. Vanessa hugged her arms tight, breath frosting in silver plumes. Ari was shivering, despite his layers. Being Tanushan, they were used to shirt sleeves even in winter. Rhian floated motionless, listening.

Tung returned empty handed. He gave them a thumbs up, floating easily back into the cabin. "Easy," he said. "Give them a moment, they'll move the stuff. We'll take the next crawler in."

"Wonderful customs system you've got here," said Ari.

Tung grinned. "This is why governments were invented, yeah? Make some makeshift bullshit admin with six big corporations sharing everything, no one trusts the other to do proper security, everyone has their own little loopholes for goods they don't want no customs agent to check, no one knows which customs agent is reporting to which corporation . . ."

"What was in those boxes anyway?" Ari asked.

"Don't ask," said Tung, tapping his nose. "We don't. They know we've got more stuff here but they won't ask further. If they see something they shouldn't, could get messy, yeah?"

Ten minutes later they went up the tube themselves. The crawler was an elevator that traversed the length of the docking funnel. More airlocks and a tight seal, then they were trundling slowly toward the main hub. Small portholes offered a floodlit view of the funnel interior, crawling by.

"We're clear in here, no monitoring possible," said Tung, indicating the control panel. "Why'd you come?"

"Surprised you?" Vanessa suggested, eyebrow raised, holding to a handle in what she reckoned might be zero point-two of a G, a gentle drift toward the outer wall.

"Hell, yeah. Boss nearly blew a wire when we got the signal. FSA didn't tell us anyone else was coming. You're supposed to clear it first."

"Something came up," said Vanessa.

And that was that. Tung looked a little anxious, exchanging a quick glance with his pilot. There was wireless here, station network, but she didn't want to risk accessing. One look at the construct told her that there was no way Ari wasn't already in it. She glanced at him. His look back was dead level, no deviation. Very un-Ari like. Immediately she knew. One glance at Rhian, and Rhian knew also. And gave away nothing.

"She a GI?" Tung asked, nodding at Rhian.

"Yep," said Vanessa.

"Low-des, right?"

"No low-des GIs in the Federation."

"Is that right?" Tung looked at Rhian, dubiously. Rhian gazed out the porthole as though she hadn't heard him.

The crawler reached the hub wall and continued into its berth like a grub burrowing into a tree hole. It paused, as airlocks crashed and clanked, then jolted forward once more, emerging into a small chamber. Big locks crashed open, and the entire side opened, allowing them to float free.

"Just through there," said Tung, pointing to an adjoining corridor, more of a tunnel in zero-G. "My cell leader's in there, he'll meet with you."

"In there?" asked Ari, pointing down the narrow space. "After you."

"No, I'm not some big shot, best you talk with the CL alone."

"No, I insist," said Ari. "You come with us, be good for your promotion prospects."

"No, buddy," said Tung, "I assure you it won't."

"I insist," said Vanessa, having floated to an advantageous position at one wall. Her pistol was out, levelled at Tung's head. Rhian similarly covered the pilot.

"Whoa, whoa, whoa!" said Tung, with a forced, nervous laugh. "Look, don't be jumpy, there's nothing down there but the people you came to meet . . ."

"How do you know who we came to meet?" Ari asked. Tung blinked.

Suddenly all three adjoining doors slammed shut and locked.

"Fuck it," said Vanessa, immediately grabbing her facemask out of a coat pocket and sealing it on, as Ari did the same. "Rhi, you smell anything?"

Rhian didn't bother with the facemask, pushed off a wall to float at a sealed door, and tried to find leverage. Tung and the pilot pulled out their facemasks also, but Ari took them away.

"No chance," he said. Sealed in like this, the room could just be gassed, or decompressed. But ISO had two of their own in here, and gas wouldn't stop Rhian, mask or no mask.

"I could punch it," said Rhian. "But in zero-G there's no leverage." She removed a small explosive from a leg pocket and clamped it magnetically to the door. Vanessa gestured Ari and the two captives behind the open elevator door, as Rhian got above her impending explosion.

Tung and the pilot chose that moment to try and grab Vanessa and her gun. Vanessa fended easily and punched one in the head, then broke the other's ribs with neat, short jabs. She had no leverage either, but with her augmentations at point blank range it didn't matter.

"It's odd," said Ari as they dragged the men behind the elevator door, one unconscious, one injured. "When I'm dealing with combat ops I'll attack the small woman last, 'cause logically she's the most augmented. But there's still so many guys that won't figure."

"I can't figure if that makes you chivalrous or chauvinist," Vanessa replied. "Rhi, we're clear."

Rhian's charge blew with a deafening crack. Rhian quickly got a hand into the hole, another on the bulkhead, and pulled. Steel shrieked and began to bend. Soon she had both hands in, and with more pulling, it was large enough to fit through.

"Guess who's going first," said Vanessa, eyeing the size of the hole.

"Me," Rhian corrected. "They'll try to shoot us coming up the passage. I'll shoot them first."

"Wait," said Ari, eyes distant, "my schematic says there's a cross-corridor halfway up, better to go around them than through."

"Never been my experience," said Rhian, making a last adjustment to the size of the hole, then pulling out weapons. "See you in a minute."

One of the corridors abruptly opened, and all weapons swung onto that space. A man emerged, empty handed, palms up, floating into the room.

"Who the hell are you?" Vanessa demanded.

"A friend," said the man. Chinese features, young, handsome, strongly built under all the clothes. "Come to help."

"GI," said Rhian, not taking her pistol from his head. "Are you ISO?"

"No."

"League?"

"No."

"Well you're not Federation because I've never seen you."

"Doesn't leave a lot of options," said Vanessa.

Ari abruptly winced, a hand flying to his ear. "Ow."

"Please don't access my uplinks without permission," said the new GI, with a faint smile. He seemed quite comfortable with the whole situation. "It's not polite. Now if you please, the ISO will realise their trap was sprung, and will be hurrying around to block this corridor even now. Let's go."

He disappeared back the way he'd come. The three Feds looked at each other.

"You okay?" Vanessa asked Ari.

"Sandy's the only GI I know who can do that," said Ari, looking quite astonished. "He went through all my layers just like that, could have fried my main perimeter if . . ."

"That's great, Ari," said Vanessa, pushing off to follow. "Sounds like a man crush."

"Is that safe?" Rhian wondered.

"Says she who was about to charge an ISO position single-handed. Move." Vanessa hand-over-handed her way up the corridor after the GI. They emerged into a new chamber, this one with walls stacked around with safety equipment and storage containers. And the floating body of a woman.

"ISO?" Vanessa asked the GI, who was checking adjoining corridors for signs of movement.

"Yes. High designation, unconscious."

"Unconscious?" GIs were notoriously hard to knock out or disable. It made non-lethal neutralisations nearly impossible.

"Fast hack," said the GI, patting the lump in his pocket. A booster cord? "This way."

He pushed off down a new corridor, with the grace of a natural spacer. Ari peered at the unconscious woman's face.

"Fast hack a high-des ISO GI?" he breathed. "No way!"

"From man crush to wedding bells," Vanessa remarked, following after. Ari had a point, though. Technically, the highest designation GI ever made was Mustafa Ramoja. That anyone knew of. ISO only recruited the highest designations and didn't have the problems with defections the League military had, because they treated them better, gave them responsibilities, trusted them as partners and friends.

Combat GIs were hard to hack. Sandy herself, nearly impossible. Fast hack meant a backdoor, something written into the barrier defences that a simple key could access and disable in a split second, but no high-des GI had anything like that in her systems, least of all one working for the League's premier intelligence and security agency. Sure, this new GI had used a booster cord, meaning direct access to the back of the head, presumably while holding her in some kind of immobilising grip . . . hard enough to do on its own. Then insert the cord, then do a fast hack and knock her out cold . . . who the hell was this guy?

Further along, the hub became busy—docking crawlers unloading goods, dock workers moving heavy crates with just light touches. Crates were then attached to railing systems down these corridors, then guided to central cargo. It was only small goods, though. Main cargo went through automated systems direct from ship to station down on the rim—the station hub was for stuff that avoided customs, though there were a few people around who looked like security, checking seals and scanning contents.

Vanessa, Rhian and Ari had their facemasks off, manoeuvering past some crates on rails, when security stopped them. "You three. IDs."

They pulled readers, established direct uplink connections while security inserted their own readers, and verified those barrier IDs on the non-invasive platform the readers presented—less dangerous than a direct uplink, for security and their targets. The security were both men, dark jumpsuits, spacer webbing with many tools, pistols included. On their readers, IDs would show as corporate—Heldig Corporation, semi-shielded background, meaning they were quite high up and couldn't be verified all the way back to home base. Ari had warned them it would open them up to greater suspicion, but it was the only way to do it—an unshielded ID could be traced by anyone, and found immediately to be fake. Higher level corporate types kept some information behind barriers, not liking to share everything with rival corporates. Station security were theoretically independent, and no corporations trusted that impartiality, so station security could only check so far.

"So," said one of the security men, in a half-bored drawl as his eyes scanned the reader, "what brings you three Heldig folks up this way?"

"Merchandise check," said Ari, a steadying hand on a bulkhead to stop him from spinning. "New arrival."

"New arrival," security repeated. "That wouldn't be that *Farseeker* ship, would it?"

"No idea," said Ari, all skeptical intensity of this man's right to ask him anything. His accent, Vanessa noted, was spot on—score one for another of Ari's fast-training upload programs. "Why not take it up with my superior?"

"And who might that be?"

"That's right!" said Ari, as though it just occurred to him. "You can't find out, can you?"

"Hey buddy," said the man with a smile, unplugging his reader. "Just doing my job. You know, we caught someone pretending to be checking on a backdoor cargo, just last week?"

"Did you, now?"

"Turns out they were just black-marketing for personal profit. Not even letting their buddies in on a cut. Someone got pissed, blew one of them out an airlock."

"You're joking," Ari deadpanned. "You know where the airlocks are?"

The security man pointed. "That way, I think."

"You know how to use them, too? Those little buttons by the door? I think there's a red one, and a blue one."

A dry smile. "Have a nice day sir. Ladies."

"You have to pick a fight with them?" Vanessa remarked as they floated on, down the next corridor.

"It was well done," said the new GI. "No one trusts anyone up here. It's neutral territory, so the corporations constantly squabble over jurisdiction. You handled it exactly as they would."

"Why didn't they check your ID?" Rhian asked him.

"I'm known to them."

"Any sign the coalition's working?" Ari asked.

"Well, they're not killing each other anymore. Or not so obviously that they can't deny it. The station staff are appointed by all the major corporations; station master's a rotating post, two months at a time. There's big government offices up here. Corporate officials run a lot of the new government from orbit. Safer than the ground."

"You don't say," said Vanessa. She knew all that, but their new friend seemed quite talkative. "Who's the new ship in port? League vessel?"

"Ghostie, Fleet recon."

"Any idea why she's here?"

"The same reason anyone docks at Antibe Station," said the GI. "Someone invited her."

"Who, and why?"

The GI smiled, gliding easily down the corridor with gentle touches on the wall to recorrect. "Wouldn't that be telling?"

More floating down corridors, and dodging station hands who spared them not a second glance, brought them to an elevator bank at the top of a station arm. Small elevators for small groups of people, larger ones for cargo or larger groups . . . further along would be a big one for shuttle and other heavy cargo, mostly an automated system.

The GI keyed in a code and they slid into a waiting elevator car. With a whine and shudder of magnetic rails it accelerated, creating faint gravity for a moment, then nothing.

"Talk," said Vanessa to the GI. "Not ISO you say, not League, not Federation. Are you just non-aligned? Gone AWOL?"

"Can't say," said the GI.

"Can't, or won't?"

"My name's Cai. I'm here to help you. I'm aware of ISO's operations on this station, and on Pantala. So of course I'm aware of the FSA, too. I knew you were coming because I was monitoring ISO networks. That's how I knew they were going to spring a trap."

"Any idea why?" asked Vanessa.

"Yes. Cassandra Kresnov's mission was betrayed. I think most of her team were neutralised, but she is missing. Given her reputation, I suppose that means she's still alive and operating. The ISO certainly think so."

"ISO betrayed her?" Vanessa's heart was thumping. Ari and Rhian looked worried. Not shocked, but definitely a little scared, in that way that only concern for a good friend could do. "Why?"

"I do not know," said Cai. There was a certain calm intensity to his eyes. Rather like Sandy's, Vanessa thought. An unblinking, intelligent penetration. "I was hoping perhaps you would know more from your end. This is an unorthodox move of you, to come. Why do it?"

Vanessa glanced at Ari. She was technically in charge, but Ari outranked her on intelligence matters. Telling a high-des GI anything was dangerous, because they couldn't be guaranteed of shutting him up if they required it.

"He's not ISO," Ari told her. "His attack barriers just now aren't like anything the ISO use. Or anything anyone uses." Watching Cai with intense curiosity. "He's not League, either; all their loyal GIs are dumb."

"Not all," Cai corrected with a faint smile. "But most. And no, not League. All that you need to know is that I'm on your side. Or more correctly, on Cassandra Kresnov's. What Chancelry does to their GIs on Pantala is evil. I want it stopped."

"I'll decide if that's all I need to know," Vanessa warned him. And took a deep breath. "League pulled an intel operation in Tanusha that we fear may have compromised Cassandra. But now you're telling me the ISO betrayed her . . ."

"It may be connected," said Cai. "ISO and League gov have only been estranged, not divorced. Perhaps the intel operation you describe uncovered something that brought them back together."

"What designation are you?" Rhian asked, as gravity began to increase, and sunlight from outside strobed the elevator car through the porthole.

"What designation do you think I am?" Cai asked her.

Rhian struck at him. Cai's hand flashed immediately to intercept. Rhian smiled, sent drifting despite the low gravity.

"High," she said. "You're as fast as Sandy."

"I wish you'd give some warning before you do that," said Vanessa, heart restarting.

"You didn't answer her question," said Ari.

Cai smiled. "I'm sorry. You'll find it's occupational."

The answer reminded Vanessa of Mustafa. And the next time she met Mustafa, she was going to kill him. These days, with her upgrades, she reckoned she might even survive the attempt.

CHAPTER NINETEEN

Sandy woke. Again, she'd slept in. Danya and Svetlana were busy with some device on their bed, while Gunter made breakfast in the kitchen. She blinked her eyes and head clear. Normally she didn't need much more than four hours, though it varied. It had been a long time since she'd slept this long.

Svetlana's device was a teacher. Its goggles were fastened over her eyes in a headset, earpieces firmly fixed. Her mouth moved silently, repeating what she was seeing and hearing.

"How did you get a teacher?" Sandy asked Danya, impressed. Even as she asked it, she realised it might not be the right question.

"A friend said we could have it if she died," said Danya, reading off a small portable.

"Oh."

Danya smiled a little. "It's not so sad, she was old. Well, I mean it was sad, but . . ."

"Natural causes."

"Yeah. She left a will and everything. Someone made sure the teacher came to us. We'd do errands and stuff for her sometimes, and talk to her. She didn't have anyone to talk to, usually."

Sandy hadn't thought of that. Most old people in Tanusha were socially hyperactive, uplinks and VR meaning that even physical immobility couldn't stop them. Though there was the phenomenon of many old folks liking VR too much, and spending nearly all their final years there. Some VR techs swore that the years of uplink time imprinted virtual personalities into the matrix, which continued to live as ghosts after their passing, sending whispers to visiting friends.

"What's Svetlana learning?" she asked.

"English. Those are the only cards we've got, that and maths. She hates maths."

"Are the drugs expensive?" Non-uplinked teachers like this used just a light sedative, to suppress the brain's natural processing. The unit itself would also learn individual users' brainwaves, and compress and order information specifically to the individual.

"Yeah." Danya shrugged. "It's worth it, even if we have to go hungry a few times. We'd never have survived this long if we didn't get smarter from the teacher. How are you feeling?"

"Better, I think."

Svetlana removed the headset. "Danya, could you adjust the input? It's getting fuzzy again." She noticed Sandy. "Hi! Feeling better?"

"Let's see." She sat up, and found that someone had laid some clean underwear on the bed. Female underwear. And pants, to replace her borrowed ones.

"A friend's," said Gunter from the kitchen, seeing her looking. "Don't ask."

Sandy smiled, and changed, her back to the kids.

"Danya!" she heard Svetlana accuse him with a playful whack. Well, she could hardly blame a thirteen-year-old boy for looking. She supposed that she could have gone to get changed behind the shower curtain, but it was her old military reflex again, to do things the simple and straightforward way in the company of people she respected. Vanessa had once accused her of being too straightforward, and for a time she'd been self-conscious about it, but these days not so much. She was what she was, and if it caused others trouble, well, she wasn't above finding that entertaining.

Then she lay on the floor and stretched. One thing with being a GI— if you wanted to stretch, most of the time the only thing you had to hang onto that wouldn't break was yourself. She tried several positions, and got her muscles up to what she reckoned was sixty percent of maximum. They'd do better if she pushed, but she didn't want to risk it.

Gunter put breakfast on the table—scrambled eggs and bacon. The kids were so impressed. Gunter went to Sandy, his hands together in imitation of Svetlana's game last night. Sandy smiled and did the same, fingertips touching his. He tried ten times, and couldn't lay a finger on her. She tried ten times, and slapped his hands on every one.

"You really are a 50 series," he observed, sitting down to eat. "Are you one hundred percent?"

"Not yet," Sandy admitted, joining the table. "Maybe tomorrow."

"I don't get it," said Danya around a big mouthful of eggs and toast. "GI designations are mostly about brains, right? I mean, physically there's not much difference between you and Gunter?"

"I have a better figure," said Sandy, with mischief.

Danya blushed. Svetlana giggled. "But, I mean," said Danya, recovering well, "if it's all about brains, why does it make you faster as well?"

"Because brains are what control how fast we are," Sandy replied. "That's what nervous systems do in most animals. It's all about movement. Intelligence came later, but it's only a small part of what brains actually do."

"But lots of really smart people aren't coordinated."

Sandy shrugged. "And lots of them are. Think of it this way—not every smart person is physically gifted, but nearly every physically gifted person is smart. And by physically gifted I mean with coordination and reflexes, like a gymnast or a tennis player. People who are just fast or strong, okay, they don't have to be so smart . . . but I've met quite a few people good at really technical sports in Tanusha—my SWAT guys have lots of friends in pro sports. The best ones are all really smart, no exceptions. Technical skill is another form of intelligence. Look at great musicians. That's not just an intellectual gift, it's a physical one, too. You can't separate them."

"So they made you really smart, and that made you faster as well?"

Sandy paused to drink juice. "My nervous system processes information faster than most, and in bigger volumes. Physical information is no different from other information, so yeah, I'm faster."

"So why don't they make all GIs like you?" Svetlana asked. "If you're so much better?"

Sandy smiled. That old question again. It was a settled, stale issue in Tanusha, but she couldn't blame Svetlana for asking—she didn't know. "Because the only reason the League spends all that money on us is so they can get an asset in return. In my case, and Gunter's, a military asset. They want us to fight, and do what we're told, or they've wasted their money. Or worse, created a dangerous enemy."

"And you left," said Danya, gazing as the answer occurred to him. "They're scared of you. They don't want GIs thinking for themselves, but GIs have to think or they can't fight."

"Exactly." Danya never failed to impress her. "So they want GIs just smart enough to fight, but not so smart that they'll really think for themselves. I've got lots of high-designation friends who've defected. A huge percentage of those who survived long enough to think about it ended up defecting, and it hasn't stopped yet. Not all of them did, but a lot. Why would any arms industry invest all that money in a weapon that one day was a fifty-fifty chance of turning around and shooting back at its creators?"

Something was bothering her, a low frequency pulse in one of her receptors. A radio signal?

"You hear that?" she asked Gunter.

Gunter frowned. "Hear what?"

"Maybe a radio frequency. Something old and nasty."

"Only people who use radios that openly in Droze are Home Guard," said Gunter.

"And they know where you live, right?" asked Sandy, rising to her feet.

Gunter waved for her to sit back down. "Finish your breakfast first. They're not stupid enough to pick a fight with me."

After breakfast, Gunter went out his front door and down the steps. Around a corner, he found several heavily armed but nervous Home Guard, debating what to do next. Gunter invited them in for coffee.

They entered nervously, four of them, in the rough, heavy clothes of most Droze residents, ideal for protection from cold and dust, and for concealing weapons. Their leader was a black man with a pointy beard, and a big floppy beret on his head.

"Duage," said Danya from by the kitchen. Hands where the men could see them, Sandy noted. "Modeg. Hi."

"Hello Danya," said Duage, but his eyes were on Sandy, sitting on the dining table, her new rifle in her lap. "Is this a friend of yours?"

"Her name's Cassandra," said Danya. "Would you like some coffee? Gunter, let Svetlana make the coffee. She's really good at it."

"Gee, thanks," said Svetlana, pretending to be upset at being told to work, but actually pleased to be complimented.

"Thank you," said Duage. "Two white, two black, no sugars." His eyes didn't leave Sandy as Svetlana set to work. Gunter had a real coffee machine like Treska's kitchen had, and she was indeed good at it. "The Tings are after you," he said to Sandy. "A blonde female GI, attacked their men. You'd best be careful."

"Tell the Tings they have that the wrong way around," said Sandy.

"The Tings have a lot of people," said Duage. "They're one of the biggest employers in Steel Town. They could muster a hundred guns if they wanted, easily."

"After I 'attacked' the Tings' people," said Sandy. "Were any of them killed? Badly injured?" Duage shook his head. "That can change real fast."

"She's right," said Gunter, offering the men some fruit. Fresh fruit was basic hospitality on Droze, precious enough that its gift counted for generosity. They took some. "The Tings were after Danya and Svetlana for stealing. But they only stole to help Cassandra; she was injured and needed drugs. Cassandra protected them from the Tings. There's no real injury here to anyone."

"The Tings' pride is injured," said Duage. "You know that pride is power in Droze."

"No," said Sandy. She indicated the rifle. "This is power. Tell them to let it go."

"You make a lot of threats," said a younger black man. Modeg, Danya had called him. There was a family resemblance to the older man. His son, Sandy guessed. "For someone who got her backside kicked by Chancelry the other night."

Sandy gazed at him, unblinking.

"It was you, wasn't it?" asked Duage. "The GI raid in MidEast? You were the target."

"What did you see?" Sandy asked quietly.

"They did an airdrop. GIs, no armour. Very quiet." Terminal velocity wasn't a very big impact for a GI; they could jump out of aircraft and land unassisted without injury, if lightly equipped. Heavier equipment tended to break, however, requiring parachutes or other landing assistance to protect the gear. "We watch all the flyers that go overhead, day or night. This one hovered, about five thousand meters."

"You're sure it was a Chancelry flyer?"

"No," said Duage. "But who else uses so many GIs like that?"

"What else did you see?"

"Nothing. We got over there fast, but by the time we arrived they were leaving. We could have had a shot at the evac flyer, but we have a policy not to shoot at them when they're leaving, only when they're coming in. We don't know who they're carrying when they leave."

Sandy's eyes flicked to Danya. He looked skeptical. She knew a lot of Droze residents said the Home Guard liked to talk a lot about how they could have done this or that, but never actually did anything. Given what she knew of corporation firepower, she couldn't say she blamed them.

"But we took some footage," Duage continued. "I'll show you, but you have to promise you'll tell me what it shows."

"I might," said Sandy. Duage considered her. They had to know roughly what she was by now. There were only so many people that Chancelry Corporation would make such an effort to take out, and only so many offworld GIs who'd be on Droze making enemies of the corporations in the first place. But he had nothing to lose by showing her. The Home Guard were enemies with the corporations no matter what, and no matter how little he trusted her, the prospect of a bit of information was better than none.

Her Tanushan reflex was to expect Duage to offer her an uplink cord to view the images internally, but instead he pulled a slate from his coat and activated the screen. He handed it to her, then sat alongside to watch as she scrolled.

The footage was shaky; a handheld, not some uplink vision monitor. There was running on a rooftop, then hiding behind cover. The user's hard breathing. Then a steadying of the camera, and the first calm shot of a black, military issue flyer hovering over a rooftop, sans running lights. Sandy recognised the building where Aristide's apartments were. Stairs opened to the roof, black clad figures emerging. They'd booby-trapped and wired those stairs five times over, but the attack had come through windows and from lower floors, and the traps stopped people from entering, not leaving.

The black figures moved with military precision and inhuman speed. Several were carrying bodies. Sandy recognised Weller, slung over a shoulder. Khan. Han. No restraints, clearly dead—hostile GIs had to be restrained if captured, even drugged. It was procedure. Unless they were dead, obviously.

Then a new figure, upright but not walking. Dragged by the armpits, his wrists locked behind him, head lolling. Sandy froze the image and zoomed. The zoom was awful, and she rewound the footage. Ran it forward at standard speed.

It was Poole. She'd bet her arm on it.

"That one's still alive," Duage remarked alongside. "Who is he?"

"Friend," said Sandy. Her voice was tight. "They all are."

"How'd they take you?"

"Gas. Through the ventilation. Something GI specific; they're pretty rare, hard to use. We were half gone before we realised we were under attack. Someone on the inside."

"Well, then," said Duage. "You'll find this next bit interesting."

A new figure emerged from the stairway, without the light assault gear of the attackers. A black man, broad shouldered, walking uninjured and unassisted to the waiting flyer on the rooftop, in the company of the attackers. He turned just once to survey the horizon, and the screen caught his face perfectly.

It was Mustafa.

A creaking from the portable warned Sandy that her fingers were about to break the screen. She relaxed her hands with difficulty.

"One of yours, yeah?" Duage asked, watching her face. "Who is he?"

"A dead man," said Sandy. And meant it. There was silence in the room. One of Duage's men shifted his weight, and a weapon clicked against a jacket zipper. Sandy's eyes shot to him, and he froze. She was in combat reflex, and everything looked like a target. Small movements leaped at her, begging retaliation. Small noises crashed upon her eardrums. No one dared move.

Save the small figure who advanced upon her from the kitchen, slim body a glow of warm and mellow shades to Sandy's vision, but for the mug in her hands that glowed soft red with heat. She walked up to Sandy and offered her the mug.

"Sandy? Have some coffee. You'll feel better. It always makes me feel better."

Sandy took a deep breath and forced the deadly focus down. Normal vision restored, slowly, and there was Svetlana before her, offering her the mug. Trying to help the only way she knew how, because small luxuries like coffee were heaven in Svetlana's world, and one learned to be happy with what one had, however fleetingly.

Sandy sighed. Accepted the coffee with one hand, and ruffled Svetlana's hair with the other. On the portable screen, the flyer lifted off the rooftop and climbed quickly for altitude.

"So what's your mission now?" Duage asked. "Now that one of your main guys has betrayed you?"

"That depends," said Sandy. "You're the one who came here with this portable, looking for information. It seems to me that you're the one who's planning something."

The basement was under a standard block of dusty apartments, guarded by a guy in a plain coat that covered an assault rifle. Duage led the way downstairs beneath flickering fluoro lights, to another secure door with big locks, guarded by two more armed men, playing cards.

The door was opened, and down some more stairs, then into the building basement, a big concrete space with generators and overhead pipes. Everything looked almost pre-technological to Sandy; this part of Droze had sprung up around the corporations without planning permission in the early days of colonisation. League law couldn't prevent the excess people from coming, so the corporations had to accept them and let them do their thing. Rimtown and districts like it were like the old shanty towns she'd read about in books, slums of poor workers springing up in the hope of profit from proximity to the wealthy. They'd built cheaply, and it showed.

Tied and chained securely to steel pipes against the wall was a woman. A GI, female, brown skinned. She sat in a chair, hands locked behind her with cuffs, aside from all the other restraints. Two armed men got to their feet at the party's arrival.

"They missed one in the evac," said Duage to Sandy, indicating the GI. "She's drugged. Someone shot out a piece of her skull, but she survived. Could have been you."

"Could have been me," Sandy agreed. She'd been so cross-eyed at the time she might certainly have missed a clean shot.

She walked to the GI. Behind her, Danya, Svetlana and Gunter stood with Duage and watched. The GI had no gag in her mouth. Her head had been roughly bandaged, a small bloody patch on the cloth, bound over very short hair. Her eyes were closed.

Sandy squatted in front of her. The GI's eyes opened. Pretty, as were they all. Her gaze seemed well focused, so the drugs weren't too serious. Targetted drugs repressed muscles, not brain function, but some did both, just to be safe.

"What's your name?" Sandy asked. No reply. Not even the flicker of a response in those eyes. "Do you have a name? Are you Chancelry Corporation? What's your designation?"

No reply to any question. And no prospect of getting one.

Sandy looked at Duage. "Got a cord?"

"Hey now," said Duage, "she's our prisoner, I'd rather you didn't do anything with her I can't see."

"Well you can torture her all you like, she won't talk. We suppress pain, and we heal more easily. If you want to find out what she knows, you'll need another GI to do it, one who's a higher designation than she is."

Duage thought about it. Sandy wasn't sure what to make of him yet. He had no military background, that was clear. But he seemed pretty smart. Whether that assessment would change once she figured what he was up to, time would tell.

Duage pulled a cord and booster unit from a pocket, and tossed them to her. One of the guards brought her a chair. Sandy sat alongside the prisoner, inserted the cord into the booster, then the back of her own head. The prisoner saw what she was doing and moved her head evasively, but Sandy smacked it back against the pipe she was secured to, and plugged in.

Big barrier elements. A huge, complex structure in the empty 3-D neutral space created by the booster. Better to use the neutral space than hack a GI directly. She established her entry point, made sure she was back-secured, then began. The GI's construct resisted, but Sandy knew these League patterns too well, and soon the feedback responses were allowing her automatics to construct new offensive codes, which she tried in turn to create new feedback . . . the loop accelerated until outer elements began collapsing, and from there it all fell pretty fast. A hard job for her by GI standards, but in real-time outside, it probably only took five seconds.

The construct still resisted, a mass of branching pathways that glowed and pulsed, looking much like a real brain in full complexity. Sandy knew from nasty personal experience that entire constructs could take long hours in real world time to break down entirely. That was okay, her needs were more limited.

A blur of visuals as she shot down various paths and junctions, it ought to be right about . . . here. Minor barriers resisted and were killed, then she found multiple matching keys to get visual functions unlocked, and . . .

Visual memory. You couldn't actually hack a GI's memory any more than you could a regular person's. Brains worked in mysterious and complicated ways; memories weren't stored as data files to be pulled out and reinserted, they were meshed into a million other things that all overlapped and interconnected in ways that made it impossible to unravel even if you could access it, which usually you couldn't. But GIs, and an increasing number of augmented regular humans in Tanusha, had memory attachments—cybernetic memory, it was often called, though the latest advances made that clunky old terminology sound quaint.

Memory attachments lightened the processing load by duplicating fuzzy "real" memory in data files, like making a copy and storing the backup. It made recall more precise, whether of people's names, faces, passcodes, or anything else a person might want or need to remember as a matter of urgency. Soldiers used them to recall procedures, regulations, technical skills learned once but rarely practised since. Instant and precise recall. And, in some very popular Tanushan thriller vids based on true stories, occasionally subject to outside manipulation and hacking, with all kinds of hair-raising results.

Sandy was only looking for images. Lower designation GIs stored them as a matter of automated function, like a camera set to record automatically whenever something walked in front of it. Here she found images, and flashed through them rapidly—corridors, rooms, meals. Bathrooms, showers, sex. Beds. Combat sims, more corridors, people. People.

Sandy reset the search function and went after faces. Lots of them flashed by. Her own memory implants had all of Chancelry's most senior known faces, and these matched with none of them. This GI didn't mix with the rich and powerful, no surprises there. But there were lists of technicians Mustafa had provided them with, ISO lists of minor functionaries in various corporations. If she could find a few of them, maybe there were some elements of her old plan that could be resurrected . . .

She paused on an image of a mess hall. The image played, a few seconds, erratic time lapse, but the purpose of cybernetic memory images was to store visual information in 3-D, not to accurately recall events in sequences. Here was a girl, seated amongst the others at chairs and benches. Dark straight hair cut short, blue eyes. A GI amongst GIs, yet all alone as GIs rarely chose to be. And then she recognised her.

Wow.

She copied the data and withdrew fast . . . and found herself blinking in the dull fluorescent of the basement. Disconnected the cord and double checked images on internal visual from her own memory implants . . . definitely her. Definitely. So what to do about it?

The prisoner was staring at her. "Why her?" she asked, voice hoarse. As though she were having difficulty speaking.

Sandy frowned. "Excuse me?"

"That one. Why her?"

"The girl alone in the mess hall. She's a Chancelry Corporation GI, isn't she?" There was no reply, but this time, a flicker of response. "Do you know her?"

The GI's mouth worked. Nothing came out. In her eyes was something new. Confusion. Sandy felt as though the room temperature had abruptly dropped ten degrees.

"Oh dear God," she muttered.

"What's going on?" Duage wondered. Then, "Hey kid, best you stay back from there."

But Danya came to Sandy's side anyway, peering at the prisoner. "What's wrong with her?" he asked.

"Nothing's wrong with her," Sandy said quietly. "She's exactly how they made her. Her neural construct patterns are strange. I'd have to spend hours looking at them and I'm not a neurologist, but they just look odd."

"What did she mean 'why her'?"

"She knows another GI in Chancelry, I pulled an image of her off the memory implants. I don't know her name, but she had a good friend who was sent to Tanusha on a mission some months back. His name was Eduardo."

The GI was staring at her.

Sandy leaned close. "You knew him, didn't you? He said this girl was his best friend. He loved her. I think he only went to Tanusha because his bosses said they'd hurt her if he didn't. He's dead now, you know that? His killswitch activated. They killed him, your bosses. I tried to save him."

The prisoner closed her eyes.

Sandy stood up. "Well, we've got something to go on, now. That is, if the Home Guard actually want to do something big for a change?"

Duage drove them through the night time streets, bouncing on rough roads, a careful eye out for activity. Their path took them through two other Home Guard sectors, some of which might not take kindly to Rimtown Home

Guard passing through their patch unannounced. But if they were going to do this quietly, there was no other choice.

They pulled down a side street several blocks from the neutral zone, this was a wealthier area, streets buzzing with light and people, and quite a bit of traffic. Duage drove the van to an underground car park, queuing behind several others at the entrance, all checked by heavily armed guards at the entrance. Being Home Guard, they were waved through. Then spiralling down into the parking space below, until Duage found an empty level and pulled the van into a park.

The passengers clambered out—Duage, Modeg and a Home Guard man named Zhao, plus Gunter, Sandy, and their two scouts, Danya and Svetlana. When Danya had first insisted they go, Sandy had refused. Then Danya told her about the salvage riches in the neutral zone near the barrier, the wreckage of technology that still lay unattended in or beneath many of the buildings. Most folks left it alone, rightfully fearful of the perimeter bots that prowled the zone, but a few times, when they'd been desperate, Danya and Svetlana had come here for a fast but dangerous score, as had other street kids. Street kids networked, and it hadn't taken Sandy many questions of the Home Guard to discover that the kids knew the neutral zone far better than they did, either first hand or from others. Sandy still didn't like it, but if this was going to work, it had to be done.

They rattled up a service stairwell until they reached a corridor along the ground floor of the apartment building above. Danya and Svetlana led the way, their usual drab, dark clothes serving the purpose of a night recce well enough, plus the dark woolen caps pulled over their heads. Sandy followed, rifle slung under her coat, a borrowed pistol in her pocket, a black cap hiding blonde hair. She'd have been happier with a second pistol, not to mention sensible webbing to secure the rifle to her back, hold grenades, and a headset for sensor enhancement plus rear vision, but beggars couldn't be choosers. Several passersby gave them odd looks in passing, four bad-news adults led by two kids.

The corridor emerged at the building's rear, then along a narrow walk against the property wall. Someone had knocked a hole in that wall, for access Sandy supposed, and they moved into a rear garden, past a long disused swimming pool that hadn't seen water in years, then up stairs to the next building through-corridor.

"It's all apartment buildings all along here," Danya explained as they walked. "It used to be real expensive before the crash. It used to be right next to Chancelry's main zone."

"Still is," said Duage from behind Sandy. "Just now there's a wall in the way."

"The apartments up close to the wall are still really nice," Svetlana added. "Some folks still try to live in them from time to time. But the bots get them. The corporations don't like anyone living too close."

"Can't imagine why," said Modeg. His coat was longest, concealing what would be a high caliber sniper rifle, once the barrel was attached.

They exited through the building's front lobby, occupied by several home- less folks heating some food on a cooker. One of them extended a hand at the passing group, dirty and bearded beneath an old blanket.

"So many apartments," Sandy observed as they trotted down stairs onto the next cross street, "but there's still homeless people."

"This here is Decision Street," Danya explained, pointing up and down. Further up were lights and people gathered around a night market. Several street vendors did a brisk trade despite the deepening cold. At the far corner, loud music thumped. "They call it that 'cause if you live here, you've got a decision to make. Live here, and pay high prices, and be safe. Or try your luck a bit further down and live for free, and risk the bots."

Danya led them along a few buildings, then up a side lane. They had to clear the gate first, and Sandy would have given the kids a boost, but they scrambled over with the dexterity of urban bunbuns. The lane got dark very quickly, though, away from the street lights.

"Broken glass on the right," Sandy alerted them, vision fading to ultra-v. The kids walked left, peering to see.

Svetlana turned to give her a grin. "I wish I could see that!"

I wish you could too, Sandy thought, wishing once more she could have left them in safety. Or as close as Droze got to safety, for street kids.

Ahead they had to climb a genuine wall, and this time Sandy demon- strated with hand signals that she had a better way for them than climbing a neighbouring drain pipe. With Danya's foot in her hand, she just had to extend her arm for him to grab the top and clamber over. Svetlana followed, then Sandy jumped up herself and helped pull Duage, Zhao and Modeg over. Gunter jumped himself, bringing up the rear, and made his own sign to his mouth, warning her that it was no longer safe to talk.

Sandy didn't need to tell the kids that; they were reverting to their own system of hand signals, manoeuvering close to a wall, then pausing beneath a broken window. Danya gave Svetlana a boost up, and she wriggled in and disappeared. A moment later came two taps on a wall, and Danya followed. The window wasn't big, and Sandy realised that there was a good chance kids were better at this than adults—fitting through small spaces and making less noise. But her desire for them to be elsewhere didn't come from doubts about their ability.

In fact, their hand signals as they crept through an abandoned downstairs laundromat were remarkably close to the military language she'd known forever, save for a few intriguing variations. Pausing to look back from a corridor, she made a few of her own signals to them, and was instantly understood.

There were no lights in these buildings at all, and the central corridors were so dark the kids must have been nearly blind . . . but the way was straight and predictable, and they walked fast enough with fingertips trailing along the walls. And as they neared the front lobby, things brightened fast. There was a lot of city light outside, coming from somewhere ahead. That was Chancelry Quarter, on the other side of the barrier, where buildings loomed tall and life was good.

The kids ducked left instead of moving through the lobby, and Sandy saw its windows were shattered and its walls peppered with shrapnel marks. Whether it was recent or crash-damage, she couldn't tell.

Danya led them up stairs to the third story, then indicated they should wait in the corridor outside an apartment. Sandy was having none of it and followed him in. Within was a regular apartment, stripped of everything valuable. A rope was tied firmly to a kitchen fitting beneath the sink. Another slim line, like fishing line, made a connection from the apartment balcony to the neighbouring building. Two lines, Sandy saw, like a little pulley system. Danya set about securing the rope end to the pulley . . . it would take the rope across to the other side. Leaving the rope there permanently would show up on some bot's scan, but fishing line would probably not. And where the hell did they get fishing line on Droze? With no nearby oceans or fish?

Sandy indicated a negative to Danya. He frowned at her, and pointed across to the neighbouring building. Walking streets was too dangerous, obviously—they were easy to monitor, and even if you didn't die immediately, the monitors would know you were there. Sandy nodded her understanding, then pointed to herself, pointed to him, and mimed a throw to the neighbouring building. Danya looked at her as though she was nuts.

Svetlana came into the room with a questioning expression. Sandy repeated her throwing mime. Svetlana jumped up and down with enthusiasm, and pointed to herself. Sandy grinned. Danya stepped forward sternly to indicate that however nuts, he'd go first. Svetlana made a face at him.

It wasn't a long throw, just four meters, but further than a kid could jump with no run-up. Sandy lobbed Danya neatly over the opposing balcony rail, then did the same for Svetlana. Then she jumped herself and left Gunter to deal with the other straights.

This time it was down to the basement, Sandy now insisting on leading the way, pistol in hand, checking back on Danya for instructions. In the basement there was no light at all. Danya pulled a flashlight and led past dead pumps and heaters to a service room. Inside, Sandy found a hole in the wall, leading to a service tunnel for power and com cables. Within was enough space for a kid to crawl comfortably, and an adult uncomfortably.

Sandy definitely went first this time, beneath the opposing road. Surely Chancelry knew about these access tunnels, and would guard or booby-trap them. But then, the corporations had never been interested in the population beyond their walls, had ignored it and been disinterested in their doings. Did they even have detailed planning schematics of the non-corporate city beyond their walls? No one here had had to gain planning approval before building anything.

At the other end, another hole was covered by a metal sheet, opening into another basement-adjoining room. Sandy cleared it and the basement beyond before clearing Danya and Svetlana to come through. Modeg stayed to guard the basement, as Zhao had remained to guard the balcony crossing . . . Danya signalled to her that he wasn't happy leaving people behind, it only increased the chances of discovery. Sandy could see his point, but Home Guard weren't incapable, bots were pretty stupid, and a random sector search that discovered their trail could be neutralised before it transmitted back. Bots were not in constant communication with HQ because HQ blocked all outside transmissions, fearing subversion. Which was why they were having to sneak inside the kill zone to begin with . . . but it did mean bots could be taken out without HQ's immediate knowledge, provided it was done fast.

And leaving people behind to guard the trail meant they wouldn't be ambushed on the way back. Though probably Danya knew several other ways.

The next crossing was six stories up, this time a hidden plank bridging three meters between close balconies. Or it would have done, if the kids hadn't had Sandy. They'd barely gotten over and inside when Sandy heard a whining sound, and ushered them quickly into the back of the apartment. A hover UAV went over, lift fans whirring. Sandy wasn't so worried about them. There was no way to make them silent; she could hear them coming a long way off. But Danya indicated the spot he knew was just one building over, so they left Duage at the balcony, meaning now it was just them and Gunter.

They took stairs down, then a fast door past a corridor and into the deserted kitchen of what had once been a ground floor restaurant. Sandy took guard by the kitchen doorway and peered out. The restaurant beyond was a wreck, destroyed by weapons fire long ago. Danya indicated out and to the side, and after a full scan, Sandy silently did that. The side door was missing, and the wreck of a crashed aircar had come down right alongside, between buildings, providing cover.

Then Sandy heard it coming—tires up the road—and gestured Danya quickly back into the doorway. Danya in turn gestured to Svetlana, who darted across to join him. None of them looked when the bot passed—most recon bots had complete 360-degree vision, and if you could see them, odds were they could see you. Best to hide, and listen. Sandy recalled old tales of Jason fighting Medusa, duelling with a foe he wasn't able to look at without turning to stone. She reckoned this one had just the four wheels, weighed perhaps half a ton. Probably had more firepower than she felt like dealing with if she could avoid it.

They left Gunter to guard that crossing, moved quickly into the neighbouring building, then took the stairs. Two floors from the top, Danya took them into a corridor, then finally to an apartment doorway. Sandy opened it quietly and cleared the room as best she could, crawling low behind the bed. The room was bright with light from nearby towers. She lay on the floor behind the bed, wondering if she should roll across to the bathroom to check it was clear. She decided against it—any one of those towers could have AI-analysed telescopes trained on these buildings, and the windows were clear to see through. Any movement could conceivably launch a high explosive round in here within a matter of seconds.

So. She took off her small backpack and began setting up the unit the Home Guard had lent her. It was a military issue encrypted radio, an ancient thing at least a century old, but in good working order and suitable for her purposes. This apartment, Danya had assured her, was the only one he knew with a view of a Chancelry com tower, and within a hundred meters. That was within the boundary of Chancelry's own chatter, and if she set the frequency right, should get confused amidst all the other signals; a lot of them were automated along the barrier, plus all those civvie signals . . . even if the location triangulation did get set onto her, it probably couldn't place her with certainty outside the barrier. She hoped.

She placed the little transmission dish against the pillow—no automated scan was sensitive enough to see that through all this light contrast—and began listening. Danya and Svetlana joined her, backs to the bed, one on either side and watching with curiosity. Sandy put the unit in her lap, then plugged the cord into her head, not wanting to leak even the smallest local transmission.

With the control panels up, she received for a moment. Lots of traffic; a genuine cacophony. Excellent. She sent her own signal to join them, modulating it to resemble them as much as possible. That took some work, but she was somewhat designed for this, too—one of those reflexive programs that just happened when she thought about it. Home Guard had provided her with thousands of local pass keys and identities, and after a little while of listening she was able to determine which ones seemed most likely to work. She tried one. A com tower asked for a pass key, which she saw as a 3-D graphic on internals, and 3-D graphics asking for pass keys was her bread and butter.

She gave the kids a thumbs-up to indicate she was in. Svetlana pulled out a little portable screen and pointed to it questioningly, wondering if she could be allowed to see what was going on. Sandy shook her head . . . they lacked the right cord. Svetlana rolled her eyes and looked immediately bored. Sandy smiled. Kids.

But the network . . . this was more like it. This was a very big network, but nothing compared to Tanusha. Lots of it looked automated, but that just made it predictable, and she flew down gleaming visual highways, looking for branch-offs and offshoots. How to find a single GI in this network? Narrow it down and keep narrowing. Experimental GIs wouldn't be allowed to just roam. Somewhere heavily shielded, then. Chancelry HQ, someplace very hard to get into.

It wasn't hard to find, but it was heavily shielded. On internals it looked like what medieval knights must have seen staring up at the walls of impenetrable castles, huge barriers designed to keep everything out. But unlike castles, network barriers had to be penetrable; if there was no communication with the outside, there was no point putting it on a network at all. She just had to find a way to fool it into thinking she was an insider. And that, with her skills in a League-software environment, was just a matter of time.

CHAPTER TWENTY

"**Y**ou'd do more good staying on station and working on the problem up here," Cai told the three Feddie agents as they sat on his bare-boards floor and contemplated a shared station graphic.

"No," Rhian said firmly, cleaning one of her pistols. "I came to help Sandy and our other GI friends. We can't do that if we're not on the planet."

"Getting down to the planet's going to be very hard without ISO help," said Ari. "Forging IDs for a downworld berth wouldn't be hard without them, but now they're working with League again, and League's at least paying friendly visits to New Torah, we can't assume ISO hasn't told everyone that we've arrived."

Cai's apartment was in a deserted quarter of the station. It was directly beside a heating vent, or it would have been freezing instead of merely cold. Big windows overlooked the docks, covered now by a big tarpaulin. It must have been quite an upmarket joint when the station was fully occupied and buzzing. Now, stripped of all fittings, it echoed.

"Look," said Cai. "League resumed contact with New Torah at least two years ago. I've been doing recon in these parts for a while, and I know this for a fact. I suspect it has something to do with whatever Chancelry is up to with their GIs. Chancelry is doing all kinds of experiments on GI technology . . ."

"Why?" asked Ari.

"I don't know. But whatever it is, League wants a part of it."

"Chancelry's a heavy arms manufacturer," Ari muttered, rubbing his forehead. "What do they even want with GIs?" He glanced at Cai. Cai said nothing. Ari's eyes narrowed. "You know something, don't you? Who do you work for, some private League corporation? Maybe Mohindi Group, worried Chancelry's stealing a lead on you?"

"You can ask all you want," said Cai, "but I'm not at liberty to discuss it."

"Hang on," said Vanessa. "ISO's entire premise for this operation was that League didn't want anything to do with New Torah. That they had no interest in intervening here, didn't want to admit New Torah was a problem, and would start a war with the Federation if the Federation tried it instead. Now you're saying League's actually been here talking to New Torah for two years?"

"At least," said Cai. "So if the ISO were upset at their own government for something, it wasn't that."

"Maybe . . ." Ari's eyes widened a little. "Maybe ISO weren't upset League wanted nothing to do with New Torah. Maybe they were upset League had too much to do with them."

Everyone looked at him.

"Okay, okay," he said, "think about this. League Gov gets involved with New Torah, the last place in the known universe they're actually welcome. I mean, they'd be more welcome on Callay."

"'Specially amongst your friends," remarked Vanessa.

"Suddenly Chancelry Corporation, New Torah's biggest surviving heavy arms manufacturer, starts making GIs. Heavily experimental ones. No media out here, no human rights observers . . ."

"Few enough even back League-side," Rhian said drily.

"Damn sight more than here," Ari retorted. "Anyway, we don't know what the hell they're up to with GIs. But that's the point, neither do the ISO. And ISO have senior high-des GIs like Mustafa, who take this stuff very seriously. They want to know what their own government is up to, but their own government won't tell ISO because they know ISO will get pissed."

"Oh, fuck," said Vanessa, blinking. "Oh, they fucking suckered us right in, didn't they?"

"They suckered Sandy right in, you mean. They made her believe—Mustafa made her believe—that ISO wanted to force League to intervene in New Torah. Instead, he knew League were already involved in New Torah, he just wanted to force them to let ISO in on the action. And in coming here, and causing all kind of chaos as Sandy is so good at doing, suddenly League and maybe even New Torah get worried, and tell Mustafa, 'hey, that's enough of your troublemaking, we'll let you in on the deal, but you gotta ditch your new Federation buddies.'"

"So Mustafa betrays Sandy," Rhian said quietly. "In exchange for getting the ISO a slice of the action." She slapped her pistol back together, with ominous intent. Chambered a round.

"Makes sense," Vanessa agreed. "There isn't much he wouldn't do for ISO. And he knew how important it was to Sandy, that she'd fall for it more easily than most."

"Yes," said Rhian. "But now he's going to regret it. They all are, you watch. Sandy's still alive down there. She's dangerous enough on normal days, but now she'll be really angry. They're all screwed."

"Even Sandy can't take out all the corporations in Droze single-handed," Ari murmured.

"No?" Rhian looked dangerously sceptical.

"If you're right," Cai interrupted, looking at Rhian, "then we have a problem. Cassandra seems very effective and determined. But I warn you—if she were ever to stand a realistic chance of compromising Chancelry HQ on Droze, League would never allow it."

Vanessa frowned at him. "League would never allow it? You mean New Torah would never allow it, surely?"

"Either," said Cai, with certainty. "But if Cassandra were successful in spite of New Torah's efforts, League would intervene. If necessary, they'd destroy Droze from orbit, whatever New Torah thought of it, and no matter how many died. With this League ship at station dock, they could actually do it. New Torah has orbital defences, but this ship is fast, and already in close orbit. Droze is relatively defenceless against it."

"Destroy Droze from orbit?" Vanessa stared at Cai, incredulously. "Ari, help out this poor head-kicking grunt for a second, does this make any sense to you at all? Ari?"

Ari said nothing. Vanessa looked at him. Ari was staring at Cai, open-mouthed. His long face seemed paler than usual in this cold, dark against his beard. He raised a finger and pointed at Cai. The finger appeared to be shaking slightly.

"I know what you are," Ari whispered. Cai stared back, with hard, unblinking eyes. Ari raised a hand defensively, as though to protect his uplinks, one covering his ear. "No, you stay out of my head! I won't tell anyone, I swear!"

"Ari!" Vanessa barked, now utterly lost. "Ari, tell anyone what?" Ari thought himself completely vulnerable to Cai? Ari was an uplink wizard—he was vulnerable to no one. Her hand clasped the pistol in her thigh pocket. "Would someone tell me what the hell is going on?"

"I can't tell you," said Ari, a little calmer now, but no less astonished. "We've got recon to do, we're in enemy territory, and if these guys captured me they might find out that way. Cai's identity needs to remain secret. Cai." Very sincerely. "Trust me on this. If you are what I think you are, I'm on your side, too. And Vanessa, Rhi, you don't need to worry. I don't know if it makes him a good guy, necessarily, but he's certainly not on their side, I guarantee it. League, ISO or New Torah, no way."

"New Torah least of all," Cai murmured, seeming to relax. "I thank you."

"No way!" said Vanessa, getting to her feet. "There is no way I conduct an operation like this. One of you will tell me what's going on!"

"So, things being what they are," Ari said to Cai, ignoring her completely, "we need to find a way to help Sandy. Perhaps disable that ghostie, certainly find out what her captain is talking to New Torah about."

Cai nodded. "It will be nice to have some assistance. I am capable, but I cannot do it alone."

"You're the only one?" Ari asked, an amazed smile breaking through.

Cai smiled back. "Yes. For now."

"Wow," said Ari, leaning back against the wall, both hands in his hair. "Wow."

"But I warn you," said Cai, "what we can find up here is limited. The true secrets are in Chancelry HQ. Only Cassandra can uncover them. And those secrets, I am entirely sure, League would rather nuke the city than have revealed."

Anya looked around. She couldn't remember coming here. She couldn't remember where "here" was. There was nothing really to look at, just a giant blank, no colour, no texture. Beneath her was something that might be a floor, but her hands felt nothing as she pressed upon it. She seemed to feel weight, though. And thus, balance. Though it would help if she could see a horizon.

Someone was walking toward her. She looked up. It was a woman, though she wasn't sure how she could tell. It just moved like a woman. The clothes were indistinct, as was the face. As though obscured by some kind of static.

"Hello," said a voice, and it was a woman's voice. She squatted alongside. "Do you know where you are?"

"I think this is some kind of VR," said Anya, puzzled. "But I'm not very good with VR, usually. How does it work?"

"I'm sorry," said the woman. "That's my fault. I brought you here. I found you hooked into the main network here, and I wanted to talk to you. This is the only way I could do it without the corporation seeing. The VR matrix hides all our activity here."

Anya knelt upright. Then, carefully, she stood. She looked herself up and down. She wore her tracksuit, standard clothes. Though of course in here, the tracksuit wasn't actually real.

"What's your name?" asked the woman.

"Anya," said Anya, still looking herself up and down.

"I'm Sandy."

"Why can't I see your face?"

"Well, the VR doesn't know what I look like."

"Can you see my face?" Anya asked.

"I can. And your hair. I like that haircut."

Anya put a hand to her hair. It was dark, cut straight about at the jawline, and straight across at the fringe. "Oh. I haven't had this haircut for a while."

The woman nodded. "The VR produces an image of how you've looked recently. Most people have those images in their memory implants."

"Where did you find me?" Anya asked. "I can't remember where I was."

"What can you remember?"

Anya thought about it. She remembered the usual routines. She remembered not passing tactical. The monitors hadn't been happy with that. They'd told her she had to take herself off the roster for more procedures.

"Not a lot," she admitted. "That's weird, that must be something to do with the VR. Are you from Chancelry, or Heldig? I mean, you are a GI?"

"Yes."

"Well I remember failing tactical, but I didn't believe them," she explained, frowning as she tried to piece it together. "I didn't think I'd done that badly, but the monitors insisted I had. I wanted to get onto active duty roster—I needed to do something. I was getting tired of waiting and doing all of their boring routines. But they said I had to do some procedures, and I hate those."

"Medical procedures?" asked the woman.

Anya blinked at her. "Do they do procedures differently from where you're from? You never said where you're from."

The woman looked aside, hands on hips. Anya wished she could see her face. "I'm not from any of the corporations," she said.

"You're from outside?"

A nod. "I'm here because I promised someone I'd come to find you. Someone who said he was a very good friend of yours. He said his name was Eduardo."

Anya gasped. "You met Eduardo? How? Where?"

"He came to where I live. He told me about you. He said you were his very best friend."

"He is!" Anya agreed. "Where is he? Is Eduardo okay?"

A pause from the woman. "He's fine," she said then. "But he can't be here right now. I said I'd look for you when I came here, and I'd try to bring you to him. Would you like that?"

"Yes," Anya breathed. "Oh yes. We were different. Did he tell you we were different?"

The woman nodded. "But I'd like you to tell me, too."

Suddenly a room appeared about them, replacing the blank space. It was a hospital ward, with rows of empty cots. Anya blinked at them.

"This place is taken from your memory," the woman explained. "And from some local schematics. I can't bring any of my own information in here past the barriers."

Anya took a seat on one cot. The woman sat opposite . . . and suddenly Anya could see her face. Blonde, pale blue eyes, both pretty and strong.

"Your name's Sandy?" she double-checked. Sandy nodded. "Well, Eduardo and I came through development together. And there were lots of others, and some of them were okay, but we just always got along better. We liked the same books and we liked the same games. Did you have any special friend when you went through development?"

"I don't remember very much of development," said Sandy. She made a self-deprecating smile. "I'm kind of old. But I've checked my files since, so I know some of my records from then, even if I can't remember."

"I'm not very old," said Anya. "I'm four. I think I'm quite a high designation, because some of the others got out of development much earlier than me. They went straight on to active rosters. But I was still struggling a lot with some of my lessons, although those lessons were more complicated than some. The monitors say high designations take much longer to get through development."

"They do," Sandy agreed.

"And my attention kept wandering. You'll tell me if I start wandering here, won't you?"

Sandy smiled. "I certainly will. But you're doing very well now."

"Yeah, but I can't remember where I was!" Anya exclaimed in frustration.

"Is Eduardo high designation like you?" Sandy pressed.

"Yes! We're exactly the same age. Eduardo thought we might be based on each other, you know? Our designs? We always thought alike. We could just sit and talk for hours. And sometimes we'd be doing something, and we'd both have exactly the same thought at the same time, and then we'd laugh about it."

"You're very lucky," said Sandy. "From my files I saw that I had a few friends in development, but no single close friend. I was always the highest designation, so I never had anyone to talk to. My best friend was a dog called Goldie. He used to come and visit, and I'd play with him."

"We have a cat," said Anya. "Her name's Ralph."

"A girl cat called Ralph?"

Anya laughed. "We didn't know that when we named her! That Ralph was a boy's name, I mean, not that the cat wasn't a boy. Eduardo called her Ralph, and then we got used to her being Ralph, so that's what she stayed. That's interesting that you had an animal to play with, too."

"They like to give animals to GIs in development because it helps with socialisation. Do you know what that means?"

"Yeah, it teaches us to play nice with other people," said Anya. "Even though Ralph's not a person. Although, I suppose she is really, isn't she?"

"GIs are very strong," Sandy added. "We can hurt people if we're not careful. Animals are very trusting, so the monitors figure that if we can be nice to animals, and not hurt them, then maybe we'll be nice to people, too."

"I'd never hurt Ralph," said Anya with certainty. "She's our friend. Though sometimes she hurts me. She scratches!"

"Eduardo said that the two of you like a TV show called Rinni and Pasha," said Sandy.

"Oh, yes!" Anya exclaimed. "That's our favorite. It's really funny. There's these two children, and one's a boy and one's a girl, and they're best friends, even though for straights girls and boys aren't always supposed to be friends. But they don't care, they're best friends anyway no matter what anyone else thinks. And they're always getting into trouble and stuff . . . did you know, our monitors didn't want us watching it?"

"Really?" asked Sandy. "Why not?"

"Because it's a show from the Federation. I think it's made on some place called Callay, and none of us are supposed to like the Federation. But I said that's silly, because you wouldn't know it's from the Federation, it's just a show, it could be from anywhere. Eduardo learned to break into the data storage on the network. He found lots of episodes in the library, and we watched them in secret together . . . we can do that. We make tacnet just between the two of us, and use the visual function to watch vids."

"That's clever."

Anya beamed and nodded. "It was Eduardo's idea, he's so smart. He said we were just like Rinni and Pasha, always doing things together and getting into trouble. Sometimes he called me Pasha, and I'd call him Rinni. Those were like our code names."

"So you're good at using the local network without monitors knowing about it?" Sandy asked.

Anya nodded again. "Eduardo's a little bit better than me, but he showed me lots of things. It's quite easy when you know how."

"Do you think you could find people here in the Chancelry buildings?"

"Yes. It depends where they are. Some places are more difficult than others, but usually I can find them."

"Okay." Sandy leaned forward a little on the edge of the cot, looking serious. "Anya, I'm here looking for two of my friends. One is a high-designation GI. I think he might be hurt, so it's possible he's in medical. His name's Poole. Another is a little boy named Kiril. He's six years old."

Anya frowned. "A child here? I can't remember ever seeing a child in Chancelry HQ. I mean, I know all the monitors have children, but they're all in the accommodation sector. HQ's only for adults."

"He was taken from his brother and sister. They're children too, though they're a bit older. The eldest is about the age of Rinni and Pasha, and they're friends of mine. They're so upset that their little brother was taken away, and they want him back. Can you imagine if Rinni and Pasha were taken away from each other?"

Anya stared at her. "Chancelry did that?"

"Does it surprise you?"

Anya took a deep breath. She looked down. "No." In a small voice. "It would have surprised Eduardo even less. He said bad things about them. He said only high designations like us seemed to think bad things about Chancelry, the lower designations never did. Why was he taken?"

"Because Chancelry don't like these two kids," said Sandy. "Only they couldn't get them, so they took their brother instead."

"Why don't Chancelry like those kids?"

"Because they were helping me. I'm from the outside, Anya. I'm from where Eduardo was sent. That's how I met him."

Anya looked up. Now she understood. Eduardo had been sent on a mission. She didn't know what, and she hadn't been able to talk to him before he'd been sent away. She knew he hadn't wanted to go. But he'd made friends once he got there. That amused her. GIs were made for fighting, but Eduardo had said once that if he ever had to fight the Federation, he'd rather make friends with them instead, since that was where Rinni and Pasha came from. Maybe that was why the monitors hadn't wanted them watching it.

"Your GI friend Poole is from the Federation too?" she asked.

Sandy nodded. "He plays the piano. It's my fault he's here. He should still be at home, playing music. But he decided he wanted to help, and he's very stubborn and I couldn't say no. Do you think you could help me to find him, and little Kiril?"

Anya smiled. "Yes. But only if you bring Eduardo back to me. Or take me to him."

"Would you like to leave here?" Sandy asked. "If I can get you out?"

"If that's the only way I can be with Eduardo, yes." And she frowned. "But Sandy, I don't know where I am right now. I mean, physically. I suppose I must be asleep, or in some procedure. When you're looking for Poole and Kiril, can you look for me, too?"

Anya had code keys to parts of the security network it would have taken Sandy dangerous ages to find. Even now there were random network sweeps pulsing through HQ's various sectors, searching for anomalous activity. She was quite good at blindsiding them, but if she stayed in here long enough, at some point they were going to get lucky.

But now, with Anya's codes, she could micro-burst glimpses of the main security net, cameras and all, avoiding the random surveillance patterns that would normally trap anyone simply leeching on the feed.

HQ was at least ten buildings that she could see, all in a complex, all connected below ground and above. Those were in turn surrounded by Chancelry Quarter City, home to at least fifty thousand Chancelry employees, a proper city-within-a-city. That she hadn't seen, but was told it looked not unlike modern cities anywhere, and completely unlike the parts of Droze that lay beyond the corporate barriers.

HQ's network was completely separate. Its various parts corresponded on the network to its physical geography, so she looked first roughly where she knew medical to be. Camera feeds showed her various wards and beds, and various patients and doctors. It all looked very normal, like hospitals anywhere. In the League, military hospitals hadn't segregated GIs and straights very much; a lot of biotech overlapped between them, unlike in Tanusha where she had to go to a separate facility to get treatment. But here, she couldn't see GIs or GI-related treatment anywhere.

Anya had been very vague, she pondered, searching further while scanning for potential intercepts in a hundred different directions. Partly it was that Anya was young, and the irony of high-designation GIs was that at four years of age, you could probably expect more rationality from a lower des. High designations just took longer to fully form—she herself had taken at least five years, another big drawback for any military power wanting to make lots of GIs as short term circumstances changed. Wars could be won or lost, and new ones started, in less than five years. Regs took a fraction of that time.

Sandy suspected Anya was indeed unconscious, either sleeping or in some "procedure," as she'd called it—common enough for an experimental GI in development. She'd had quite a few of them herself. GIs were never made perfect. In their early years development wasn't just about allowing the brain to mature—it was about ironing out the kinks, entailing various medical procedures, most of them small scale involving micro treatments to adjust implants, or immune system balances, or to enhance motor skill pathways, or some such. Anya had not been able to help Sandy any more than give her these key codes. And her memory access had been poor, suggesting temporary limited function.

She broke off her ponderings, noticing some active monitoring where it didn't seem to belong. It looked like . . . residential? Dormitories? She took feeds from several cameras, and saw corridors and classrooms. Children's drawings on the walls, and rooms filled with toys. A class for science experiments, big displays of galactic charts, the composition of a binary star system. A cool holographic display system. It was far too late for school; regular city kids wouldn't come to school in HQ, so these would be special kids kept separate . . .

She traced the active monitoring to the floor below, and wasn't surprised to see a boy at a table, drawing. A woman sat alongside, talking to him, though Sandy didn't have audio. Praising his work, which did indeed look good—it was an interactive screen, and the boy drew shapes that he could then manipulate and animate with controls. He seemed to be drawing animals, then animating them with the holographic display, which brought them to life before his eyes. He laughed with delight now as a giant lizard-like creature he'd just finished drawing appeared upon his table top, then half-galloped, half-slithered across the table. The woman clapped and praised him.

The boy looked about six, sandy-brown haired, and now as the camera caught his face, Sandy recognised Kiril from their brief meeting. So, thought Sandy. Not mistreated at all. A few more years of this, and he'd be a Chancelry kid. She understood his siblings' distress to lose him, but wondered again if Kiril hadn't gotten the best deal of the three.

She returned to where she'd found Anya's uplink. This one wasn't geographically contiguous. She'd only registered the uplink because she had special functions searching for them, and recognised the signature as being similar to Eduardo's. But it could be coming from anywhere. There was nothing for it but to search geographically, floor by floor.

Things looked familiar in the sixth building she scanned through, on the seventeenth floor. Here the barrier elements about the security nodes changed—a whole new level of security. Even Anya's codes couldn't crack these. She tried a whole bunch of tricks, ran into a bunch of dead ends, then finally found a com relay that repeated origin codes it shouldn't have when queried. That gave her bits of a puzzle to assemble, which combined with other bits gave her the foundation for a blind key . . .

. . . which worked when she tried it. For how long, she neither knew nor trusted. She scanned quickly, one room then the next. Heavy duty biotech medical, rooms rigged like something set up to monitor sub-atomic experiments. Sensors everywhere, wiring, reinforced doors and walls, bed restraints. Heating, coolling, cryo-tubing, triple redundant systems ... she scanned through it rapidly, looking for active systems, rooms that might be occupied.

Found one, and locked into the security camera. A bed, and a GI, locked down in restraints, heavily monitored and sedated. A zoom upon the face, and it was no one she knew. Probably a local.

Further along, she found another, and repeated. This one was Poole, upper body swathed in bandages, tubes in his mouth and nose, heavily restrained, and no doubt sedated. Sandy took note of the room layout, its position in the corridor and the rest of the building, the full schematic. She didn't think they'd move him soon; he looked hurt. But alive, and possibly recovering.

One to go. Past more barriers, teeth on edge now, expecting to be discovered at every turn ... smashing barriers was more her style than sneaking through them; this was more Ari's game than hers. And then two floors above Poole, as she accessed the level, a whole new construct appeared that had been hidden from a distance. This was big. Almost industrial, like they had a small factory running up here; lots of small generators, pumps and conduits. The layout made her blood run cold, just to look at it. She'd seen this layout before.

She camera-scanned on a room, now dark and empty, workers gone home for the night. Here was a giant cradle rig, with 3-D x-ray and multiple electrode attachments. A GI would lie on that slab, and be studied. Alive, she saw, given the life support built in by the wall. The electrodes would do things. The tubes would siphon off blood. The laser scalpels would cut.

Here in the next room was refrigerated storage. She could make out limbs behind transparent glass. Organs. From live subjects. GIs only gave decent life readings while alive, obviously. She'd found stuff like this on Tropez Station. She'd had it done to herself, upon first arrival in Tanusha. But with far less professional and industrial sophistication than this.

Another room had bodies in storage. These were deceased, in floating rows, preserved until recycled. Men and women, GIs in their usual physical dimensions. There was no telling if they'd lived and died, or ever lived at all. Nor how Chancelry had decided they would end up here. Chancelry GIs saw very little combat, and lived mostly secure lives. There might be one or two fatalities a year. In here was provision for hundreds. Chancelry production capacity was estimated at similar hundreds per year. They didn't have that many in active duty, really. It had always been a mystery, where those hundreds of new ones ended up, and why they always needed more.

Now she knew.

In the next room were the live cases. She knew she shouldn't look, but like those dark nightmares from which there was no awakening, the pull was magnetic. Besides which, she wasn't asleep, and this was all real. She couldn't look, but she had to, because here lay her darkest fears.

These GIs were alive. They shouldn't have been. They lay on suspended cots, restraints and tubes and wiring all feeding back and forth like some nightmarish high-tech jungle that had reached out and snared them. There were limbs missing, and ghoulish wounds temporarily covered with transparent bandage. You could do all kinds of things to GIs that would kill regular humans rather quickly, yet still GIs would live. Sandy had thought she'd seen her life's share of this sort of thing. Now she learned otherwise.

A lot of them were rigged for tests. The neural systems could be accessed more easily this way, once the brain had matured, and you could manipulate the nerve endings in the limbs or spine with direct stimulation. The whole GI nervous feedback system remained a mystery; how it grew was a never-ending series of surprises. Accessing it all was difficult, in live subjects interested in remaining that way.

And here, in a next cot along, was a woman. Face up, torso pried open, feedback circuitry fed into the lower spine and at the base of the skull, alongside the uplink connections, to read a full schematic of all the brain activity. Life support cycled, keeping air in the lungs and the heart pumping. Giant pins kept the head in place, driven through the neck like a pair of huge knitting needles.

The face, tube in mouth, eyes closed, was Anya's. The pretty dark hair was gone, just a shaven scalp, red across one side from recent incision . . .

. . . Sandy woke back to the apartment with a start, where she sat against the bedside with Danya and Svetlana, the uplink reality fracturing like a china plate thrown upon the floor.

Svetlana had crept to the doorway, and now looked back with concern. "Sandy?" she mouthed. "What's wrong?"

Sandy was crying. She couldn't stop shaking. Danya put a hand on her shoulder, and she looked at him through tear filled eyes. He looked frightened.

Sandy shook her head. "No," she whispered, very low, as Danya and Svetlana put their heads close to hers to hear. "Not Kiril. I saw Kiril, he's safe. They're looking after him."

They both looked unutterably relieved. "Thank you," whispered Danya, and hugged her. Svetlana hugged her, too. Sandy hugged them back. It felt nice to have someone to hold on to, given what she knew she had to do now. Given the scale of Chancelry's defences, she doubted she'd be alive much longer. But by God, she was going to take a lot of them with her.

CHAPTER TWENTY-ONE

They were barely out of the hotel room and into the corridor, when Sandy held up her fist for a stop. The kids stopped. A faint whine. A click. Beneath human hearing range, but within Sandy's. Whine. Click. Coming down the adjoining corridor.

Sandy moved very quietly to the next hotel door and tried the handle. It opened, and made an unavoidable noise. She pointed Danya and Svetlana inside. Svetlana went in immediately, but Danya paused, questioning. Sandy pointed ahead, and around the corridor. Made a two-legged walking figure, then a single index finger.

One humanoid, around the corner. She pointed to herself, then around the corner, then a cutting motion across her throat. Danya nodded and retreated into the room, pulling the door in but not closed. Sandy pressed herself into the doorway of a room opposite. And waited.

There was no noise now. It would have heard the door open, and stopped to listen. Sandy could not sense any transmissions. An independent operator, as were all the bots in the secure zone. Sandy didn't trust it. It was too convenient, this thing turning up right now as she was about to leave. It was possible she'd triggered some alarm in her net infiltration. She doubted it—when she fucked up on the net, usually everyone knew about it—but it wasn't impossible. More likely was that one of their Home Guard friends had betrayed them. She'd known that was possible too, but there hadn't been any choice. It also meant she couldn't count on Modeg, Duage and Zhao being where she'd left them on the way out. Gunter though, she was prepared to bet on. He was downstairs. Maybe this unit had come up the rear way, away from Gunter.

Click, whine. Click, whine. There it was again. The corner was just a meter away, and the noise maybe five meters beyond that. Most likely it was an AQ-9 through 12. Chancelry didn't make them—that was Dhamsel Corp's department—but they did use them. Humanoid robot, ideal for sentry duty in urban environments, could climb stairs, open doors, all the things a wheeled street bot couldn't. Very fast, very tough, and heavily armed. She didn't like them within the same postcode as the kids. Federation pop culture had whipped up almost as much of a fearful frenzy about them as they had about GIs. Steel-skulled and unemotional, they looked the part.

Sandy waited until it came right to the corner. It put its gun around first, looking on armscomp vision. Sandy pressed herself flat in the doorway. It couldn't see her here. Then the bot took a step around, and she went low, knowing their balance was weakest when changing face. She took a leg, pulled an arm down, and it spun rather than fell, trying to decapitate her with a reverse swing. Sandy caught it, broke the arm, smashed its head into the wall, bent its lower spine with her knee, then tore its head off.

"Quickly!" she called to Danya and Svetlana, reaching into the bot's spinal cavity to pull out connections where her memory implant schematic told her the locator beacon was. She pulled, and it came out in a shower of sparks and shuddering limbs.

The kids came out running, with a wide-eyed look at the dead bot, but Sandy was already up with rifle out, scanning the corridor, then running on to the stairwell. But shit, even a bot could read a schematic, and AQs didn't operate alone.

Near the bottom of the stairwell she punched a hole in the wall to the corridor and dropped one of her grenades through it. It blew the corridor to hell, doing very little to the bot waiting there at the stairwell door, but disorienting it considerably. She needed her weapon to cover down the corridor, so she knocked its weapon arm aside as she went through the door and leaped for a spin kick at its head; very fancy, but it allowed her to point her rifle somewhere else whilst hammering the bot into a wall.

Sure enough, the second bot was waiting there, Sandy shot it through the eye, then landed as the first one came back at her, despite its caved-in head. Its swing smashed the wall as she ducked, then kicked it in the chest, knocking it flying, then ducking sideways and returning fire as the second bot shredded the air where she'd been, her own fire putting holes through eyepieces and armoured faceplate until it lost armscomp and began spraying wildly, tearing apart the walls and ceiling. But it didn't protect its face, so Sandy put another ten rounds through the right eye until the head casing came apart and it fell in a jerking heap.

The first one aimed at her, point blank and flat on its back, and Sandy just sidestepped whilst emptying the rest of her mag up under the chin plate, into the brain case. Big armoured beasts that they were, no personnel-sized armour really stopped a Teller 9 rifle at this range, least of all with accuracy like hers. When armour contested firepower in modern warfare, firepower always won, and for all the bots' fearsome reputation, they were no match even for a lot of regs.

"Sandy!" she heard a shriek from the stairwell, and peered inside, back up the stairs. Svetlana was being restrained by Danya from rushing down— half the stairwell wall had been caved in by the bot's last swing. Svetlana had seemed to think she might be dead . . . well, it must have sounded from the stairs like the corridor were being torn apart.

"Come on," she beckoned them from amidst the smoke. "I'm too advanced for a walking dishwasher. Let's go."

They continued downstairs until they reached Gunter, at the side entrance where the crashed aircar made cover to the neighbouring building.

"Everything will be coming down on us now," said Gunter, barely looking at them, his attention on the road outside. "We'd have a chance if we sprinted, maybe we could carry the kids."

Sandy shook her head. "Even I can't target very well while running at speed, especially not with one arm occupied." And if we can't shoot what's trying to shoot us, she didn't need to add, we're dead. The tech here might be no match for a high-des GI in a close fight, but it could certainly hit a moving target on a road. "You take the kids back the same way, move fast and stay hidden. I'll give you cover and make a distraction up top."

"Two would make a better distraction."

"No," said Sandy, very firmly, and grabbed Gunter by the shoulder. "Guard the kids," she told him. "With your life. Promise me."

Gunter considered her for a moment. He liked Danya and Svetlana, Sandy was certain, but a lot of mid-des GIs just didn't get why kids were special, on that emotional level that straight humans did. But he could see the look in her eyes, and nodded.

"With my life," he assured her. "I promise."

"No, Sandy!" Svetlana protested. "Come with us, it's safer!"

"If I go with you we're all dead," Sandy said firmly, peering out the doorway. "Trust me Svet, this is what I do. Danya, go with Gunter."

Danya nodded, and followed Gunter in a fast dash out the door, pulling Svetlana with him. Immediately a hover UAV appeared between buildings, homing on that noise. Sandy shot it through the CPU. It veered into a building side with a crunch of shattering fan blades, then vanished. They'd get smarter now, she thought, as she dashed after the others and into the next building. Even a dumb AI network could figure out it was facing high-designation GIs and stop using small units at close range. Now it got interesting.

Gunter, Danya and Svetlana ran through the abandoned restaurant opposite and into the building's lower corridor, heading for the rear. To cross to the next building behind without UAVs getting them, they'd need a distraction. As Sandy took up cover in the abandoned restaurant, she could see that distraction rolling quickly up the road outside, with six wheels and an angular armoured turret.

Rotary cannon opened fire on the restaurant floor as it saw her, and she rolled neatly for cover behind a concrete wall corner as high velocity rounds tore whatever was not already destroyed on the restaurant floor to pieces. Sandy checked her rifle settings amid flying splinters and glass. The instant the firing paused, she put her rifle around the corner, aiming by rifle arm-scomp, and emptied the rest of her magazine directly onto the tank's main vision sensors—it had three of them, heavily reinforced, but they'd now be cracked and blurred.

It opened fire again, and she pulled back to a safe distance from the corner, and waited. Even tank bots knew when they couldn't hit something, and against infantry in urban environments, the textbook said use explosives, not guns. A rocket screamed in, and blew the restaurant to hell. It would have knocked a straight human senseless where she was, but Sandy just shielded her face, closed her eyes, and with her ears still popping from the pressure shock, ran straight out into the dissipating explosion.

Half the ceiling nearly fell on her as she ran, chemical flames scorching skin and clothes, and then she was out, streaking at full acceleration toward the tank. It tried to declinate its turret to hit her, but with damaged vision and the explosion smoke and debris covering her for half the distance, it couldn't adjust fast enough. She slid in on one hip, got directly under the tank's front wheels, lifted and flipped it onto its side with a crash.

Something launched missiles at her, she couldn't see from where, but she got a clear sense of homing frequencies squealing in her inner ear as they came in . . . but no way they could track an unarmoured person, and she leaped for a nearby building rooftop. It was eight stories tall, and she was at the fourth when the tank exploded. The shockwave blew her trajectory off, and now she was falling off the edge . . . only she caught the lip one-handed, and hanging there, shot another hover UAV as debris rained around. Just one shot to the head—these things weren't armoured, just relied on stealth.

She flipped back onto the rooftop and ran, crouched low, knowing that somewhere high a recon UAV would be locked onto her, circling well out of range, coordinating all of Chancelry's slowly awakening firepower down onto her. And she was right on top of the building that Danya, Svetlana and Gunter were in. She zagged right, leaped low for the adjoining building rooftop, hit the building edge rather than the top, not wanting a high trajectory that would get her blown from the sky. Even then, something shot at her from a nearby window, bullets whipping past. She flipped and rolled onto the rooftop, nearly swearing—she wasn't armed or armoured for this.

She lay flat a moment, just waiting, hearing mostly the ammo from the tank cooking off in the street below. For the first time, she had a good view of the Chancelry Sector buildings here. Nothing too tall—there was no need in a relatively small city like Droze. But wealthy, flash rooftop pads, with com gear, weather shielding. Lots of them, a real city, if a little functional on the architecture.

A UAV hummed beneath the wall to her side. She saved ammo by pulling her pistol, aiming briefly downward by sound alone and firing a single shot. And pulled back as she drew fire from that window again, followed by a crash as the UAV hit the ground.

Then she heard the next one, only this was much bigger, huge fan blades cutting the air. And not a UAV, she realised, looking right. Perhaps a kilometer off and coming her way over the Chancelry wall, a combat flyer, much like she used in SWAT.

She moved immediately, running across the rooftop as even now a sensor squealed in her ear at the active tracking. She selected a window two floors down on the next building, jumped, shot out the glass, then tucked into a little ball to smash through remaining shards without hitting the rim. Hit the bed in the abandoned apartment, bounced sideways into a closet with force enough to smash it, rebounded off and out the door.

Missiles blew out most of the building wall behind her, knocked her momentarily off her feet as half the corridor collapsed, but she smashed through it, broke down an inner door into another abandoned apartment, then kicked and punched herself a new hole in that wall, into an adjoining apartment. The corridor beyond was at the building core, safe from missiles unless they decided to bring the whole building down. She reckoned they'd need authorisation for that. Unless someone figured out who she was in the next few seconds. Maybe they already knew.

A howl of engines overhead. Flyers operated in pairs; if she exposed herself on the rooftop to shoot at the first one, the second would nail her. She bounced off walls in her haste to reach a window on the far side. Once there she didn't have a clear angle, so she dashed to the far end, furthest from Chancelry Sector. The flyer was turning clear of there; Home Guard had reasonable anti-aircraft weapons, and concentrated them here near the Chancelry wall. They'd all be awake over there now, hearing all this commotion in the neutral zone. But the flyers weren't hovering, they were making strafing runs—hovering made pilots nervous, and she was pretty sure these were flown by real people, two standbys kept waiting for situations to arise. Strafing runs made flyers harder to target with modern weaponry . . . but it was risky of them. She only had a rifle; if they hovered out of range she couldn't hit them. And then they'd struggle to hit her, with all these buildings for cover. Strafing runs gave them a chance to get her, but brought them into her own range, and created patterns. Sandy liked other peoples' patterns.

She could hear one of them coming in from the non-damaged building side, and skipped away from the window, back into the building core as cannon rounds tore holes through that wall across several stories.

"Not that side," she said to herself, visualising it as she sprinted across, and then bounced up two flights of stairs to the top floor. She sprinted down that corridor, sections of right wall missing from the missile strike, was nearly surprised by a walking floor bot on four legs that she shot before it could shoot her, hurdled it and crashed through a door to a Chancelry-side apartment. Skidded over a bed and took up brief residence by the window. "Come on. This side, just once."

A flyer roared overhead, coming the wrong way. But given neither of them were game to overfly Home Guard territory, they had to circle this way eventually, back to Chancelry Quarter. One curled across in front of her, exposing its canopy, and she put fifteen rounds right onto the pilot's head from four hundred meters. The canopy was armoured, of course, but no pilot enjoyed that, seeing the armoured glass fracture and crack all across their eyeline.

The flyer jerked away like a frightened bird, and now his buddy was coming around to support.

Sandy sprinted back the way she'd come, out of the apartment and back down the corridor. The next explosions took out the whole building front, and would have knocked a regular human unconscious. Then came the strafing cannon, tearing through the wreckage and dust. Sandy hit the first intact stairwell, bounded up it, smashed through the door to the rooftop. It was booby-trapped, but the mine was only big enough to blow a limb off a straight, and damaged only her clothes.

Up on the rooftop, she had a lovely view of the flyer breaking off its attack run and roaring in right past its target. Sandy shouldered her rifle and sprinted. She took off like a bullet, hit the flyer's exposed underside, and stuck on with sheer force of synth-myomer fingers. Then she overhanded her way to the wing root, got a leg over in the slipstream, and smashed a fist through the canopy. It stuck in the hole, so she pulled, and a whole chunk of canopy came away. She pulled herself up to the canopy, tore the pilot's harness off, threw him out, then climbed into his seat. The front seat weapons officer protested, so she kicked him in the head.

Controls weren't that different from what she was used to. The flyer was now falling into a dive, so she pulled it up and banked back the way it'd come, eyes narrowed and hair blowing in the gale. Her brain kept trying to catch up with what she'd just done. She'd not even been aware it was possible until now, although she'd heard tales of other GIs doing it during the war to low-flying, slow-moving aircraft.

How to aim . . . she couldn't access by wireless; if hacking into a war machine was that easy no GI would ever have to fire a shot. The weapons officer's helmet should give her access . . . but it was the direct interface that made flyer systems work. Cords dangled free where the pilot's helmet had been attached . . . were they the right size? Of course they were, it was all standard League designation, and she grabbed them, yanked and inserted directly into the back of her head.

The raw feed struck with a force, dazing her, but then her reflexive tacnet matrix established itself and compensated, and things began to make sense. Weapons, armscomp, navcomp, engines, attitude, trajectory, full spectrum scan, communications. The other flyer was coming around, not yet having figured out what had happened. Sandy locked it, selected something big and high explosive, and pulled a trigger. Armscomp protested, saying it was friendly, and Sandy shut down IFF entirely as the network routines began to make sense to her, and pulled the trigger again. The flyer blew up, and what was left scattered flaming across various buildings.

Now, however, that could easily be her. Sandy swung the flyer into a low, sideways flight, skipping over rooftops and targeting the major com relays atop Chancelry buildings nearby. They'd be locking big weapons systems onto her even now, overriding their own Identification-Friend-Foe routines to get a shot at her. She fired everything she had, missiles leaping off weapon racks and streaking over the Chancelry wall toward tall buildings. Defenses lit up like a fireworks display—rockets, lasers, chaff, flares and rapid cannon all erupting at once—but her range was too close, and the rockets too fast for most of it. Huge explosions ripped dishes and antennae from the tops of buildings, then a big com tower came down right on the barrier, and all her com traffic went crazy, and navcomp disappeared in a blizzard of static.

She dove away behind buildings, zooming up a road, and redirected armscomp to search straight above her. There it was, a little recon UAV, and she fixed on it, then fired, and watched a missile fly a hundred meters in front then shoot straight up. Ahead a road tank traversed on her, and she killed it with cannon fire. High above, the UAV exploded. And now they had no overhead visual.

Gunter, she was fairly sure, would have led the kids directly back through the buildings, none of this sideways sneaking around, not with the sizeable distraction she was providing. She flew low about those buildings anyway, keeping out of any line of sight from Chancelry Sector, and shredding several ground bots with the cannon turret, a simple enough task to operate with tacnet, despite the weapons officer's incapacity. She wondered if Gunter had figured out yet what had happened, but didn't dare contact him lest something still in and around these buildings managed to trace those transmissions—she didn't control this battlespace, she'd only acquired the capacity to shape it a little.

With plenty of bots in the secure zone, she ought to have been receiving more ground fire by now, except that the bots were not in constant communication with Chancelry, and would have to receive an override priority target to allow them to fire on a friendly flyer. She'd just taken down a bunch of com relays, so perhaps that was stopping a lot of them . . . except for the big tank bots, but she wasn't so concerned of them.

Scan registered big missile fire from Chancelry Sector, streaking straight up into the sky. Sandy was pretty sure she knew what that was, and didn't want it coming down anywhere near where Gunter and the kids were. She roared up a street, then pulled into a tight hover next to a building. Overhead, the seeker missiles ceased their climb, one circling, the other pulling into a dive as it acquired. It wouldn't have as good a lock without the UAV airbourne, but on the vertical trajectory, these buildings ceased to be a problem.

It dove in, and she put a missile into the upper floors of the building before her, diving under the exploding debris and releasing full countermeasures—electrostatic charged particle mist to add to the confusion. The flyer was only prop powered instead of jet powered, and barely got clear in time. The seeker's explosion sent her lurching forward, struggling to control the swinging aircraft. She barely made the next right corner, nearly standing the thing on its side to avoid hitting buildings ahead, then losing altitude abruptly and skimming the road to recover. She could nearly hear one of her SWAT pilot friends snorting derisively at her piloting skills—having crazy battlespace capabilities, and actually using them on unfamiliar equipment, were two very different things.

The second seeker fell on her, and she thought about pulling up into it with a steep climb, but that would expose her to line-of-sight weapons from Chancelry Sector. Hanging dead in space, they'd nail her even if the seeker didn't. There was no choice but to go full countermeasures and turn sharply down another road, and hope. The seeker blew a huge hole in the road behind her, and this time she didn't nearly crash on the corner. Great, she thought. She was improving as a pilot fast enough that at this rate, she might live another sixty seconds, tops. There'd be another UAV up shortly, and then the seekers wouldn't miss by so much. She had to either ditch this flyer, or put it somewhere they couldn't hit it.

Even now, scan showed her more flyers coming airbourne, first two, then four, then . . . they multiplied, someone had obviously shouted scramble, and they scrambled. They'd know there was one hostile pilot in the air . . . maybe she could get in amongst them and fool their IFF for long enough so they wouldn't know which was the hostile? But she was kidding herself, and she knew it. She had okay piloting skills, but it was hardly her specialty, whatever her innate natural talents. Twelve to one and climbing was pushing it, and so much of this form of warfare was technology; she couldn't make a flyer defy physics and if one homing missile got a good lock on her, that was it. Only worse, because built as she was, she'd possibly survive with damage, only to be salvaged by Chancelry operatives in some extremely unpleasant way . . .

Sandy's inner ear crackled as someone made a direct microwave com connection. *"Sandy, stay low and pull back to Home Guard airspace, we have aerial cover."*

It was Gunter's voice. Aerial cover? Not air support, surely. Perhaps Home Guard had moved up all their air to ground launchers; surely they'd have them prepped by now?

She didn't know how to reply on that channel—the flyer wasn't similarly equipped; she just turned away from Chancelry Sector and hoped the Home Guard knew friend from foe. To make it more obvious she spun around between buildings, moving in a backwards hover, weapons trained in the Chancelry direction, her rear completely exposed to Home Guard. An AQ bot stepped around a corner below and aimed at her, but on auto targeting she was faster, and cannons tore it into bouncing pieces. More fire zipped by below, coming from behind her. That was Home Guard, shooting at . . . something. Her scans showed nothing. Well, they were enthusiastic, and most importantly, shooting past her, not at her.

"Here they come," said someone on that microwave frequency. *"Six in the main wave, six behind. Fire when they breach the zone."*

Which might have meant a fire zone. That was tacnet terminology. No damn way Home Guard used tacnet. Who were these guys?

She couldn't see any of the flyers approach, only that they were all closing in on her, six units angling around for a run. In a low hover between buildings, they couldn't see or hit her, but were protected by the same. And now, as the first pair came zooming on the diagonal within two hundred meters, missiles leaped from all across the Home Guard front. Not crappy little mid-tech missiles either. These twisted and fizzed, acquiring and adjusting at startling speed.

The Chancelry flyers were still low, and that saved them as missiles hit buildings, or darted after countermeasures and clipped rooftops instead, a cascade of explosions racing after the twin flyers between buildings . . . Sandy lost scan feed for a little, there was so much jamming and low level flying going on, it wasn't showing her more than two or three targets at a time.

"*He's gone,*" someone said. "*One down.*" Smoke boiled up behind nearby rooftops.

The other flyers were milling, unable to operate against that kind of ground to air tech in these concentrations. Chancelry HQ would not view this as a positive development. What would the button pushers do, confronted with a tactical disadvantage?

Fuck. She quickly enabled a main frequency broadcast, and patched it onto external speakers as well, just to be sure. "All civilians get to shelters! Get to shelters NOW! Everyone take cover immediately!"

She was only ten seconds early. Then, utterly predictably, a cluster of missiles leaped into the air from multiple locations within Chancelry Sector. Having acquired optimum targeting altitude, they fanned out, and dove. Sandy spun her flyer about and ran, full power, straight down the main street into Home Guard territory. Behind her, explosions swept the row of occupied buildings closest to Chancelry Sector in a wall of flame.

Someone found a frequency she could access on a directional com, and directed her to a disused factory building three kilometres from the Chancelry barrier. She didn't particularly like the look of the neighbourhood, as she came in low to hover—it was old industrial, most of which had survived the crash physically, but not the economic consequences. Factories were disused and stripped now, or had been converted to something other than their original purpose—weathered steel rooves that had never been high tech facilities to begin with, just opportunist investments from the free settlers who had followed the big corporations unasked to Droze.

Sandy also wasn't certain why she was being directed to stay here in the Chancelry control-neighbourhoods, those Droze neighbourhoods in a quarter-arc of the city out from Chancelry Sector. The six big corporations dominated the central section of the city, surrounding the Free Zone, which was not actu-ally free, being reserved for corporate folks only . . . but it was not owned explicitly by any one company, which meant "free" in corporate language. Chancelry's UAV system had been hammered thanks to her strike. They seemed to be having trouble talking to them, and her scans didn't register anything airbourne in this part of the city, but still she reckoned Chancelry would have other means. And they'd be angry now, and possibly worried, now their bots had gotten a look at her. They'd know who was after them, and more importantly, what she was after.

A few Home Guard wrapped up against the cold night opened the factory's big doors for her, and she hovered inside amidst great swirls of dust. Landed, killed the engines, but left weapons systems live as she began writing some very specific key codes to protect the flyer's CPU. This might just be the most advanced weapon system in Home Guard territory, and if it was, she wanted the only person with the key to be her.

Some vehicles roared into the deserted factory through a back way, lights off, armed men jumping from the back. Sandy recovered her rifle and got out through the place where the canopy should have been.

Home Guard approached her, weapons ready. Several aimed them at her. Sandy activated the cannon mount beneath the flyer's chin, and aimed straight back at them. With her uplink working, she could kill everyone in the factory without having to move a finger. Some others saw the turret target them, and pushed their companions' weapons down.

"Who are you?" a man shouted at her, approaching angrily. "Duage says you're Federation?"

"That's right," said Sandy.

"And what gives you a right to start a fucking war against Chancelry?"

"So the Home Guard signed a peace deal with the corporations?" she answered. "When did that happen?"

It was contrary to all their propaganda. Home Guard insisted the war went on, preached eternal vigilance. It was on all the posters, and graffiti scrawled on the walls.

"We have at least twenty dead civilians!" the man shouted, gesturing back toward Chancelry Sector with his rifle. "A hundred wounded! You provoked an artillery strike!"

"That happens in a war," said Sandy. "Corporations kill people all the time. If you were actually at war, and not a bunch of frauds posing as soldiers, you'd know that."

Someone else raised a gun at her. Sandy spun the flyer's cannon barrels, prelude to mass slaughter. It made an unearthly, shrieking whine that echoed off the steel beamed ceiling. Many flinched, and ducked for cover.

Sandy felt bad about the artillery strike. She might not have done it that way if she'd suspected Chancelry would use heavy weapons on a civilian area if it went wrong. But then, she'd had no idea that eruption of missiles would come from Home Guard territory, compelling Chancelry to target them. Home Guard weren't supposed to have any weaponry like that, and she'd been planning to leave civilians out of it. But now, if Home Guard thought she could be intimidated by threats of force, they needed to have made very clear to them just what treacherous ground they were treading on. Force was her domain. She was well past doing favours for those who didn't yet "get it."

When she was no longer being directly threatened, she let the barrels whine down to nothing. "What's your name?" she asked the man who'd shouted at her.

"Hector." He hadn't flinched all that much. He stood and looked like a tough guy, not especially big, but with a scarred face and attitude.

Sandy recalled a name from a briefing. "Sylvan Hector? Droze Home Guard commander?" Hector nodded. So she'd found the head. "Was that you with the missiles?"

"No," he said, lips twisted with what might be contempt. "Not us."

"Who?"

"People who should stay the fuck away from where they're not wanted." He pointed at the flyer. "You've landed on Home Guard territory. That flyer's now our property."

Sandy smiled. "You all just came within one stupid move of dying. I'd quit while I'm ahead if I were you."

New vehicles roared into the factory, lights also off. Men and women climbed from these, an equal division of gender. Some wore full assault armour, League issue, even the stenciling visible on shoulder plate—Fleet, Company, Squad. There were modern weapons, full headset rigs, and the armour rigs even had back-mounted launchers, smaller versions of what she'd used on Pyeongwha. This was where the missiles had come from.

They came through the Home Guard without really paying them much attention, and the Home Guard seemed to shrink from their path. And then, weaving through their midst, came a skinny girl sprinting toward her.

Sandy knelt as Svetlana ran into her and hugged her. She was crying. Sandy frowned, pulling back enough to see, and brush the tears away.

"Hey, come on, tough street girl," she said. "I'm about the hardest thing to kill that's ever lived."

"I can see that," said Svetlana, with glee. She let her go, and stared up at the flyer. "Whoa! You just jumped up and caught it?"

"Thought it might be useful," Sandy agreed. "Oh, and there's someone still alive in the front seat. Best send someone to get him out." That last more loudly. "Who are these people?"

"They're GIs!" Svetlana said excitedly. "They're Gunter's friends! I mean, can you believe it? We always thought Gunter was just Gunter, but it turns out he's got all these important friends living out in the sands! This is Kiet, I think he's in charge."

Kiet was a GI, Vietnamese looking, in League Fleet Marine armour. He wore a headset, had a teller 9 rifle, and various other weapons besides, including a back-mounted launcher. For a moment, Sandy had such a strong flashback, it gave her a chill. She really was back in the League now.

"Kiet," said Kiet. "Former groundie, Tac Sergeant, 13th Colonial. Designation 4186."

"Kresnov," said Sandy. "Captain, Dark Star, retired." Kiet's eyes widened slightly. "Designation 5074." The eyes widened a little more. "Currently FSA, special ops commander."

Kiet exhaled. "Wow."

"You guys got left here?"

Kiet nodded. "In the crash. League stationed a security force here, a bit over six thousand GIs. Of course when they started evacuating, naturally we got first preference." The sarcasm was strong. Coming from a GI, Sandy loved it.

"Naturally," she agreed, smiling.

"We kept strong chain of command right up until the shooting started. Then some took the companies' side, some took the civvies', and the rest of us packed up and moved elsewhere."

"Where elsewhere?"

"Somewhere safe," said Kiet. And smiled. "Somewhere amazing."

"So you've been living on your own out in the desert for five years?" Sandy asked in amazement. She'd never heard this in any briefing, never even hinted at. "Six thousand GIs and no one thinks to figure where all the originals ended up?"

Kiet shrugged. "Four fifths of us were regs, and you know regs. Most of them died in the fighting. Too brave to stop, too dumb to run away. The other thousand, well, there's guys like Gunter, decided to stay here, make money. It's probably more comfortable here. Because we're GIs, you know, no one ever bothered to do a proper headcount."

"How many of you?"

"Can't say," said Kiet, faintly apologetic. "Sorry. Been a secret for a while."

"And why come in from the cold right now?"

"Because of you," said Kiet, completely matter-of-fact. "Gunter told us. He's kept our secret for a while, he's one of our eyes and ears in town. He said what you're trying to do. Not all of us agreed, but some of us thought we should help. We've got some Chancelry runaways amongst us, too. We know what Chancelry's doing."

"Make you mad?" Sandy suggested.

Kiet's face hardened, and his grip shifted on his rifle. "Damn right. We've been free for five years. Some of us still aren't completely free, if you know what I mean." He tapped the side of his head. "But a few of us have figured out what freedom actually means. And we know it sure as hell doesn't include Chancelry Corporation."

"Hey," said Hector, pushing unwanted into their conversation. "Sorry to break up the happy skinjob reunion, but it's not safe here and we've got things to talk about."

Kiet was going to let it pass. Sandy gave Hector a look that might have turned men to stone. "If you use that word on me again," she said icily, "I'll skin you."

Hector snorted, and left, waving his men to follow. Kiet just looked at her, faintly puzzled. "It's just a word," he offered. "Everyone uses it."

"I used to think that," said Sandy. She thought of what she'd just seen, in Chancelry HQ. Of Anya, lying in that bunk, all a mess. "But then, I used to think the League were the good guys. Svet, where's Danya?"

Danya was with Gunter and a bunch of the new GIs who had taken up temporary residence in a warehouse. It was owned by some big local family, but Gunter was friends with the GI who worked security for them, so getting in was no issue. GIs sat about on bales and boxes, and checked their gear, or heated meals on small cookers, or stretched out synthetic muscles. Most of them took the time to look at Sandy as she arrived in Kiet's truck and walked in amongst them.

Danya was helping to pull steel fragments from the back of a female GI who lay on a soft bale. It was slightly gruesome. He was having to stick his fingers into holes in the woman's skin and feel around. But Sandy could see why he might be more suited to the task than a GI—a lot of GIs actually lacked the fingertip sensitivity of regular humans; it just wasn't one of those things GIs needed very much. Plus, Danya's fingers were smaller, so he could feel around and find fragments of splinter another GI might miss.

"Kresnov," said Sandy to the woman on the bale. "Name?"

"Kuza. 3515." Which meant she wasn't likely to say much more—a 35 series was significantly smarter than a reg, but in Sandy's experience they weren't big on conversation.

"Hi," said Danya, very pleased to see her, but unable to take blood smeared hands from Kuza's back. Sandy kissed him anyway. "She got this in the artillery strike. She was on a rooftop with a launcher, so she might have saved your neck."

Sandy wasn't comfortable with the idea that all these people were suffering for her, civvies or GIs alike. But she was here to stop Chancelry and GI experimentation, the long term consequences of which could spell a terrible fate for billions. Compared to that, these few casualties were nothing. Her own life included, if it came to that.

"How close were you to the strike when it came in?" Sandy asked somberly.

"Right under it," said Danya. "Gunter got us in the middle stairwell, lots of concrete. A lot of people in the outer rooms got hit, though." He found a splinter, pulled it out and put it on a plate someone had provided.

"Serves them right," Svetlana snorted, jumping up to sit on a bale alongside and watch. "Everyone up against the Chancelry wall are shit, running the smuggling routes, bribing all the poor folks and street kids to risk the bots for them."

"Svetlana," said Danya, in a very stern, older brother voice, with a firm stare. "Not all of them are like that. And they don't deserve to get blown up."

"Hmph," said Svetlana. And changed the subject. "Does your skin work like that, Sandy? I mean, it looks a bit rubbery." Looking at Kuza's shrapnel-peppered back.

"It's not quite as permanently attached to the muscle as yours, no," Sandy agreed, looking around for Kiet. She found him, talking to several others whom Sandy took to be his senior command group, for this unit at least. "In an injury it comes away more easily for access. You two stay here and look after Kuza. Svet why don't you look for something to use as disinfectant? Alcohol works well. GIs can get infected just like straights."

"Straights?" Svetlana asked. "You call us straights?"

"You haven't heard that before?"

"Maybe. Is it offensive?"

She'd threatened to skin Hector, Sandy recalled, for using a word she didn't like. "I don't know. Do you find it offensive?"

"I'll think about it," said Svetlana with a cocky smile, jumped off the bale and ran to look for some disinfectant.

Sandy gave Danya a puzzled look. "Is she okay?"

Danya nodded, attention divided as he worked. "She does this. We saw some nasty stuff from the artillery strike. Would have stayed to help, but we were with Gunter and these new GIs, and the locals didn't want their help, so we left. Svet won't admit when she's upset, she says stupid stuff like 'they had it coming,' you know. She copes."

Sandy did know. "Shit," she muttered. "I'm sorry, Danya."

"Why? It's not your fault."

Sandy sighed, put a hand on Danya's shoulder, and left to talk to Kiet.

"It doesn't make any sense to me," said Kiet after Sandy had explained what she'd seen when she'd hacked Chancelry HQ. A number of other GIs sat and listened also, and in the warehouse, all speaking had ceased. Sandy sensed a low level network, powered off some small, portable equipment, obviously transmitting this conversation to all other GIs beneath this roof. "Our lives are cheap to them, but not that cheap. What you're saying is that they're making us just to kill us. To take us apart and see how we work. Why?"

"I'm not sure." Mustafa had betrayed her. The ISO, at odds with the League government. They'd been puzzled too. Only . . . she took a deep breath. "I have an idea."

All eyes fixed upon her. Kiet was the highest designation here, and he was a 41. That was about par for the course in her experience, in Dark Star. The majority here were high to mid thirty-series. They looked up to her immediately, not with trust, but with respect. Sandy wasn't sure she liked that. It was the automatic respect that GIs paid to higher designations, like a caste system. She didn't think she deserved more respect than anyone else by some accident of birth. It didn't seem right. And yet it was the world that GIs were consigned to live in, because designation really did matter, and it was the reason she was immediately senior-most GI present, and all the others had to pay attention when she spoke. Unlike the old human caste systems, the synthetic human caste system was based on something real.

It was the reason she was always uncomfortable with well-intentioned folks in Tanusha attempting to equate her own situation in society with that of racism amongst straights. Racism was bullshit, a discrimination based on something so utterly insubstantial that even the most cursory knowledge of genetics should have been enough to allow its immediate dismissal. The things that separated her and other GIs from straight humans, however, were not bullshit. Those were real. And regular humans, she couldn't help but conclude, had some very sensible reasons to think discriminatory thoughts about her.

"The corporations here don't have much money," she explained. They sat on bales and crates, arranged around a common center. "Their standard of living remains high enough thanks to all the infrastructure they built when they were rich, but the crash was an economic collapse more than anything else. Running that infrastructure is expensive, especially on this world. Now they're burning more resources to make big numbers of GIs as little more than lab rats. Like Kiet says, it doesn't make sense. Unless someone else is paying for it."

Frowns from the group. A few looked at each other. "Who?" asked one.

"Well there aren't many options," said Sandy. "Sure as hell it's not the Federation. It's so hard for even independent Feddie agents to get into League space, let alone Torahn space, something like this would take so much organisation they'd get caught. Plus the only interest a Federation biotech company might have in research here would be in shipping it back to the Federation to make money . . . so why have it all wasted by killing subjects here? And why not just do it through the usual communication ratlines back into the main League worlds? FSA knows a lot about those; it's so much simpler than coming here."

"Are you saying the League government might be paying Chancelry to do experiments on GIs?" Kiet asked.

"It would make sense, wouldn't it?" Sandy looked around at them. One thing with GIs, it was harder to read them, as a group. They didn't react so much, and it hid their thoughts. "League society reacted badly to the news that Recruitment had gone much further in developing GIs during the war than they'd admitted. They're being watched. There are still places they can do research without oversight, but nothing with a full industrial infrastructure. This is the only place where GIs are made large scale, where there's no oversight at all. They can violate synthetic rights out here and no one will know or care. And if the League foots the bill, the corporations have a much needed source of revenue."

Was that what the ISO really wanted to find out? Had Mustafa known all along that the League was funding GI research out here? Was the real cause of the conflict between League government and the ISO really that the government had tried to keep the ISO out of the loop? She recalled Duage's footage—Mustafa walking unguarded to the waiting Chancelry flyer, amidst Chancelry GIs carrying the bodies of her dead friends. Was that all that had happened? Chancelry had agreed to let Mustafa and the ISO in on the deal, in exchange for calling off the attack, and sacrificing all her friends?

"Of course," Sandy added, "no one in the Federation has any real idea why there's any GI industry out here in the first place. Pantala's a heavy industry world. There's no real advantage to building synthetic biotech out here, and we're pretty sure there was no GI industry here during the war."

"There was research," said Kiet, solemnly. "When I first arrived. Seven years ago. Big labs, very secret. They've been here a long time. Since Pantala was settled. I saw secret files I shouldn't have, when I was League military. They confirmed it."

Sandy gazed at him. She'd not heard that before either. Kiet was only a 41-series, fairly high as GIs went, but he wouldn't have been privy to much high intel. But then, she knew how curious GIs sometimes ran into information they weren't supposed to. "Really?" she asked. "Why build a research lab out here?" Pantala was settled 120 years ago. GIs themselves weren't that old, though the technology had been approaching takeoff right about then. Chancelry had had GI research labs out here during technological inception?

The GIs looked at one another. There was no reply. Sandy recognised an uplinked conversation when she saw one, and remained silent until their discussion had ended.

"Can you process VR?" Kiet asked.

Sandy frowned. "As of very recently, yes. Only on my own matrix though, it takes a while to process a foreign system."

"What I'd like to show you is not a big system at all," Kiet assured her. "Seven Tigs, no more."

"Why does it need to be VR?"

Kiet smiled. "It just does. I'd take you there in person, but it's a long way out, and we've no time. VR is easier. You need to see it to believe."

He rummaged in a kit bag, and found a booster unit and a cord. Sandy accepted it, and inserted the cord. A small unit like this was no conceivable threat; it lacked processing power, even if GIs of this lower designation did have some VR system that could overwhelm her, which she doubted. Kiet inserted also.

It clicked, and the construct appeared before her. Sandy accessed. It didn't look all that large, as Kiet had said. Newfound VR compatibilities kicked in, and . . .

. . . she stood in a vast chamber. It was natural, smooth hewn yellow rock. Local Pantala sandstone, she supposed. There had been oceans on Pantala once, long ago. Now, only the sandstone and limestone remained. The curving walls made a perfect sphere, as though carved by some laser geometry. Except that the chamber's perfect sides were broken by natural fissures, like any cave system, breaking the curves with crevasses, and rough slices.

In the middle, enormous, was a statue. It was a hand, carved of rock, at least ten meters tall. Its fingertip nearly touched the cavern's ceiling, frozen in some evocative pose, like the hand gestures of classical Indian dance. Sandy wondered what this hand might signify. And why it looked like no human hand at all.

"Looks odd, doesn't it?" said Kiet. Sandy looked at him. As she did so, the construct blurred, then resolved with a new layer of additions—sleeping bags, equipment crates, tents, cooking supplies. A camp, settled upon the sandy floor. Fissures leading from the chamber made huge corridors, sand ploughed by many recent footsteps. Sunlight fell through several fissures that exposed the chamber to the ceiling, making stripes of bright and dark.

"This is your camp?" Sandy asked.

"Yes," said Kiet. "These caves go a long way."

"How far from Droze?"

"Can't say, sorry. We agreed not to tell anyone not in the group. As military we had access to some survey maps left behind by Fleet before they left. Stuff Fleet never shared with the corporations."

Sandy frowned. "The corporations have mining operations all over Pantala. Surely they've surveyed the whole thing?"

"Actually no," said Kiet, walking slowly around the giant stone hand, gazing upward. "The corporations found their major mineral deposits and that was enough for them. They've everything they need right there, more than they could mine in hundreds of years. Fleet controlled all space lanes, did a lot of the corporations' surveying work for them. And this landscape, it's just so metallic, there are zones here in some weather where your basic compass won't work, the coms are all static, and radar surveys just return a big mass of blobs. Lots of magnetic interference."

"So Fleet kept these caves a secret," said Sandy. Beams of sunlight through the overhead crevasses crept slowly along one wall, making brilliant yellow where they struck. "Why?"

"Oh, there are other caves like this," Kiet admitted. "The corporations found a few of those. Fleet just kept the best charts, and from those charts we were able to find a few telltales that led us here. One of the caves the corporations will have a real hard time finding."

Sandy nodded, looking up at the hand. Elongated, and so slim it looked like it might have an extra knuckle in there somewhere. She wondered what the sculptor was trying to say.

"So who carved this?" she asked.

"No idea. Long dead. Look at this." Kiet pointed upward. Sunlight reached a carved fingertip. The fingertip was inset with reflectors of some kind, maybe fibreoptics, inlaid through the stone. Beams of light refracted in all directions, spearing the chamber with golden rays.

"Wow," said Sandy. The effect was extraordinary. "I've never seen that before." Long dead, Kiet said. But Pantala had only been settled for 120 years. Long dead? "How long dead?"

"We dated the molecular residue left by the tools used to carve it," said

Kiet. "It makes some telltale residues from friction with the rock that degrade at a steady rate. It's nearly as reliable as carbon dating. Our results say nearly two thousand years."

Sandy stared. No. It could only mean one thing, but there were some truths a brain just struggled to immediately accept, no matter how obvious.

"That's just after the fall of the Roman Empire," she whispered. "Humans were fourteen hundred years from powered flight, let alone FTL space travel."

"Yeah," Kiet agreed, with a lower-des GI's laconic acceptance of amazing things.

"And that's not some kind of avant-garde version of a human hand, is it?"

"Not unless they were visiting us and taking samples," said Kiet. "But look, it's so precise. Artistic realism, I think."

Sandy put her hands in her hair and gazed up at the blazing fingertip. She wanted to laugh, but the impulse was lost. It had been common speculation for ages—synthetic biology of the kind that created herself was *so* advanced. Yes, it had sprung out of a field of League technology that had been evolving before the League had even officially declared itself a separate entity, but there'd been a number of huge leaps in understanding that a lot of very smart people, Federation and League, who were not directly involved in the field, had struggled to understand.

Of course, speculating that the technology had actually received a kickstart from elsewhere was sacrilege with the League, who preached faith in human comprehension and rationality, and scorned such talk as superstitious anti-progress. When the first micro-circuits had been developed in the 20th century, they'd said, some unsophisticated fools who didn't understand basic science or engineering had presumed that it must be aliens, that human beings couldn't possibly have thought up these things by themselves. And to transpose that argument onto the 26th century, and to propose that human science alone was insufficient to allow for the mapping of human brain function onto synthetic systems to allow for the replication of human sentience on pseudo-biological materials that were not organic, but behaved just like they were, only different . . .

Well. The riddle answered itself, when you looked at it like that. Confronted with this.

"Research labs," she breathed. "This is why you found research labs on Pantala, isn't it?"

Kiet nodded. "Chancelry were the primary sponsor of the first New Torah expeditions anyway," he reminded her. "On the condition of first crack at commercial rights."

Sandy gasped, recalling that information. Chancelry Corporation hadn't just exploited Pantala's resources, they'd settled them. They'd mounted the first expeditions, and made the first footprints on these sands. The first human footprints. "Talee," she said. "They came here and found Talee settlements."

And this before her, self-evidently, was a Talee hand. Reaching toward the sunlight, and dispensing warm glow to all surrounding.

"Presumably they found stuff more high tech than just a statue?" she asked, circling to view from another angle.

Kiet shrugged. "No one knows. I don't know that even most of Chancelry knows, just the top few executives. But what we do know is Chancelry came here first, made a few small outposts, and stayed for a while. 120 years ago."

"But there was no viable reason to stay here," Sandy breathed, recalling FSA intel files on New Torahn history. "It's hard to live here, so settlements aren't self-sustaining without some core economic resource, and the only resources are for heavy mining, for which you need to export because there's no domestic population base. And exports are so damn expensive from here because of the distances, it's only the war that made arms exports viable. So why else would they stay? And why would Chancelry start getting rich around that time?"

It all fit. Exploratory ventures like Chancelry Corporation had hoped to find systems worth settling. Pantala wasn't. But on it, they'd found something far more valuable than real estate.

"But they never expanded into actual production," Sandy wondered aloud. It felt incredibly odd, to be discussing the secrets of her own origin in this location, with another GI. Perhaps like some people felt travelling to holy places. A strange sense of belonging, and of things in the higher cosmic order clicking into place.

"No but they get intellectual property," Kiet reminded her. "That's the real money. Chancelry wasn't a very big corporation when they came out here, just an exploratory venture put together by some speculators back Leagueside. If they hadn't found something in the Torah Systems, they might have gone bust."

"So they licence their IP and get a royalty," said Sandy. "Assuming they found some kind of lab. A high tech settlement. Hell, maybe they just found data records. That could have taken a while to put together. What little I do know of the Talee from the FSA is that they're plenty more advanced than us. And that they've got a bunch of settlements on the far edge of League space which were apparently abandoned."

"In Fleet we called them 'no-see-ums,'" said Kiet. "After those no-see-um bugs. We'd get some radio traffic every now and then, spacers would report it, say it was the spookiest thing to be on the bridge, get traffic maybe a few hours old, but the Talee themselves had gone, or were lying silent somewhere once they saw us jump in. Not real sociable."

"Yeah, I remember." Her old friend Captain Teig had told her once of an encounter far closer than that, where the damn thing kept following her right across one system, just on the edge of range, like some shadow that vanished every time you turned to look. Longest three days of her life, Teig had said. Not the worst, and possibly the most exciting, but definitely the longest. "No reported hostilities, though."

"Yeah. Unless you believe the stories."

Sandy didn't. They sounded too much like old fashioned human xeno-phobia to her. Talee just weren't as enthusiastic about alien contact as many humans were. She knew from FSA reports that many in the League were quite disappointed that the Talee wouldn't talk to them, the enlightened League, and were worried their alien neighbours would make a terrible mistake and talk to the Federation barbarians instead, and share things. That kind of human politics made Sandy think the Talee had been damn smart to avoid humans from the beginning, lest one side think they were hostile because they talked to the other. And that humans might be damn smart to avoid talking to the Talee, for similar reasons.

"So Chancelry find some Talee technology," she repeated, determined to piece this together. "Maybe just a database. Salvage it, translate it and report it, because they have to under exploration law. League government sees this as national significance, classifies it to within an inch of its life, puts its own labs onto it, comes out with . . . what? Let's say synthetic neuro-science. The neuron replication breakout, across the sigma barrier. That's always been the suspicion—that was one technological leap too far for even League ingenuity."

Kiet nodded, arms folded, watching her. As though wondering where she'd go with it.

"They use it to replicate human brains in synthetic form," Sandy continued. "That makes GIs. Chancelry aren't big enough to go into full production, and League government won't allow a monopoly anyway, so that's where the licencing system starts, with Thurtel Corp, Tirvukal Engineering and Zhijue Inc. Those were always the big players. And, damn," she said, as another thought occurred to her, "that would explain why League government were always so involved from the beginning, when usually they're so free market about everything, and how no single corporation ever got credit, it was always suspiciously well spread. They must have made it that way, to avoid monopolies and retain central control."

"Above my pay grade," Kiet remarked. "But go on."

"Hobby of mine," said Sandy. Sunlight moved across the carved Talee fingertip and the spectrum of beamed light changed, from yellows to reds and violets. GI origin history. Ari had called it GI theology theory, which Sandy hadn't found helpful. "So Chancelry give up sole rights, but get a big royalty payment . . . only that doesn't work, because ongoing royalties will get the financial watchdogs asking questions of what they're for, so maybe a big lump sum, plus promises of big future government contracts. Which is why Chancelry is one of the League's favorite corporations when the war begins, wins lots of big weapons contracts."

"Starships," Kiet agreed. "Trying to build new ones right here."

"But this is just the local arm of Chancelry Corporation," said Sandy, frowning. "Chancelry became a League-wide conglomerate, arms in every system. Torah Chancelry was the one that started the deal, but after expansion it was just another branch. And after the crash its own parent company cut it loose, like they all did. Damn, that must have been a decision."

Because this was where Chancelry had started. The other corporations had followed once the war began, as Chancelry landed huge weapons contracts and starship facilities based on the incredible mineral wealth of the systems, and League government had insisted that Chancelry share, if only to keep up appearances. They'd set up their operations in parallel to Chancelry, cooperating with them mostly, competing occasionally, serving huge government orders for starships, flyers, tanks, robotics, microsystems, everything League needed to win the war.

But Chancelry was born here. This was where Chancelry's core intellectual property resided, and damn sure they weren't about to share that with the other corporations. It was well known they had small bases in various places around Pantala, places it hadn't always made sense for them to be, if they were only interested in mining. Surely they'd surveyed the entire world, and all the Torah systems, whatever Kiet said, just to keep other corporations from discovering variations of what they'd discovered.

Unless they'd somehow known their source was the only source. And Kiet was right. Chancelry had been small when they'd first discovered it, with no capabilities to survey that much space. If the first thing they'd done was tell League government what they'd found, League would have sent Fleet to do the surveying, like Kiet said. And however big Chancelry got, and however many ships and other capabilities they acquired, no one pushed Fleet around, not even the League mega-corps. In that, League and Federation were alike. Fleet would have retained that responsibility, even if it meant threatening Chancelry at the point of a gun. National importance. National security. The government will take it from here, we'll tell you what we think you need to know and no more. She knew Chancelry and League government had had their share of strains before, during and after the war, but this put it all in a whole new light.

"Cut the sim," she said. She needed her real mind back, the one unencumbered by VR simulations, however spectacular.

The real world reappeared, GIs seated around, watching her. Sandy wondered how much of that conversation with Kiet they'd been privy to.

"Amazing," she told them. "Not especially surprising. Some of my friends in Tanusha have been insisting it's the truth for years, but these are people who think the government puts micro-recon colonies in drinking water. Amazing to find out they're right for once."

"How does the joke go?" Gunter asked her. "Even paranoids have enemies?"

Sandy smiled. A few of the GIs laughed. That was amazing, too. The joke worked on an abstract level that GIs of this designation rarely responded to. Some of these guys had been kind of old by GI standards before the crash. At least fifteen, some twenty or older. That was five years ago. So quite a few were older than her. Even low-des GIs began to show real sophistication at this age, and it was wonderful to see. It made her hopeful for her people. And made her wonder if even regs would start to demonstrate a comprehension of abstract concepts if they lived long enough. Sadly, few had. But what about now that the war was over?

She took a deep breath, and ran a hand through her hair. "So we really all are products of alien technology." It would take a long, long time to figure out how she felt about that. The knowledge made her feel different somehow, she just couldn't put her finger on how. Maybe it was just that being a GI had always been something hard to define. Was she really a human? Or did synthetic creation make her something else? She'd always leaned to thinking of herself as human, just made of different stuff. But this . . . this made her reconsider.

"We don't talk about it," said Gunter, slicing a pear with his knife and eating. "One, Chancelry will have us exterminated if they know we know. Two, people won't understand anyway. They struggle to accept GIs as things stand; now they'll think we're actually aliens or something. They won't understand that the technology just allows humans to replicate human function, and it's not like we're part Talee. I don't know if anyone actually has access to Talee DNA at all. Assuming they have DNA."

"Do we know what happened to them?" Sandy asked. The FSA didn't. Or, not that they'd told her. These days, there wasn't much that they wouldn't.

"No," said Kiet. "They were here once, a long time ago. Then they left. Haven't been here for nearly two thousand years. No idea why. Geological survey doesn't find any natural disaster. It's like they got bored, or something happened elsewhere that required them to leave."

"What if Chancelry are doing experiments on the original data?" another GI asked. A woman, African appearance, Sandy hadn't learned her name. "The original stuff they used to create the technology? Maybe they have stuff they never pursued, and now League want to know what's in it?"

"Yeah, but why?" countered another. "Chancelry wouldn't have ignored anything they'd found. There was a war on."

"And money to be made," Kiet added. He seemed to Sandy a little cynical. She always liked that in a GI. It wasn't common enough. All of them impressed her. Lower des or not, this was a real debate, and worth listening to. In her experience it rarely happened.

"And they do hate the League," the other continued. "That part's not bullshit, we've seen how they hate the League, after the crash. They were abandoned and got slaughtered. So why work with them now?"

"I bet it wasn't Chancelry's idea," said another. "I bet it was League's. And League don't do anything unless there's profit in it, or advantage."

Sandy's eyes widened. "Or unless they're scared," she said. Mustafa. Seated on his surfboard, asking question after question about Pyeongwha. Neural Cluster Technology. Prepared to send the ISO into what was effectively a small scale war against his own government, to find out what they were up to on New Torah. The government hadn't told the ISO. League and its own primary security agency, working at odds, fighting each other. The government running top secret tests on GIs in New Torah, and not telling the ISO why. The ISO desperate to find out. She'd thought of the usual motivations, strategic advantage, greed, power. She hadn't really thought of fear.

Fear about what? The Federation? The war was over, and while League remained paranoid about Feds, they weren't so dumb as to believe the Federation were the slightest bit interested in resuming hostilities. The Talee? Talee never hurt anyone, at least not that was known.

"I'm missing something," she murmured. "Something big. I need to talk to Duage's girl again."

CHAPTER TWENTY-TWO

Rishi found herself in a play room. It felt like waking up, but she wasn't tired from sleep. It was just that one minute she wasn't conscious, and the next she was. The play room was like her own, only different. Bean bags and cushions were in different places, and the toys were different. Everything was in the same bright colours though, and the wall displays showed colourful scenes in brilliant definition. This one showed a rain forest, emerald green and dripping. Cicadas shrilled and keened.

The woman was there. The GI from before, blonde, blue eyed, sitting on a table. She tossed a ball in one hand. The ball looked old, and well worn.

"Where am I?" asked Rishi, cautiously. "Is this VR?" It had to be VR. The woman nodded.

"This was my play room," said the woman. "Or as near as I can remember it. It's odd, I have hardly any memories of events at this time in my life, but I do remember places. The more I worked on this room, the more I remembered. I guess it was cathartic."

Rishi didn't know what that meant. "Where was this room?"

"I'm still not entirely sure." Still tossing the ball. "Either Angelo Three or Matawari, certainly. Those were the two main pre-service facilities Recruitment ran. I remember some of these games, and these toys. I remember this ball. The ball was for Goldie. Goldie was a dog, a golden retriever. He was my friend. He'd come here, and I'd play with him. I hardly remember him at all though. I had to read about him in a pre-service file I stole a look at."

Rishi looked around. She'd never seen VR this complete before. Usually when her minders let her into VR, it had safety controls, a panel she could activate if she wanted out. This world had nothing. But then, in the real world, she was drugged and restrained. There was no way out of that world, so it made sense there'd be none out of this one either.

"What's your name?" asked the woman.

"Rishi."

"I'm Sandy. I'm twenty-two years old. How old are you?"

"Four."

"Designation?" Rishi said nothing. "I'm 5074J."

"There's no such thing," said Rishi, with certainty.

"There's every such thing," said Sandy. "You came to kill me and my friends the other night."

"You were here to attack the corporation," Rishi retorted.

"Why is that a bad thing?"

Rishi blinked. Opened her mouth, and shut it again. Sandy's blue eyes watched her, patiently, awaiting a reply. "Attacking the corporation is bad," Rishi said finally.

"Interesting," said Sandy. "Why?"

"It just is!" Rishi said in frustration. "People live in the corporation. You shouldn't hurt people."

"What if those people are hurting others?"

"The executives don't hurt others."

"They do," said Sandy. "They're hurting you."

Rishi frowned. "They never hurt me."

"They keep you from being free. That's the same as hurting you. Do they ever let you out? Can you walk wherever you want? Do whatever you want?"

"No one can. It's a corporation, we all have jobs."

"And you're a GI."

"Yes," Rishi agreed, more comfortable on firmer ground.

"And it's a GI's job to fight, and do what she's told."

"Yes." Even more comfortable. "That's how the corporation works. It's not always fair, but nothing's fair." She felt pleased with that. She'd been told that once, and it seemed to fit this situation. It was a clever thing to say, she was certain.

"Ah," said Sandy.

The room disappeared in a blur. It was replaced by a city. The scale of it was extraordinary. Rishi stood on a sidewalk as people in business clothes hurried by on all sides. Traffic whizzed on the road, and huge images splashed and danced colour up and down the sides of towers. High above, aircars whined, turning and flowing in streams.

People everywhere! She'd never seen so many people. Not all of them wore business clothes. Some wore saris, and some bright jackets, or coloured scarves, or strange eyewear. Ahead, a woman was playing an instrument and singing. Passing people tossed coins in the case at her feet.

"This is where I live," said Sandy. She stood at Rishi's side on the sidewalk, suddenly wearing jeans and a leather jacket. "This is Tanusha. Bhubaneswa District; it's a big business hub. There's maybe seventy districts this size in the city. Come on, I'll show you around."

Sandy walked, beckoning Rishi to follow. Rishi knew she shouldn't, Sandy was her enemy. But she walked anyway, because she was a prisoner and had no way out of here, and because the street just looked so amazing. The flow of people never stopped, no two ever alike. There were brown people, white people, black people. A group of old people, following a guide who was shouting to them over the noise and explaining what they saw around them. Some kids, balancing on strange boards on wheels that clattered on the pavement. A pair of police, in uniforms she'd never seen before.

Sandy turned down a street, and Rishi was astonished to see that this street was completely different from the first. How big was this VR construct, anyway? Staring up past the sidewalk trees, the towers seemed to go on forever against a blue sky.

"This is a great street," said Sandy. "Have you ever seen a street like this before? There's lots of functions and conventions in Bhubaneswa District, so this street became a catering hub. Lots of food shops."

A big van had pulled to the curb, and some people were carrying huge cakes in protective covers to the vans. In the shop window, more cakes, with crazy decorations. The next shop was chocolates—Rishi had never seen so much chocolate in her life. Then pastries, and the VR was truly amazing, because the smell made her feel instantly hungry. Then a sweets shop, crowded with many Indian women in clashing saris who laughed and chattered while selecting big containers.

"They're dressed that way because they're going to a wedding," said Sandy, pointing to them as they walked. "Indian weddings are the biggest; some go on for days. Ever been to an Indian wedding, Rishi?"

Rishi shook her head, staring about. In a small garden alcove between shops, men and women in robes were singing chants, and dancing, banging tambourines. "Hari Krishna, Hari Krishna!"

"What does that mean?" Rishi asked.

"Praise Krishna," said Sandy. "Krishna's a god. Hindus have lots. You believe in God, Rishi?"

"I don't know."

"Never thought about it? Ever wonder why not? Everyone else believes in God, or believes in something else. Ever wonder why they don't want GIs to think about it?" She took Rishi's arm, and guided her about the next corner. "This is the best bit. I hope the VR doesn't crash. This can get a little crazy."

About the corner was a lane with no cars, filled entirely with people. It was crowded with stalls, mostly food stalls, and here crowds made a press so thick Rishi and Sandy had to dawdle and edge sideways to get through it. Stalls of live fish and crabs, stalls of hanging meat, stalls of piled vegetables, stalls of multi-coloured spices and smells so thick it was like breathing fumes. Sellers shouted prices, buyers clamoured back, and at the back of stalls, newly arrived vehicles were unloaded, men manoeuvering automated carts directly from a tower's service elevators in a nearby lane, trying not to run people over. More of a street than a lane, wide and long, and filled with people. Thousands of people.

"The cruisers land in the service parking!" Sandy shouted over the din, pointing to the elevators. "For the seafood they come straight from the ports; the fish gets here within a few hours of being caught."

"Why do it all like this?" Rishi shouted back, jostling through the confusion. "This is so crazy! There must be easier ways!"

Sandy made a grand shrug. "This is what human civilisation gets like when you let it free! It just happens. Market forces, social demands . . . no one plans it like this, it just evolves naturally. But you'd never know it if you don't get to live free, yourself."

They got past the worst of the crush, and now it was flower stalls, huge multi-coloured garlands dangling from every post. People were buying them in bunches, with bundles of incense.

"How much of Tanusha is like this?" Rishi wondered.

"Oh, only small bits. But every bit's different, that's the fun of it. There are plenty of markets. This is the Bhubaneswa market. It's sometimes called the Jain Market; it's quite famous. The Ranarid gold souk is even more famous, and even bigger, but myself I like food and flowers more than gold."

"Why the Jain Market?"

Sandy indicated to the left as a big gap between buildings opened up. Nestled within soared a great, white marble temple, with winding spires and a facade carved with dazzling, detailed patterns. More crowds ascended and descended from its wide stairs, carrying the garlands and incense from the market, plus offerings of food.

"The Bhubaneswa Jain Temple," she said. "Do you know about the Jains?" Rishi shook her head, mouth open. The temple was stunning. She'd never seen anything quite like it. "They're pacifists who don't believe in harming any living thing. Ironic location, in this market with all this meat around. See those funny looking crosses on the walls? Those are called swastikas. That's a Jain symbol. Over three thousand years old now."

Rishi didn't know what to think. She'd never even imagined a place like this. It was amazing.

"You say your executives never hurt you," said Sandy. "Why won't they let you see a place like this?"

The place vanished. They were back in the play room. Rishi felt a sense of loss. Tanusha was fascinating. She wanted it back, and didn't know what to do with this sensation. Dissatisfaction.

"I'll tell you why they don't," said Sandy. "Because GIs process information. High-designation GIs especially. We like complexity. Confusion appeals to us. We're like kittens, dangle a shiny ball in front of us and we'll chase it round and round in circles, we can't take our eyes off it. You know how many League GIs have defected to the Federation?"

Rishi blinked. "No."

"Seventy-six so far, last I heard. All high-designation. You didn't tell me your designation."

"4505," said Rishi, dazed.

Sandy whistled. "High. Very high."

"Not as high as some," Rishi murmured. "The girl you found. Her image, in my memory implant. She's higher."

A pause from Sandy. Her stare was very intense. "You know her?"

Rishi nodded. "She was very high. And her friend, Eduardo. They were always together. Executives tried to find things for them to do, separately, but they preferred to be together. Everyone talked about them, because they were strange. I suppose that's what happens, when you're strange."

"Are you strange, Rishi?"

"I don't know." Helplessly. "Maybe."

"Eduardo came to me, in Tanusha." Rishi stared at her. "He was very strange, but I liked him. The executives killed him."

"No!" Incredulously. Defiantly. "You're lying."

A new image replaced the lush green rainforest on the display wall. An autopsy table. Gruesome images. Eduardo's face, lifeless in the cold light. No images that belonged in a colourful play room.

"My own memory implants," Sandy said quietly. Rishi stared. "See how the implants melted, in the back of the head? You know what does that?" No reply. "They put killswitches in all of our heads, Rishi. Me too. All the high-designation GIs. In case we start doing things they don't want. Then they melt our brains."

A VR control panel opened in empty space in front of her.

"On here are the schematics and images I recorded of Chancelry HQ when I hacked in just now," said Sandy. "You know the medical research building, floors 12 to 17? The ones you're not allowed into? Here's what's in them. Anya's in there. You take your time, and look them over yourself. Then you tell me what you think. I promise if you want to go back to Chancelry after you look at them, I'll let you. You won't be a prisoner here anymore. It's your choice. Life without choices is no life at all. Remember that."

Sandy unplugged from the back of Rishi's head. She lolled, unconscious against the chains that bound her to the cellar's rusting pipes. Monitoring the portable processor, Kiet gave Sandy a questioning look.

"VR works amazingly," said Sandy. "I showed her Tanusha, and a full schematic of Chancelry HQ. She's processing that now."

Home Guard had given her drugs that knocked her out, but that wouldn't stop the VR construct from working, a little bubble of consciousness within the enfolding dark of sleep.

"Not waking up," Kiet observed. "Try slapping her?"

Sandy shook her head. "I don't want to interrupt. Sometimes they wake up, sometimes they don't. What I showed her was traumatic. She'll wake when she wants to."

"Can she process the schematic without this?" Kiet tucked the cords away into the processor in its carry pack.

"It's just a schematic, it's not full VR. Tacnet will handle it easily. Every GI has tacnet built in."

"Amazing you can keep a VR construct that size stable," Kiet observed. "There's so many unstable parameters."

"There's a formula. I've got a new system worked out. It's self-adjusting, monitors the construct and keeps it stable."

"Automated systems find it nearly impossible to stablise a construct that big," Kiet said cautiously. "Especially with a subject who doesn't want to be there."

Sandy shrugged. "But run automated systems with conscious oversight, and the capabilities exponentially increase. That's always been a GI advantage. Augmented straights have it too, but they just don't process the volumes that we do."

They left the basement, past Home Guard with weapons at the door who looked displeased with their presence. Outside the door was a blaze of cold morning sun, and Sandy wrapped her scarf beneath her raised collar, eyes adjusting to block the glare. It was only a short walk to the nearby garage where their vehicle and its guard were parked, but there were people in the street. Too many people, looking their way.

Sandy didn't need to tell Kiet. He immediately walked wide, hand in pocket for a weapon. On the right, immediately past a battery recharge store, Home Guard emerged from a coffee shop where they'd been waiting, smoking hookah pipes. Their weapons were not particularly well concealed within their heavy coats, berets askew, hoods raised against the chill. Sandy had never been much on dress discipline, but this was unprofessional. Raised hoods blocked the ears, restricted peripheral vision. Heavy duty boots were good for soft-footed straights, but slowed running. Weapons access was blocked by clothing, or otherwise poorly positioned.

One of the men was Sylvan Hector. "Who gave you permission to talk to the skinjob?" he asked. Ordinary folks were gathering around, and it didn't take a GI's vision to spot more poorly concealed weapons.

"I did," said Sandy, not wanting to get Duage into trouble. She had asked, she wasn't impolite.

"From now on," said Hector, "consider that permission revoked."

Sandy would have kept walking, but their path was completely blocked. Ordinary folks looked angry. Which made this a setup, because it could be no coincidence that all these people would gather in this place by chance. But a setup by whom, and for what?

"Listen," said Hector, "you don't control anything around here. This is

Home Guard territory. We've shed blood for five years to keep Outer Droze free from the corporations. You want to do anything, you talk to us first. Otherwise, we end up with Chancelry artillery attacks and a bunch of dead and wounded."

Angry growls from the crowd.

"Noted," said Sandy. "Move aside."

"What did she tell you? In there?" Hector jerked his head toward the doorway they'd emerged from.

"Nothing," said Sandy. "Your people gave her drugs to knock her unconscious."

"So what did you tell her?"

"You've got a strange conception of the term 'unconscious.'"

"Listen Feddie," said Hector, "I know you GIs have tricks. You didn't just go in there to play visitors. What's in the bag?" Looking at Kiet's backpack, where the processor was stored.

"It's not safe for so many people to gather like this," said Sandy. "Chancelry's not the only corporation with UAVs. Kiet's people can't shoot them all down, it'll just invite counterstrike. And now, like a bunch of geniuses, you're not concealing your weapons."

"And now she gives us lectures on not inviting a counterstrike!" snarled another onlooker.

Now Sandy was truly concerned, but not for herself. She raised both hands, palms out. "Look, I don't know who told you that confronting high-designation GIs physically could intimidate them, but they're idiots. I'm going this way," she pointed through them, "and trust me, you can't stop me."

She indicated with a brief flick of the finger to the surrounding windows up and down the street. Kiet turned to look, scanning in full combat mode as the red shift descended upon Sandy's own vision.

"Twenty-six people are dead because of you!" another person shouted. "Fucking skinjob, who's going to answer for all our dead?" More shouts. It was becoming hard to be heard.

"Listen!" Sandy shouted. "Someone sold us out! I was doing recon in the neutral zone about the barrier and we triggered no alarm, just suddenly the Chancelry bots knew where we were! If you want someone to blame for that artillery strike, blame whoever told Chancelry we were there!"

"Oh right!" Hector laughed, angrily. "Because it's our fault! And all you skinjob freaks turning up on Chancelry's doorstep with your heavy weapons had nothing to do with it!"

"Go back to where you came from!" someone shouted, and others joined in the chorus. It was a crescendo of yells, pointing fingers and angry faces. Even in Tanusha, with its multiple extremist elements, Sandy had never experienced anything like this.

But despite the noise, her hearing was sensitive enough to detect Kiet's muttered reply, intended for no one but himself. "Go back to where I came from? You fucking made me, I came from you."

Shots. Someone fell, then another. Screams, yells, people running, ducking for cover as Sandy pulled two pistols and targetted on both sources, but they were gone as fast as they'd come.

"Go!" she yelled at Kiet, and he sprinted for the vehicle. Sandy walked slowly, in full combat vision and watching the windows she was certain the snipers had been in, but knowing better than to expect those windows alone to yield more snipers.

No more shots came, and now the truck was roaring toward them, doors opening, and Sandy jumped on the rear tray, weapons out, still scanning. The truck dodged more running people, and now some of those were aiming weapons. Sandy put a shot through an arm, a leg, then another arm, as again people ducked or ran for cover. Then the truck skidded about a dusty corner, and Sandy clambered around the cabin to crawl into a door that a GI inside held open for her.

"You see them?" Sandy asked Kiet.

"No," said Kiet, weapons out at the opposite window, as were the other three GIs, including the one driving, a pistol on the wheel. "Two guns, that's all."

"Why didn't you shoot them?"

"Dammit," said Kiet, "not all of us are as fast as you. I only had a second, they were well covered and didn't expose themselves."

Crap, thought Sandy, lateral thinking returning as combat reflex dimmed a bit. She hadn't meant it as an accusation, just an honest question.

"Fucking setup," she muttered. "Whole thing."

"Whose?" asked the driver, roaring about another corner.

"Home Guard. I had to wound a couple just now who tried to shoot at us. Now we'll get blamed for the whole thing, all of Droze will turn against us."

"Hey!" said Kiet, as something occurred to him. "Rishi, the girl! They'll kill her. We have to go back."

"For a Chancelry drone?" the driver asked sceptically.

"She's not a drone, she's high-des. We were trying to bring her around!"

"Keep going," Sandy told the driver.

"We're not abandoning another one!" Kiet turned on her, angrily. "I've had enough of these fuckers, I've had enough of being treated like shit, and if they're stupid enough to pick a fight with me, that's their problem. We went to all that trouble to try and bring her around, and . . ."

Sandy held up a hand. "I know," she said, with a calm, knowing look. "She'll be fine."

Kiet blinked, as the truck bounced on some rough road. "You slipped her something?"

"Drug neutraliser. When you weren't looking. Home Guard won't let the mob have her, she's an asset. But when she gets free of those chains, there's plenty of ways out of that place without her having to kill any Home Guard. You see those high sidewalls? Led straight to the alleys."

"Wouldn't care if she had to kill a bunch of them," Kiet growled.

"We might have to kill a bunch of them," the driver agreed. "If they come after us."

"Then what?" asked another.

"Maybe she comes to find us," said Sandy. "Maybe she won't. We'll see."

CHAPTER TWENTY-THREE

"**W**ell that settles it," said Ari, sliding in beside the others. "They're definitely following Cai."

They were huddled in a cold, abandoned storage compartment, behind the cover of steel air ducts and empty cargo rails. Nearly four hours ago, they'd been forced to abandon their reconnaissance, based from Cai's empty apartment, when both Ari and Cai's tripwires had been triggered, warning them of an approaching ambush. Since then they'd been moving continuously, deeper and deeper into Antibe Station's cold, empty bowels, cautious pursuit never more than a few hundred meters behind.

"We're being herded," said Vanessa, working her pistol mechanism to prevent jamming in the cold. "I hate that."

"Herded where?" Rhian wondered. They all had station schematics uploaded, but didn't dare access the station network to monitor something real-time. Only Ari and Cai had the network kung fu to risk it, and they'd do it disguised as any number of other functions, and wouldn't check something so obvious as a schematic. If it came to a fight, Ari had his booster they could run tacnet off, but they didn't dare use it until the bullets were flying. Anything that generated a transmission range they could use, their pursuers could also monitor, even if they couldn't interfere with it.

"Somewhere they have a trap waiting," said Vanessa, eyes fixed on doorways. They communicated only at a whisper, unable to use uplink formulation for the same reason they couldn't use tacnet. Being in a communications unfriendly environment was getting old.

"I'm not sure it follows they're definitely chasing me," Cai said with a faint frown.

"You accessed docking matrix from gridpoint CF-92, like I said?" Ari asked. Cai nodded. "And immediately my mole reported a feedback spike on that grid, and two minutes later we hear footsteps coming down the best corridor access to CF-92. Somehow they know what to look for when you access the net."

"Best you stop for now," Vanessa suggested. Her stomach grumbled.

Being on a big, empty space station was like being stranded in a giant steel desert. Most services to these parts had been switched off, excluding air. No water ran through the pipes, and the nearest food was only available from retail outlets a kilometer away, or warehouses, both guarded and visible.

"I've been on this station for several months," Cai replied. He looked concerned, possibly even worried. That was a first. "They've never been able to trace my interface before."

"Yeah," said Ari, staring intently at the surrounding walls. "I wonder. That League ship, the ghostie. Any other League ships visiting while you've been here?"

"No," said Cai. He and Ari looked at each other for a long moment.

Vanessa got a chill that had nothing to do with the cold. Ari thought that super advanced League warship had been sent all this way to warn the station about Cai? That brought a thousand questions to mind.

"Shit, Ari!" she whispered in frustration. "Who the hell is he? I can't think my way out of a tactical situation if I don't even know what we're stuck in! And like it or not, I am ranking military here, however advanced he is!"

"Perhaps we should tell her," Cai suggested.

"No." Ari shook his head, adamant. "Ricey I'm sorry. You can kick my ass later."

"You better believe it," she muttered.

"But I think I've got some idea what's going on out here," he continued. "Why Chancelry's making GIs out here, where GI technology came from. We're getting chased right now. If they catch one of us . . ."

"Yeah, yeah," she growled.

"Tell me," Cai interrupted. "You three seem too smart and too senior to just get yourselves trapped on this hostile station. Do you have support? Out there?" With a nod toward distant, empty space.

"Now who's asking for secrets," Vanessa said drily. A thought occurred to her. "Do you?"

Cai smiled a little, and shrugged. It was a subtle smile, with a hint of irony. The kind of expression only the most mentally developed GIs would offer. Like Sandy.

"Well, whether you guys will talk to me or not," she said, "I've only got one plan when people come after me."

"Ha," said Rhian, checking weapons and ammo. "Thought so."

Ari blinked, looking from one to the other. "You're going to attack them?"

"Not all of them," Vanessa replied. "Just the ones that matter."

The ambush was easier than she'd thought. With their pursuers tracking Cai's network access points as they moved through the station, it was a simple enough matter for Ari to find a way to fool the network receptors to thinking Cai was somewhere he wasn't. Almost immediately the pursuit deviated in that direction, with flankers to guard the main corridors to prevent any backtracking. A simple study of the schematic told Vanessa the logical spot for that, and she made sure she got there first.

Rhian did it herself. There was no cover for any more than one person, and the others were needed to make sure they themselves weren't flanked in the maze of corridors and empty rooms and service crawlways. Vanessa didn't see exactly what she did, just heard a fast commotion, then peered down her corridor to see Rhian already dragging one body, boots disappearing around a corner.

One last check to see the corridor remained clear, then Vanessa ran in, meeting Ari at the ambush cross-corridor, Ari tapping his ear then pointing outward, indicating his jamming had worked; no one else had heard these two go down. No, three, Vanessa saw as she ducked into the side room where Rhian was dragging bodies, two already in, a third lolling unconscious outside. Ari grabbed that one, then Cai came in from his end of the corridors.

Vanessa checked vitals—two concussions, one severe, and one with a knife in the throat, fast dying and very messy.

"Fucking stupid patterns," Rhian pronounced, all business as she went through their clothes for anything useful. "Two is standard for that spot, three's overkill, I had to stretch with the knife or he would have shot me."

Vanessa checked the dying man's vitals . . . and found with the position of the knife, missing the jugular, he might yet survive. Maybe. "Fuck it," she muttered. Killing hadn't been the plan. Yet.

She glanced at Rhian, ruffling through IDs, gear, passing an ear com to Ari in case he could do something with it. Rhian was a mum now. It had changed her, for sure. But today, she was all combat GI, no doubt still deep in combat reflex. Some things wouldn't change. Couldn't.

Cai stood guard at the door, leaving it open. His hearing would detect anyone approaching before they heard anything themselves.

"Rhi, help with the knife. If we get a bandage on it, he might make it."

"Oh, we're doing that, are we?" Rhian asked blandly, moving to help. "We're caring?"

"Fuck it, Rhi, just get the knife." Vanessa held the head still while Rhian pulled, then used it to slice off some uniform to use as bandage. The man kicked and spluttered, blood bubbling between his lips. "You miss on purpose?"

Rhian pressed the cloth down, then cut more to tie it with, giving no indication she might reply.

"Ricey," said Ari, fiddling with the ear com, "you got some idea of what Chancelry's doing down on Pantala?" Vanessa shot him a hard look. "If you were a GI, how'd you feel about the people who were part of that?"

"So we're doing that, are we?" Vanessa said sarcastically. "We're going all revenge crazy and bloodthirsty? Or are we doing our fucking jobs?"

Rhian finished tying the bandages, looking a little subdued. Vanessa had never seen Rhian belligerent before, not even in combat. She understood that. But they were all pros, or she and Rhian were, and God knew what Cai was. Pros did it right or not at all, and blood lust only turned you into an amateur. Unless you were Sandy.

The less-concussed man was waking up, groggily. Vanessa pointed her pistol at him, more to get his attention than from any concern. "Hey," she said. "You awake?"

An awkward nod. His hands felt to his weapons, finding nothing.

"What corporation?" No reply. "Quickly, or I'll start blowing bits off."

"Dhamsel," the man mumbled. Put a hand to his head, wincing. "Hey, who's doing . . . stop that."

Vanessa blinked, then looked at Cai. Cai seemed to be concentrating. "You in?" she asked him. Cai said nothing.

"Fucking wireless direct access," Ari muttered incredulously. "Even Sandy can't just barrier hack a security pro like that."

"Who are you chasing?" Vanessa persisted. "Who told you what to chase?"

"Man," muttered the Dhamsel Corporation man, "I don't fucking know. I'm just a grunt, yeah?"

"Welcome to the club," said Rhian.

"Who are you after?" Vanessa snapped, raising her voice.

"A GI! A GI like you, right? You are one, yeah? Can smell the fucking synthetic blood from here."

"Thinks I'm a GI," Vanessa said to Rhian.

"Be flattered," said Rhian. "I always am."

"Well it's either you or her," said the man. "'Cause it's not him, he doesn't look like it." Looking at Ari.

"Well fuck you, too," said Ari.

"Not him?" Vanessa asked, pointing at Cai. The man looked, frowning, then looked back.

"What are you fucking talking about? Who?"

"Him. There. By the door."

"I don't know who you're fucking with, lady. There's no one there."

Vanessa was puzzled for a moment. Then heard Ari mutter, "Oh, no fucking way." Then her eyes widened. She stepped over the man, who raised hands to defend himself, but she swatted them aside, knelt beside him, grabbed his head and pointed his face directly at Cai.

"There. Look right there. What do you see?"

"See?" The man was now frightened and confused. "What are you trying to pull?"

"Oh, good God," said Rhian. Rhian was not given to great exclamations of any kind. Vanessa stared at Cai. Cai was still concentrating. Now he seemed to roll his eyes, with a flicker of disgust, and suddenly the man was unconscious again.

"That's impossible," Vanessa said flatly. It wasn't smart to disbelieve what you'd just seen, but she was tired of being baffled. It didn't suit her. "No one has the technology to do real-time visual override. It's a technogeek myth, the holy grail of Ari's crowd. It barely works on undefended subjects with a week's preparation, sure as hell not real-time against a conscious security pro working for an arms corporation."

Cai shrugged. "Well then, there you are. It's not possible. We'd best move before their friends notice they're missing, I've got most of his files. We can do some good things from here."

And suddenly she saw it. Why Ari was so in awe of this man. What could make all this impossibility possible. She'd just seen him do something no human technology could allow. No *human* technology.

"Oh, for fuck's sake," she exclaimed, angry at herself for not having seen it sooner. "You're Talee."

Silence in the room.

"So where are the tentacles?" Rhian asked. Vanessa nearly laughed.

Cai sighed. "No, I'm human. But humans didn't make me. Talee did."

"Why?" Vanessa demanded. It was all very fascinating, but there were people trying to kill her and she was more interested in the tactical applications. "What's your mission?"

"Scout," said Cai. "Recon. I can make myself invisible to heavily uplinked individuals; there aren't many places I can't go."

"We shouldn't be talking about this," said Ari, fingers pressing the bridge of his nose, wincing. "We should all just shut up and . . ."

"No, it's all right," said Cai. "I'm allowed to make myself known in extreme circumstances, I deem that . . ."

"No, just shut up for a second," Ari interrupted, walking between them. "Please. I've been saying for years GI brain tech is so obviously not human, no one believed me, not even Sandy . . . in fact, especially not Sandy . . ."

"Because you're a paranoid conspiracy theorist," Rhian said helpfully.

". . . and we just shouldn't talk about it," Ari continued, "because this blows everything out of the water. This is why League will fucking blow Droze off the map if they find out Sandy knows, they'll nuke this station too, just to get us, if they know we know. This knowledge is dangerous, do you get that?"

"So what do you want to do?" Vanessa demanded. "Pretend we don't know? I'm not a big picture strategist like you and Sandy, I just know what I know. And I'm going to use it to kick some ass!"

Ari rolled his eyes. "Damn, could you use some subtlety just once? I'm going to have to say it out loud, aren't I? What if this guy . . ." jerking a thumb at Cai, ". . . would rather commit suicide and take us all with him rather than let that secret get out?"

Everyone looked at Cai. Cai looked faintly affronted. "Do I look suicidal?"

"Does anyone?" said Rhian.

"Well if you argue like that," said Cai, "then there's nothing I can do to convince you. You'll just have to trust that I'm not. Quite honestly, I'm not that sort of guy. And neither are my employers."

"Maybe they should be," said Ari, with sinister intensity. "Maybe even they don't realise just what a mess this is."

Cai smiled. "I think they do. And it's worse than you know, trust me."

"You have backup out there?" Vanessa demanded of him. "Since we're being honest with each other?"

"I'll show you mine if you show me yours."

"Let's just say we're not alone," Vanessa confirmed.

"Me neither," said Cai. That gave Vanessa another chill. He was talking about a Talee ship. Somewhere out there, beyond the solar system rim, where the dust and debris of the middle-system dust cloud made for good cover. Spacers told spooky stories about Talee hiding and spying on them. Cai was talking about one that was his friend.

"Maybe yours and mine should get together so we don't make any unfortunate mistakes."

"Oh, don't worry," said Cai. "Mine will know exactly where yours is."

"I don't doubt," Ari murmured.

"Great," said Vanessa. "Your ships can see a pea in orbit from a billion clicks, and you can disappear before a person's eyes by hacking their brain. If they're prepared to nuke the station to get us now we know you exist, let's take it from them first. The bridge is probably the only place we're safe now, anyway."

Ari stared at her. "You're not serious."

"No I'm not serious," Vanessa said drily. "I'm just talking because I like the sound of my own voice. Can you see my lips moving?"

"Are you really just going to attack them?" Danya asked.

Sandy sat against a wall before windows in a derelict apartment, fifteen floors up. They were in Whalen sector, ten kilometers southwest of the Rimtown. Here amidst the crumbling urban sprawl they had a mediocre view over Heldig Corporation's perimeter from four Ks out. Any tower with a better view would have been suspect, and even now Sandy sat low to hide her silhouette in the dust stained window.

"That depends," she said, peering through the scanner she'd acquired from Kiet's equipment store. Her own visual zoom was too restricted at this range, particularly at night. A lot of the corporate zone's lights were off. Clearly they were nervous of surveillance.

"On what?"

"Whether I can find a way in or not.

"Cassandra, I know you're a top soldier and everything . . ."

"Call me Sandy."

"But, I mean, these are the corporations." Danya's expression was pained. "Even you can't beat them all. What about all those reinforcements?"

He was right, there were a lot of reinforcements. Shuttles had been landing from God-knew-where—Batu Mehra probably, and Tivu. Even one reentry shuttle, direct from orbit, that had come down on landing pads atop Heldig Corporation's HQ roof. Pantala was an arms factory world, and there were a lot of weapons here. But after her brush with Chancelry's defences, Sandy had doubts about the training of the people using them.

"I just need to get in past that kill zone," she said. "All the heavy weaponry in the world won't help them in a built-up environment. Once I get in there, they can't shoot without destroying their own city and their own people."

"Kiet's only got about two hundred people. Sandy, there's tens of thousands in there, plus all those robots . . ."

"I know. We'll get their command and control, first targets."

Danya said nothing. Sandy glanced at him. He looked unhappy. Frightened. Sandy thought about it for a moment. Then she realised.

"Hey." She reached, and put a hand on his knee. "This isn't a suicide mission. I'm good at this."

"Nothing good's ever happened to me without it blowing up in my face and making everything worse," Danya said bleakly. He gazed at her, with frank honesty. "You're something good."

Sandy didn't know what to say. It was confusing. These kids were amazing. She'd never felt so strongly about anyone so soon after first introductions, save for maybe Vanessa. They saw in her . . . something. A parent figure, perhaps. A protector, certainly. And these were tough kids. They'd seen a lot of people come and go, often violently. They were tough judges, sceptical at best, brutally cynical at worst. She'd seen veterans like that, eyeing the new recruit and concluding he'd be gone within a week. And keeping their distance, because you couldn't get attached to such people. If they were gone in a week, better they didn't take any of your soul with them.

Dangerous to be a 50-series GI around such kids. A 50-series GI wouldn't be gone in a week. She'd exude power, and protection. A kid might yearn for such things, and think to have found them in her.

But a 50-series GI wasn't cut out to be a parent. She'd avoided it for precisely this reason—Rhian might be able to settle down and adopt, but Sandy had seen this coming. Not specifically, but in general, the collision of two opposing worlds. She was a soldier. A killer for a cause. There'd been a time she'd thought her causes had evaporated, and with them, she'd hoped, her killing days as well. But events had proven that a false hope. And now she had Danya, seeing in her something that she could never be for him, and wishing that she could stop being what she was, because he feared the outcome. Well, so did she. But she feared the alternative worse.

Besides which, she'd never felt stronger about a cause than she did about this one. That didn't just mean passion, that meant fury. When she got this angry, lots of people died. How could she be that, furious and deadly, and also this . . . this whatever it was that Danya wanted her to be? Motherly? What was she going to do . . . launch an all-out attack on the corporate headquarters of Droze, then return to embrace adopted children with bloodstained hands?

Those two parts of her life, of her soul, had to remain separate. She couldn't see them blurred, combined . . . the prospect filled her with a dull heart-thumping panic she could not put words to.

A flash lit up the horizon. Then another, close to the first. Sandy looked, zooming on the fireballs, debris raining down. Whatever it was had taken the top floor off a pair of buildings. Then another, five hundred meters from the first two.

"Shit," she murmured.

"Artillery again?" Danya wondered.

"Yeah. I guess this is why Home Guard don't pick fights with the corporations any longer."

Boom, as the sound reached them. And again. Footsteps in the corridor outside, and a burst of short-range transmission—Gunter. He entered a second later, sliding through the half-open door and keeping low across the bare concrete floor.

"We okay?" Sandy asked him. They had directional coms across the city that could be used in short bursts without the corporations seeing them, but they had to know where to point them first. That meant small groups of people who knew where other people were going to be stationed—a security risk, but a necessary one.

"I think so," said Gunter, peering out the window above what had once been a kitchen bench. "They're shooting blind. Probably they saw movement. It happens sometimes when they're on high alert."

"Yeah, and they kill some people for walking around in their bedroom," Danya muttered. "Hector's gonna love this."

"There are reports of Home Guard following us," Gunter confirmed. He had a laser com sight mounted on his short rifle, the easiest way of pointing. "We've had to warn them off."

Sandy exhaled hard. "They're going to give us away. With those UAVs back up." They'd shot a couple of UAVs out of the sky with missiles, but those missile firings had immediately been targetted by corporate artillery. Their shooters had barely got away in time. A few more civvies killed, Home Guard even more furious, it had become clear they'd have to let the UAVs operate unmolested once more.

"They'll give you away on purpose," said Danya. "Like they gave us away in the neutral zone. Spies everywhere."

"Don't know about everywhere," said Gunter. "But some, certainly. With Home Guard against us, we can't operate freely in this city. The corporations don't care how many civvies they kill."

"Which means we have to go in sooner rather than later," said Sandy. "I think we can do it into Heldig Corporation here. Those networks are pretty invulnerable from the outside; that might change once we get in. But I can see a geometry here between a few buildings that blocks line of sight for their second layer defences, and if we can drop a few missiles into their roads a block or two in, bring down a few walls, cut off mobilisation of those secondary assets . . ."

"Straight explosive entry?" Gunter asked. Perhaps dubiously, but the man's bland expression made it hard to tell.

"With a diversionary attack. There are ways."

"And once inside?"

"Go fast straight across Heldig Quarter. We go through the buildings, a few floors up. They can't stop us without bringing buildings down, we only expose ourselves leaping over roads between buildings."

Gunter scratched his jaw. "I've never done that before."

"I have. For fast movement in an urban zone it's the only way to go. Straights can't do it, so few people have thought of defence against it. Least of all League or ex-League, who've never expected attack by GIs."

"Then all the way to Chancelry? That's a long way, corridor by corridor."

"Their defences will diminish further in. And the crossing into Chancelry territory will be lightly defended. They're not expecting direct attack from another corporation's territory."

"What do you figure for casualties?" Gunter asked somberly.

Sandy pursed her lips, still watching the dissipating explosions. Thick smoke now rose, blocking city night lights. "Not light. Conservatively twenty percent, if it all goes well."

"And not conservatively?"

"Attacking into a vastly superior force means we'll be completely sur-rounded," Sandy answered. "If it doesn't work, getting out will be nearly impossible." She took her eyes away from the scanner to look at him. "But I think everyone knows that. If they don't want to come, no one will think less of them."

"Yes they will," said Gunter, gazing toward the lights of corporate terri-tory, between various buildings ahead. "I know I will."

Danya said nothing, back to the wall beside the window, with no interest in the view.

Gunter's com unit flickered. Gunter frowned, and looked at the hand screen, dialling frequencies and adjustments in his head. "That's broadband," he observed. "Must be corporate, anyone else would be dead in seconds."

"Can you put it on?" Sandy asked.

Gunter took Danya's place by the window so he could show the screen without that illumination registering on any distant scan. Danya crouched by Sandy, watching. On the little handscreen was a man in a suit.

"That's Tarasan," Danya and Gunter said simultaneously. Emilio Tarasan, that could only be. Chairman, Chancelry Corporation, New Torahn Division.

"Apparently," Tarasan told the screen, with an air of dry contempt, "there are violent, dangerous people out in Droze tonight who seek to attack Chancelry Corporation and its allies. As you are now observing, recent attacks have been answered in full. Our retribution shall be harsh, and further security measures are being pursued even as I speak."

He paused, leaning forward a little, with great seriousness. A square faced man, heavy browed, humourless. "It gives the corporation no pleasure to do this."

"Bullshit," said Danya.

"But corporate policy is clear and unwavering—security is paramount, and we will accept no alternative but total security. Should any attack be received, civilian casualties from our response shall be enormous. I appeal to the common sense of the ordinary citizens of Droze, do not allow this folly. Stop them, or alert us to their location. Rewards shall be high, we've proven that in the past. Penalties shall be final.

"Furthermore, I would finally address the leader of last night's unprovoked attack. Chancelry Corporation has in custody someone dear to those close to you. Remember that. I'll say no more."

The screen flickered, and then the message began to repeat. Gunter silenced it.

Sandy made a face. "Well, he's dead," she said sourly. "He's made my list."

Danya looked terrified. "Kiril," he breathed.

"We'll get him out, Danya."

"Sandy you can't!" Danya exclaimed. "They'll kill Kiril!"

"Danya, listen for a moment . . ."

"No! No more listening . . ." he made to get up, but Sandy grabbed him, pulled him back down.

"No sudden movements," she reminded him.

There was no use struggling in that grip, but Danya gritted his teeth, pressing against it. "Danya. Danya, stop." He stopped, breathing hard. Sandy put her forehead against his. "Look, kid. I know you're scared. But Tarasan just made a huge mistake. Relations with the other corporations are shaky, and he just dropped his bundle. I don't know how much the other corporations know about Chancelry's GI experiments. I'm betting a lot of them don't like it but have gone along with it until now . . . but it makes Chancelry the most powerful of the bunch. They won't like that, and now Chancelry's causing them trouble, too.

"I can get my message out. I have enough intel now to get the Federation coming down on this world pretty hard, and they'll all be neck deep then. I can stop that. I just want Chancelry to stop, that's all, and one of those other corporations can give them to me."

"You're playing games with Kiril's life!" Danya shouted, fighting away from her. Sandy let him, and he knelt by her side. "That's my brother you're playing with!"

"Danya. I didn't take you for a naive boy. Don't be naive now. What do you think I am?" Danya said nothing, staring at her. "This is what I do, Danya. Whatever you might want me to be, and whatever I've come to feel for you, Svet and Kiril, this is what I am. Now, I can save Kiril's life. But there are GIs dying in there, in all sorts of horrible ways, and I just can't allow it. I can't allow this to be all that my people are, in human society. Objects to be experimented on. Our lives must have value, Danya. Do you think I should just live with that?"

"I don't care!" Danya retorted, his voice trembling. "That's my brother's life! My family's all I've got, and it's not the same!"

"So when you say you care about me, is that the only reason why? Because I might protect you, Svet and Kiril? Because I might do something for you? Is that really affection, or is that just selfishness?"

Danya didn't know what to say, his eyes darting. Hell of a tough question to ask the kid, in his circumstance. Sandy nearly hated herself for asking it. But she was asking him to consider the difference between being a boy and being a man. That was what parent-type figures were supposed to do. Wasn't it?

Danya got up. Sandy caught his arm. "Let me go," Danya muttered.

"It's not safe out there, Danya."

"It's never been safe out there. I survived five years on my own before you got here, then you got Kiril kidnapped and now you're going to get him killed. I can do without your help."

His stare was cold, his manner abruptly less childish by the second. It hurt about as badly as anything anyone had ever said to her. Sandy let him go. He moved quickly to the door and disappeared.

Sandy squeezed her eyes shut and leaned her head against the wall. When she opened her eyes, Gunter was before her on one knee, awaiting her response. "What are you going to do?" he asked.

Mother or soldier? Whatever Danya thought, she could see only one way to get Kiril back and shut down Chancelry. Abandon her goal, just to save Kiril? Ridiculous to even think it. How many civilians had already died in this mess? Who was she to decide that one was more important than all the others?

No, that path was impossible. She was a soldier. Pain was in the job description, and this pain was just one more she would bear.

"I want a secure com line to Dhamsel Corporation," she said. "We'll route it remotely, directional link on a micro-UAV. They can torch it, won't cost us anything, but I think they'll want to listen. And I want that uplink to Antibe Station. My team should have arrived by now. We need to get the latest report back to Callay ASAP."

CHAPTER TWENTY-FOUR

"*N*o deal, *Ms Kresnov,*" said Dhamsel CEO Patana in her earpiece. "*I'll take my chances with the Federation Fleet.*" The sarcasm suggested how little he thought of that possibility.

"You might not live that long," said Sandy, munching a snack bar from the store shelf. "You'll have to take your chances with me first."

"*I'll risk it,*" said Patana, with contempt. "*The fact that you're talking to me now shows clear enough that you can't break our defences.*"

"Can," said Sandy, still eating. "I don't know if you know my life history, Mr Patana, but I'm pretty much knee deep in blood by now. I was really hoping I wouldn't have to kill everyone. Again." She put a foot up on the stool opposite at the bar. "I want Chancelry. You give me them, I'll leave you out of it. They're doing things to GIs over there that I object to. I'm going to stop it, and that'll leave you top of the tree here on Pantala. Win-win, as I see it."

"*You know, Ms Kresnov, fuck you. The day I cave in to the pathetic threats of a Feddie skinjob who's upset because a few of her plastic pals lost a few bits next door . . . you know, you all deserve it, you're not good for anything else.*"

"Well," said Sandy, taking another bite as Gunter made some coffee behind the bar, "I'd like to congratulate you on making my list."

"*What list?*"

"My kill list. No one's ever survived it yet, and buddy . . ." she gave an amazed laugh, ". . . you're on it. Have a nice final few hours, and if you change your mind, you know my frequency."

She cut off, and sipped the coffee Gunter put in front of her. The store was dark and deserted; most of Droze was in shelters or basements, sleeping, or trying to.

"Let's see if we can reorient UAV3 down to mid-west, get a line of sight on Navaran Corp, get Mr Wellington on the line," she said.

Gunter nodded, and began making adjustments on his hand unit—they had a system set up: transmission from here on the local building network to the rooftop unit Gunter had set up, which made a directional laser com to the small network of mini UAVs they had flying tonight, little more than the size of insects, matte black and hovering behind buildings, nearly impossible to detect.

An explosion lit up the night outside, then a thud that shook the windows. Then another, further away.

"Patana's not happy," Gunter observed. Sandy snorted, sipped her coffee.

An explosion hit the street right outside, blasting the windows in a shower of glass. Sandy shielded her coffee, not wanting glass or dust in it.

"Seems pretty frightened, for a guy who's not scared of my threats," she remarked. As dust swirled in through the store, coating her hair and jacket. She took another sip as more explosions walked away, giant footsteps falling across further neighbourhoods. "We still connected?"

Gunter nodded. Then frowned, looking at his display. "Message traffic from near the Chancelry neutral zone. Put it on?"

Sandy indicated yes. The unit connected, and now she could hear chatter. A couple of GIs whose names she didn't know, talking on directional com about activity in Chancelry.

"Dahisu," she said, "this is Sandy, what's going on?"

"*Looks like gunfire,*" said Dahisu.

Gunfire? "That information might be useful to me if I knew where it was coming from?" Sandy suggested. Some of these guys hadn't seen real combat in years, if they ever had. Their com etiquette was a little scratchy.

"*Chancelry HQ. You want me to feed it through?*" And before she could reply, "*Whoa, big explosion.*"

"Inside Chancelry HQ?" Sandy had been doing this too long to be bothered wondering what was happening. She had to see; guessing was pointless.

The feed came through, vision carried on laser com . . . and now she could see a blast taking out an upper floor. Another, smaller pop, removing one window.

"That's anti-personnel," she observed. What the hell was going on? The visual feed shifted to another building, rapid strobe flashing, heavy machine gun fire. Now she could see ricochets. And more flashes, moving from window to window through the building.

"*Someone's clearing that building floor,*" Dahisu observed. "*It's not us, unless Sandy's doing something she didn't tell us about?*"

"Not me, no," said Sandy. Trouble in Chancelry? She was still figuring how to get through the defences. Was someone inside saving her the trouble? The only people that could possibly be . . . but no. She shouldn't leap to that conclusion. That was an old dream, and a dangerous one. A dream she wasn't entirely sure if she wanted to come true. "Keep an eye on the network perimeters," she said urgently. "Whoever it is might be trying to bring the barriers down."

Suddenly there was a new broadband transmission. The com booster said it came straight from Chancelry, but the vision, when it came up, was not some Chancelry corporate suit sneering at her. This was shaky cam vision, filled with muzzle flashes and explosions, currently sheltering by a corner as other people exchanged fire nearby. The firefight was moving fast, dark shapes leaping past, then exchanges further away, and shooting in this corridor ceased. GIs, making rapid flanking moves, as only GIs could.

The cam flashed around, to resolve on a woman's face. Brown skin, shaved head, wrapped in a thin bandage. Rishi. Staring at the camera, with hard intent.

"Hey, Sandy!" she said. "You coming or what?"

"Rishi got out!" Kiet was shouting on the network from somewhere up ahead. Sandy sat on the back of the truck tray as it bounced and roared along broken, dusty streets, no lights and hoping no one at the cross streets would be stupid enough to be out this pre-dawn morning. *"Your drug must have worked! Home Guard didn't report her missing, probably too embarrassed!"*

"She must have got back through the barriers," someone else added. *"They'd have recognised her, let her in, she must have convinced them she was friendly . . ."*

"Damn, Sandy!" said Kiet, excitement obvious in his voice. *"What did you tell her?"*

"Enough to make her angry," said Sandy, scanning the sky between the hurtling, dark concrete shapes of buildings. "Looks like she shared it with friends . . . Kiet, I need tacnet up ASAP! I don't want you to wait for me. If that barrier gets compromised you need to hit it immediately, get everyone concentrated on the Chancelry perimeter, forget going around the long way!"

"If we convert the UAVs to broadband they'll get toasted!" Kiet retorted.

"Not if we keep them low amongst the buildings! We'll make enough confusion they won't be targetted! And once we get into Chancelry, we can tap into their network . . . Rishi might even get us hooked in before that!"

The truck braked hard into a roundabout, skidding and throwing Sandy about in the open tray. She held on with one hand, rifle tight in the other. Somewhere behind and above, their little UAV was buzzing on little props to try and keep up, maintaining directional com down to the truck. Someone would see that soon, Sandy was certain.

"*Well, we can't talk to Rishi now without giving away our location . . . Sandy, we're suiting up and positioning, get here as fast as you can.*"

"That's the idea. And get ready to knock down those corporation UAVs! You'll just have to dodge the counter strike before it arrives. We can't have them up there when we go in."

"*Yup,*" said Kiet, sounding busy.

Damn the lousy timing, Sandy thought. Rishi had been a longshot, maybe an intel assist, some useful codes to access Chancelry network once they were in. She hadn't expected a full scale uprising. This was truly "revenge of the synthetics," the old vid thriller title come to life, the scenario she'd gotten entirely sick of seeing all over the Tanushan entertainment networks. It had only happened before in isolated pockets, individuals like herself getting sick and tired and unwilling to take it anymore. But what she saw going on here was entirely different—the formation of a collective identity. GIs were "us" now, everyone else was "them." It was exhilarating. And it was frightening.

But the detour to talk to the other corporate honchos had taken her halfway across town, to the southern neighbourhoods where UAV coms could gain a direct line of sight, away from Chancelry's perimeter. Now she had maybe fifteen kilometers to travel, along awful, potholed roads. There were Home Guard road blocks along here that could turn hostile anytime. And there was corporate artillery raining down on anything suspicious-looking.

"They're going to see us any second now," Gunter said, reading her thoughts. There was little activity on the streets; a lone pickup hurtling along with no lights would be an obvious target. But it was too early to take out the corporate UAVs yet. Chancelry artillery might be too busy to spare rounds, but the other corporations were helping now, the entire central ring of corporate zones primed on highest alert. With Kiet's GIs gathering, shooting down the UAVs now would only give positions away and cause a mad scramble to reposition, right before they were needed elsewhere. Damn, she wanted tacnet. She needed to see where everyone was!

Their own UAV's feed relayed her an orange missile trail rising from

Heldig Quarter, accelerating fast. "Here we go, one up," said Sandy. That one zoomed away on a different heading. Then another. "Two up. That one's heading our way. Right turn, please."

The truck screeched and slid right, fishtailing violently. Sandy steadied and raised her rifle. "Steady," she told the driver.

Teller 9s were high powered and deadly accurate out to a kilometer and more. For most people, including GIs, shooting at incoming missile artillery with rifles was futile. Even for her, it was iffy—there wasn't much she couldn't hit from any range, provided she could see it. But at the speed these things came in, even hitting it was no guarantee. Doubtless it would keep coming, it was just a question of how much damage she did in the second before it arrived.

Combat reflex zoned in as intensely as she'd ever felt it before. Interface established with the Teller. She could feel its balance, microscopically. Found the weight, the trajectory. Locked it in. Focused ahead. The tray bounced, and her body absorbed it like built-in suspension.

Here it was, a flash of contrail, two Ks out. Crossing the road, acquiring a good look down between buildings. Disappeared, then zoomed back, zagging, then hurtling high overhead, then the death dive. Even in time-slowed combat reflex, it was fast. Sandy's rifle tracked, her legs extending to a higher crouch to absorb any sudden bump, and fired. Hand and index finger shuddered, blurring at a rate of fire comparable to the rifle's automatic setting. A whole string of hits, she could see flashes lighting the incoming projectile all over, eight hundred meters down to four hundred down to one hundred . . . it tumbled, broke up and crashed in eight places behind them, dust and debris and no explosion.

"We're clear," she said, changing her mag. "It broke up, supersonic things don't take punishment well."

"I'm glad you can do that," Gunter remarked, as the truck veered left once more, back to their original heading. *"I can't."*

If she hadn't been making her own continual upgrades and enhancements to software and augment hardware in Tanusha, Sandy knew she wouldn't have been able to do it either. Not all of her performance improvement in the past years was from experience. She was a long way better than her original design specs, and those design specs were still largely unmatched.

"Yeah, well," she said, "if they figure out that one was shot down, they'll figure who's on the truck and send ten of them after us next. Let's hope they think it was a dud. Kiet, do me a favour and take out those UAVs now."

It was bad timing, but she had no choice. She was the command asset and the command asset was worth saving. Kiet would fire immediately, and, given the pause of a few seconds to assess the situation . . .

The UAV feed showed a whole string of launches, from all the corporate zones. She counted seventeen in four seconds. Only three of them came from Chancelry.

"Well, that looks like Christmas," she observed.

"*What's Christmas?*" Gunter asked.

"You know what Dewali is?"

"*Sure.*"

"Same thing."

Kiet's shooters would be abandoning their firing positions, sprinting and leaping away for new cover. She hoped they made it. High overhead, UAVs fired countermeasures and dodged . . . and exploded. Kiet's missile tech had no patience with countermeasures.

Then explosions hit just beyond the Chancelry neutral zone ahead, seeking those shooters. Another missile streaked overhead, zoomed back, then dove. Sandy shot it down. This one hit a neighbouring building and blew its upper facade all over the street, crashing down mostly behind them. Another missile came down from their front with little warning; Sandy barely turned and acquired in time to put the other half of her mag into it. It tumbled, broke up and blew up the street in front of them.

The shockwave blew Sandy off the truck, and bits of truck in all directions. She rolled, came to a stop on her back, and checked her rifle. Still worked. She changed mags fast, acquired on the next incoming missile amidst dust and debris from the explosion, and shifted her sights just a little to one side. Hits from nine hundred meters shaved off one side's stabiliser fins, and it spun, turned sideways, and smashed into building rooves fifty meters away with a deafening thud.

Sandy got up amidst the new rain of debris and went to check on the truck. It was a mess, bonnet smashed in where it had nosed into the crater, roof peeled back, windows and doors gone. Gunter and Tim, the driver, were climbing out dazed and bedraggled, but apparently okay. Except that Gunter was pulling a piece of shrapnel the size of his fist out of his midriff, amidst what was left of his clothes. If he were a straight, there would have been guts everywhere.

"You okay?" Sandy asked.

"Can you believe we're designed to take this shit?" Gunter marvelled, tossing the shrapnel aside. If not for combat reflex, Sandy would have laughed. Thank God she'd had that fight with Danya, and he wasn't in the car. Though if she hadn't, she'd have let him out before now.

"That should be the end of them," said Sandy. "With no UAVs they can't see us. Anyone good at stealing cars?"

"You're sure you don't want me to plug in for support?" Vanessa pressed.

"Just . . . guard the damn crawlway," Ari said, waving her distractedly away. He arranged a backpack to lie on, head propped against a cold pipe, implants plugged in and waiting to go.

"I'm not completely useless stabilising a big field matrix," Vanessa persisted.

"If some corporate gets in here with a gun, we'll all be completely useless. Go and shoot stuff—it's what you're good at."

The engineering crawlspace was on the perimeter of red sector, getting toward the heavily occupied parts of the station. Best of all, it was only three hundred meters from the bridge. Any further, though, and the corridors became seriously guarded. Cai was up ahead somewhere. Augmented individuals couldn't see him. Station security cameras and sensors were another matter.

"See you in a bit," he told Vanessa. "Wake me if something interesting happens."

It was Cai's construct before him almost immediately, filling all view. Perspective shift had to zoom in enormously to grasp its detail, and then the scope of it blew him away. No, not Cai's actual construct, just something he'd built in the past few hours. With Cai's codes in his own interface, he could see it: intricately interlocking functions and gateways, astonishingly beautiful in this format's vis-field, like some crystalline life-form flickering and gleaming as it did various things he couldn't guess at. Locked out of this processing level, Station wouldn't see any of this.

"*Like it?*" asked Cai's voice from somewhere.

"Well, I mean, the colour scheme has a certain post neo-mechanist inspiration . . ."

"*You don't know what it does, do you?*" Cai was responding to teasing with teasing. Very high-des.

"No." He accessed a gate with a simple key. It let him in and guided him along coloured streams of light. Everywhere was not merely structure, but function. And when he applied his own functions, it responded, allowing him to see the station functions within the system, integrated, wrapping around, rarely directly interfacing. Streams of information bent, were distorted, without being aware they were being distorted . . .

Ari laughed. It sounded odd, in netspace, an echo without restraint or repetition. A reverberation off nothingness.

"It's VR," he said. "It's VR for advanced networks. You're not just fooling a human brain into thinking it's in a virtual environment, you're fooling the entire station network."

The computational power required was . . . off the scale. By a factor of millions, he reckoned, with reflexive sums in his head. Human brains were comparatively easy to fool. Once the initial stimuli was accepted the brain would process within that established containment, essentially fooling itself without further assistance. But complex computer networks had no such self-perpetuating mechanism. The illusion had to be constantly reestablished every microsecond, and the sheer volume of calculation . . .

"Talee are double-brained," he said then, abruptly as it occurred to him. "I read that. Is it true?"

"*Not at liberty to say,*" said Cai.

Intellect, then, arose from not the one hemisphere or the other, but somewhere in the middle, an abstract between two cross-referencing processors. God knew how that worked, but like an abacus it exponentially increased its rate of calculation by the combination of two separate yet coordinated processors. Perhaps a similar principle was at work here. Only, the exponential processing from separate, coordinator processors continued ad infinitum. Humans ran into laws that stopped it. Maybe the Talee had found a shortcut, something only a double-brained person could conceive. Shortcuts in mathematics, like shortcuts through the consciousness, or space/time. Conceptual wormholes. A lot of people had theorised how double-brained Talee might see things humans missed. And probably there were things humans knew, had invented early in their development, that Talee would find astonishing.

He thought of Cai, walking through corridors, augmented guards unable to see him, their vision hacked in real time. You didn't know what you didn't know, or didn't see. Couldn't see, because your brain wasn't structured to conceive it. Even if it was right in front of you . . .

He stared about him, utterly mesmerised, as his visual function unveiled more and more of the self-replicating system before him, burrowing into ever greater detail. Surely the first humans to set foot on other planets hadn't felt anything more profound than this. Direct human meetings with Talee remained things of rumour and secrecy, but here, he felt he was seeing something even more profound. The inner workings of the Talee mind, through their network technology. Here was a blueprint of how they thought, on the technical, structural level. And by God, as he gazed across a billion pulsating, gleaming nodes and currents of information, he'd never seen anything as beautiful.

"So what can I help you with?" he asked.

"*Nothing,*" said Cai. "*I just wanted you to see it. Log out and walk toward the station bridge. You'll find the way clear.*"

Ari laughed. "You can't just brain hack the entire station."

The construct abruptly disappeared. Now he was in bed. With him was a girl. Beautiful, smooth skinned, warm against his body. Blonde hair fine through his fingers, her lips tasting his, her breath sweet and warm. Blue eyes, gazing, with infinite depth. Sandy.

Then back, at the construct. Just like that, like flicking a switch. His heart was pounding, in a way that had only a little to do with that shock of arousal. That had been a memory. Cai had accessed a memory. A real one, with full sensory depth, not just some memory implant facsimile. And translated it into replication language. He'd grasped technological explanations for everything else Cai had been able to do to this point, but this one completely eluded him.

That was scary.

"*Just walk,*" said Cai. "*I promise you.*"

Vanessa walked, Ari behind, Rhian guarding the rear. The corridor was nearing the bridge; a busy place, with offices and control rooms, security bulkheads with bright, black and yellow stripes, and multiple layers of scanners. Some stationers were standing, staring blankly into space. Others sat with their backs to walls. A few were lying down, perhaps sleeping, though some had their eyes open.

Vanessa was stunned. She moved at a fast crouch, pistol ready in both hands, expecting someone to awake at any moment, or a station alarm to go off. She didn't understand how the station sensors weren't registering them in the corridors. She certainly had no idea how it was possible to brain hack so many senior station security personnel at one time. She knew what Sandy had done in the President's Office Incident, but even that was not so significant as this. She'd had a lot of help, and time to set up. Cai was doing this largely alone, given just a hundred and five minutes preparation once they'd snuck into red sector near the bridge.

"What are they doing?" she asked Ari, edging past several more standing, vacant-eyed stationers.

"Their usual," said Ari. "They're working, talking, taking a lunch break. Using the toilet." Ari was not at all perturbed. He strolled the corridor, pistol in hand but expecting no trouble. Vanessa guessed he was uplinked, watching both Cai's world and this one simultaneously. He waved a languid hand past stationers' eyes in passing, or felt at empty space in the corridor where he seemed to see things in the air. If a techno geek could experience the rapture, it would feel something like this, Vanessa thought. For Ari, this was a religious experience, and he seemed to be floating.

"So they're still functioning?" Vanessa pressed, peering cautiously down side corridors before continuing on. "They're not knocked out?"

"Just another VR program," said Ari. "Their brains are still running real time, they're just not experiencing the real world. They think they are, but they're not."

"So they'll be rearranging things on station, doing their work . . . and they'll wake up and find otherwise."

"Yep," said Ari. "This is a one-time deal. Cai can't use it again. But it gets us into the bridge, and control of the station."

"For how long?"

"Until someone outside Cai's zone of control intrudes and raises the alarm."

"How big's the zone of control?"

"Most of this sector, I think," said Ari, as they approached a security post. The heavy door hummed open to admit them.

"Any idea how he's doing it?" Vanessa pressed.

"None," Ari said happily. "I mean, I can make you a list of all the reasons it's not possible. It's a damn long list."

"He's an alien," Rhian explained from the rear.

"Not at all," said Ari. "No more than you are."

"Semantics," said Rhian. "Speaking functionally, he's an alien. He understands concepts and technology a thousand years beyond what we've got. Things that our brains might not even be structurally equipped to understand."

"And yet Sandy's already started messing with her own invasive VR," Ari replied. "More like fifty years than a thousand, I think. If Cai's an alien, then Sandy is, too."

"Would explain a few things," Rhian admitted. Vanessa thought she was kidding.

Doors to the bridge opened as easily as the others—massive, blast resistant interlocking plates that hummed on triple-redundant hydraulics. Bridge design was different from what Vanessa had seen before, arranged semi-circular about large display screens on the front wall—an extravagant use of space on any station. In each of the bridge posts sat a man or woman, staring blankly into space.

"Wow," said Ari, strolling inside. "Just wow."

Not wow, Vanessa thought. This was frightening. Uplinks weren't supposed to make people this vulnerable. VR was a completely separate application. You couldn't just impose it onto people who hadn't signed up. And even here, with League-tech equipped personnel, brains weren't supposed to be so integrated with the tech that anyone could just reverse-infiltrate and take over.

Cai used technology far beyond what humans had today, yet the point remained—this was the future of technological possibility. She was a security operative, and the security implications of this were horrifying. As evidenced by what she was doing here now.

"Ari, get me traffic control central please," said Vanessa, striding to the stationmaster's chair. "Monitor their attempts to break in, people outside the control zone will be wondering why bridge isn't responding. Can you keep these people quiet or do we need to toss them outside?"

"We can leave them here," said Cai, leaning past the motionless com operator at her console, plugs inserted from his portable unit into main com systems. "People are quite hard to move in these numbers."

"Depends how gently you do it," said Rhian, moving to station systems, no doubt to check security system.

"Then close the doors and seal us in," said Vanessa. The stationmaster's chair swivelled behind a bank of screens, systems to be monitored within a virtual control bubble. "Can I get in?"

"Sure," said Cai. "Just access."

Vanessa did so, established a basic connection, and . . . security perimeter, station network, shielded functions, bridge controls, all rushed past at crazy speed. Cai had accelerated it, given them rapid access. The speed and ease of control was insane.

"Okay," she said, now locked into flight control, multiple sensory systems giving her a complete 3-D picture in her head: the station, three smaller support stations, the planet, facilities on two small moons, trans-orbital shuttles en route, atmospheric shuttles on or departing station approach . . . whoa, a whole mass of trajectory information that zoomed and swivelled as she mentally manipulated the picture, giving her such vertigo she nearly lost her balance. And here, immediately leaving the station, was . . . "Cai, what's this ship?"

"That's our ghostie. No idea what it's called, the name doesn't appear on station charts. But it's leaving. Left dock nine minutes ago, just after I arrested control here."

"Any idea why it's leaving?"

"Chancelry HQ in Droze has issued a condition black. Requesting immediate support, downfall imminent."

"Get me full coms," she demanded. "Route them here." Visual displays appeared before internal vision: internal functions, external functions . . . she sorted, found Droze uplinks, zoomed on those. But station was a long way away. Broadband transmissions wouldn't reach Droze, only what the companies thought to put onto the dish.

There was a dull news bulletin, daily routine service announcements . . . a teleconference meeting on promotions and salaries . . . daily trading information and commodity prices.

"I'm not getting anything in relation to the condition black," she told

Cai. She could see the general announcement, a warning panel with black colour coding, and a short statement that said, in total, "Condition Black." Nothing more. "What are we missing?"

"Outer com satellites," said Ari. "Intel said Home Guard often transmit up to the geo-stationary to get word out. Companies jam them but they might be a bit busy right now."

"I tried that," said Cai, "there's nothing, complete blackout."

"Someone's scared of someone finding out what's going on," Rhian observed.

"But if Chancelry's scared they're in trouble, they'll be asking other settlements for help," Vanessa insisted. "Where are those messages?"

"Narrowband," said Cai. "They go direct through satellites, they don't pass through here."

"We can reprogram the damn satellites from here, though," said Ari, determinedly. "Cai, get me access?" Whatever he did took barely ten seconds. Then, "I got it, it's talking."

A woman in a nice jacket appeared on screen, hair askew, looking scared. *"Look, I don't care what your reserves policy says, send us everything you've got now!"*

"Not without a full sitrep," came the reply, *"you know the policy on reserves, we have to keep something here so . . ."*

"We don't know!" the woman shouted. *"Nothing got past our barriers but suddenly we've got shooting in the perimeter! Look, they started taking out key installations five minutes ago! We can't engage with full firepower because we'll take out our own buildings . . ."*

"So what use are the reinforcements going to be if you can't use what firepower you've already got?"

"Send us everything!" the woman shouted, quite terrified. In the background, distant but not too distant, Vanessa heard an explosion. Then gunfire. *"Kresnov is out there, she's been threatening us the past couple of days! She's going to come in here and kill us all!"*

"You better believe it, darling," said Rhian.

Vanessa froze the transmission . . . it was several minutes delayed, at least, recorded on some com unit's processor. "Did our Ghostie hear this?"

"I'm betting yes," said Ari. "Or something like it."

"Fuck. What's their acceleration profile?"

"Indirect to Droze," said Cai, and a trajectory path lit up, circling up over the northern pole, then around to intercept Droze as it rotated past on the far, daylight side. "They're carrying the station's orbital V. Changing orbit like that is a hard burn, but that thing can accelerate at ten Gs if it has to."

"Why the long way around?"

"It's dodging defensive emplacements," said Ari. "Look, they've anti-ship missiles here, here and here . . ." spots lit up across the planet's surface, ". . . but they can't get a weapons fix where they are. The satellites are out of position, and that ghostie can outrun nearly anything that's not a direct intercept . . ."

"Can ground defences make an intercept on that trajectory?" Vanessa demanded, staring at her display.

"Not without better targeting than they're going to get with their satellite placement at the moment," said Cai. "ETA twenty minutes, they'll have a firing position on Droze." Surely they wouldn't actually nuke an entire city? That was over a million people down there. But there were secrets in Droze Chancelry HQ, Cai insisted. Secrets worth a million lives. She didn't have the luxury of hoping.

"Cai," she said, "if anyone can calculate an intercept, you can. Can you talk to those emplacements and feed them the data?"

"Yes," said Cai, "but likely we can't get a hit. He can make evasive with those engines of his and anti-ship works better further out in the gravity well. This is far too close."

"But we'll make him dodge and he'll miss his strike run."

"He'll reacquire. We can force him to do another orbit, but on that second orbit he'll be so low the missiles won't acquire, and he's not vulnerable to atmospheric missiles because his own defensive systems can neutralise anything slow . . . that will push the ETA out to eighty-four minutes, give or take."

"That'll have to do."

Vanessa accessed station's main com, redirected the antennae, and fed it some very secret coordinates. Station registered confusion at being told to transmit into empty space. She overrode it, and opened the channel.

"Hello Big Hat, this is Jailbait. I have a target for you. You must acquire and destroy in less than eighty-four, or Droze and everyone in it dies. Bear in mind I'm reading slightly better than an hour for this message to reach you, you'll have to break every shipping lane rule in the book to get here."

CHAPTER TWENTY-FIVE

The firefight in front of Chancelry's perimeter wall was as crazy as anything Sandy had seen, and she'd seen a lot. The neutral zone between inhabited Droze neighbourhoods and the Chancelry wall itself was four blocks wide, and now as she took cover at the first corner behind a pile of new rubble, most of it seemed engaged. Contrails streaked up and down the roads ahead, amidst rapid cannon rounds, small and large explosions and occasional crazy ricochetes. Every now and then a big explosion hit, probably missile artillery, though Sandy knew Chancelry had been positioning a lot more heavy weaponry in the last few days.

She'd taken the time to suit up. Kiet's forces had brought additional armour and prepositioned some of it in a big van, parked underground nearby. The suit was League mil-spec, a little less advanced than her SWAT armour but good enough. It received and generated tacnet, as did every other suit, boosted further by their mini UAVs. They were in such close contact now that Chancelry couldn't jam it without jamming their own tacnet. Sandy knew they had to get much closer.

"Sandy has command," said Kiet, acknowledging her arrival at the fight. *"What's your plan?"*

"Get in fast!" said Sandy. "Before the other corporations can bring reinforcements around, and before Rishi gets her ass kicked. Once we get in amongst their population, we're safe. They can't use big weapons among their own civvies."

Kiet had a hundred and thirty-six operational GIs concentrated here. They followed standard GI ground ops in pairs, fours and twelves—sections, squads and platoons respectively. Four platoons made a company, so she had less than three companies, with no heavy support. Chancelry defensive forces were making interlocking fields of fire all across the roads ahead, making it impossible to advance quickly without significant casualties. With a force this small, she couldn't afford casualties.

She sprinted, straight into the opposite building, a dive through a window then fast down a corridor. Tacnet showed her where her friendlies were, mostly pinned down two or three blocks in, trying to manoeuver against heavy positions—Chancelry had tanks and AMAPS blocking the streets, and a shitload of bots in the buildings to block any flanking moves. It was turning into a slugging match, but GIs were best at fast manoeuvering.

Even as she ran, she saw a big building take a hit from heavy artillery, and several IDs on tacnet went blank, followed by lots of shouting after squadmates lost under collapsing rubble.

"If they get us pinned down they'll just pulverise us with heavy support!" Kiet was yelling, gunfire in the background. *"We've gotta move!"*

Sandy dashed into a new building, Gunter and Tim close behind, down a deserted corridor. Missiles were flying on tacnet, GIs launching mini-rockets at Chancelry defensive positions, tacnet coordinating those strikes but failing to make much impact.

"Someone get me a visual on those missile strikes," said Sandy, skidding to a halt at the corridor's exit onto a main street. Burning vehicles made cover in the street. Gunter covered and she ran. "Do they have defensive screens established?"

"Yes!" someone shouted. A visual appeared, a shaky view out a window, missiles streaking by towards what appeared to be a hovertank behind rubble up the road. Countermeasures shot the missiles down before they reached, a stream of rapid autofire. "I think it's the AMAPS; they're anti-missile equipped!" The visual ducked back as return fire blew out half the wall.

Fucking arms factory world, Sandy thought, shooting a bot that tried to hit her from a high rooftop, then skipping sideways through a new hole in a wall. Chancelry would throw everything at them. Something shot at her through a window as she dashed through ruined corridors, shrapnel ripping off the walls.

"Gotta separate those AMAPS from the tanks!" she said. "There's no clever back way around; we've just gotta work our way through the buildings and take out those AMAPS—they can't defend the tanks without them. Don't waste missiles unless you've got a clear shot!"

The next cross street was chaos, the third block beginning and nothing safe anywhere. Wreckage burned in the street, bot tanks, AQ walkers, walls riddled with holes and collapsing in parts. A GI in a wall hole opposite waved up and down the street, warning her of multiple hostiles. Sandy threw a piece of concrete out, drew fire from both directions, an eruption of dust and flying fragments.

She indicated for Gunter to put fire to the left, as tacnet triangulated fire from the right . . . she made her own adjustments by eyesight, matched that trajectory against tacnet's map of the skyline, and found the apartment window the bot must be located in. Locked a mini-missile from her back launcher and fired. Big explosion a few hundred meters down, ammunition cooking off. More fire ripped by, but lighter . . . Sandy kicked off the wall and flung herself explosively across the road, caught sight of more bots in doorways. Rolled, covered as fire sent concrete fragments pinging off her armour, then put an arm out long enough to bring two of them down with precision shots.

And left the road quickly, as the inevitable missile fire streaked in and blew a big hole two meters from where she'd been—GIs weren't the only ones with tacnet coordinated missile fire. Gunter got across also, then Tim, and they pressed through increasingly ruined walls, past one wounded GI who gave them thumbs-up slumped against a wall, her buddy checking a small ammunition reserve, grabbing more grenades.

Up ahead, the volume of fire was staggering, the building constantly shaking and convulsing, dust raining down. Sandy skipped past one dead GI, several ruined bots, then a hands and knees scramble over rubble and a crouch behind what remained of the only wall left between here and the road heading into Chancelry. Down this street everything was flying—chain guns, auto-cannon, rapid grenades and rifle fire. This was why they had to go through the buildings for cover. The end of this street was so blocked up with weapons systems, anyone sticking a head up here would be dead before blinking.

She scrambled back the way she'd come. Even loitering in the open was deadly—seeker artillery would do wide circles above a target area on low power for several minutes, doing their own recon before finding a target to destroy, so even Chancelry's lack of UAVs didn't make her safe.

Here she found a hole in the ceiling, and sprang through it to the next floor, dashed along and found a stairwell to ascend another. This built-up environment was perfect GI terrain. These buildings had at least ten levels each, and Chancelry bots had to guard each one. Sandy didn't think it possible. Tacnet showed her GIs on the seventh level of this building, more on the fourth, so she pressed down this corridor . . . and was immediately confronted with an AQ bot at the corridor's end. She blew its arm off before the chain gun could fire, but the torso had missile mounts, and she flung herself through a side doorway before the missile reached her and blew all the walls to pieces.

Amidst dust and confusion, she crashed through an adjoining wall and dashed up the next corridor, shot a mini bot, a third made a smoke screen before she used it for a football, then ducked sprawling as another minigun just fired through the walls with no warning, pulverising everything around her.

She fired a grenade at it, ran again and took cover behind a heavier, reinforced wall. The ceiling blew in ahead of her, where she would have been if she'd kept running . . . something upstairs had been tracking those footsteps. There was now dust everywhere, and it was getting hard to breathe. Certainly she could see why there'd been such slow progress—Chancelry had deployed the full robot army into the buffer zone before their wall. And they hadn't even reached the wall yet. God knew how they'd get past it.

Explosions behind alerted her to Gunter and Tim's approach as they caught her up. This time she was grateful for the support—this wasn't the same kind of mad dash she'd made through the underground caverns on Pyeongwha. These quarters were too tight and too well defended; here some teamwork would be welcome. Tacnet made a little three-person loop between them. Sandy fired a grenade into the wall of a cross corridor ahead, and they moved.

This time the bots didn't stand a chance, as one GI drew a bot's attention, while the other outflanked and killed it. They advanced in leapfrog through the building. A booby trap blew the floor out from under Gunter, but he bounced back up to this level immediately and kept fighting. Above them, on tacnet, Sandy saw one of her GIs put shots into an AMAPS guarding a hover-tank on the corner, only to receive fire from three places at once and abruptly vanish from the grid.

"Demo charges," she said to Gunter as they covered behind the last heavy bulkhead before the end of the building. They weren't more than ten meters from the tank-guarded intersection here, and one city block from the Chancelry wall. She showed him on tacnet where she wanted them placed— she didn't have more than a basic knowledge of demolition, but this under-built building didn't require any genius.

She slapped her own to the wall, then another further on, set it for tacnet activation . . . and ducked flat as something outside opened fire on this part of the wall, heavy shells tearing through multiple walls like tissue paper. She ran without waiting for it to stop, nearly lost her head to one near miss, and saw Gunter simply wasn't there anymore, just bits and pieces blasted across the corridor.

She grabbed Tim on the way through, hauling him back from the blast zone, took cover and activated. The blast rocked them, then an external feed from tacnet showed another GI's perspective, half this building wall collapsing on the tank and AMAPS position on the corner. They vanished in a crash of debris and dust . . . the tank would be fine, but the AMAPS wouldn't. Missile fire followed immediately, and the tank, without anti-missile protection, took multiple hits and detonated with a blast that made the demolitions seem small. Yells and victorious swearing over tacnet. Sandy had never heard GIs do that before in combat, either.

"That's for you, Gunter," said Sandy. And to Tim, "Come on, let's get some."

The crossroads were less well defended than the roads that lead straight to Chancelry. GIs now leaped across this part of the last crossroad, from building to building, and only received a little crossfire. That changed as Chancelry defences realised their line had been breached, and began pulling units off the line elsewhere. A tank appeared from Chancelry's wall, AMAPS support sprinting alongside. Sandy sat in the rubble of her demolished building corner and picked off multiple AMAPS from several hundred meters, joined by fire from other buildings. The tank fired at someone else, who leaped as rapid cannon fire tore the building facade in half, but others further up the street were already firing missiles that accelerated to Mach two in just two seconds, tipped with mod-uranium heads that melted any armour yet devised on high velocity contact. This tank, too, exploded.

Chancelry pulled several tanks off their intersection positions further up the cross street, but again, GIs had time to fire here with less risk along the cross street, picked off the AMAPS with rifles, then blew the tanks with missiles. Another tank made a slow advance with AMAPS walking, shooting down incoming missiles while the tank's rapid turrets backed by bots on high rooves further along, made sniping uncomfortable. GIs aimed missiles for the walls, trying to bring them down, but the missiles were anti-armour and couldn't bring down the structural supports required to collapse an entire facade. But by this time GIs had made enough progress within adjoining buildings to blow a wall onto the advancing tank from within, and missiles did the rest.

With tanks lost and defensive positions crumbling, missile artillery began to rain down. GIs retreated into building interiors and pushed forward. The artillery lacked penetration, blowing off top floors where it hit buildings, or landing on roads to keep them clear. It killed mostly bots, something that no doubt registered on Chancelry tacnet, and artillery paused once more. Combat flyers tried to engage, but missile tech had made that tactic obsolete two centuries ago, and soon any that strayed from above the Chancelry wall's built in anti-missile defences were almost instantly shot down. Worse yet for them, GIs were now close enough to target flyers with rifles, and even without Sandy's degree of accuracy, that was often lethal.

Soon Sandy found herself with a third-story view directly over the Chancelry wall itself. There had been apartment buildings here once, but only the faint outline of foundations remained visible, having been razed years ago. In their place was a wall, three stories high, reinforced concrete within a steel frame, topped with electrified wire and heavy guardposts. It might have been impressive to a Droze non-corporate resident, or a scavenging street kid, but to three companies of advancing high-des combat GIs, not so much. But the wall itself was not the problem. It was the seventy meters of open, featureless ground before the wall that made things difficult.

"*Big kill zone,*" someone suggested, viewing what she was seeing on tacnet. There was just no getting across that with the guard towers operational, to say nothing of artillery raining down from above. They'd be lucky to make it ten meters, let alone seventy. The guard towers were largely immune to missiles—their own anti-missile systems were high-tech and functional, and the GIs didn't have enough projectile weaponry to knock them off at this range.

Behind the wall were tall buildings. Those nearest the wall were squat and ugly, with few windows—a defensive precaution no doubt. But shortly behind them rose buildings of glass and bright lights, and beyond them, genuine towers. Like one of Tanusha's many urban districts, but heavily defended, an island of propriety in a sea of poverty. So close.

"*What's the plan?*" someone asked. They hadn't come this far just to turn back.

"Corey," said Sandy, "is that tank at grid 35-42 still working?"

"Yeah, I think so."

"Let's see if we can get it running, take out a few of those guard posts . . ."

She stopped, seeing something strange. A new round of missile artillery, five missiles climbing up together. Something in their spacing looked odd. Five simultaneous targets? Someone called warning on tacnet; several GIs retreating from viewpoints, assuming they'd been spotted . . . but Sandy stayed where she was. Obviously the missiles weren't tracking for her location near the wall. In fact, they were following no pre-programmed trajectory that seemed logical . . .

They dropped, all five together. Straight onto the Chancelry wall, with no fore warning. The wall disappeared in a series of rapid flashes, concrete debris and steel frames cartwheeling away.

"Rishi!" Sandy shouted in delight.

"*She must have hacked and acquired fire control for one artillery unit,*" someone observed.

"*Let's go!*" said Kiet. "*Before the smoke clears! Full sprint, then straight for HQ!*"

Vanessa could hear laser cutters over surveillance microphones, as Antibe Station crews tried to get through lowered defensive doors and retake their bridge. It was going to take them longer than they had available.

Most of her attention remained on the ghostie's orbit. Multiple ground missiles had been fired at it so far, none acquired. It had counter measures, and had once even dipped into an aerobraking manoeuver that generated a heat signature so intense an incoming missile had become utterly confused, hit the atmosphere too shallow and detonated short. Anti-ship missiles were a deep space or mid-orbit defence. Big ships weren't supposed to skim the atmosphere, and most captains avoided planets like ocean ships avoided reefs. But having missed once, this League captain was determined not to miss a second time.

Now they had eight minutes. He couldn't fire until he was right over Droze. Orbital artillery was supposed to be fired far further out, giving it time to equalise with planetary orbit so it wouldn't burn up in reentry. If it did enter the atmosphere too soon and decelerated to manageable velocities, it would run out of fuel in slower atmospheric flight before it reached the target.

"Come on," Vanessa muttered, seated in the station master's chair, hooked into multiple displays and nav systems. The stationmaster lay in a pile with others further down the row, still unconscious, as were they all. Cai admitted it might be doing them damage by now, but she had other things to worry about.

"Should be coming in any moment now," said Ari, also plugged into navcomp and calculating possible intercept trajectories—not strictly Ari's speciality, but Vanessa had never seen him fail at these mathematical simulations yet. "That's actually a pretty rare thing, to see the lightwave of arrival get here before the departure."

"That's great, Ari," said Vanessa, staring at her display.

Suddenly it appeared, jump entry, a massive wave of energy dangerously close to the planet. Alarms wailed, automated bridge systems putting the station into emergency modes. Ships weren't supposed to come in this fast, this close to planet. Normally an arrival would jump into the outer system and coast in over several days.

"He's carrying . . ." Ari did some fast calculations, ". . . point zero six L, God damn that's fast." Trajectory lines calculated, adjusting for the curve of planetary gravity . . . missing the planet's atmosphere, but not by much.

"Can he make it?" Vanessa asked, heart hammering as she tried to read the frantic scroll of data across the feed. "Is he short?"

The data wave hit them now, just behind the initial light wave . . . *"This is Captain Reichardt of Federation warship* Mekong. *This is an emergency manoeuver! All vessels stay clear, this is an emergency manoeuver, all vessels stay clear . . . !"* And repeated, over and over.

From navcomp's seat, Ari's eyes were wide, calculating furiously. "I think he's short! Fuck it, I think he's short!"

"What about weapons V?" Rhian pressed.

"No he's six percent of light speed, weapons V won't make a damn bit of difference . . ."

"Oh, God," said Vanessa, hands to her face. "Oh, God, what can we do?" Ari's intercept line was showing *Mekong* definitely short, one minute and thirteen seconds so. As soon as the ghostie had launched, it would manoeuver and jump, and possibly kill itself doing it so close to the planet, but that was no comfort for anyone on Droze. The mathematics of trajectories in space were pure and simple: Reichardt had carried as much velocity from the energy of jump as physically possible, but still it was not enough. Jump speeds were a function of jump engines; burning the regular mains at full power would make no observable difference now. "Get me that damn channel to the ship again!"

"He won't answer," Rhian said quietly.

"I don't care, we have to try!"

"New arrival!" Ari shouted, as something else flashed on the nav screen. A big surge of energy, a unique signature. "He's close, real fucking close!"

Navcomp didn't recognise the signature, nor the data wave that followed. Because there was no data wave.

"He's heading straight for the ghostie, shallow approach, projected V . . . seventeen percent!"

"Fuck me," Rhian breathed. Rhian had spent a lot of time on ships. "We can't do that. That's Talee."

Vanessa turned to stare at Cai. Cai sat at the auxillary post, staring intently, unspeaking. Navcomp was giving them strange readings, trying to make sense of an alien ship jumping into close planetary proximity at a fraction of light speed that should have turned them all to mush.

"What the hell?" Ari muttered. "I think . . . I think he's fired? I can't tell, but it looks like the signal's fracturing, he's on intercept and . . ."

"*Antibe Station, Antibe Station, this is* Mekong*!*" came Reichardt's voice on coms. "*What the fuck is that?*"

"*Mekong*, this is Antibe Station!" Vanessa called back. "New contact not hostile, not hostile!"

She had no idea if it was true, but it was the only chance they had.

"Intercept in ten!" Ari called. "Five! Mark!" The alien trajectory skimmed the atmosphere, tangentially. Dear God, if he actually hit the atmosphere at that speed . . .

"What happened?" Vanessa asked. "Where's the target?"

"Navcomp's not sure," said Ari, sifting furiously through incoming data from multiple satellites. "Hang on just a minute, he might have manoeuvered."

There was a long, deathly silent pause.

Then, "*Antibe Station this is* Mekong. *We read that ship as dead, there's a big reentry cloud just short of projected line. No other reading available—he's gone.*"

There followed a huge surge of energy, a ship jumping. No one had to ask whose. For a moment, they all just sat and stared at the screens, dumbly.

Vanessa's com crackled. "*Uh . . . Antibe Station, this is* Mekong." Captain

Reichardt's voice, an understated Texan drawl, warped by massive velocity shift in the light wave. *"Was that thing what I think it was?"*

A Talee ship had just killed a human ship. Even in the relief that she felt, and her utter disdain for the lives just lost, Vanessa could feel the enormity of what they'd just witnessed. And furthermore . . . what the hell was so important down in Droze that the Talee would violate all established norms of their interaction with humanity to protect it?

She took a deep breath. "Antibe Station to *Mekong*. Good shot, Captain. Congratulations on a first class piece of manoeuvering."

A pause from Reichardt. *"Yeah, copy that, Antibe Station."* Reichardt was not a politically stupid man. He'd understand why this should not be talked about. *"Now pardon us while we slow down before we hit something tiny and die."*

"Well, shit," Ari remarked. "Talk about first contact."

Inside Chancelry Quarter, it was a rout. Sandy kept to the inside of buildings, then running on rooftops, then crashing through windows to run through hallways and open plan offices. It was early morning now, all streets deserted of civilians in the pale yellow glow. There were security vehicles and domestic police, and some AMAPS and tanks, but without the coordination and overlapping capabilities of the outer defences. Tacnet identified targets and eliminated them, mini-missiles whizzing along streets and turning corners, setting streets aflame as tank ammunition detonated, shattering every window within a hundred meters.

Police and domestic security had position on rooftops, but wasn't prepared for GIs running through the center of buildings, then leaping across roads to neighbouring buildings, without needing the roof or the ground floor. From within buildings, GIs paused to shoot anyone on a rooftop with a head raised high enough, and vehicle reinforcements rushing along streets ahead were missile-struck with terrible results, bodies strewn across the road. Sandy had barely progressed three blocks into Chancelry Quarter and already she could see the defensive coordination breaking down.

She paused at the edge of another office building, shot down a UAV trying to move along the street beyond, fast scanned the skyline for defences and saw three soldiers two hundred meters away and a bit below, trying to set up a defensive position on a rooftop. Three quick shots dropped all of them, and with a mental signal to her armour, she amped leg myomer to maximum and leaped across the thirty-meter space to the opposing glass office wall, and smashed through. Tim followed, moving fast down the next hallway, bashing through doors that got in the way, not taking any fire from adjoining buildings. Tacnet showed their strength at ninety. They'd lost about forty on the way through, though some wounded remained behind with a few others to care for them. Chancelry Quarter had maybe fifty thousand inhabitants, but by appearances, they'd become very reliant on bots and heavy weapons around the external perimeter. Bots were strictly not allowed inside the safe zone; no one trusted dumb AI with that much firepower around civvies. Opposition here was all human, and simply not trained for the task, whatever their weapons.

At the far side of this building she paused again. There were civvies running on the streets below, some with weapons, others just panicked. The street was all shops, cafes and foyers to apartment buildings, like any middle class urban neighbourhood. Directly ahead, just a block away, was Chancelry main HQ, a series of fifteen twenty-story glass buildings, like modern office complexes anywhere.

A scan of the skyline showed several more rooftop positions, some new UAVs, some vehicles on roads below, the beginnings of roadblocks. They didn't realise they couldn't defend in the open against GIs. Sandy took a knee, Tim taking position beside her, and opened fire until everything hittable within weapons range was either dead, destroyed or behind cover. A human sniper could take ten seconds or longer to acquire a new target at over a kilometer—she took barely one, Tim about three. Other GIs were moving through neighbouring buildings, also firing, forcing everyone Sandy had no line of sight on to take cover also. Grenades hit nearby armoured vehicles on the roads; missiles destroyed more distant ones. Return fire was sporadic, perhaps reluctant to use heavy weapons in civvie zones, and shell shocked, because everything exposed was getting killed before they could use it.

Sandy thought she might need some cover approaching the HQ, so she leaped onto the opposing apartment rooftop, a twenty-meter drop, then jumped the remaining twenty meters to the road itself. A few civilians were cowering behind benches, public transport stops, behind plant holders. Sandy ignored them and took off running up the road. She paused at an intersection, but it was already occupied by several GIs who waved her through, and she raced on.

At the next corner, she peered around and found an odd-angled intersection, public transport rail across the road, and a hulking great hovertank guarding the main doors to the HQ building. She stepped back, tacnet fixing the tank's location now that she had a fix, and locked on her last missile. Fired, the missile shooting out and turning abruptly left around the corner. The tank blew up. God knew what use they thought it could be against modern missile tech.

The blast knocked over a nearby AMAPS, another shredded the corner cafe beside her with chain guns. Sandy waited until it paused, then fired a grenade through shattered windows that struck the AMAPS's nose and blew it through a wall. More longer range fire engaged targets further along the HQ perimeter, and Sandy dashed toward the HQ entrance, accelerating into long, flying bounds like a triple jumper. She crossed fifty meters in five progressively lengthening strides, and crashed through the front doors at eighty kph, sliding across the lobby amidst a tangle of metal door frames, prepared to shoot any defenders. But there were none.

Others followed her in at similar speed and she was off, sprinting along wide, polished hallways. The building looked deserted. Sprinting down shiny, empty hallways in dusty, explosive-scorched armour was surreal. Tacnet abruptly illuminated a central courtyard between HQ buildings as one GI acquired a visual on it—there were armoured vehicles there, and soldiers, frantically redeploying weapons that had been trained on the other several buildings ahead. Sandy didn't need to say anything—she just illuminated those buildings as "friendly," and the forces around them as "enemy," and watched the shooting start.

She crashed out through a window and found cover along the side of the big garden courtyard where a sunken path went around the landscaping, as soldiers ahead scattered, fire pouring in from newly arrived GIs. Vehicles and weapons exploded; several soldiers were running for cover ahead of Sandy, who shot them as she came. Now she had a crossfire going, ran out of ammunition and pulled her pistol rather than waste time reloading, shooting left-handed as soldiers who weren't dead fell flat and pretended they were.

The building ahead was a mess, windows smashed from incoming fire, smoke billowing from many floors, countered by a spray of automated fire retardant. Sandy reloaded, dashed in a window, shot someone point blank who tried to shoot her from a corridor, then slid out into that corridor with rifle and pistol blazing in both directions simultaneously, felling the assault team waiting there and putting a grenade into a wall for good measure, spraying others with shrapnel. More shooting, as some of them had armour to survive the initial shots, and then others were falling to her teammates crashing in from the court-yard behind, a flurry of point blank shooting and then just bodies, sprawled on the ground as GIs rushed over them like a wave and kept going.

"GIs!" Sandy yelled ahead, moving at a fast, ready crouch. This corridor too was already shot to hell, bodies on the floor that had been there a while now, blast marks from grenades. "GIs, we're friendly!"

"GIs!" came a reply around the corner, and a hand waved. Sandy rounded the corner, and found three, crouched in little more than tracksuits, two of them bloody, armed with rifles. Clearly GIs, and somewhat amazed to see them.

"You came!" said one of them, with a lower-des appreciation of obvious things.

"How many of you?" Sandy asked as others rushed past, heading around the perimeter to clear the other Chancelry soldiers attempting to retake their HQ from the rebels.

"Isn't it easier if we just integrate tacnets?" one replied.

Sandy blinked. "Of course! Where's your link?"

She found it quickly on the local network, and it let her in without query . . . codes matched and suddenly her tacnet and theirs began to merge. Abruptly the space in her head expanded, and she could see dozens of new markers. Friendlies, rebels who had fought for their freedom, and now occupied this central cluster of main HQ buildings, holding them off against concerted Chancelry efforts to take them back.

"They transferred command functions," said one of the GIs, apologetically. "We tried to shut it down so you wouldn't have to fight through that perimeter, but you can't shut it down by just destroying one post. It transferred to somewhere remote and we can't find it."

"Never mind," said Sandy. "All their main corporate functions are still routed from here, and we've got them now. They can't shift their mainframes. Chancelry belongs to us now."

CHAPTER TWENTY-SIX

Head offices for mega corporations were usually found on the highest floor, but Chancelry's central office was deep underground, beneath the basement complex. To get to it, Sandy descended stairs as the lift was not working, past multiple security barriers that GIs had blasted open with high explosive, and finally down a ferrocrete reinforced corridor that provided the chamber's only entrance or exit.

Within, it was like the Intel briefing room at the Grand Council building, completely shielded. There was no accessing the mainframe here from outside—not by wire, nor by wireless. Lethal defences at each guard-post should have killed the attackers, but Rishi had hacked enough internal systems to alert them. Slow progress had finally forced a way inside.

When Sandy arrived, Rishi and several others were seated by the long table, working at the exposed mainframe behind a removed wall panel. Rishi was sweaty and dusty, as were they all, barely fitting in the leather seat in her armour. Sandy wanted to hug her, or pat her shoulder, or exchange something meaningful, but Rishi only acknowledged her with a nod. She seemed entranced at something, her eyes vacant.

Sandy noticed the booster on the table and uplinked to the local network . . . in a flash she was in, and it was a monster. Cyberspace on a grand scale, harbouring perhaps the biggest set of barriers she'd ever seen in her life. This construct was completely isolated, an autistic entity. It talked to nothing and no one, and could only be accessed by the highest clearance. Even then, Sandy didn't doubt that for all the microsecond computing power in the galaxy these days, it would take many minutes to process entry.

Within the network, she could hear the GIs talking to each other, quite calmly, trying to find a way in. Several of them seemed quite expert. No doubt these were their best, brought downstairs for the purpose.

"Why didn't they fry the mainframe?" Sandy wondered.

"Maybe they can't," said a GI, distractedly. "Who would they trust to carry whatever's behind these barriers on a portable?"

And if there had been a contingency plan, Sandy thought, against most threats they would have had hours. Mostly they were scared of other corporations, and spies. Chancelry was heavily armed enough to resist those threats, and corporations had no interest in attacking each other so vigorously as to capture each other's HQs. No, the level of inter-corporate warfare on Pantala had never reached anything like that intensity; they all ultimately relied upon each other to maintain the infrastructure that allowed them to survive on this barren world.

And if the League or Federation had attacked, they'd have had lots of warning. Days of ships arriving in orbit, then big attack formations that took many hours to assemble. They'd never expected their own GIs to attack them. They weren't set up for it. It hadn't been thinkable. Because . . .

"Rishi," Sandy said. Rishi looked at her. "Why didn't they use the killswitches?"

"There's a channel," said Rishi. "We were never supposed to turn it off. We weren't able to, most of the time. They said we'd be in trouble if we tried. But Eduardo found out a way to turn it off, him and Anya, but make it look like it was still on. A few of us knew how to do it. I showed the others when I showed them what you showed me, the medical research building. We agreed that must be how they'd use the killswitch, so we used Eduardo's trick before we started shooting."

"They didn't have an active response frequency?" Those would be built into a GI's com uplinks, and would answer an active signal whether the GI wanted it to or not.

"Maybe," said Rishi. "We killed them so fast they didn't get a chance to use it. Com centers first, Beta building, fourth floor. Blew it to bits."

On her way upstairs, the pushback started.

"*Ms Kresnov,*" said Ms Kaif of Heldig Corporation, very coldly. "*The New Torah Council Board has been in emergency session. You have ten minutes to vacate Chancelry HQ and leave Droze completely, or we will use full firepower upon those Headquarters.*"

"And I will reply in kind," said Sandy, climbing stairs. "We've captured several artillery units within grounds perimeters, we are targeting your own Headquarters as I speak."

"*And we have the anti-missile defences to neutralise the few offensive weapons you have present,*" Kaif replied. "*You have nothing like the defences to withstand ours.*"

"Ms Kaif," said Sandy, emerging into the lower floor office, and then to the hallway beyond, "if you'll look skyward, you'll notice that there is currently a Federation carrier positioning to orbit about this planet. Federation forces also control Antibe Station. Be assured that any act of aggression upon me will bring down the full weight of Federation firepower upon your heads."

"Then you've just committed an act of war against the League, you idiot! We may not consider ourselves League space, but League certainly does!"

"Maybe, but that won't help you, bitch. Nor will God himself if you continue to piss me off."

She broke off, and walked across the landscaped courtyard, heading for the medical research building. The day was bright, hazy, sunny and cold, like most days on Droze. Wrecked vehicles still burned upon the landscaped grounds, amid sprawled bodies. In the near and far distance she could hear sirens, flyers, and the occasional burst of firing. The other Droze corporations were mobilised, encircling Chancelry Quarter with their own forces, a tightening ring of bristling armament. They were all trapped in here now, and almost certainly, there was no fighting their way out. She had enough firepower to ensure her perimeter against infiltration, but no way to ward off a bombardment if it came. Only the fear of orbital firepower could stop that.

Whoever was now in charge of HQ communications directed some new orbital transmission to her. It was Vanessa. *"Hi Sandy, what's your situation?"*

"Gonna get pummelled if Reichardt doesn't convince them not to."

"I think he can do that. You understand the amount of collateral damage that's going to cause?"

"I do. Tell Reichardt I'll understand if he has a problem with it, but if he doesn't, all us GIs are dead, and all evidence of what Chancelry's done here will be destroyed. Which means this shit will happen again and again. It has to stop somewhere."

"I know. He'll agree. He didn't volunteer to back us up for nothing."

Captain Reichardt was their personal guardian angel, and had bailed them out of trouble several times now. Every time he'd managed some shore leave in Tanusha the past few years, Sandy and Vanessa had organised to show him and his officers a good time, SWAT-style. On one of those eventful nights, Reichardt had met a very pretty FSA analyst, to whom he was recently engaged. Sandy didn't know if that made them even, but the captain seemed to think his role as guardian angel had paid off handsomely so far, and kept volunteering. Or maybe he was just a crazy Texan who liked trouble.

"*Ari tells me you're struggling with the barrier construct of their secure mainframe?*" Vanessa continued.

"Looks like it could take days," Sandy affirmed. "Even for the likes of me and Ari."

"*Well we have . . . a guy, up here. I think he can help. Can you get him an uplink direct to the construct?*"

"I don't know how much one guy is going to help, but sure, I'll arrange it."

"*I think he could help quite a lot.*"

"Are you guys safe up there?" Sandy asked, as the medical building loomed ahead of her.

"*Station crew stopped trying to cut their way in once Reichardt threatened to board with marines. We'll be okay, we've food and water for a few days. Toilet facilities, thank God.*"

"Good, I gotta go. Stay safe, and thanks for saving all our asses."

"*You betcha. You know, we might have to actually sleep with Reichardt after this. Both of us.*"

"Ha," said Sandy. "That first night out, after Nehru Station. Who says I already didn't?"

Vanessa laughed. "*You slut.*"

The secure level of the medical building had visitors. Lower designation GIs, most in standard issue tracksuits, filing slowly through the facility floor. They stared unblinking at the bodies, the parts, the "examination rooms," with their cutting horrors and heavy restraints. And with silent respect through that part of the ward where some of Chancelry's experiments still lived.

About some of those beds, there was activity. Some medicos worked at gunpoint, attaching tubes, detaching others, applying medicines. These were straight humans, looking very scared. Sandy wondered where the rest of the Chancelry working population were, who hadn't run away in time. Perhaps she didn't want to know.

She could guess why the lower designation GIs were here. Chancelry employed a mix of lower and higher designation as a combat force, then siphoned off selected higher-des GIs for experimentation—probably when those hit a certain age, and the results of genesis-experimentation came to maturity. That would also be the age when a GI might start to ask questions. From what she'd gathered of Rishi's uprising, they'd managed to lock most of the lower-des GIs in their building for most of the fight. Some others had fought and died, and yet others had had a crisis and sat it out, not knowing which side was right.

Now they were filed through these ghastly rooms to see for themselves. Even a lower-des would be affected by this. She could see it in their eyes as she walked past their slowly shuffling line. Could see some of them bending to peer at names and designations listed on patient boards at the end of the beds. Mouthing them, silently to themselves. *This could be me*, they realised. *This is me, or someone just like me.* And then, one hoped, the first, faint glimmering of a concept known to the rest of the world as injustice.

At Anya's bed, the horrific monitoring gear had been removed. No more pins through the spinal cord, surveying signals, compiling maps of feedback and response on whatever odd things they'd done in creating Anya's nervous system. It made so much more sense now, knowing that so much of it was Talee technology from inception. Even the most advanced human laboratories still didn't know how a lot of it really worked, thus all this experimentation and research. Of course, they could have made non-combat GIs; it might have been possible to study those without mutilating them, while combat GIs were built so tough there was little choice but to crack them open. But it would be equally expensive either way, and combat GIs were required for the hostile combat environment Chancelry so often found itself in here on Pantala, so why not kill two birds with one stone? It had been an executive decision, no doubt. A matter of sensibly employing available resources. The kind of thing that executives got promoted for.

There was no medico by Anya's bed. Just a GI Sandy didn't know, who sat by her bedside and watched. And met Sandy's eyes, and gave a faint shake of the head. Sandy knew. Whatever they'd done to Anya was degenerative, she'd been told. Chemicals were breaking down her internal systems. That degeneration gave good data readings, apparently. Sandy didn't know why—she wasn't a biotech medico. She could quite happily have lived the rest of her life without knowing why.

Anya blinked at her, sleepily. "Hello," she murmured. "You're Sandy."

Sandy grasped the girl's hand. "I am Sandy. I told you I'd come to you."

Anya smiled. "You did. You kept your word."

"You inspired a lot of people," Sandy assured her. "If you hadn't helped me, this wouldn't have happened. Now all of the GIs here in Chancelry have a chance to be free. And those GIs working for other corporations too." And one day maybe, she might have said, far more than that.

"Free like Eduardo," said Anya, her smile growing broader. "When you see him again, tell him I love him. Tell him to be happy with his freedom."

Sandy's eyes spilled. "I will. He loves you very much, Anya. He told me he did."

"I know," Anya said quietly. "Thank you for coming. But it's sad here, and it hurts. I'd like to go now."

Sandy kissed her. Then indicated the GI by the life support. The GI nodded, and pressed the sedative. Soon Anya was sleeping. Then the life support was turned off.

Sandy sat by Anya's bed for a while, holding her hand and gazing at nothing in particular, in her heavy, battle-scarred armour, as lower-des GIs filed past the bed. Then, after a long moment, she got up, and left.

As she left the ward, she saw through the doorway of a side room, bodies lying on the floor. Lined up and shot, execution style it looked like, one to the back of each head. They wore the clothes of lab technicians, Chancelry workers. Regular humans, sentenced to death by those who were to be the next victims of this program. Sandy was too sad to feel any satisfaction at the sight, yet neither was there a shred of remorse. She merely wondered, with vaguely academic curiosity, exactly what she'd started here. And what the history books would record had happened on this day: the day that synthetic humanity had finally turned, en masse, upon its makers.

And not before time either, she thought, shouldering her rifle and heading for the stairs.

The next level down was secure rooms, all sealed glass and once-sterile environments like the upper room, but all the doors now flung open, people passing back and forth in numbers. Someone had said there was someone here she should see, but no further information, and she always thought it best not to wonder, because she'd had times in Dark Star when she'd wondered after a fight, and been disappointed at what she'd found.

The medical ward was open and some GIs were here, armour discarded in piles upon the floor, sitting on chairs or on beds for treatments to bullet wounds, mostly. Treating them were other GIs, possessing only basic medical knowledge, but bullet wounds on GIs usually didn't require much, just pull out the slug, disinfect, patch and wrap. And here was one woman sitting on the edge of a bed, treated by a man, who was assisted by a boy of perhaps six. The man was pulling out slugs and handing them to the boy, who gave him disinfectant gel and bandages, and a sip of water to the wounded GI from a flask. The GI took it, observing the boy with curiosity.

"Kiril!" said Sandy. The boy looked at her. Recognised her, grinned and waved.

"Cassandra!"

Sandy went to him, dropped to a knee and hugged him. The boy seemed surprised, his hands full of bandages, and not really knowing her that well . . . but Sandy felt like she'd known Kiril an age.

"You know," said Kiril, "I didn't know you were such an advanced GI? But I was talking to your friend Poole, and he said you were the best GI ever, and that you'd be here real soon . . ."

"Poole!" Sandy stared at him. "Poole's alive? Where?"

"Here, you fool," said Poole, still treating the woman on the bed. She hadn't even recognised him with his back turned. "Someone said the kid was your friend. I thought you'd be mad if I didn't look after him."

Sandy wanted to hug him too, but he was busy. And, she recalled past the emotion and relief, had never really been that kind of guy anyway.

"Thank you," she said, squeezing his shoulder. "You're okay?"

He shrugged. "Drugs, restraints, a few injuries, I'll be okay. The first I knew about all this was GIs crashing into my room, releasing me, and giving me a gun. Not much more than two hours ago."

"Yeah. Long two hours."

"Cassandra, where are Danya and Svetlana?" asked Kiril, urgently.

"They're fine, Kiril." Even as she said it, her heart set to thumping. She couldn't really be sure, Danya had stormed out on her over in Whalen neighbourhood . . . a good thing in that it had been a long way from the fighting, but now he'd have to make his way over to where Svetlana was on his own. But Danya was more adult than most adults. Moving around a city was a simple thing for him, even a city in the state this one was in.

Svetlana worried her more—she'd been in the warehouse with Kiet's forces, but all of them had advanced; they'd not been able to leave any reserve behind. So now Svetlana was all alone too, with only the Home Guard for protection . . . and the last Sandy had seen of the Home Guard, they'd been shooting at her.

"I don't know exactly where they are," she explained, "but I'm sure they're very safe. You know how smart they are. I couldn't bring them with me—I had to attack through the neutral zone to get here, you understand? Danya and Svetlana aren't soldiers, so I couldn't bring them. I promise I'll try to find them, but honestly, I think they might be safer where they are. It isn't very safe here at the moment."

"That's okay," Kiril said confidently. "They're really good at staying safe. And you don't really have to find them, they can find you—that's what Danya always tells me. He says if I'm lost I shouldn't look for him, he'll find me. He always knows how to find me."

Sandy wasn't at all surprised. And that should have been that—she couldn't do anything more about it, there was a wall of firepower encircling them now, there was no way of getting Danya and Svetlana here, and if there was, it would be ridiculously unsafe. Plus, as she'd told Kiril, they were probably safer where they were. So why this unsettled sensation of . . . of what? It felt like panic, heart thumping, mind unsettled. A very low grade panic, because of course she didn't *do* panic. She did affection, and love and friendship, and all that good human stuff, but not the kind of maternal mode, high intensity attachment that Rhian had discovered. So why this creeping desperation?

Then she noticed the light bandage on the side of Kiril's head for the second time—the first time she'd assumed he'd had a light, recent scrape. But this looked like something else.

"Kiril, what happened to your head?"

"Oh, they did an operation," Kiril explained, offhandedly.

"An operation?"

"Yeah. Uplinks, I think. They're not working yet."

Uplinks augmentation. On a six-year-old boy. Now she wanted to kill people again. Line them up like those corpses upstairs, and blow holes in their heads. It was medically unsafe to do mental augmentation on children below the age of at least sixteen, everyone knew that. Doubtless Chancelry had been doing similar things to abducted street kids for a while now.

"Does it hurt? Do you feel any different?"

"Not yet. But uplinks are cool, right?" With enthusiasm. "I've always wanted to have uplinks!" He handed Poole some more bandages as he worked.

"Tell you what," said Sandy, "as soon as I find the right medical facility, we're going to get that looked at. Just to be certain." An urgent call registered on her uplinks. Rishi. "Crap . . . Poole, you look after Kiril for me?"

"No," said Poole. "I'll look after Kiril for everyone." Pointedly. Sandy managed a faint smile. She'd always liked Poole. He was a contrarian. "You think there might be a piano around here somewhere?"

Sandy rolled her eyes and walked for the door. "Kiril, you stay with Poole. I'll be back when I can!"

"That's okay," Kiril called after her. "I want to stay here and help!"

Of course he did, Sandy thought, smiling as she left. A friendly, generous boy, just as his siblings had described him.

Back at the basement office, she found that the impossible had happened, and Rishi's people had cracked the mainframe barriers.

"No, not us," Rishi corrected. "Cai."

"Cai?" Sandy took a seat by their open wall panel, frowning.

"Your friend Vanessa's friend. Up on the station. We linked him in directly, he solved it in fifteen minutes."

Which wasn't possible, Sandy knew. She herself was likely one of the fastest to break such a barrier, and she didn't think it was possible in less than ten hours. But whatever, she'd solve that puzzle later.

She uplinked to the local network and found the giant, spherical side of the barrier looming before her. At first glance it looked intact. But then she saw the slim, gleaming wire of a data link, like a loose thread in a huge ball of yarn. Plugging into that was entirely simple.

Within were simple data files. Not a phenomenal volume of information, but it was big enough. Data was filed under various headings. Rongyao. Hadiah. Angel.

"These are planet names," said Sandy, puzzled. "League systems."

"I know," said Rishi. "There's a lot more. I've no idea what it means; I was hoping you would."

Sandy did not move too fast this time. This wasn't the kind of data she could just whiz through. It looked like a sociology rundown, the kind of thing she'd read in Tanusha, where sociologists compiled news clippings as footnotes to their various databases that attempted to track social trends. Government departments loved them, and attempted to tailor government services according to the statistical models provided. And yet Sandy had always been sceptical, a scepticism reinforced further by Ari and his underground friends, who'd never failed to point out to her how the grand sociological theories always overreached and overexplained, and never failed to identify social patterns that truly only existed in sociologists' heads. No coincidence that a lot of sociologists hated Compulsive Narrative Syndrome theory, and tried constantly to disprove it, with efforts that usually served to confirm it instead. Sandy concluded that a lot of this stuff was really Rorschach Tests for sociologists rather than an objective model of anything real.

Her eyes flicked over one series of reports from Angel—a large League world of nearly three hundred million, a wealthy place but now struggling with various troubles. The articles listed were obscure, almost trivial—a shooting, the description of a political squabble, an incident of road rage, a first person account of a big social event . . . this was the contents of Chancelry's top secret vault? You could find this stuff anywhere, Tanusha included. This was what a League warship, Vanessa had hair-raisingly informed her, had been trying to nuke Droze over, rather than have the outside world find out?

News clippings were grouped by planetary heading, and then further grouped into a broader statistical framework that at first glance did not seem to make sense. That framework organised into various charts and graphs, with strange letters for heading that might be acronyms.

These in turn linked into more files. Public opinion surveys. Interface polling. Aha. Very large scale interface polling . . . damn, it looked like every world in the League had been comprehensively polled. Something that large could only have been run by a very coordinated central government program. Spying on its own citizens, attempting to discern public preferences, opinions, social breakdowns by net traffic intensities across various indices. And there were other references she didn't recognise . . . she herself had come across her little psychological profiling trick for large network constructs that had so freaked out her CSA friends, probably League operatives had their own little tricks. Was that what this was? A giant attempt to psychologically profile the entire League population? Well that would certainly be a bombshell if League media ever got a hold of it. No doubt the government would come crashing down, a scandal of monstrous proportions. But enough to try and nuke Droze? Not even close—politicians were scared enough of losing office, to say nothing of their lives. The League had used their death penalty far more often than the Federation during the war, sometimes even against wayward or traitorous politicians. No doubt a few would like to use it on her, if they could.

And here on various graphs, whatever-it-was that they were measuring, was absolutely taking off across the last . . . five years? Sandy frowned, trying to make sense of it all. On one world after another . . . well, the curve was inconsistent, but it was definitely rising, and now she was seeing a pattern in the organisation of all these files. They all led back to that series of uprising graphs. Measuring what? A preference for chocolate? Group sex? Damn stupid sociologists, what were they trying to . . . ?

She flipped to some new graphs, and suddenly, a series of acronyms she recognised. FD. Fifth Dispersal. That was the technical term for a form of synthetic neurology, one of the means of achieving sentience. But that was purely GI-specific. Nothing from that strand of research had ever made it into regular humans. What the hell was it doing here, in a study of a huge population of regular, organic humans?

Oh no.

Time stopped, and her blood turned cold. The other acronyms. DPO. Delta Pattern Osmosis. MD. Mitochondrial Duplication. Shorthand terms for microscopic processes that took entire volumes to explain. GI tech. Talee tech. But the indices were clearly measuring trends directly across the entire League population.

"Oh, fuck you!" she shouted, tearing away from the uplinks. She kicked the wall so hard she put a hole in it. And stumbled back around to a chair, pulled it out and sat in it, hands to her face, then in her hair. Staring at the wall in blank horror.

"Sandy?" asked Rishi, a little nervously.

"They never admitted GI technology came from Talee," Sandy said. She could barely hear her own voice. Could barely comprehend the monstrosity that she saw before her, emerging from this data. It was too horrible to contemplate. And too huge. "So of course, they never admitted they used Talee tech in standard human uplinks. Like all people have, in League society."

"And Federation, right?" said Rishi.

"Not like this," said Sandy. "Because the Federation never kept big secrets like this. League kept this secret. Our secret, our Talee origins. And once they kept a big secret, the little ones didn't seem so bad. Especially once the war started, and suddenly secrecy was everything. They used the same Talee tech in standard uplinks that they used to make us. Federation never did—they used their own indigenous tech instead. League loves all high tech, it'd give them a big economic boost over the Federation, League loved to stick it up the Federation. What a great idea, so long as you don't admit where it came from.

"It went wrong, Rishi. It's like Pyeongwha all over again. They used neural tech they didn't fully understand and the technology's great, but it's causing second and third generation mutations in human brain function, and League society's going nuts. That's what all this documents . . ." and she waved a finger at the exposed mainframe in the wall, ". . . it's all this stuff in League society, it's not just the dislocation following the war at all. It's Neural Cluster Tech again. It's Compulsive Narrative Syndrome, and it's taking off exponentially. They're getting weird behaviour they've never seen before, strange social divisions, cults, political movements . . . and if it all keeps building up at this rate, they'll tear each other apart." Suddenly one of the graphs she'd flicked over made perfect sense. "Three years. Maybe. This whole segment of humanity's on the verge of becoming homicidally dysfunctional. Billions of people. And all because these fucking League elitist bastards think they can run everything themselves without sharing with the rest of us."

Rows of bodies in the caverns. Six hundred thousand casualties on Pyeongwha. Pyeongwha had been one world, with three hundred million people. League had five billion. She just couldn't believe what the League leadership had done. It was unspeakable. Sandy was Federation, and didn't like the way the League worked, but this was so far beyond any concept of petty tribalism or revenge. League civvies were just people like people anywhere—it wasn't their fault their system sucked. They sure as hell didn't deserve this.

"No wonder League wanted to nuke us rather than let it get out," someone said quietly. Sandy could only nod, still staring at the wall. No wonder also that Ramoja had betrayed her to get at this. His civilisation was dying, his government had been trying drastic covert things to fix it, and he'd wanted in. At any cost.

And the Talee must have known what was going on here. Somehow, they must have known, and decided it shouldn't be covered up. Perhaps they were scared too. Perhaps they knew things about this technology, this horrifying phenomenon, that they'd not yet shared with humanity. Evidently someone over there felt strongly about it, to have destroyed a League warship in full view of everyone, to keep the truth alive.

"So . . ." Rishi said slowly, "they've been working with Chancelry to . . . try and find a cure?"

"Looks that way," said Sandy. "Try all kinds of new stuff. Try it fast, because they're running out of time. I'm sure League's trying lots of other stuff themselves at secret bases, but New Torah Chancelry's the only corporation with access to the original tech. So if they want to find a solution at the source, they've no choice but to come here, and since they're using GI tech in straights, experiments on GIs directly might be the best way to find answers. This way you can separate the synthetic results from the organic interference. God knows what Chancelry asked from them as payment."

"Independence," said Rishi, with certainty. "I bet you."

Sandy nodded slowly. It made sense. "Starships. Sovereignty. A guarantee of non-interference from League and Federation both." Thus the League going to such lengths to keep the Federation out of it. And the ISO, whom they obviously didn't trust. Probably Mustafa and his friends were a big part of that, given the kind of research being done on Pantala. Wherever the hell Mustafa was now—no one had found him yet. More unfinished business.

"So what happens now?" Rishi asked. "You think there'll be another war?"

"Oh, only if we're lucky," Sandy said bleakly. "A war like the last one would be a best case scenario. Pyeongwha was only getting started when we intervened—if left alone, it would have gotten much worse. If this is as bad as Pyeongwha, spread over five billion people with the firepower the League still has at their disposal, we could lose half the species. Unless the Federation does something fast. Probably something very violent and very unpopular."

Given the Federation's track record on such recent matters, it seemed a small hope at best.

ABOUT THE AUTHOR

Joel Shepherd is the author of seven SF & Fantasy novels, including the Cassandra Kresnov Series, and the *A Trial of Blood and Steel* quartet. He is currently completing a PhD in International Relations, for which he's living for a year in India. He also has a short screenplay in development, has had an "interested" Hollywood feature producer, and other entertaining distractions.